I0639819

BOOKS BY OLIVIA ASH

Nighthelm Academy

City of the Sleeping Gods

City of Fractured Souls

City of the Enchanted Queen

Demon Queen Saga

Princes of the Underworld

Wars of the Underworld

Mistress of the Underworld

Sentinel Saga

By Dahlia Leigh and Olivia Ash

The Shadow Shifter

The Demon Prince

The Rogue Alchemist

STAY CONNECTED

Olivia Ash occasionally takes over the Wispvine Publishing social media channels on Facebook, Instagram, and Twitter. She also has her own Facebook page.

Olivia also likes to hang out with Lila Jean in their Facebook group specifically for readers like you to come together and share their lives and interests, especially regarding the hot guys from their reverse harem novels. Please check it out and join in whenever you get the chance! Everyone in there is amazing, and you'll fit right in.

https://www.facebook.com/groups/LilaJeanO-liviaAsh/

Sign up for email alerts of new releases AND exclusive access to bonus content, book recommendations, and more!

https://wispvine.com/newsletter/demon-queen-saga-email-signup/

Enjoying the series? Awesome! Help others discover the Nighthelm Academy by leaving a review at Amazon.

PRINCES OF THE UNDERWORLD

DEMON QUEEN SAGA

OLIVIA ASH

WISPVINE PUBLISHING

BOOK DESCRIPTION

Four immortal demon princes. One strong-willed human. A bewitched amulet that makes her queen of the Underworld—and binds the five of them together.

Sadie's world is crumbling beneath her, and she's starting to wish for a way out of her lonely life in Seattle. But when her sister Blair arrives unannounced in the middle of the night, covered in blood and carrying a glowing medallion, Sadie has no idea her wish is about to come true in the most violent of ways.

All of hell is after the amulet's vast power. And when Blair puts it around Sadie's neck, all of hell is suddenly after *her* as well.

Separated from Blair and with hardly any information to go on, Sadie finds herself surrounded by four stunning men—the warring demon brothers of the Underworld. The princes hate each other with a passion, and yet they're bound to her side, captivated and ensnared by her magic.

In an instant, the amulet gives Sadie everything she ever wanted—wealth, power, even a fortress with a mind of its own. But she also inherits the amulet's enemies, and they're about to kick down her door.

Sadie has no idea who she can trust—except for her men. As she spends time with each of the supernatural princes who won't leave her the hell alone, she falls for them. Hard. Though they can't stand each other, she can't imagine ruling her new kingdom without them all.

But this is the Underworld, the land of monsters and warlocks, of angels and deadly treachery.

The shadows of the Underworld hold secrets, and as her enemies close in on her new life, Sadie has to make a choice—surrender her newfound power, or stand as Queen and fight for the last remaining ounce of integrity and justice left in the Underworld.

There are armies at the gate. Traitors in the fortress. Blood on the walls. Good thing Sadie is too damn stubborn to quit.

CONTENTS

CHAPTER ONE

SADIE

"Jesus," Sadie muttered, rubbing her eyes as she got into the passenger seat of the ambulance. "What a night, Joe."

Her assigned partner didn't say anything as he shut the driver-side door. Keys jangled in the darkness. The ambulance rumbled to life, and the veteran paramedic just sighed. "This job wears on you, kid. It really does."

Sadie stared out the window as they drove away from the hit-and-run. Their tires crunched over the glass as a police officer Sadie hadn't met before waved them through the backed-up traffic, clearing the way for them. She gave him a grateful nod, which he returned, but it was all she could muster at the moment. As they left the chaos behind, she groaned and sank into her seat.

Three years into this job still wasn't enough to completely numb her from the gore. Judging from old-timers like Joe, it would never really get better.

Multiple units had been called, and even though this was what Sadie had been trained to do—what she had known since she was a kid she was *meant* to do with her life—she was still kind of grateful another crew had taken away the woman who barely clung to life.

As they turned onto the main road, Sadie saw a beige stiletto on the side of the street a good three yards from the impact site. Cheeks flushing with nausea, she squeezed her eyes shut. She tried her best to shove down the chilling dread that came with the thought of what was happening to the person that shoe belonged to.

At least tonight, she wouldn't have to watch another person die. It had been happening so often, lately. Every shift for the last three weeks, someone had died on her.

Every shift, a heart stopped.

Every shift, someone sobbed as they bled out.

Every shift, someone asked her what it was like to die, if she'd seen it before.

Every shift, she lied to them and told them they'd be fine.

Well, tonight, come hell or high water, no one would die on her.

Thankfully, Sadie was almost in the clear. One hour left of her twelve-hour shift, then three glorious days off. She'd had one close call, a girl who had been mugged and beaten on the way home from her waitressing job, but thankfully they'd gotten there in time to stop the girl from bleeding out.

Sadie tensed at the memory of the gashes on the girl's arm, and she instinctively tapped her fingers on the knife she kept strapped to her calf for her own protection. The cops didn't always make it to the ambulance calls, and sometimes a paramedic needed to protect *herself.* Between the knife and her Tuesday night MMA lessons, it was enough to make her feel a little more secure on calls to dangerous areas or situations.

A little. She wasn't about to go pro or anything, but Sadie could still hold her own in a fight.

Joe sped along the road, slipping away from the densely populated areas to their assigned stakeout spot somewhere in the Highline district of Seattle. This was half the job—sit and wait. And tonight, so close to the end of her shift, Sadie was just fine with boring.

From this vantage point, she could see down the Seattle hills to the interstate below, and the flashing blue and red lights of their fellow paramedics caught her eye as they raced toward the hospital. Joe turned down the chatter on the radio as he watched them fly down the highway, probably for his own peace of mind more than anything, and it made Sadie grateful. For the moment, she wanted to just watch, to hope that they got to the emergency room in time, that the woman would make it.

"I need a beer," Joe grumbled. "But since I can't have one on the job, let's get a soda."

"Fine by me." Sadie yawned. "I could use the caffeine."

He turned left, veering away from the freeway and heading toward a string of fast food chains a little down the road. The tree-lined road curved, the yellow line snaking through the darkness, illuminated only by the headlights and the occasional dim yellow street-light passing overhead.

They sat in silence, Sadie lost in thought, eyes slipping out of focus, when a blaring horn sounded behind them.

"What the—" Joe swerved just as a pickup truck flew around them, racing over the double yellow line into the other lane at twice the speed limit. Tires screeched. Sadie's blood ran cold. The truck veered and fishtailed, plowing into an oncoming minivan.

The minivan never stood a chance.

One second, peaceful quiet. The next, bloody chaos.

But this was her job. This was what Sadie excelled

at—chaos. Panic. Blood. She could stuff the emotions away, deal with them later, hurt *later,* so that she could help the wounded *now.*

And it seemed like someone always needed help.

Joe flipped on the lights and blocked traffic as best he could, but Sadie tuned him out. They were both operating on autopilot now, running through their training to get the job done and save whatever lives they could.

She grabbed her kit and threw open her door before the ambulance even pulled to a stop, hopping to the asphalt with the effortless ease of years of practice. Joe could handle the admin stuff—calling it in, getting the gurney, setting up the most basic of perimeters so that she could just get to work. Sure, she hated calls where they didn't have police backup, but she wasn't about to let someone die just because there were no cops to cover her.

First things first—triage. Assess the damage. See who needs the most help.

She peered into the truck's window and the driver slowly turned his head back at her. He slurred something through the shattered window about fish sticks, and though her instinct was to tear him a new asshole for driving under the influence, it wasn't her job to assume. Not yet, anyway, not until he had been properly treated. Yeah, he was probably drunk—but he could've had a stroke. She scanned the rest of the truck, but he was the only one in it.

Still, he was breathing, he was moving, and his car wasn't about to explode. He could wait.

"Joe, one in the truck!" she shouted.

"On it!" he answered.

Sadie ran to the minivan, and as she took in the sight of the crushed engine and shattered front windshield, she briefly froze in place. It was almost flat, and in the dark she could barely see inside. She clenched her jaw and pressed onward, peering inside to find a man, unconscious and buckled into his seat, the airbag covering most of his torso. She checked the other seats, but thankfully, they were empty.

A thin trail of blood leaked from the driver's mouth, and he wheezed with every strangled breath. It hurt to even listen to him breathe. Sadie swallowed hard. Not good. That meant he might have punctured a lung.

"Stay with me, sir," she said firmly, pulling on her gloves as she leaned in to check his pulse. "We're going to get you out of here. Everything is going to be okay."

To be fair, she wouldn't know until later if it was a lie. All she cared about right now was keeping her people alive. And in this moment, for however long this stranger was in her care, he was one of her people.

"Sir, can you hear me?" she asked the man as she

looked over the gathering crowd. Some were already filming her on their phones, too busy with the spectacle to ask if she wanted help.

She didn't, but still. She hated when these assholes filmed her.

Within seconds, she had her kit sitting open on the ground beside her, everything neatly arranged and ready. Her hands ran through the motions, assessing the damage, looking for anything she could mend on the way to the hospital to try to stave off death.

Anything.

~

SADIE

*I*n the end, Sadie failed.

It had been an impossible situation. With his internal bleeding and the logistics of a head-on collision, there was no way Sadie could have helped him, but she had done everything she could think of regardless, everything she had been trained to do.

But she couldn't save him. His pulse had stopped, and she never even learned his name.

For situations like this, for times when someone died on her at work, Sadie had one very important rule—no sobs, no emotion, no sadness. Nothing, not one tear, until she got home.

But today, she felt numb. It was so hard to think. After twelve hours on her shift and three years of this job, she didn't know how much longer she could do it.

How much longer she could lose people.

She moved on autopilot, barely paying attention, not really noticing anything until she was standing at her front door, in the hallway, staring at her apartment number. A door slammed shut somewhere down the hall, but she didn't flinch. Normally she would be more aware of her environment, more interested in who was around her, more cautious as a single girl in a big city, but today she just couldn't.

With a deep sigh, Sadie blinked away the tears that welled up in her eyes. As a paramedic, she was familiar to these situations, but it didn't mean she wasn't affected by the loss of another life.

In her numbed haze, it took a moment for her to register the blood-smeared doorknob of her apartment. She looked at her hands—they were clean, thanks to the gloves she was mandated to wear. A sinking sense of dread broke through the sadness. Tenderly, just to test it, she twisted the knob, finding it locked. Whoever opened the door had stumbled inside and closed it after them, locking it once more.

A chill crept up her spine as she realized the intruder could still be inside.

With a renewed sense of self-preservation sweeping away her sadness, she grabbed the knife from her boot and slowly, quietly, opened the door, her ears alert for the slightest sound.

Oh, please, give me an ass to kick tonight, she thought to herself, body humming with adrenaline. With her shitty evening, with all the grief and anger and loss, it would be one hell of an outlet.

As she entered her apartment, everything was bathed in darkness. Silver streams of moonlight cut through the open windows.

The problem? Sadie always left the living room light *on*.

Uneasiness thrummed through her as she searched the shadows for an immediate threat. She didn't see anyone. Keeping to the shadows, she crept into the room, leaving her front door open in case she needed a quick exit.

Her heartbeat quickened as she followed a trail of blood on the floor that led into the living room. She took a deep breath and raised her knife chest-high, body positioned in a fighting stance. She swiftly turned the corner, ready to attack, but stopped when she saw a familiar figure slouching in her favorite armchair, swathed in dim moonlight.

The figure held a gun at her. The hand gripping the pistol shook.

Sadie squinted in the darkness, warily glancing

between the familiar figure and the shaking gun. "Blair?"

Sadie flicked on the light switch to her right and stared at her sister.

With a sigh of relief, Blair lowered the gun, resting it on her lap and leaning her head back against the chair. She looked worse for wear. Bruises and scrapes covered her thin, muscular body. Her clothes were tattered and covered in grime. Sadie paled as she took in the bleeding gash on Blair's right shoulder. Her sister's dirty fingers clutched the wound, trying to stop the bleeding.

In that moment, Sadie shifted into emergency paramedic mode. It was fast as lightning. Instantaneous. No feelings. No thought. Just her training. Just her doing anything she could to help.

Sadie's knife hit the floor with a thud as she rushed to the bathroom to get the first aid kit, turning on more lights as she went. She quickly grabbed the kit from her bathroom drawer and then rushed back to the living room.

Eyes scanning the wound, she knelt beside the chair where her sister slouched. Sadie gently removed Blair's hand that had been pressing against the gash and cut through the scruffy sleeve, revealing a deep, ugly slash that appeared to have been torn open by a jagged blade.

"What did you do this time, Blair?" Sadie asked as

waves of worry and confusion tangled in her mind. "What happened?"

Blair only grunted in answer.

"Jesus, Blair. Tell me," Sadie said, begging clear in her voice. "Do I need to call the police?"

"No!" Blair tried to stand but immediately collapsed back into the chair, hissing in pain. "No," she said, weaker. "A job just fell through." She gritted her teeth. "I only need a place to crash. I'm going to be fine."

If you say so. Sadie sighed. It always seemed like it was "just a job fell that through."

As she began to clean the outside of the wound, she asked, "What job, Blair? No one knows what you do."

"I hust—"

"Yeah, yeah, sometimes you hustle pool." Sadie rolled her eyes. "I had hoped this time you wouldn't lie to me, though."

Sadie's family thought Blair was unemployed, bumming off boyfriends since her fiancé died eight years ago.

But there was obviously more to Blair's life than she had let on.

"What's *really* going on?" Sadie pressed, tossing a bloody, dirt-covered gauze to the floor, picking up antiseptic and clean bandages. She gently cleaned out the mud caked in the gash.

Her sister didn't answer, only groaned in pain

while Sadie nursed the wound, but Sadie wasn't going to let this one go. Not this time.

Neither of them spoke for a minute.

"You need stitches," Sadie said with a frown.

"Then stitch me."

Sadie snorted impatiently. "This isn't a damn hospital, Blair. You need to go to the ER."

"No," Blair said firmly, glaring down at her. They stared at each other for a second before Blair softened, and her gaze flickered to the floor. "Sadie, I can't. I can't go to the cops. Please, you're a pro at this. Please, stitch me up?"

Sadie sighed, shoulders drooping in defeat. "Fine."

She could bring people back from the edge of death, run into danger and tend to gunshot wounds, but damn it all, she couldn't say no to *Blair*.

After gathering a few more supplies from the bathroom, Sadie sat beside her sister and quietly rubbed a bit more alcohol on the wound, not entirely looking forward to stitching up her sister. This would hurt, and she didn't really have the right supplies.

"I have friends on the force," Sadie said, pausing as she inserted a suture into the wound to seal it shut, meeting her sister's eyes. Blair's breathing slowed but grew heavier. Sadie continued, "I can call in a favor and get you some protection, if you're worried. If someone's after you."

Blair gripped Sadie's arm as if it were a stress ball and sucked in a pained breath through her teeth as the needle broke through her skin. "I told you. No cops." She rested her head on the back of the chair and gazed at the ceiling. "There are too many cops on *her* payroll."

Sadie hesitated, finally getting somewhere with her sister. Apparently, her enemy, the person after Blair, was a woman. Interesting. Maybe the loss of blood had made Blair delusional, or maybe Sadie was about to get some much-needed answers. She remained silent, diligently stitching her sister's wound.

"Besides, no human can protect me now," Blair said softly, almost a whisper. "No one can protect me from what's after me."

Sadie furrowed her eyebrows, pausing as she stared at her sister. Okay, now that didn't make a lick of sense.

Delusions—this was a bad sign. Perhaps there was head trauma Sadie had missed, but in all likelihood, Blair was probably just disoriented from the blood loss.

Worry clutched at Sadie's chest. She needed to take her sister to the hospital, get some scans done. She could have brain damage. Or a lesion, or even some internal bleeding.

Shit.

Hesitantly, Sadie wrapped up the final stitch and tied it off, not altogether pleased with her makeshift handiwork, and ran her fingers through her sister's hair, gently checking for lumps or soft spots.

There were none. As far as she could tell, no head injuries. It could have been a side effect from the trauma, but—

"Sadie," Blair said, a bit of a hard edge to her voice.

Sadie snapped out of her thoughts and caught her sister's eye. "What?"

"It's not safe for you if I'm here. Please, let's finish so I can get you someplace safer."

With a sigh, Sadie reluctantly finished bandaging the superficial cut on Blair's shoulder. She tended to a small scrape on her sister's jaw when the young woman reached into the discarded jacket beside her and pulled out a beautiful amulet: a teardrop-shaped ruby, the size of her palm, bordered by a thin, silver strip encrusted with tiny diamonds that dangled from a golden chain.

It glimmered and glowed as Sadie gazed at it, her eyes slipping out of focus, as if she were hypnotized.

"*Sadie,*" someone said softly in her ear.

Sadie gasped and looked around, hand on her chest in surprise at the voice, but no one was in the room save for her and Blair.

She gave the amulet a sidelong glare, her skin crawling this time as she looked at the enchanting object. She leaned in toward it, fascinated, her fingers lifting to touch it, her curiosity getting the better of her. To her amazement, it glowed brighter, humming. She snapped her hand away.

It felt almost... *magical.*

"What is that?" Sadie whispered. She turned her gaze to her sister, seeing fear reflected in Blair's wide eyes.

Fear for *her.*

"Shit." Blair pocketed the amulet then stood. She mumbled to herself, limping while pacing, completely ignoring her injuries. "Shit, shit, shit. This is bad. This is bad. This is really, really bad."

"What's bad?" Sadie jumped to her feet. "Will you *please* start making sense?" She gripped Blair's shoulders to stop her from pacing. She couldn't tolerate the confusion any longer. "Blair, you can't keep stumbling into my apartment like this. I've let you get away with this long enough. The least you can do is explain to me what in the world is going on!"

Blair's expression softened as her eyes took on a haunted glint. "I've done bad things, little sister. I've gone after terrible people. People who want me and everyone I love dead. I'm sorry for always barging in here, but all my contacts are gone. I don't know if they're still alive or—" Blair choked, tears welling in her eyes. "I have nowhere left to go." She sat back on the chair, wincing and lightly rubbing the bandage on her shoulder. "I'm afraid these people found out about you, and if they did, they're going to come after you next. I have to find a way to keep you safe."

Sadie crouched in front of her sister to readjust the bandage, puzzled and apprehensive from everything Blair had said. She had never seen her sister like this. Blair had always been the strong one, the badass sister who could wield any weapon and make even the scariest dude in a bar steer clear.

It gutted her to see Blair afraid, lost, and in so much pain.

That's it. Hospital it is. "We need to go to the ER," Sadie said, helping her sister up. "You've lost too much blood, you—"

"No!" Blair seized Sadie's wrist, nails digging into her skin. "No, please. They'll find me. They'll kill me. They'll kill *you.*"

She's hysterical. "Who, Blair? Who is going to kill us?"

Blair didn't answer.

Sadie unwrapped her sister's fingers from her wrist, torn and anxious from the fear and exhaustion in Blair's eyes. Did Blair really have dangerous people after her? Aside from getting mugged in an alley, Sadie couldn't think of any reasonable explanation that would result in an injury like this.

Pushed to the brink, already exhausted, and now

stressed beyond what she could handle, Sadie took a calming breath.

She had seen stabbing victims in this state before, and they had not survived. She was scared for her sister's life. She scrambled to clear her mind. This was her sister. She needed to be objective and do what would save her sister's life, even if it wasn't what Blair wanted.

Blair sagged against the armchair, looking at Sadie, face slack, but her eyes were serious, sad almost. She seemed to be making her mind up about something. She opened her mouth to speak, but before she could say a word, her gaze darted to the door over Sadie's shoulder and her eyes widened with horror. Without a word, she shoved Sadie to the side then stood in front of her.

Sadie tucked her arms and rolled as a bolt of fire shot past them, hitting the wall and leaving a dark patch of soot.

"What the—" Sadie hunkered behind an armchair and peeked around it to find a tall figure in the entry. The gorgeous woman sneered wickedly, all white, sharp teeth and vicious, glowing, red eyes.

The woman walked into the room, and pointed, antler-like horns, velvety wings the length of her body, and a spiky tail came into view. Gilded armor scantily clung to her body, and her harsh features were unearthly.

Beautiful.

Deadly.

Sadie could have taken a moment to appreciate the dark elegance she exuded, but the woman stared right at her, eyes narrowing. She looked ready to kill. "You must be the sister."

CHAPTER TWO

"Mara." Without missing a beat, Blair raised her pistol and pulled the trigger.

The deafening boom echoed throughout the room. Sadie flinched. Her adrenaline pumped through her, flooding her body in shock. It was as though she were dreaming and drowning, all at once.

The bullet hit the woman Blair had called Mara square in the chest, but she barely flinched. She grinned wider, those wicked teeth gleaming.

Great. Beautiful and *bulletproof.*

"This isn't happening," Sadie said softly to herself.

It couldn't be.

Mara smirked, her ruby red lips perfect. "Nice to see you again, too, bitch." The woman raised her hand, and a blaze of fire erupted from her palm.

Magic.

This woman, who looked for all the world like a breathtaking, winged demoness, had summoned fire on a whim. Sadie briefly looked back at the singed patch of her wall, and it all clicked.

This was very real, and this woman had not only hurt Blair—she intended to kill them both.

Fuck *that*.

Sadie shook herself free from her daze and charged Mara, knocking her off balance. Mara's armor heated bright red, scalding the skin on Sadie's arms and chest and forcing her to back away. She ran to Blair's side, who was already on her feet. Sadie was surprised at how remarkably well her sister moved despite her injuries, but adrenaline was one hell of a hormone.

Blair looked at her, panting for breath. "You all right?"

Sadie nodded, the sting of her burns already fading. "What are we going to do?"

"Run," Blair said softly. "As soon as the moment's right."

Across from them, Mara crouched, snarling at Sadie. "You're as annoying as your sister." Almost too fast to see, she cast a ball of fire in Sadie's direction.

Sadie ducked, grabbed a snow globe from a nearby shelf, and sent it crashing against Mara's head. Sadie did *not* expect her reflexes to be this enhanced by her unapplied martial arts training, but she was thankful nonetheless. With a smirk, she rolled away from the woman's wings and knelt, ready to dodge another blow if needed. "Pleased to meet your acquaintance, Mara."

Adrenaline surged through Sadie's veins as she dashed to the side, grabbed a stool, and then swung it into Mara's back, sending wood splintering into fragments. The impact seemed to have jarred her more than it had Mara, who only smirked. If bullets hardly did anything, what did Sadie think a piece of furniture would do? Her heart pounded. Her eyes went to the knife she always kept with her, though it now lay on the carpet next to the door, but she doubted she could do anything with it.

She needed to come up with a plan. How could she disarm Mara and get herself and her sister out of there alive?

Mara's serrated tail descended on Sadie, and the woman's wings stirred a small breeze in the confined space. Sadie twisted to her right, dodging a blow to the ribs but not the painful scratch to her shoulder. She quickly inspected the area as beads of blood oozed out. It wasn't deep but would sting in the morning.

Blair propelled herself from the coffee table, lunging toward Mara and smacking the woman's temple with the butt of her pistol. The woman's head twisted to the side. Sadie then crouched down, hooked her leg around the woman's calf, and yanked Mara's legs from underneath her. There was a loud pop. The deadly woman screeched as she fell to the ground, wincing. Her skin might have been impenetrable, but she could clearly feel pain. She was only hiding it.

Good to know.

Between the gunshots and the screeching, the cops would be here soon. Sadie could use that to her advantage—maybe. It all depended on if anyone witnessed the demoness spewing fireballs or if that was going to be left exclusively to her testimony, because if so, she might not have a job in the morning.

Sadie shifted her attention to Blair, who wobbled on her feet and shook her head, rapidly blinking her eyes. Sadie quickly stood and went to her sister's side, helping to steady her while Mara writhed on the ground from a dislocated knee.

"You ripped your stitches," Sadie said.

Blair shook her head. "Doesn't matter. Here."

She handed Sadie a knife, predominantly reddish brown with an iridescent blade. Sadie gripped the carved handle, her thumb brushing over the engraved symbol of a snake eating its own tail—an ouroboros, if she remembered correctly. Embossed scales and spirals brushed her palm, but she would have to examine the carvings on the knife later.

Mara climbed to her feet, the action catching Sadie's attention. Mara had somehow recovered and prepared to hurl another fiery assault as she held her hands out to her sides. Her palms ignited with balls of fire, growing bigger and blue.

"The sooner you die, the sooner I can get what is mine. So, let's just get this over with, shall we?" Mara hurled the balls of fire toward Sadie and her sister with a growl.

Both Sadie and Blair dodged in opposite directions, avoiding the blast of heat as the balls of flame hit the far wall of Sadie's living room. The curtains caught fire, the overhead light burst, and Sadie's favorite armchair was caught in the inferno.

"Shit," Sadie muttered, watching her home become consumed in the aftermath of the fire strikes. They really needed to get out of there, and fast.

Sadie advanced, sidestepping another fireball aimed at her. She ducked, evading another one that sailed close to her ear. The smell of burnt hair hit her nose, but she pressed onward.

"Damn it," she muttered as she charged the demoness. Frustrated that her raven locks got included in the crossfire, she bent low and then sliced Mara's thigh with the exquisite dagger.

Sadie expected the attack to hurt, for Mara to scream, or groan, or at least stagger a little at the sheer force of the blow.

It was so much *better.*

She didn't expect the wound to spurt dark liquid, black as night—it looked like ichor, a supernatural river of blood, hissing and bubbling as it streamed to the floor. She paused as Mara scowled, enraged.

So, she can bleed...

Before Sadie could move out of the way, Mara bent her left wing and impaled Sadie's forearm with the giant thorn on the wing's apex, slamming her against the wall. Sadie screamed as pain erupted through her arm and into her shoulder. Mara twisted to face Sadie, holding up a single, glowing hand, red eyes glowing, ready to burn her to a crisp.

"Time to die," Mara hissed.

Sadie's heart pounded as she shut her eyes, wincing, waiting for the pain to hit her. A jerk came, and she was released from the wall, falling to her hands and knees. She opened her eyes to find Blair on Mara's back, a dagger in hand—plain compared to the magnificent weapon she had given her—aimed and ready to be plunged into the woman's chest. When the dagger sank into the leather of her armor, right where Mara's heart should have been, it didn't hiss or pop, or sizzle. No dark ichor seeped from around the blade.

Sadie took note of the differences in the daggers. There must have been something special about the one that she wielded that could cause the damage. A poison, maybe. Sadie made sure to carry the knife carefully, so she didn't accidentally cut herself and in case her sister didn't have an antidote nearby.

Mara used her wings to get Blair off her back,

sending her flying to the floor. Blair shifted in the air, tucking her feet under her and landing gracefully in a crouch. She stood, maintaining her usual confidence. Sadie stared at her sister in wonder.

A throb pulsed in Sadie's shoulder. She grasped the puncture on her arm, knees buckling. It baffled her how her sister could endure this much fighting with all the injuries she had. What had her sister gone through to turn into this kind of a warrior? Blair looked like she could still fight for hours despite the numerous injuries she had endured already.

Through Blair's mask of confidence, though, Sadie spotted signs of exhaustion. Her sister's knees shook, her chest heaved a little too hard, and she swayed a bit. Subtle, but to Sadie, it was obvious, and that worried her. If Sadie didn't find a way to get herself and Blair away from this demoness and somewhere safe, they both may die tonight.

"Where is it, you wench?" Mara shot a column of fire in Blair's direction.

Blair ducked, staggering sideways. The fire hit the bookshelf in the corner of the room, setting it, and the books, aflame. The fire spread faster, smoke wafting from the flames. Sadie crouched low and covered her nose with the neckline of her blouse. The smoke burned the back of her throat and she forced back the tickle of a cough.

Think, Sadie, think. She quickly scanned the area for

an escape, but Mara blocked the exit, and her home was too filled with smoke and flames to find an alternate escape route.

"Where's what? Your manners? I was about to ask you the same thing," Blair retorted, breathing deep and then coughing from the smoke.

Sadie's clothes were drenched in sweat from the heat. She fought to keep her head clear and find a way out before succumbing to the fire that was rapidly igniting everything she owned. Mara shifted, briefly turning her back to Sadie. On instinct, Sadie raised her dagger and charged, but her attack was sluggish from the smoke. Mara turned to face Sadie, tail whizzing from the side, striking Sadie's abdomen. As Sadie sailed back, she swung her iridescent dagger, piercing Mara's wing and dragging the blade through the thin fibers.

Sadie struck the ground, knocking the air from her lungs. Dazed, she struggled to climb to her feet as Blair joined her, helping her up from the floor.

Swing by swing, moment by moment, Blair and Sadie fought against Mara, side by side. But as Sadie noticed Blair's movements slowing, her advances growing slower by the second, she realized they were losing.

"The pendant is mine," Mara said, glaring at Sadie and Blair. "It doesn't belong to you."

"Well, since you asked nicely..." Blair threw the

knife, landing it hilt-deep in Mara's throat. It would have killed a human, but Mara only flinched.

She bared her teeth and yanked the knife out of her throat. "You think a little human like you can stop me?" She threw the knife in Sadie's direction. Sadie sucked in a surprised breath and tumbled to the side to dodge the attack, jarring her arm as she fell. The knife whistled close to her head, grazing her cheek. A sting pulsed where the blade sliced her skin.

Sadie instinctively touched the spot, pulling her hand back to find her fingers coated red with fresh blood. Anger boiled in her gut. "How dare you barge into my house, set it on fire, and attack me and my sister, you psychotic freak!"

Mara turned an annoyed gaze toward Sadie. She pointed at her. "You have it, don't you?"

"What—"

What happened next blurred by, almost too quickly for Sadie to register. One moment, Mara had stretched her wings and charged, nails extended and teeth sharp, ready to bite her throat, ready to kill. The next, Blair stood in front of her, blocking Sadie from harm.

Mara's tail curled around her body and, in one fluid motion, stabbed Blair clear through the heart.

A scream lodged in Sadie's throat. Seeing red, unable to think about anything but saving her sister, she lost control.

With clenched fists, Sadie launched herself at the woman's back, gripped Mara's blond hair with one hand and, with the other, drove the dagger in between the woman's shoulder blades. She quickly jumped out of the way of her flailing wings. The wound hissed, and bubbling ichor streamed out. The sight gave Sadie some satisfaction.

Mara's tail slid out of Blair's body. Sadie watched her sister drop to the floor and go limp. Mara dropped to her knees and clawed at the dagger. Her dark, pointed nails failed to grasp the hilt.

Sadie had to make a choice—yank the dagger out of Mara and have a weapon once the demoness recovered or leave it in her and hope it distracted the vile woman long enough for Sadie to drag Blair to safety.

"Damn it all," Sadie muttered, making a split-second decision she hoped was right. Once Sadie was sure Mara would never be able to reach the blade, she dug it in to the creature's back as deep as it would go and ran to her sister.

It was time to leave. Now or never.

Blood pooled around her sister's body, and Sadie tried to ignore what was already obvious—Blair was going to die. Pushing that thought away, she gently pulled her sister into a sitting position. "Let's go. We need to go, Blair."

She ripped the lower part of her shirt then wrapped the cloth around Blair's stomach. She took

Blair's arm, hooked it around her neck, and with all her strength, attempted to pull Blair to her feet.

Instead of standing, Blair hugged Sadie, and then a cold weight was placed around her neck. Sadie looked down to see the ruby pendant that had so mesmerized her earlier, the very thing this heartless demon bitch had so badly wanted. The gem glowed bright red and emitted smoke, though the stone didn't burn Sadie's skin. The enchanting magic she experienced from earlier flowed from the ruby to her fingertips and down her spine and welled deep within her core. The energy stretched and swelled, invading every part of her body. It didn't hurt, it didn't ache, it just felt— beautiful. Perfect. *Right.*

Sadie clasped the pendant. "What—"

Mara squealed in pain, wailing as if she had just lost a loved one. The ugly, mournful sound ripped Sadie from the wonder she felt from the pendant. She tugged on Blair's arm to help her sister stand while Mara furiously thrashed and scrambled for the dagger lodged in her back.

Blair didn't budge. "I'm sorry," she said, eyelids drooping, barely able to stay conscious as she looked at Sadie with a sad expression. "I—I have condemned you to darkness and pain, but it's the only thing that will keep you alive." Her breathing became shorter and ragged. "I hope you can forgive me one day."

"What are you talking about, Blair? Let's go. We

have to go!" Sadie kept tugging, but her sister remained motionless, growing heavier. Tears welled in Sadie's eyes. As she blinked the tears away to clear her vision, Blair handed her a glass orb that filled her palm with an electric sensation.

"I love you, little sister. I always will."

"Blair! Let's go. Please, let's go," Sadie said, voice full of desperation as tears flowed down her cheeks. Mara made one last growl then sighed. She had successfully yanked the blade out of her body and dropped it on the floor, the hilt burning her skin as she touched it. The woman stood then arched her back, taking in a deep breath and cracking her neck bones with a few flexes. She glared at Sadie, eyes burning with malice.

Sadie mustered all her strength to try and carry her sister, but her muscles ached and she hardly lifted Blair at all. "Let's go! Come on!"

Blair cupped Sadie's cheek and smiled. "Find those worthy of your trust and guard them with your life," she closed Sadie's hand around the glass orb and whispered, "Safehouse."

As Mara strode toward them, leering, Blair shoved Sadie away. Sadie fell backward, thrown off balance, and a surge of icy numbness spread through her from the orb.

Whatever this thing was, it was doing something to

her—something bad. Something that was stopping her from saving Blair.

As Sadie stared at her sister in shock, the world around her warped. The colors melded together and turned darker. Before she was consumed in absolute darkness, the demoness's hands wrapped around Blair's neck while Sadie's living room burned.

Sadie screamed. "No! Blair!"

The darkness swallowed her whole.

"Blair!"

Sadie kept screaming, but her voice sounded muffled. Frustrated, furious, and desperate to save her sister, she screamed again and again, until she couldn't hear anything anymore. Until she couldn't move anymore. She tried to smash the orb on the ground, but she couldn't feel her body.

All she could see, all she could feel, all that surrounded her, was the darkness.

She thought she would be trapped forever, but she a force jerked her out of the orb's confinement and she hit the ground hard. There was a sound of glass shattering somewhere near her. Her right arm went numb. Nausea gripped her, and she groaned in pain. Her vision was spotted. Just when she thought the worst was over, the ground tilted again, and her world faded to black.

CHAPTER THREE

SADIE

*S*adie blinked herself awake on the floor of what seemed an abandoned house, judging by the litter, debris, and lack of any semblance of home. Her head throbbed, and her muscles ached. She sat up, gritting her teeth against the protesting muscles being forced to move. Her bruised arm ached as she gripped the wound created by Mara's wing, but by the looks of it, it would be fine. Just a flesh wound. Ripping a strip of fabric from the bottom of her already tattered blouse, she wrapped the cloth around her forearm, using the moon as her only source of light.

Her chest burned a little, and her entire body felt warm, as though she had spent the entire day in the sun. Which was odd because Seattle wasn't warm, and her shredded blouse barely covered her upper body. Cool night breezes that should have felt cold against her skin swept in through the broken windows around her, ruffling her dark hair, but she felt only a simmering heat deep within her core.

And through it all, the soothing enchantments of the amulet against her chest reminded her that nothing in her world was going right.

She tried to make sense of the night's events as she took in the ragged mattresses, the floor covered in trash and discarded clothes, and the colored graffiti on the wall. Then she found a familiar symbol on the farthest wall of the room, illuminated by moonlight. An ouroboros. Just like the one carved on the knife Blair had given her.

Blair.

She scrambled to her feet. Flashes of everything that had happened to her sister rushed through her mind. Her hands shook, and her chest tightened as she remembered how Mara's tail impaled Blair, how Mara strangled her sister just as the strange orb swallowed up her vision.

Sadie needed to get back to her apartment.

She shuffled to the window, peeked outside, and recognized a sleazy area of Seattle, perhaps two miles from her neighborhood. Not a great place to be for a girl alone at night, but not far of a walk.

Across the silent, garbage-littered street lit by a single, flickering lamplight, a row of dead trees guarded withered lawns and more abandoned houses. At least, they *looked* abandoned. She didn't know how she could be in an abandoned house when, moments ago, she and Blair were getting reamed by a she-demon with bat wings and a dragon's tail.

And *horns.* Sadie shivered at the memory of the woman.

Though her muscles burned with the most minute movement, she maintained her composure, looking outside for signs of danger and coming up with a plan. She had been in too many close calls before working as a paramedic. Logic and a cool head were the only things that got her out of those brushes with danger.

The same would be needed for this situation.

Her body grew warmer and the burn in her chest intensified. An itching sensation spread from her sternum to her collarbones, and she absently scratched at her chest to soothe the odd ache as she walked away from the window and made her way through the dark house.

Sadie needed to go after Blair, but now there was a problem—she had the amulet Mara so desperately wanted. If Mara was smart, she would keep Blair as leverage to get the pendant back, and that at least bought them time.

Hopefully.

The itching on her chest intensified, and Sadie groaned with discomfort. She needed to figure out what the hell this amulet even was. Looking at the ceiling, there were no light bulbs and she figured no electricity either. Even if there had been electricity, she wouldn't have used it as it would probably draw unwanted attention.

Wading in the moonlight, she found a shattered mirror on the ground next to empty bottles of beer, a few feet from the broken orb. Kneeling and bending toward the largest fragment, she pulled down her shirt's neckline enough to see the pendant.

Her eyes grew wide with shock and wonder as she stared at the ruby that had embedded itself in her chest. The golden chain that held the red gem was draped around her neck, ends dangling above her breasts. She ripped the fabric of her shirt to inspect the amulet.

Wispy, black tattoos radiated from the glowing stone, resembling runes and sigils that shifted and moved with a life of their own, like living ink, crawling on her skin in what little moonlight reflected.

When Sadie touched the stone, it glowed brighter. Her pulse quickened. She wasn't just wearing an amulet anymore—this object was now *in* her body.

Part of her.

Fused to her.

Though a brief surge of concern shot through her, she knew Blair wouldn't have given her something that would hurt her, so she shoved away the thought that this could kill her. Instead, she focused on what to do next.

Blair had given this to Sadie to protect, and this was all the leverage she had to get her sister back safely… if Blair was even still alive.

"She's alive," Sadie hissed to herself, killing the thought as it hit her. "She has to be."

The pendant is mine. That was what Mara had said. And from the way Mara had screeched in pain and frustration when Blair put the necklace on Sadie's neck, it was clear Blair stole the pendant from Mara, and that the woman wanted it back. She wanted it *bad*. Bad enough to kill.

She wanted to blame her sister for what happened tonight, but Blair was still in trouble. Sadie needed to get to her. She could play the blame game after she and Blair were safe and sound. She stood and started to form a plan. She would need a phone, several of her cop buddies on the force, and maybe a psych ward.

While formulating a plan to get back to her sister and both of them to safety, a slight movement of shadow flickered in the moonlight within her periphery.

She whirled around to find a huge, ugly, shaggy man silently standing in the darkness, glaring at her with cold eyes beneath a mane of wiry, dark hair. She gasped, more from surprise than fear. He was so bulky, yet so quiet, sneaking into the room unnoticed like that. She tensed for another fight. This guy couldn't possibly be good news.

He pointed at the pendant fused with her body and scoffed. "Oh, you are in deep shit now, little girl." He stepped closer, the faint light bouncing off his exposed biceps as he continued to glare at her. His lips pulled into a grin, baring rotting teeth. "Didn't anyone tell you not to mess with dark magic?"

Magic. The word gave her goosebumps, the hair on her neck stood on end. As much as the logical and reasonable part of her wanted to explain everything away as completely scientific, there was no possible way to do so, not after what she had seen. Magic was the only explanation for everything that had happened.

Magic was very real, and right now, magical beings were trying to kill her.

He shuffled even closer. "Pity. Waste of a pretty face." He drew a hunting dagger from his belt.

This guy was going to kill her.

First Mara, now this *stranger*, all over a pendant.

Her blood ran cold, and a frosty blast of nerves sailed clear to her fingertips. Just like that, she snapped. The good girl with the perfect GPA and the clean apartment at the edge of town was gone.

As long as Sadie had this pendant, she would have people coming after her, trying to kill her, trying to slit her throat. She had to choose whether or not to keep going.

It was a sink or swim moment, a fight or flight decision—and Sadie was a *fighter*.

With one glance at the knife, Sadie scoffed then planted her feet into a fighting stance, fists held at eye level. "You don't want to mess with me, honey."

He snorted in answer, apparently entertained by the comment. He quickly closed the remaining gap between him and Sadie, pointing the dagger at her.

Fine. A beat down it is, then. At the last second, Sadie spun to the side and then swiftly scrunched down, extended a leg and caught her attacker's legs mid-stride, sending him face-first to the floor. He landed on glass fragments that used to be the weird orb.

"Name's Sadie, by the way." She got up and back into her ready stance.

The man pushed himself to his feet, scowling. "You're going to pay for that, bitch."

"Nah," she said nonchalantly. He was a scrub, barely trained how to fight, and even though she wasn't a pro, she could take him, knife or no.

She returned to the broken mirror and grabbed a sizable glass shard from the scattered pieces. Rapid, thumping footsteps approached her. She turned then jumped back as the man's knife whistled past her exposed midriff, barely scratching her skin. The man growled and swung again. She turned to the side, dodging the attack, ignoring the sting and ache of her sore muscles. She maneuvered behind him, avoiding another swing of his knife and drove the glass shard into his left shoulder.

The goal was to hurt him. Bad. To make him stop. To make him limp away, body and ego bruised enough to give up. She didn't want to kill him—but if he made her, if he pushed her, she absolutely *would.*

She ignored the sting burning through her hands. The man cried out as his knees buckled and he crashed to the floor. Sadie climbed onto his back, clenching his torso between her thighs and wrapping an arm around his throat. She released the knife from his grip by applying pressure to the soft skin between his thumb and forefinger then tossed it across the room.

Applying the last of her remaining strength, she squeezed her arm tighter around the man's throat. He wildly scratched at her, hands clawing at her arm, peeling layers of skin. Sadie sucked in a pained breath, letting it out slowly as she fought through the sting of his nails on her arm. When his movements slowed, Sadie thought she was gaining the advantage, but then the man started to crawl toward the knife.

Why won't he just pass the hell out? Sadie wrapped her other arm around his throat, pulling even tighter, and although the man seemed to crawl slower, he showed no signs of stopping.

This guy was a *tank*.

He was about three times her size and it would take more of an effort to incapacitate him. With a strangled groan, he finally collapsed on the ground, crumpling in pain. Sadie held on a little longer, thinking the moment was finally ending.

Nope.

To her surprise, he reached toward his weapon, fingers fanned out. Sadie rolled her eyes and tried to summon extra strength to get her attacker to pass out from lack of oxygen. His fingers grazed the handle, spinning it in his favor. He gripped the handle and quickly jabbed it into her right thigh, startlingly fast.

Blistering pain tore through her body. She released his throat and fell off his back, hands clenching the wound. Her attacker coughed a few times, taking in large gulps of air and then pulling himself to his feet. He faced Sadie.

A dark chuckle rumbled from his throat as he limped toward her and kicked her hard in the side. He did it again. And again. Each time she tried to stand, he kicked her once more. Sadie's vision lit up with dots with each blow. She tried to place distance between herself and the attacker by crawling on her hands and knees, but he took the opportunity to ram fists into her back, making her collapse to the floor.

Sadie's mind was consumed by the pain and the need for escape. She needed to do something —*anything*—to get away from him. She rolled onto her back, prepared to kick out one if not both of his kneecaps. The man loomed over her, rubbing his fingers over his throat. Sadie lifted a foot. He caught it, twisted it. She cried out. He chuckled again and straddled her, pinning her arms to her side and sitting on her injured leg. She yelped in pain.

Sadie writhed under his heavy weight, determined to fight, to get out of this ungodly place and find her sister.

The man slapped her across her face. "That's for being an annoying bitch."

Sadie's head snapped to the side. Her cheek throbbed, the pain reverberating. Her eyes watered instinctually, blurring her vision. She blinked them away, and the sharp tip of the man's knife descended on her face.

She lifted her hands instinctively. It was intuitive, perhaps not the most advanced martial arts move she'd learned, and she fully expected the blade to pierce her palm.

It didn't.

Instead, her chest began to burn, right beneath the amulet.

The heat became unbearable, and energy surged

through her. It was all-consuming, as though a star had come to life within her body.

Just then, bright flames exploded from her hands. It was violent and sudden, completely out of her control. She squeezed her eyes shut against the intense heat and light.

The burst lasted for only a few seconds, but the weight on her lifted. A knife clanged on the floor.

She opened her eyes, finding herself alone in the abandoned house, covered in ash. The amulet on her chest glowed like molten gold, or a chunk of amber.

She looked at her hands. Flawless. Clean. Not a scratch on them anymore. Nothing seemed different. No scars or burns… nothing.

I did this?

Sadie gasped and crawled backward, shaking off the ash that had fallen on her. She stared at the remains of the first person she had ever killed. She wanted to cry, but she held it in. Whatever she did wasn't her fault. She only defended herself from the man who tried to kill her. She had to choose to save herself. And she would *keep* choosing to save herself. Not only would Sadie get out of this alive, she would stop whoever was coming after her and her sister. She would end this.

For herself.

For Blair.

Weary and injured, she stood then walked to the

man's knife, bent down, and picked it up. With the way her night had been going, she was certain she would need a weapon again. She sighed and glanced at the pile of ash, wondering what the hell Blair had gotten her into.

CHAPTER FOUR

SADIE

*S*weat dripped along Sadie's hairline as she removed the remains of her shirt and wrapped it around the gash on her thigh. Covered in wounds and a bra, she limped to the pile of discarded clothes on the floor and picked up a ragged, navy-blue coat that reeked of spilled beer and vinegar.

At least, she *hoped* it was vinegar.

Breathing through her mouth, she put on the coat, grateful for the coverage. The warmth she felt from the amulet slowly faded. She shivered and tucked her hands inside the smelly coat's pockets, slipping the knife into one.

She limped toward the nearest shelf and opened the cabinets, hoping it would contain something that would help her tend to her wounds. Alcohol, aspirin, anything. Maybe there was even a first aid kit stashed in here somewhere.

Hey, a girl could dream.

But after looking through all the overhead cabinets and counter drawers, she found only cobwebs, dust, and the occasional rat scampering away from her. She sucked in a breath as she walked around the room, scanning the debris and the messy bookshelves, looking for anything that might possibly aid in her healing.

There was nothing. Nothing but trash, anyway.

Blair must have sent her here for a reason. Maybe her sister thought it was safe for her to get here. But it was also possible Blair had no control over whatever the orb had done to her. After all, her sister had been critically wounded by a monster just before she handed Sadie the orb.

She walked around, kicking the litter on the floor, sucking in a breath when she put too much force on her injured leg. She crouched over the broken glass orb and examined it. Some fragments had a bit of a yellow color to it, and when she picked up larger fragments, the yellow tint looked more like melted topaz that crystallized inside the transparent orb. She might have found it beautiful at any other time, but under the current circumstance, the orb was useless.

She stood with a grunt and approached the large ouroboros painted on the nearby wall. Around the image were different sigils and runes painted black. She unbuttoned the first few buttons of the smelly coat she wore and traced her fingers over her chest. It still itched and burned a bit, but the sensation had dulled compared to earlier.

Inside the ruby, she felt the energy. The movement. Something stirred within her chest. If she was being honest, she loved the sensation the amulet gave her. And even when she felt ashamed with what she had done to the man that had attacked her, the sensation that overwhelmed her body—the warmth, the *power* —overshadowed every negative feeling.

The amulet made her comfortable and provided a sense of safety. It made her feel *strong*.

She closed her eyes and tried to reach for that power again. Her eyebrows pinched together. Although she felt a stir within her chest, and her mind brushed the edges of the energy, she couldn't tap into it. The power stayed out of her reach.

Sighing, she lightly rubbed the red jewel on her chest and continued walking.

A crashing sound—something like clay pottery falling onto stone—came from the door on the right of the ouroboros. Sadie halted in her steps, straining to hear anyone, or any*thing*, approaching. Her heart raced. The darkened doorway seemed to lead to other parts of the abandoned house. If occupied, the fight with the man she turned to ash could've been heard. Maybe a buddy was coming to finish her off.

Well, not if I can help it. She narrowed her eyes on the dark, searching for movement, and pulled the knife from her pocket as she cautiously approached the doorway.

As she neared, without further sound or movement, she reasoned the sound was probably just a pesky rat knocking something over. She calmed herself and walked to the wall farthest from the dark doorway, to where the front door stood. She should leave this house soon, but first, she needed to plan what she would do next.

Despite the plan, she found herself nodding off. After sixteen hours awake and twelve of those hours on the job, it was understandable, but she couldn't stay here.

Her body slumped from fatigue, and her eyes wanted to close. She wanted sleep, but she had a plan: find a safe place, properly tend to her wounds, rest a little, and find Blair.

Nearby, the sound of boots shuffling broken clay fragments caught her attention. She stayed still for a moment, looking at the doorway as she gripped the knife's handle, waiting for someone to jump at her. When no one appeared from the doorway, she eventually relaxed her grip on the knife, though her eyes never left the dark space beyond the door. The window next to it overlooked an alley. Her muscles went rigid, and the hair on her neck stood on end.

There. It shifted again. It could be nothing, but her body warned someone watched her.

"Who's there?" she asked, her voice ringing through the quiet with thick command.

Silence.

She waited for a moment, her eyes glued to the window. The shadows shifted one more time.

"Show yourself," she said, again commanding.

Still, no answer.

Whoever it was, he had no intention of showing himself. She glared into the shadows, ready to take him on, but there wasn't any more movement. And everything was silent, save for the sound of the occasional rat crawling through the walls and her harsh breathing.

Her gut, however, told her that someone was there, and he was watching her every move.

Time to get out of this place. She hastily headed out the front door.

After she flung the door open and rushed out, she tucked her hands into her coat pockets, knife hidden away. She carefully kept her head down and stayed in the shadows as she limped toward help.

She had never been to this place before, especially at this time of night, but she only needed to walk a few blocks and enter the nearest store. Hopefully, the clerk would let her use a phone. Blair had said she couldn't go to the cops, but Sadie had friends on the force who weren't corrupt. They were good and honest people who would do her a solid.

Disregarding Blair's aversion to seeking police aid, she followed her intuition and planned to call a friend for help as soon as she could. She didn't know what on Earth she would say, but she had to start somewhere.

She stayed close to building walls and walked as quietly and as fast as she could. She had never been so thankful that the streetlights weren't working. When she had passed a few blocks, the sound of a fight wafted toward her. She halted and then pressed her back against the wall of a crumbling brick house.

She peeked around the corner, finding a few men at the end of the alley. They appeared no older than teenagers, actually, and she counted five of them ganging up on a scrawny guy. The bulkiest of the five shoved the skinny kid to the ground. The five guys then took turns punching and kicking him, but as far as she could tell, none of them had any weapons.

She probably should have left. She had Blair to worry about, and her injuries needed tending to lest they got infected and left her much, much worse than she already was.

But she couldn't turn her back on the poor kid that clearly needed help.

Knowing she would probably regret it, she grabbed

a rock the size of her fist and threw it at the bullies. It hit one on the back and he cursed loudly as he turned to glare at her, cradling the back of his neck. She knew she couldn't outrun them because of her injured thigh, so she took her knife and walked toward the middle of the alley.

Well, she couldn't go back now.

"Do you want to be next?" the largest of them asked as the group approached her.

She looked over their shoulders and saw the scrawny guy stagger to his feet. Through the glow of the moonlight, he met her gaze, nodded once in gratitude as his face bled, and scampered out of sight.

She raised her knife and took on a fighting stance. The five guys looked at each other then laughed.

"Ooh, I'm terrified," a blond who stood at the back said as he pulled out a swiss knife from his pocket and flicked out a blade. The others did the same.

She wasn't sure what happened next, but those punks looked over her shoulder and their eyes simultaneously widened. Without another word, they turned on their heels and ran. Her eyebrows shot up and she turned around to look at what had scared them. She prepared for another ambush, but the street behind her was empty and silent.

Soon, she stood alone in the alley, baffled but secretly grateful she didn't have to take on anyone else in this injured state.

Deep between her shoulder blades, the sensation of being watched returned. She frowned, glaring at the darkness around her, wondering if she'd gotten a tail from the abandoned house, wondering if something worse than a few teenagers had followed her.

Just great.

Her heart thudded in her chest, but she pressed on toward the convenience store, limping from her leg injury and doing her best to keep her pace steady. She clenched her fist around the knife's handle within the pocket of her smelly coat, ready to draw it if need be.

If she hurried, she would look scared, and that would make her an easy mark for whatever lurked in the shadows. It would make her look weak. She had to keep her resolve and remain calm despite the urgency of the situation and how desperately she needed to get to Blair.

But the fear in those boys' eyes… she lost herself temporarily in thought. If whatever was following her was another magical creature, though, she wanted to catch him alive.

She needed answers. Come hell or high water, she was going to get them.

CHAPTER FIVE

KAISER

*K*aiser kept to the shadows as he watched the stunning woman limp down the barely lit sidewalk. Even with ash smudged on her face and grime staining her beautiful skin, she captivated him. The fire in his blood burned hotter every time she got close to him.

He craved her.

As he watched her, he shifted and changed his form to become more inconspicuous, hiding his wings, tail, and horns. Even his armor shifted to a grey hoodie, faded denim jeans, and sneakers.

The human world was no place for a demon to go un-glamoured.

The neighborhood she was unknowingly leading him through was close to abandoned, but he wasn't going to chance letting a criminal, or worse, another demon hunter, touch her. She hadn't needed his help back in the abandoned house, but at this rate her luck wouldn't hold out.

She didn't know what she was. He did. She needed him—almost as much as he needed her.

He crossed his arms and kept his attention toward the entertainment for the night.

Sadie. A name fit for royalty.

She seemed athletic, but he hadn't thought she could hold her own against that ogre of a man back in the demon hunters' safehouse. As she walked down the street, she hugged the coat close, but he knew what lay beneath—he'd seen her beautiful body as she'd dodged the man's blows with graceful movements, the torn flaps of her shirt's neckline separating to reveal luscious cleavage glistening in sweat. His eyes had lingered on her curves, her sensuality igniting something primal within him.

He shook his head and furrowed his brows.

What the hell am I doing?

He was never one to be affected by an ordinary, human girl.

But that was just it, wasn't it? She wasn't *just* an ordinary human girl. She was more. So much more. And by the looks of it, she had yet to learn that. And the way she'd burned that man to mere ash—

Kaiser grinned, equally impressed and turned on. He wanted this girl—and what he wanted, he got.

Hell, she had just killed a man without any real weapon, without conscious control of the immense power she wielded. And from the shock written all over her face, this was probably her first time taking a man's life.

This tall drink of deadly water was a welcome distraction to the hunt for the demon who killed his brother, and though he thought he'd had a lead after his followers captured that accomplice, a solid week of torture had turned up nothing. So far, he wasn't any closer to an answer. Kaiser gritted his teeth instinctively, the flare of anger habitual at this point, but he couldn't let himself think about Cedric's murder.

As with everything in the underworld, there was so much more at play than even he realized, and if his suspicions were even remotely correct, everything he knew was about to unravel.

He needed help. He needed *Sadie*.

And this girl didn't know what she had become the moment she put on that amulet. The girl had no idea what sort of hell was about to come after her.

Oddly, he felt protective. He wanted to rush in, to sweep her out of this frail human realm and down to the underworld where she could be a little safer—for a time.

It didn't make sense. He didn't even *know* her. And yet... his eyes trailed after her as she turned a corner, and his jaw clenched as he fought with making a decision.

He knew exactly what a first kill felt like, how lost and uncertain she must've felt, and for a moment, he wanted to run to her and take her in his arms. But that was a bad idea. He kept still, though his entire body wanted to go nearer, pulled by her unique energy.

By her *power.*

This was it—his chance. He needed her power, her abilities. She would help him get everything he needed. This was all too perfect, and he wouldn't miss this chance to make her his.

More than that, she was special. He *felt* it. He needed more of her. But from what he had seen, this woman was dangerous. Especially since she didn't have control over her newfound powers.

For now, he needed information. He needed to know her resources, her plans, her followers—if she even had any. Before he made himself known, he needed to know the kind of woman he was dealing with.

And so far, he was impressed.

As she kept to the shadows and walked as fast as her injured leg allowed, he silently traced her steps. He kept his eyes on her and never strayed more than a block away. Aside from the practical need to watch her, he also felt the need to protect her, to make sure she safely arrived to wherever she was planning to go.

This woman is one of a kind.

Eager to see what she would do next, Kaiser lifted the hood on his jacket and followed behind the woman who was so much more than she realized—the woman who had hypnotized him without even a word.

CHAPTER SIX

SADIE

*S*adie was definitely being followed.

Her stalker made the mistake of a slight shuffle of a boot half a block behind her. The faint sound almost went unnoticed, but between that and Sadie's gut instinct, she knew someone followed her from that abandoned house.

Not wanting to let her pursuer know she was aware of his presence, if it even was a he, she kept her pace steady. She bit her cheek against the throb in her leg as her hand griped the knife in her pocket a little tighter.

She wondered what her stalker wanted and who they were. It could be Mara. The woman was beyond pissed when Blair draped the necklace around Sadie's neck. If she wasn't hellbent on killing Sadie before, she certainly was now. But why wait on attacking? If

Mara truly followed her, she didn't want to know what that meant for her sister. She could be dead. She could be barely clinging to life, crawling from Sadie's burning apartment. Hell, Blair could be the one following.

Sadie wanted to risk a glance behind her, but that was a serious no-no. The last thing she wanted was to alert her stalker and provoke an attack. Blair or not. Mara or not. Sadie's best bet was to stay the course. If she turned and the person following her turned out not to be Blair, Sadie would have to fight again.

A small gas station was just a mere two blocks away from her. She would clean up in the bathroom then use the phone to call in a favor from one of her cop buddies.

A small warmth pooled in her chest, filling her with renewed energy. The pain in her leg ebbed. Her mind cleared.

She glanced at the amulet in her chest. Dim, red light emanated from the ruby. She smiled, feeling stronger. Powerful.

Though she wouldn't dare risk a look over her shoulder, she could duck around a corner and wait. She'd catch her stalker in the act. Find out who followed her and why.

Taking the first right she could, she ducked behind a dumpster. She plugged her nose to keep from breathing in the sickening, sweet and sour scent of decaying garbage. A few rats scurried away from her, squeaking in their flight from danger.

The awareness of her follower's presence centered between her shoulder blades. The sensation chilled her spine. She could *feel* him drawing closer. Her deadly predator.

But Sadie wasn't prey.

She pulled out the dead man's knife from the pocket of her "borrowed" coat. Footsteps shuffled closer.

A shadow appeared from behind the dumpster, and the figure of a handsome man came into view. He stopped and turned his head toward her, calmly taking her in. God, he was gorgeous. But he could also be dangerous.

Not taking any chances, Sadie jumped up, dagger held out. She lunged toward him. He shifted out of the way effortlessly.

"Who are you? Why are you following me?" she asked.

She shook her head. Weapon raised and left leg shifting back, she readied herself for another fight. He put his hands inside his pockets, adding to Sadie's confusion. He remained collected, quietly observing her.

"Answer me, dammit." Sadie jutted her chin forward. She didn't lower the knife, waiting for him to make a move.

"You need to come with me," he said, unfazed by the dagger in her hand. He stepped closer, removing his hood, revealing soft, tousled brown hair.

Her arm wavered slightly as she felt the strong urge to run her hands through his locks. She tightened her grip on the knife's handle. "And why would I do that? You do realize how creepy that sounded, you asking me to come with you?" She looked around before settling her gaze back on him. "We're even in a dark alley."

"I know that," he said, voice remaining calm and unaffected. "But it's not safe for you here."

She snorted. *No shit, it's not safe.* "Thanks for the offer, but I can handle myself."

"You can, to a point," he said, lips quirked. "You have quite a skill, taking down a demon hunter as beautifully as you did."

She kept her features even and remained in her fighting stance, trying not to show her surprise.

So that was a demon hunter.

He must have been a human who had been after creatures like Mara. She wondered why he had attacked her. She wasn't a demon. But then this man knew she had gotten into the fight. He was there—he saw it happen.

"You were there?" she asked.

He nodded.

"And you just stood there? How chivalrous of you."

She had half a mind to stab him in the heart just for that. But she still needed answers. "Who are you?" Her eyes narrowed. "*What* are you?"

He chuckled.

She scoffed and was about to ask what was so funny when he moved in the blink of an eye. He effortlessly grabbed the knife she held and pinned her to the wall, pressing her back against cold, wet stone. She winced from the impact. Strong hands restrained her arms behind her tailbone. His fingers grazed her hips as he used her body weight against her.

The unnatural speed and grace he had used to disarm her should have answered her question. But she was too consumed by his touch that stimulated her skin. Strong, electric sensations tingled throughout her body. Her injuries stung again, but with the way his lean, powerful body pressed against hers, she *liked* it.

He wrinkled his nose, toying with her coat's collar with one hand as his other arm kept her pinned to the wall. "This kind of stinks, doesn't it?"

She cleared her throat and said, "It's a creep repellant. I wonder why it's not working."

He laughed and looked at her in a way that made her toes curl. "Allow me to do something about that, shall I?" Without waiting for an answer, he snapped his fingers.

She tried to wiggle free, but he held her firm. She

could have been pushing a mountain for all the progress she made. A sensation overcame her, stilling her movements as she realized the smell of beer and vinegar disappeared.

She looked down at her coat and saw that it was now bordered by some sort of thin mist. A silver film shimmered on top of the fabric. It moved and shifted, mesmerizing her. She wished her arms weren't ensnared, so she could touch it.

"Magic…" she whispered softly, hypnotized by the wondrousness of it. The sight distracted her for a moment. She met the man's intense gaze, his hazel eyes rooting her in place. The close proximity of this stranger turned her on. But she couldn't let him know that.

Snapping out of her wonder, she clenched her jaw. *You can shove it, traitorous body.* Shaking herself from this handsome man's effect on her, she refocused on getting answers.

"Cool trick. Now, tell me, who the hell are you and why are you following me?"

She bent her knee to kick him in the groin, but he released her arms and jumped away with unnatural speed. He still had her knife, giving him the upper hand.

"Tell me what you are." She stepped away from the wall and took a step toward him.

In answer, he tossed the knife to the ground. It

clanked against the stone of the alley and flipped end over end, landing inches in front of her feet. She glared at the man, questioning the point of his action, wondering if it was a trick. She prepared herself for another fight as she knelt down, keeping her eyes on him, and picked up the knife.

"Tell you what," he said, putting his hands back in his pockets. "If you can nick me with that sorry excuse of a knife, I'll answer your questions."

She didn't budge. "I don't have time for games. Tell me now."

The man stepped closer and then extended one hand to grab the knife just as he did earlier. She swiped with the knife, throwing her fist in an upper-cut. He swerved to the side and, in a heartbeat, stood behind her, stealing the knife from her again. His arms wrapped around her torso, pressing his chest against her back, his legs on both sides of her. Her skin prickled in excitement. Adrenaline surged through her veins.

He leaned his head closer, and his lips brushed her ear as he said, "Surely you can do better than that."

She heard the smile in his voice and shivered as ripples of desire ran through her core. Rolling her eyes, she refocused herself again.

She clumsily wiggled herself free, whirling around and facing her pursuer with a fighting stance. His eyes sparkled, and the corners of his lips twitched upward as he handed her the knife, hilt first. She yanked it from his grasp then immediately advanced, swinging her blade in ferocious strikes. Once she bested him, she would get the answers she needed.

Hands once again tucked in his pockets, he ducked when she slashed at his head. She jabbed at his chest. He sidestepped, dodging the attack. She swung again, frustrated. Again, and again. Every time, she sliced only the cool, night air. He was incredibly fast and annoyingly relaxed.

She realized he was playing a game with her, but she had run out of patience to play along. Dropping her armed hand to her side, she glared at her ridiculously handsome and frustrating stalker. She didn't have time for games. She needed answers, and if he wasn't going to give them to her, then she would find someone else.

"Have you had your fun?" she asked. "Because I have more important shit to do."

She slipped the knife back into her pocket. The handsome man continued to observe her, a gleam of humor in his eyes.

"So, if you're gonna fight me to the death, I suggest you do it now," she said, tilting her chin defiantly. "Otherwise, I'm done with this game."

He didn't answer. He didn't move. He only stared, eyes intense and lips betraying a hint of a smile. Her heart fluttered in her chest. She bit the inside of her cheek. They stood in silence for a few moments that trickled by like hours. Having lost patience, she said, "Suit yourself."

She side-stepped, turning her back to him. "I highly suggest you stop wasting my time, stop following me, and leave me the hell alone."

Her voice echoed into the alley that remained as silent as death as she continued toward the only convenience store she knew of on this side of Seattle. She ducked her head again, keeping to the shadows and avoiding the light cast by the streetlamps.

As she moved, she touched the film of mist that coated her stolen garment and kept its reek at bay. It felt cold, and when she slightly pressed on it, it left a shallow indentation on the mist's surface, shimmering like foil. She smiled. *How amusing.*

She played with it as she walked, somehow knowing the farther she got from her strange stalker, the magical mist would disappear and leave her with a smelly coat once again. But as she passed more buildings, and the lit streetlights grew more abundant, the thin film of mist lingered on her coat. Even when she emerged from a street and came across a huge, empty field covered in withering, brown grass that she recognized as South Park Playground, the magical mist remained just as strong.

She rolled her eyes. That could only mean one thing. That man still followed her.

"I told you to stop following me and leave me alone." Her voice carried behind her and she knew the man backed off, because the sensation of his eyes on her back subsided.

That man is so...

Obstinate didn't seem to fit. There were a few stronger words Sadie could think of, but she abandoned those thoughts as the convenience store finally came into view. Not far from here was a friend's house —a cop—and he owed her a particularly huge favor. Now she just needed to get cleaned up and give her friend a call.

Sadie picked up the pace a little and continued to play with the mist bordering her coat. She didn't think the magic could possibly be permanent. With the sensation of being followed gone, she wondered how much longer the effect would last.

She reached the corner of the convenience store then stopped to scan the area. She didn't see anything, but that sneaking sensation of being followed pressed on her shoulders again.

Of course, he wouldn't obey my command. She sighed, knowing she would have to confront him again. Maybe she'd be forced to fight him. Hopefully, not kill him. But, like the man at the abandoned house, the one her little stalker referred to as a demon hunter, she would do whatever it took to keep breathing.

CHAPTER SEVEN

SADIE

*T*he cashier in the convenience store eyed her suspiciously as she stepped through the entrance. She must have been quite the sight, covered with blood, dirt, and who knew what else. Nevertheless, she didn't let that stop her from following through with her plan.

She immediately went into the bathroom to clean up a little, taking care of the blood, dirt, and soot on her face and hands. Though she really couldn't do much about the condition of her clothing, she felt better.

As she cleaned, she once again took in the amulet embedded in her chest. The lines of ink swirling in flame-like patterns reached across her entire chest. The amulet pulsed with a dark red glow as she gently rubbed a finger over the surface. Warmth spread throughout her body, and her nerves hummed with joy.

"Magic," she whispered and smiled. She loved the way the energy that pulsed through her felt.

After tossing the used paper towels into the trash, she returned to the cashier to borrow a phone.

The cashier stared at her from behind his counter as she approached. His eyebrows knitted together. "A-are you all right? Do you need any help?"

"A phone would be great." She waited as he walked to pick up a cordless phone and brought it to her.

"Thank you," she said and turned, nearly bumping into a cop with a large cup of coffee. She started to mumble an apology when she recognized the squared jaw and broad shoulders. "Carlos?"

"Sadie?" His eyebrows shot near to his hairline, and his eyes scanned her briefly, as if he hadn't recognized her at first.

Sadie had met Carlos six months ago on the asphalt, and her first words to him were something along the lines of *"Don't die on me."* He had been shot in the back and was close to death, but she'd been able to keep him alive on the way to the hospital and visited him often out of pity, if she were being honest with herself. His prognosis hadn't been good. His career was over. He would never walk again. Never fight crime in the streets of Seattle.

All because of a response call gone downhill.

But Carlos was a fighter, and he'd proved the doctors wrong—all of them. Her pity had become pride, and she was beyond impressed with her friend.

Now, he stood in front of her as if that injury never happened. And he never stopped thanking her for that. He gave her the credit when, really, it was all him. Sure, she saved his life. She'd do that for anyone who needed her help. That was why she had become a paramedic.

His expression shifted from surprised to concerned. "What are you doing *here* of all places—and at this time at night?" He squinted and scanned her again, as if he couldn't believe his eyes. "Christ, girl, what the hell happened to you?"

"That is a *long* story."

"Well, I guess you're in luck. I just got off duty and have no life, so I have nothing but time. Let's get you out of here."

Though Carlos wasn't the first on her list of cop buddies to call, he was on there, nevertheless, and was definitely available. He didn't owe her any favors, but he had always been good to her.

She could trust him... even though she wasn't sure how he'd respond to the rampaging demons part of her night.

Sadie smiled. "Thanks. I'll owe you one for this."

"Nonsense. Go grab yourself some coffee. I have a

feeling this is going to be a long story and an even longer night."

"You have no idea," she said.

After Carlos paid for both coffees, he escorted her to his squad car. "I'll have you back home in no time, then we can figure this out."

"No. I can't go home."

He seemed a bit taken aback by that. "All right, then."

Sadie sat in the passenger seat and buckled in as Carlos walked around the front of the squad car and climbed into his seat with a small grunt. He stared at her for a moment and shook his head. He placed his key into the ignition, giving it a twist, and the car roared to life. "Where to?"

"Anywhere I can get a change of clothes and maybe a bite to eat," she said and blew into the tiny hole of her cup before taking a small sip. Hazelnut creamer danced along her tongue, and she smiled at the small comfort the taste brought her.

"I have some stuff at my place that may fit you. Might be a little big on you, but certainly much more comfortable and cleaner than that coat has to be."

Sadie chuckled. "Yeah, I grabbed the first thing I could find. The smell is starting to grow on me."

Carlos laughed. "Only you, Sadie. Only you."

He put the car in gear and backed out of the parking spot.

Meanwhile, Sadie couldn't get over how well Carlos looked. No hint of his previous near-death experience showed. He was happy. Energetic. Not a trace of the mind-numbing pain that had almost crippled him.

"I'm proud of you," she said. "You didn't let your injury get the best of you. You beat it."

"Yeah, it's great what tenacity and a bit of luck can do for you."

She smiled. "I don't think luck had anything to do with it. Still, you look good. I'm surprised at how well you are getting around."

"I still have you to thank for that." He smiled at her and returned his gaze to the road. They spent the rest of the trip to his place in relative silence. Only small talk. Sadie was grateful for that. She wasn't prepared to share the details of the night with him just yet. She needed to collect her thoughts first and find the most reasonable way to explain things.

After all, if it were someone explaining everything to her, she'd probably find the nearest psychiatric ward and admit the poor soul. Then again, maybe that's what she needed.

SADIE

*A*fter unlocking the door and turning on some lights, Carlos told Sadie to have a seat on the living room sofa. He gave her a glass of water and went for a first aid kit to clean her wounds.

Not long after, he arrived with bandages, antiseptics, and gauze. He watched silently as she patched herself up. She winced at the antiseptic's sting while she gently worked to clean the cuts and scrapes.

Carlos, frowning, leaned forward and attempted to take the gauze from her. "Let me do it."

She dodged his hand. "No, I'm fine."

"Are you ready to tell me what happened?" he asked, sitting back into his seat and taking a sip of his coffee.

"Yeah, I'm almost…" Sadie trailed off as she untied the remnants of her shirt and ripped the leg of her pants around the wound in her leg.

The deep gash from where Mara had stabbed her— it was almost entirely healed. The opening was nearly completely sealed, leaving only a small cut less than half the size it was at first. It was still stiff and sore, but the wound was healing much faster than medically possible.

Warmth pulsed in her chest again, and she started to piece things together. The magic fire that turned the demon hunter to ash, the renewed energy she felt as she walked, the strange ink that danced on her skin around the amulet embedded in her skin... they had to all be connected.

Magic, she thought to herself, her body bristling with power. It felt so overwhelming. So raw. So *right.*

"Carlos, do you mind if I get those clothes now?" she asked as she started to clean the remnants of her leg wound.

"Sure, be right back." He stood with a grunt and left the room, heading for his bedroom and flicking on the light as he entered.

A few moments later, he returned with a small bundle of clothing. "Use whatever you're comfortable with. Like I said earlier, some of it may be a bit big on you."

"That's fine. Thank you." She stood, taking the handful of clothes from Carlos. "I'll be right back and explain everything."

Or as close to everything as possible.

She grabbed the ones on top of the pile and entered the bathroom to change. She replaced her torn jeans and the smelly coat with an oversized, plain white t-shirt and comfortable, dark green cotton pajama pants. She gathered the ruined items she previously had on and took them to the kitchen, stuffing them into his trash can.

She turned, and Carlos was opening a kitchen

cabinet, pulling out a couple of cans of soup. He had replaced his uniform with black jeans and a blue, button-down shirt checkered with yellow lines.

"Are you going somewhere?" she asked, pointing to his clothes.

He shook his head. "Nah, I just figured this is going to be a long night. No use in getting into pjs if I'm not going to bed for a while." He opened the cans and poured them into two bowls already sitting on the counter. "Will you tell me what happened now?"

"Where the hell to begin?" she muttered and took a seat on a high-backed stool at the bar-height kitchen table.

After placing the two bowls of soup into the microwave and starting them, Carlos joined her at the table, taking a seat of his own across from her. He sat looking at her expectantly, waiting for her to start her story.

"Brace yourself," she said. "This is hard enough for me to process, so I know it's going to be hard for you to believe. If it hadn't happened to me, I wouldn't believe it myself. So, just bear with me, okay?"

He nodded. "You'd be surprised by what I would believe. Why don't you just worry about telling me what happened, and we'll worry about the believ-ability later, hmm?"

She nodded as well and took in a deep breath. On

the exhale, she said, "My sister and I were attacked in my apartment this evening by a winged woman with incredible strength and unbelievable powers. That's why I can't go home."

Right. Now, let's let that sink in.

Sadie winced, pausing to taking in Carlos's expression while waiting for him to start laughing.

Instead, he sat there with his eyebrows pinched together, slowly nodding. "And?"

He seemed to be taking the story remarkably well considering he wanted to hear more instead of wanting to take her to the nearest psychiatric ward.

She pulled the knife from her boot, placing it on the table between them. Its rubber handle and regular blade paled in comparison to the one Blair had given her to wound Mara with.

"What's that for?" he asked with a nod to the blade.

"Oh man," she muttered. "I took this off the guy I killed tonight, Carlos."

The words spilled from her mouth. Once she started telling her story, she couldn't stop. Sadie told Carlos every detail of how Mara appeared in the apartment, her sister's injuries, how she got the necklace and ended up in the abandoned house. Even the demon hunter she turned to ash. She told him everything. She didn't want to leave out any details.

And most of all, it felt good getting everything off

her chest. Telling someone made everything more real and not like some crazy nightmare, but Carlos didn't seem affected by the story.

It was odd, honestly, that he wasn't losing his shit, even though a small glimmer of fear in the back of her mind warned her he was probably just preparing to lock her in a padded room.

"Do you have the necklace, now?" Carlos asked.

"Of all the things I just told you, the necklace is what you want to see?" she asked. "Of course, I have it. It's embedded in me."

"Can I see it?" he asked.

There was something in the way he asked the question that set Sadie's nerves on fire.

She hesitated at first. But what did she have left to lose?

She eventually pulled the neck of the t-shirt down to show the ruby along with the strange, moving lines of ink on her chest.

He whistled. "Damn, Sadie. 'Rough night' doesn't even begin to describe it."

"You're taking all of this rather well." She narrowed her eyes with suspicion. "What gives? Any person in their right mind would question my sanity."

"I know you wouldn't make up anything so far-fetched if it wasn't true. I can't say that I understand, and my gut tells me you aren't revealing everything, but I do believe you. My suspicion is someone drugged you at some point. Hallucinogens are good at portraying the impossible in very believable ways."

Sadie let go of the shirt and again covered the amulet's brand on her skin. She clasped her hands on the table to keep them from shaking. Everything that had happened felt so surreal, so horrific. She questioned the events being real herself. Maybe, somehow, she did ingest something without remembering when or how.

But her sister...

"Let's say that I did hallucinate everything that happened," Sadie said with a shrug. "How do you explain what happened to my sister and how I got across town and into an abandoned house?"

"It's possible, though not necessarily medically documented, that you had a sort of black out. That could explain the change in location."

Sadie nodded. "And my sister?"

"Do you have a way to call her?"

Sadie shook her head. "No. She doesn't use cell phones. She just decides to show up when she needs help or a place to stay."

Carlos leaned back in his stool and tapped his fingers on the tabletop. "Well, first thing we can do to help you figure out exactly what happened is run you by your apartment. If it's burnt down as you recall, then we can safely assume that part is real."

Sadie wasn't sure she was ready to do that, but if

that meant she could find her sister, then that's what she would do. "All right."

She grabbed the knife and slipped it back into her boot.

"Don't bother with that. I'll bring my gun."

"I need a weapon," she said. She wasn't leaving without it.

"Look, Sadie," he said with an endearing chuckle, "I've been trained to protect civilians. I'm bringing my gun. Let me handle things from now on. Hallucinogen or no, you've already been through enough stress for one night."

"All the more reason to keep it," she said, holding her ground.

He raised his hands in surrender. "Fine. If it will make you feel better."

"Maybe we should look in hospitals for my sister after we're done looking at my place," she said as they exited Carlos's apartment and made their way to his squad car.

"Let me make a few phone calls, first."

After they climbed in, he called a few places about reports of fires or anyone matching Blair's description showing up in a hospital with what appeared to be unusual stab wounds. Sadie remained quiet, trying to pick up anything from the other end of Carlos's call.

He hung up and shook his head. "No one by Blair's

description has shown up in a hospital, but I cashed in a few favors. We will be notified if someone matches her description shows up. Unless she was wearing a wig, or not as injured as you described her to be, she'll be found."

"I guess that's probable," she said. "Still, maybe we should try the hospital closest to the apartment."

"And then what? Check every bed in the hospital? We'll just waste our time."

Sadie groaned and slumped against the passenger seat, resigned. She guessed looking for clues in the apartment was their best bet. Not that she had hope of finding much. The sheer force of the flames that consumed her apartment would likely leave charred bits of furniture and framing. She didn't even know how feasible it would be to even walk into the apartment, much less find any clues to support her story.

She wasn't hallucinating. Everything she'd seen tonight—everything she had endured, it was all very real. Carlos would see that for himself soon enough, and...

Sadie cast a wary eye to her friend. Hopefully, he would still be willing to help.

"What about the fire in my apartment?" she asked.

"That was confirmed. But there wasn't enough structural damage to evacuate the entire building. Be grateful for that. With your story, I may still have to hold you for questioning on possible arson charges. For now, though, I'm going to play dumb. Let's see what we can find out, okay?" He sighed and clenched his jaw. She could see the reality of this all starting to crash into him.

Bit by bit, he was starting to realize she was telling the truth—and she could tell he wasn't comfortable.

Worse than that, Sadie's heart skipped a beat at the thought that her friend might be forced to take her into custody for something she didn't even do. "Good to know."

She took this as a good sign, though. Blair had to be alive. It was possible Mara held her captive or that she was alone somewhere and badly injured, but those were better than being a corpse on her apartment floor.

Carlos looked tense beside her. His stiff arms gripped the steering wheel, his knuckles white as his fingers squeaked against the leather-like plastic. Carlos shifted his gaze, meeting hers briefly, and loosened his grip.

"We're going to find her, Sadie." He reached out his hand, giving hers a tight squeeze before returning it to the wheel again. "We're also going to get to the bottom of what happened tonight."

Her pulse steadied a bit. She believed him, and she was grateful she had one friend through all of this.

When they reached Sadie's apartment, they were

greeted by police tape zig-zagged across her door. Flashes of earlier events raced through her mind. Her pulse quickened as the reality of what really happened stared her in the face.

It couldn't have been hallucinogens. It was real.

She clutched the knife with one hand as Carlos pulled on the tape and twisted the door knob. There was blood on the handle before. Now it was just the normal, shining brass reflecting the light above her door.

There *was* blood there. She'd seen it. She'd touched it. She *knew* it. But it was no longer there, wiped clean from evidence.

With a sigh, she ducked inside, following close behind Carlos.

"Watch where you step. The floor could fall through," Carlos whispered, clicking on his flashlight and carefully testing each step before taking another.

Traces of smoke filled her apartment, and the doorway leading to the living room was sooty and charred. She made sure to keep her footsteps light and close to the walls so as to avoid falling through the floor.

Her living room felt like a different place. All four walls were scorched with pieces of surviving wallpaper peeling off. All her furniture and decorations had either combusted or were debris scattered along the floor, except for her sofa and favorite armchair that were blackened and flaking but otherwise still usable.

At least she had the evidence of her apartment left in charred remains to help solidify her testimony to her friend. She couldn't blame him for being skeptical. But this only proved her story. Her truth.

Sadie carefully made it to the spot where she had last seen Blair. There was no evidence of her sister being burned to a crisp, just the charred remains of carpet that was once a vibrant, deep blue. Now it was charcoal black and burnt.

"This is it. This is where I last saw Blair," Sadie said in the dark, her voice echoing with eerie calm.

When Carlos didn't respond, she turned to see where he had gone off to. She expected him to be off in the bedroom, looking for evidence.

Instead, he stood in the corner of her burned living room, his gun aimed at her chest and his finger on the trigger.

She gasped. "Carlos, what—"

"I'm sorry, Sadie," he said. "Stay where you are and drop the knife."

Mara walked up from behind him, solidifying from the shadows themselves. She smirked at Sadie.

She cast a weary glance to her friend. "Hallucinogens? *Really*? I trusted you." She balled her hand into a fist, nails digging into her palm while the other tightened on the knife. "You son of a bitch."

Carlos shrugged. "It wasn't a miracle that cured me, Sadie. It wasn't even you. It was a deal with the devil that let me walk again." He nodded toward Mara and looked to Sadie again. "Sorry you got caught up in all this."

CHAPTER EIGHT

SADIE

Mara shot a ball of fire at Sadie. She sidestepped. The blaze of heat warmed the skin on her shoulder, barely burning her as the flames rushed toward Carlos. He jumped away just in time to avoid being set on fire, but he toppled to the side, tripping on a broken chair.

Mara's focus remained on Sadie. She didn't so much as cast a sideways glance toward her ally. Clearly, Mara didn't care about him. Nor did she care about Sadie. Sadie knew Mara wanted the necklace, and the demoness was going to kill Sadie to get it.

Not if I can help it.

The veins in Sadie's neck throbbed and her lips curled in disgust. Carlos had wasted his loyalty on such a shitty creature. Even more disappointing was that he burned a bridge with her to gain health—and for what? To stab her in the back and be cast aside like garbage?

Sadie dodged another ball of fire as she watched Carlos climb to his feet on shaky knees. He grunted, still half-pointing his gun at Sadie. Rolling her eyes, she tucked the knife into her boot and made a quick downward strike with her hand, forcing the gun from Carlos's weak grasp and swiping it for herself.

Mara growled as she threw another ball of fire, hitting the wall adjacent to Sadie and Carlos, setting the remnants of wood aflame. Sadie knocked Carlos to the side. He may have betrayed her and accused her of being drugged, but she didn't believe in the whole "eye for an eye" adage.

He was still Carlos. Somehow, she had to believe that he wouldn't have betrayed her if Mara wasn't involved.

Sadie turned and pointed the gun at Mara, screaming as she pulled the trigger several times and emptied the gun. But Mara only had to hold her arms in front of her to block the bullets. They bounced off her armor, landing on the floor in spent shells of ammunition.

The gun clicked as Sadie continued to squeeze the trigger. She dropped it to the floor and glared at Mara. "Where's my sister?"

Mara sneered and charged at Sadie, gliding through the room, wings folded back, and sharp claws extended. She landed toe-to-toe with Sadie and wrenched her hair, jerking her head backward.

"I will claw your heart out if it means getting back my amulet," she hissed.

Mara's talons tore at Sadie's chest, drawing blood. Sadie thrashed, trying to break free from Mara's hold, and slapped a hand behind Mara's horned head, yanking Mara's hair. The demoness's head snapped back.

Two can play this game.

Kicking her foot up behind her, she gripped the dagger in her boot and she stabbed the demoness's thigh. Mara yelped. The grip on her hair released as she twisted away. Sadie looked down to her chest as the deep gashes from Mara's nails left trails of blood along the ripped, borrowed shirt. They moved as the amulet glowed, the tendrils of ink reaching for the gashes and slowly working to seal the wounds.

"You bitch." Mara's talons descended on her again. Sadie gripped the demoness's wrist and twisted.

Mara squealed.

Sadie's eyes narrowed. "You barge into my apartment, destroy my living room, attack me and my sister, and *I'm* the bitch?" she asked. "You should be more self-aware."

She flipped the blade in her hand, the tip pointed toward Mara's body, and with a swipe, sliced Mara's side.

The weapon didn't wound her the way the intricate dagger her sister had given her had, but Mara still staggered from the cut, holding her side and pulling her hand away to reveal dark blood staining her palm and fingers.

"You'll pay for that." She charged.

Sadie side-stepped and evaded Mara, causing her to land in the charred remains of her recliner. Mara turned toward her, palms heating and glowing with the promise of another ball of fire.

Movement shifted in the corner of Sadie's peripheral. She faced Carlos, holding a sharp fragment of wood from the broken chair he tripped on. He advanced on her.

He apparently had recovered from his fall and wanted to add salt to the proverbial wound of his betrayal by also trying to kill her.

If Sadie ever did find Blair, words were going to be had. And not so nice ones either.

She ducked the balls of fire and rolled from the swing of the splintered wood. She stuck her leg out, tripping Carlos, sending him crashing to the ground. His feeble weapon flew across the floor.

Keeping an eye on Mara's next move, Sadie crouched beside him. "You brought this on yourself." She smashed the dagger's hilt against his temple. His body went slack, head lolling to the side.

Mara rushed to Sadie, moving wickedly fast and

slapping her across the face. The demoness's nails sliced her cheek. "Give it to me!"

She hit the ground hard. Her cheek stung, and her knife fell to the floor. She scrambled away from Mara and pushed herself to her feet.

Mara bared her teeth. "You're quick for a human. But not quick enough." She raised her hands, and balls of fire exploded from her palms.

Sadie threw herself behind the charred sofa as fireballs careened in her direction. Her arm collided with the floor. Heat enveloped her as the sofa combusted into flames. For the second time that night, her living room was being engulfed in flames. The inferno licked the walls and the ceiling, consuming the wooden remains that survived the first fire.

"One way or another, you're going to die, girl." Mara growled as another raging ball of fire crashed into another wall. "I'll get that necklace if I have to pry it off the charred remains of your retched body!"

Sadie poked her head around the sofa. Mara shot fireballs in every direction. She had a feeling the fire wouldn't kill a creature like Mara, but it would end Sadie for sure. A few feet from her, Carlos's unconscious body erupted into flames. Her pulse hammered in her chest.

She needed to find a way out of the apartment and fast.

Within seconds, the cop's skin blistered and blackened under the fire's heat. The stolen dagger lay beside him.

Sadie wanted to crawl over and get it, but Mara didn't show signs of stopping her heated rage.

Sweat soaked through her clothes, but the heat didn't seem to burn her as much anymore. She should've been screaming in pain, but she only crouched behind the couch that started to burn itself and tried to figure out a way to escape the apartment before the entire floor collapsed.

She reached for the ruby's magic, the energy she had felt in the abandoned house. She sought for its warmth, but it wasn't there. If she wanted to live, she had to get out of here.

This is a good time to save me again, amulet, she thought.

Mara stopped setting everything ablaze, apparently content with just waiting Sadie out and watching her burn like Carlos. Sadie's path to the knife cleared, and she sprung from behind the sofa and reached for the dagger. She grabbed the knife and threw it in Mara's direction, lodging it her throat.

Sadie didn't stop to admire the amazing shot. Instead, she sprinted through the burning doorway. She skidded along the hallway and scampered down the steps, every step making her breathe heavier. She reached the bottom of the stairs and halted as a familiar figure stood in the entryway, an intense glint in his eyes.

The handsome stranger, her stalker, knew where she lived. Or, he somehow followed her. Her heart skipped a beat. She hadn't expected to bump into him. She lost him at the convenience store.

Sadie swallowed hard, prepared to fight him off as well, figuring him to be another one of Mara's henchmen. But his eyes softened as they met hers.

"Are you all right?" he asked.

Before she could answer, he moved, swiftly stepping past her. She turned and saw him holding the tip of the demon hunter's knife between his thumb and middle finger. At the top of the stairs, Mara stood gaping at him, seeming extremely perturbed by his saving Sadie's life. She must have tried to throw the dagger at Sadie's back. And he saved her.

Maybe he wasn't so bad after all.

"Demoness," he said, his deep sexy voice nearly growling the word.

Shivers raked down Sadie's spine. She shook her head, clearing the daze from her mind. She needed to run. But her body wouldn't move. There was something about the man that stood in front of her that kept her still. Mara actually feared him.

Sadie's hesitance to leave could have been pure exhaustion from an entire night of fire, fighting, and running. Either way, she didn't have anywhere else to go. No one to turn to. The handsome stranger had just saved her life, and she needed to know why. Though she wasn't willing to trust him with the one time he managed to protect her, he was her best bet for the moment.

Mara said, "The girl has something that belongs to me. Step aside."

"This human girl is under my protection," he said.

Mara's face contorted, as if struggling with something internally. The demoness glared at him, though her hands shook at her sides.

"She stole something from me," she repeated. "I want it back."

He twisted to look at Sadie and returned his gaze to Mara. "She never stole anything that wasn't rightfully hers."

Mara snarled. "She's a thief."

The demoness flew down the stairs, arms raised. The guy jumped with unbelievable speed, meeting Mara in between. He slammed the demoness to the stairs, with one hand around her throat, shattering the wooden steps. Wrapping his fingers around Mara's ankle, he lifted her entire body, smashing it against the banister. Sadie covered her face with her arms as splinters flew everywhere.

Sadie stepped back, slumping against a nearby wall and watched, mesmerized, as her handsome rescuer battered Mara with strong, effortless blows. It would have to take someone of equal strength, someone like her, to do the damage he was doing. Sadie didn't want to face the explanation staring her in the face. She had enough of demons and fire, and betrayals. She just wanted to get this night over with.

Her rescuer swung the dagger and slashed Mara's arm, wing, and calf in one swift motion. His movements blurred as he moved too quickly for human standards. Mara tried to dodge each blow, but her movements were too clumsy compared to his. He dug the blade into Mara's shoulder and twisted it. He yanked the blade from the demoness's body, and just as he aimed to plunge the blade through her heart, Mara released a strong blaze of fire that engulfed the impossibly fast man.

Mara retreated up the stairs and disappeared into the shadows.

Sadie pushed herself from the wall, ready to go to the man's aid, but the fire dissipated, and the man stood in front of her, unscathed. She let out a loud sigh. *Of course. More Magic.*

"Well, let's just hope we never see her again," he said in a nonchalant tone.

Sadie highly doubted that would be the last time. Mara had already proven she wouldn't give up until she got the amulet back.

The handsome stranger dusted off his hands and held his arm out to her. "Shall we?"

She furrowed her eyebrows and didn't move. He shrugged, dropped his arm, and turned his back to her, walking through the emergency exit. She stared at his back as he moved at a normal human's pace. It was almost too slow compared to how fast he moved just moments before. With a sigh of resignation, she followed.

He led her into an alleyway, walking close to the buildings. Sadie maintained his speed, remaining a few paces behind him. Her mind worked overtime trying to figure out what he was, why he saved her, and why he came into her life so soon after the amulet was, for lack of a better phrase, gifted to her.

The stranger stopped and turned around. His gaze scanned her from top to bottom, lingering on her wounds and torn t-shirt stained red with dried blood. Without a word, he approached her and lifted the shirt, revealing the deep scratches that had already begun to heal.

She smacked his hands away. "What are you—"

Unaffected by her attempts to keep his hands off her body, he still proceeded to examine the wounds, tracing his fingers over the surface of her skin. He nodded to himself and mumbled something to the effect of "it was working." He released the shirt.

"What?" Sadie pulled the shirt down past the waist band of her pants.

"I'm Kaiser, by the way," he said and held out his hand.

She hesitated. But she did owe him a form of gratitude for saving her life. She lifted her hand and returned the gesture. "Sadie."

His skin was soft, warm, and smooth for such a skilled fighter.

"I know," he said, hazel eyes staring at her. She could drown in them. He added, "We should go."

He turned and started walking again.

Sadie didn't move. "I'm not going with you. Not without answers."

He faced her again and looked her in the eyes. "You have nowhere else to go, and you don't know who your allies are."

"That's not true," she said, but he continued as if she didn't speak.

"You can probably handle yourself, but you'll most likely die out here on your own. You don't know what you've gotten yourself into." He took a deep breath. "Come with me, I'll explain everything. But not here. We need to go somewhere safe." He held his hand out again.

She only looked at him as she debated her options. She could go with him where any number of unpleasant experiences awaited her. Or, she could try to get out of this mess on her own.

He had yet to give her a good reason not to trust

him, though he would still need to work on gaining that trust. One good deed didn't win her trust or faith in anyone. Tonight was a good reason to hold onto that way of thinking. However, he did seem to know more about everything she was just thrust into than she did. He had answers. She needed answers.

Finally, she made up her mind, extended her hand toward his, and when their fingers touched, the world shimmered around her. The ground beneath her gave way. She fell into a dark plummet.

The last of the world around her faded as she realized she could be falling toward hell.

CHAPTER NINE

STEELE

*S*teele bolted upright in bed. Naked succubae yelped beside him, some angrily hissing at the disturbance in their sleep. He shivered as a chill creeped through his veins. As a prince of the underworld, he had a deep connection to the demon realms. For years, his home felt empty, dead. Now, it felt like every part of the underworld burned with energy, humming with renewed life and vigor.

The succubus on his right rubbed his chest, her flaming blue hair framing her porcelain skin, making her look like an innocent damsel, not the ruinous monster she truly was. "Come back to bed," she said, purring the words with hungry need.

Tempting... but not tonight.

He flung her hand away and hopped off the bed.

Pulling on his pants as he moved toward the door, his thoughts ran circles in his head. He knew what the feeling meant. The queen has returned. And he needed to be the first to her side. Dashing into the hallway, he almost collided with the red-skinned demon servant standing ramrod straight next to the door.

"She's here," Steele said, heart thudding with excitement in his chest.

The servant nodded in agreement. "Our spies confirm that the demon queen has returned."

Steele grinned. *I guess I should pay her a visit.*

∼

SADIE

Sadie's feet planted on solid ground. Everything she saw tilted. Her knees buckled, and she almost collapsed, but strong arms held her steady. Kaiser stood beside her, looking as calm as ever.

As her world came into focus, she found herself standing before a massive wrought iron gate with silver and sapphire stones along its finials, casting a soft light in an otherwise gloomy atmosphere.

A more massive fortress stood behind the gate, majestic stone pillars and columns looming over her.

Larger glowing sapphires shone brighter from balustrade posts and parapets. She craned her neck upward and beheld the rock-strewn sky, colossal stalactites jutting down through the mist. All around her, obsidian and granite pillars towered over the rampart where she and Kaiser stood.

Her chest warmed the way it had when she found herself teleported to the abandoned house. The blood in her veins ran faster, and her fingertips tingled. She felt a connection to the place. She didn't even realize her mouth was open until Kaiser walked closer to the gate, the sounds of his footsteps shaking her from her daze.

Kaiser lifted his hand to knock on the gate, but it creaked open before he could.

"Your Highness!" a high-pitched voice called out.

Sadie heard the voice before she saw the horned and winged creature that emerged from the gate. She instinctively jumped back. He was a gargoyle, she guessed, as the creature looked exactly like the stone figures that stood guard over the gothic churches and buildings she had visited before. Except this gargoyle was talking and moving, his sharp teeth glinting against the eerie light as he fussed over her like an old grandmother.

"My name is Hobson," he said. "I am your butler."

Sadie only stared at him. She tried to process the creature standing before her, but her mind couldn't make any more sense of it than it was all an effect of the magic she gained from the amulet.

Hobson walked around her, hands shaking off the dust and dirt from her clothes. He stood in front of her and cupped her cheeks with both palms, his touch was cold but surprisingly gentle for hands made of stone.

"Are you okay, Your Highness?" he asked. "Are you hungry? Would a sweet bun cheer Your Majesty up?"

"I—" Sadie slowly pulled back, unable to find eloquence, still processing the bizarreness of having a gargoyle butler.

Kaiser shifted beside her and Hobson glanced sideways, eyes narrowing. The butler pointed a finger at Kaiser and screamed, "Detain this man!"

Metallic vines shot from the ground and wrapped themselves around Kaiser's limbs and torso, rooting him in place. Bolts of white light fired from his hands, but the metal only seemed to absorb them.

"What did you do?" she asked, more confused than accusatory. She stood still for a moment and grinned, amused to see Kaiser squirming, unable to escape from the vines. She already liked her butler.

The gargoyle remained unperturbed. "This is Bitterthorn, the demon queen's fortress," Hobson said. He turned to her and added, "We have been waiting for you for a century. You're safe now, Your Majesty."

Demon queen? Sadie furrowed her eyebrows. *I can't be royalty. That's impossible.*

She looked up at the fortress. The gothic design wasn't exactly her style, but as her gaze roved over the imposing metal spirals, ornate crystals, and pillars that decorated the façade, her heart swelled in admiration. Her pendant grew warmer. She felt a tug in her chest, like the fortress called to the pendant. To *her*.

It felt like going home. A welcoming reunion.

She had never been one for intuition, but this was clearly where the pendant belonged. And now that the pendant was a part of her, this was where *she* belonged.

"Any minute now," Kaiser said.

She turned to face him. "Oh!"

She wasn't really going to leave him there detained. She just got caught up in the amazing awe of her newfound position. At this point, it wouldn't hurt to release Kaiser. He could have done anything with her, but he had proven himself to be trustworthy several times. He even brought her to this place—this place that felt so right.

She looked at her handsome rescuer while saying, "Hobson, you can release him. This man saved my life."

Hobson's eyebrows shot up. "My apologies. My apologies."

The gargoyle snapped his fingers and the metal

vines slithered back to the ground. Hobson walked over to Kaiser and shook his hands with heavy enthusiasm. "Oh, you saved our queen. I shall forever be grateful. Come, come. Let's go inside."

Hobson turned his back on them and entered through the gate. He commented on Kaiser's appearance as he led them into the fortress. "Why do you hide your form? Is this the new custom?"

Sadie shook her head, smiling. Her butler acted as though he had never imprisoned Kaiser to begin with.

∼

SADIE

Hobson gave Sadie a tour of the fortress. Well, some of it. The place was *huge*. Hobson had led her through the throne room, dining hall, and sitting room. Kaiser silently followed behind her.

Now, Hobson opened the door to her sleeping chambers. Sadie gasped as she took in the rich, golden vines that climbed up the red walls and the matching brocade curtains that covered the windows.

But what caught Sadie's attention the most was the queen-sized bed carved from ebony in the middle of the room. Silky black sheets and cushions covered the mattress, inviting her to lay down. She desperately wanted to dismiss her two companions, so she could fall into bed and sleep, but she wanted to get answers from them first. She approached and sat on the edge of the bed.

"Your fortress is impervious, Your Majesty," Hobson said. "Nothing, and no one, can get in or out unless you allow it."

Sadie sighed contentedly, loving the ambiance of the place. The castle called to her. She stood up and walked to the nearest wall, touching a golden leaf from a vine. Her fingers grazed the wall and she felt it hum beneath her fingertips. She smiled to herself, knowing everything she had been shown belonged to her and felt better than she had felt in her entire life. As she toyed with the gold embossed vines on the wall, she recalled what Hobson had done with Kaiser upon their arrival.

"Can I do what you did with the vines?" Sadie asked her butler.

Hobson nodded. "Yes, indeed, Your Highness. And a lot more. This place is an extension of you." He clasped his hands behind his back. "It will take time and practice, but the longer you stay here and become more familiar with the place, you'll be able to explore all the fortress's secrets. You can even ask it to summon me," he said, eyes alight with anticipation. "Even if I was on the other side of the fortress, you could reach me."

Although excited, Sadie was still confused on how she inherited all this in the first place. She frowned. "I —I'm still lost. How can I be the demon queen? I'm just an ordinary paramedic. I'm not that special."

"The amulet, Your Majesty," Hobson said. "The first demon queen was a powerful sorceress who possessed immense power, but she didn't always acquire it by, shall we say, *honest* means. That left her with numerous enemies as well as people who wanted to use her power for their own gain. She was eventually killed, and her power was removed. But that much magic couldn't be destroyed easily. Most of what remained of the queen's magic was preserved in that pendant you're wearing."

Sadie furrowed her eyebrows. "So, whoever holds this pendant is the queen?"

"Not just anyone, Your Majesty," Hobson said. "The magic it contains is ancient. Through the years, it has evolved. It has become more lethal than ever. One can even say it has a mind of its own, because it *chooses* who can access the power within it."

Sadie touched the ruby, remembering how she had killed the demon hunter by wielding the amulet's power without realizing it. She remembered how she had pleaded for that energy to come back when she had been fighting Mara. It didn't. And now, it made sense why.

Sadie looked at Kaiser. "I think I used its power.

Back in that house." She returned her attention to Hobson. "But I can't control it."

"Fret not, Your Highness," Hobson said. "If you train, you will be able to master the amulet's magic. With practice, you'll grow stronger. I can help."

She sat on the edge of the bed, physically *and* mentally overwhelmed. It was definitely a lot to process. In one night, her entire life had changed. She learned more about her world than she ever knew existed. If she was going to survive even the next few days, she knew she had to keep up and just roll with the punches. More importantly, she needed to sleep.

She touched the amulet and stared at a single spot on the hardwood floor. *Demon queen.* It was so formal, so regal and dark. And yet, now, that was her. A hint of a smile tugged on her lips. Queen of the demons was a far cry from broke paramedic working the slums of Seattle.

"There had never been a human demon queen before," Kaiser said.

Hobson pouted, clearly not liking Kaiser chiming in and stealing his thunder.

Ignoring the gargoyle, Kaiser sat on the bed beside her. "The fact that the amulet chose you means you're special." He tucked her hair behind her ear, and her breath caught. "Over time, you might grow horns." He brushed her hair back and his arms rested on her shoulder. "You might even grow wings. I can teach you how to fly."

Sadie sat with her arms frozen at her sides, every nerve ending of her traitorous body flaring from his touch. She leaned slightly closer, needing more. Realizing what she was doing, she shoved the feeling away, reminding her body that this was a man even Mara had feared. Sadie couldn't let her guard down, not quite yet. If she was going to trust him—and damn it, she wanted to—she should wait until he proved himself completely.

Hobson cleared his throat, and Sadie blushed from forgetting someone else was in the room with them. "If you want, Your Majesty, I can teach you how to access your power," the gargoyle said, taking over once more.

She smiled. "I would love that, Hobson, thank you."

"Y-you're welcome," Hobson stammered, his eyebrows raised. "It's quite easy, once you get familiar with it. Magic is all about the manipulation of energy. Close your eyes, if you will, Your Highness."

She closed her eyes.

"Just concentrate and feel everything around you," Hobson said. "Be aware of your surroundings. Listen, smell, *feel.*"

She did as she was told, focusing on the sensation of the silk beneath her hands, the softness of the mattress. She breathed in remnants of old fires, perfumes she couldn't place, and the scent of Kaiser's skin. She listened to the breathing of Hobson and the air that moved through the room.

"Reach deep within you for the amulet's magic. Believe that you're one with its power, and you can gather the elements to do your bidding. All you have to do is focus."

"Okay," Sadie said. "I'll try."

She took a deep breath. *Concentrate. Focus. It's not that hard.*

With every breath she took, she let her awareness flow over every part of her body. She felt the amulet in her chest, just *there* at first, but it began to tingle, brimming with energy, with magic. She felt the amulet's warmth and power reaching out to her and connecting with her. Connection not just to the amulet, but to the fortress, the air, the ground, to *everything*.

She extended an arm, palm facing upward. She gathered the energy around her. The black tattoos grew warmer, pulsating in her skin. A prickling warmth emanated from her sternum and it spread throughout her body.

Fire, she thought.

The warmth dissipated but her palm tingled. She opened her eyes and saw a small flame burning on her palm. She willed it to grow, and it did. She let her newfound strength pervade her body. She let it overwhelm her. She willed the flame gone, and it sputtered.

Hobson nodded, eyes alight with appreciation. "You got it on your first try. With a bit of rest and more practice, you'll be a woman no one could mess with. I hope you're not tired yet, Your Highness, because I have one last thing to show you."

"I'm exhausted, but I'm willing to see one more thing. That's it for the night though."

"Of course, Your Highness."

Hobson led them out of her chamber and they meandered through lavish halls lit by clam-shaped sconces. Sadie took everything in. Opulent chandeliers, paintings, and figurines filled her vision. She practically drooled over the magnificence of it all. It was so much better than her shitty apartment.

They turned a corner and walked down a hallway that seemed plain compared to the ones they had just passed. What set this one apart from the others, though, were the twelve or so portraits hanging on the walls. She stopped by the first one—a painting of a demoness with free-flowing hair as white as her pale skin. She looked so regal and beautiful. Sadie couldn't help but linger.

"Who are they?" she asked.

"Those are the past demon queens," Hobson said.

She faced her butler. "What were they like?"

"Nothing like you, Your Highness," he said. "That's

a compliment." His eyes wandered over the portraits. "I'm not even sad they all had unfortunate fates."

Her eyebrows shot up. "What do you mean?"

"Majesty," he said, eyes softening toward her. "Your crown has a curse. Everyone who wore it had short reigns and mysterious deaths." He took her hands in his and looked at her with a haunted gaze. "I can only hope Her Majesty's fortune won't be the same as theirs."

A shiver ran up her arm. She wondered what horrible fate she was doomed to and how long her reign would be now that the queens of the past had a history of dying mysteriously. "Thanks for the heads up," she said. Exhaustion plagued her mind, pressing against her eye lids, willing them to close. She squeezed them shut and refocused on Hobson. "What were you going to show me again?"

"Yes, yes," he said. The intensity in his eyes disappeared. "Right this way."

They walked farther before stopping in front of huge double doors with metallic lion heads adorning the doorknobs.

"What's inside?" she asked. "I bet it's a library."

Hobson's smile looked mischievous. He opened the door, and Sadie gasped as she beheld a treasure hoard. Loads of gold and silver coins, golden sculptures and ornaments, and various gems filled every surface of the floor of what seemed to be a ballroom. Massive, turquoise columns formed numerous archways inside the cavernous space. Circular mirrors hung from the walls, reflecting beams of light from the enormous emerald chandelier hanging in the middle of the high ceiling.

"This is your inheritance," Hobson said.

Sadie's gape turned into a grin. She was rich beyond belief and was definitely going to enjoy this upgrade to her life.

She would have loved to examine every bit of treasure in the room, but her stomach growled. As much as she enjoyed the tour, she needed to eat. More than that, she needed to rest.

"Hobson?"

"Yes, Your Highness?" the butler asked.

"Can I get something to eat on my way to bed?"

"Of course, Your Majesty."

Sadie faced Kaiser. "I'm headed to bed. I came off a twelve-hour shift to this madness. It's time I had some sleep." She again turned to Hobson. "Can you find Kaiser a room, please?"

Hobson stared at her, grey eyebrows lifted. The corner of Kaiser's lips seemed to twitch.

"Is there going to be a problem with that request?" Sadie asked, her own eyebrows drawing together. "Don't tell me this gigantic fortress doesn't have more bedrooms?"

"O-of course, it does, Your Majesty," Hobson said.

"I'm just used to harsh orders, is all, not polite requests."

She almost laughed. *That's the big deal?* She just rolled her eyes and headed to her room. She had enough to process and would figure out the rest in the morning. First a bite, then sleep.

Beautiful, blissful sleep.

CHAPTER TEN

SADIE

*U*pon waking up, she felt renewed. Powerful. She parted the velvet curtains that led to her chamber's balcony and walked outside to examine the demon realm's atmosphere. The "sky" had changed. With the mist gone, millions of azure crystals glowed in the ceiling high above her, covering every inch of dark earth.

Even the stalactites were encased by the glowing gems. They changed color from time to time, and there were so many of them that she couldn't even differentiate the colors anymore. The beads of color blended together like a classic Monet painting, shimmering with light and wonder.

She wondered if they simulated daylight. If so, the view was even better here than in the world above.

She took in a deep breath, surprised she didn't

inhale a lungful of damp and moldy, dirty air. Instead, it was better than breathing in Seattle's morning environment. It was like dew on grass, sunshine, or flowers blooming. She wrapped her arms around her body and closed her eyes as she took in a deep breath, becoming intoxicated by the new world around her.

She should be lost, stressed out, or downright losing it, having been transported to a place like this. But this place *felt* right. She felt powerful, and whatever problems came to her, she would rise above them all.

She peered into the distance. With brighter illumination, she could now see a copse of trees close by.

Trees.

Underground!

Farther away, a forest surrounded the perimeter of her lands. There were cliffs, too, and lakes, and even a waterfall. The land was massive, and it was all hers.

A new home, new power, and a treasure hoard. She had acquired them overnight. She suddenly didn't want to blame Blair anymore, but thank her for the wonder, the magic, the gift.

She needed to find her sister and have her stay at the fortress. She would keep her safe from the things that kept bringing her injured to her apartment. Then she could handle Mara.

Sadie just hoped it wasn't already too late.

"Had a good night's rest?" a deep voice asked from beside her.

She jumped, startled, and turned to face her intruder. *Kaiser.*

He walked toward her in his plain white, button-down shirt tucked in navy pants and a brown belt. His shirt hugged his torso and seemed nearly painted on over his massive biceps. He shoved his hands into his pants pockets and leaned against the opening to her balcony, eyes glinting.

She wanted to shout at him to get the hell out of her room, to tell him this was *her* space and he needed to respect her privacy. Never mind being unsettled by how stealthily he entered her room. Not so much as a whisper of footsteps alerted her to his presence.

But she remembered everything he had done for her. He brought her to her fortress and saved her life. And being that she was fully rested, she could think a little more clearly. She still didn't know what his intentions were, but he had helped her time and again even when he didn't have to.

She decided to let it slide. Just this once.

"Thank you," she said. "For saving my life."

He only looked at her, eyes crinkling at the corners, lips tightening from a suppressed smile. She wanted to touch those lips, tell him to just go ahead and smile. For her. Instead, she looked away and stared at the crystal sky, more for distraction than to admire them.

"Mara," she said. "Do you know her?"

"The demoness that tried to kill you?" Kaiser asked.

She faced him. "Yes."

He shrugged. "I don't know much. Based on how she fought, I'd say she's an abyssian."

Sadie slowly nodded. "What does that mean?"

"They're a deadly group of assassins and radicals. They dwell deep underground, far from the reach of any ruler in this realm. I'm not exactly sure what they're up to. Some say they're forming a resistance, but against whom, I don't know."

She processed the new information for a moment. If Mara was indeed an abyssian, what did she want with the amulet? Was she acting on her own, breaking free from whatever she felt enslaved to? Did she just want the power or to become queen? What was her story?

Sadie leaned her backside against the edge of the balcony and crossed her arms. She chewed on her lip as she thought. "Why do you think she wants the amulet so badly? Is it so she could be queen? What would she use its power for? What does she really want?"

Kaiser shrugged again. "Who knows with her. But we can figure it out."

"Speaking of hidden agendas and motivations, how about you? What do you want?"

He stared at her for a moment, already poised to carefully choose his words. Sadie wasn't sure if that was a good thing or a bad thing.

"I'm a prince," he said, which really didn't answer her question.

"Really?" she asked, dropping her hands to her sides.

"Yes. My father is the King of Shadford, the largest kingdom in the demon realms." He looked at the horizon as if he could see his father's kingdom from where he stood.

Sadie glanced in the same direction, squinting her eyes to try and catch a glimpse from the horizon, but nothing defining a kingdom could be seen. Just the immense trees, cliffs, and rivers.

"He threatened to kill all his sons, and now my brothers and I are at war for his throne."

Sadie returned her gaze to Kaiser, frowning. *That's why he saved me. To use my power to defeat his father and win his own throne.*

"So that's why you sought me out," she said. "You want my magic to win your birthright back." A knot twisted in her chest, but she convinced herself she shouldn't be surprised. She kept her posture straight.

He looked at her, a wrinkle forming in his forehead. "Yes, but it's not just that. I—"

Before he could explain further, a vase crashed to the stone floor in the hall outside her bedroom. Her chamber doors flung open and Hobson entered her room, huffing.

"Your Majesty, you need to see this," the gargoyle said, panting. When he saw Kaiser, he frowned, his eye twitching, perhaps bothered that Kaiser was in Sadie's room without him knowing. Hobson placed his hands on his hips. "What are you doing here uninvited? Your Majesty, do you want me to throw him in the dungeons?"

Sadie chuckled. *Tempting.* "Not at the moment, Hobson." She winked at Kaiser. "Maybe later." She faced her butler again. "What did you want me to see?"

"Follow me, my queen." The butler led them out her chamber.

Sadie and Kaiser followed Hobson to an adjacent room not far off from her bedroom. The entire room was massive and dim, its cobalt and silver walls lined with gigantic windows bordered with elegant, spiral designs.

The room was devoid of furniture, except for a small, white marble table in the center. And there was no lighting aside from an orb that sat atop it. It reminded her of the crystal balls she saw in films, where fortune tellers stared into the orb for visions of people's futures.

Hobson gestured to the very orb. "If you would take a look, Your Majesty."

Sadie slowly approached the object. Through the glass, a green and red haze shifted and moved.

"What am I supposed to see, Hobson?" she asked.

Hobson didn't answer. Perhaps because of the fact that images already started to take shape within the ball of glass.

Her fortress solidified first. The image shifted, panning out to show two more demon men. One had black wings and the other green. They fought each other, each trying to beat the other to her fortress.

"Oh dear," Hobson said.

Beside her, Kaiser sighed. Sadie shifted her attention to him. He ruffled his hair and shifted his weight between his legs.

"You know these two?" she asked.

He grimaced. "Those are my brothers."

Interesting. She could sort of see the resemblance between the three. Similar noses and jaw shapes. But Kaiser didn't have wings, a tail, or odd colored skin.

She looked to the orb again, fascinated with learning more about Kaiser and meeting two of his brothers. They had reached her gate and waited, still bickering with each other. She wondered what the beef was between them, and if it was about winning their father's throne.

Finally, she said, "Why don't we go pay them a

visit? But first, I need to get dressed. Meet me at the gate."

Hobson and Kaiser nodded and left. Hobson pushed Kaiser out the door and turned and said, "By the way, Your Highness, your wardrobe is fully stocked within your room. Do you need my assistance?"

Sadie shook her head. "I'll be fine, Hobson. Thank you."

After taking one final look into the orb, Sadie turned and made her way back to her room.

When Sadie opened the huge double doors to her wardrobe, she wasn't expecting a huge room filled with lavish items. She was captivated as she took in the lush, dark purple carpet covering the floor and the array of bathrobes. So regal. So comfortable looking.

On the other side of the room, designs of armor were propped on mannequins, standing like warrior queens. Some of the battle outfits were Samurai-like, and some seemed more fit for Amazons.

She grazed her fingers along some of the lavish dresses that hung on the walls and nearly drooled over the expensive gem-encrusted tiaras that stood on display.

This is all mine?

She surveyed the endless array of clothing at her disposal. She needed to quickly think of something that would show her command and gain the attention of the men. She needed to make the best first impression.

A smile stretched her lips as she settled on a long-sleeved black dress that shimmered as it caught the light. Its neckline plummeted, which would show off her amulet well.

Oh, this is going to be fun.

CHAPTER ELEVEN

DAMIEN

*D*amien swung Lightbane, his broadsword, at Steele. The blade flamed, sending tiny sparks of fire into the air. His brother ducked the flames, narrowly missing his throat. The warmth Damien's blade emitted was familiar and comforting. His sword's guard was a bronze crescent that extended to the pommel, and it protected his hand from the sword's scalding heat, which should have hit his brother, had Steele not cheated by casting an illusion of Damien hitting a tree instead of his brother.

Steele wore his usual form-fitting, silver and blue armor. Even Damien had to admit his brother looked as dashing as ever, though that only added to his annoyance.

"Stop being so uptight. Stress is a real killer, brother." Steele laughed as he dodged another blow.

Damien groaned. *This son-of-a-bitch never takes anything seriously.*

Why did his brother have to be here as well? Why couldn't he just stay away for once. It's not like he really cared about anything but himself. He seemed perfectly content to lie in the beds of sexual predators even when Cedric had died. What could he possibly want with the new queen?

"Hold still so I can kill you. And none of those hallucinations. Fight me like a real man." Damien swung his sword again. The flames of his broadsword singed Steele's dirty blond hair.

Steel gasped. "You burned my hair!" He narrowed his eyes and swung his axe at Damien. The axe clanged against the sword.

Damien took note that the metal of Steele's weapon was entirely indigo, and the handle was lined with bronze fleur-de-lis carvings.

"Nice weapon. Where did you get it? Or should we say, who did you kill to get it?" he asked as he swung his sword. He struck the flat surface of his brother's weapon.

"I'm glad you like it," Steele said. "It's called Bloodrage, though I like its nickname better."

Damien rolled his eyes and said, "Which is?"

"Party Pooper." Steele smiled and bobbed his eyebrows.

"Accurate." Damien swung again, but his brother

parried the blow. "That's diamantine isn't it?" He referred to the rare metal Steele's weapon was made of.

"Aren't we supposed to be fighting, not chatting?" Steele asked with that stupid smirk still on his face.

"You attacked first!" If only Damien could land a blow to his brother's face, earn him a well-deserved scar. That would make this squabble so worth it.

"Huh…" Steel paused to rub his jaw and leveled the weight of his stare on his brother. "I wonder why."

Damien growled. He spun and smacked the sword's pommel on his brother's side. But Steele's golden tail wrapped around Damien's ankle and snapped back, knocking him on the ground. Steele's axe descended on Damien's face, but he rolled away, tucking his wings behind him. When Damien stood, brown dirt smudged all over his white and gold cloak. He had worn his best attire just for this day's purpose, and his brother was ruining *everything*. He jabbed at the tail that had yanked his feet from underneath him. It recoiled when the flames licked it.

Damien had enough of this. He sheathed his weapon, extinguishing the flames, and glided toward his brother. He collided with Steele, and they crashed to the ground, limbs and fists slamming against each other. Wings and tails whipped back and forth. He shifted his weight, gaining needed leverage, and wrapped an arm around Steele's head, pinning his brother to his chest.

"Give up, brother," Damien said, gritting his teeth as Steele tried to wrench himself free. "Stick to your petty games and brothels."

"Tempting," Steele said through clenched teeth. "But not as tempting as kicking your ass."

Steele twisted under Damien's hold, striking his elbow against his brother's ribs and breaking free from the headlock.

Damien lifted a fist to deal another blow, but Steele's eyes widened.

What the...

"Look out!" his brother yelled. Steele shoved Damien away and jumped back.

Damien gracefully landed in a crouch, but he scraped his palms against the ground trying to steady himself. A strong blast of fire hit the spot where they had been grappling. The small explosion ruffled his hair. He searched for the source of the attack and gawked as a beautiful woman sashayed toward them with a thunderous expression. Her raven hair cascaded over her shoulders, and the sexy dress she wore accented every curve well.

He spotted a figure a short distance behind her. Narrowing his eyes, he recognized his brother Kaiser's human form. A snarl erupted in Damien's throat.

Great. Now I have to contend with two brothers.

The woman approached closer, and Damien took in her stern features. She appeared human, which would likely explain Kaiser's form. Either she preferred the human form, or she was...

He squinted, discerning no hint of enchantment or glamour. His mouth fell open. What in the hell was a human doing in the underworld?

A red ruby in the center of her chest glowed as her hands took on the aura of fire. That pendant was unique, special, and only meant one thing. The demon queen was *human*. He didn't see that coming. To make matters worse, Kaiser somehow beat them to her.

Steele quietly came to stand beside him and was uncharacteristically speechless, gawking at her beauty and probably surprised by the fact that she was human just as much as Damien was when the realization hit him.

"What are you doing here?" Kaiser asked, lips curling.

"Family reunion," he said, shifting his gaze to Steele.

"Enough!" the human demon queen said in the most commanding, attention-grabbing voice.

She's fierce too.

Damien cleared his throat, returning his mind to his task at hand. "Your Majesty. It was not my intention to cause any inconvenience. I am here on a diplomatic mission, to talk to you about matters of utmost importance."

Steele snorted behind him. "Way to man up, brother." He approached the queen with a devilish smile on his face. "Please, allow me to introduce myself. You see, I'm—"

"Not interested. Now, tell me why are you two on my land and fighting." She narrowed her black eyes on Damien. His world tilted for a moment as something within him became completely consumed by the woman in front of him.

Damien stammered, finding himself at a loss for words and unable to articulate his reason for being there.

Steele muttered something under his breath that Damien couldn't quite catch.

She bit her lower lip, the space between her eyebrows slightly creasing in concentration. He could almost see the cogs turning in her brain. She shook whatever thoughts she was processing in her mind away with an eyeroll and said, "You know what? Never mind. Just follow me."

She turned in the direction of the fortress, not bothering to wait for a response. He and his brothers glared at each other, neither dumb enough to turn their back to the others. Damien particularly couldn't stand being in his brothers' presences, but he did not want to lose his chance to ally with the queen.

Damien relented, following directly behind her, keeping himself aware of his two brothers and their movements. His eyes wandered over her back to her slightly swaying hips as she walked. He knew he shouldn't underestimate her. She had just arrived, and she could already wield the amulet's magic better than she seemed capable of. To him, that showed strength and capability.

He felt drawn to her, as he had always admired women of power. But he could tell this one was different. She was special. Beyond being human and the demon queen. There was more to her than what met the eye, and he had to know more.

CHAPTER TWELVE

SADIE

*S*adie sat on her black throne and crossed her legs, her fingers brushing the golden armrest. She felt at ease in the seat, like she belonged there. The fortress felt more like home than anywhere else she had ever lived. Her gaze swept across the glistening, green marble floor of the throne room, and the majestic diamond pillars that stood on each corner.

She sucked in a deep breath as her affinity for the place grew even stronger.

She finally looked at the three men—well, demons —standing side by side on the floor in front of her throne. They waited silently for her to speak. Even from her post, she noticed how tense Kaiser was. His eyebrows met, and his lips were in a tight, thin line.

Beside Kaiser stood the handsome demon with black wings and horns, his dark-hair lay slick and polished, despite scuffling with his brother. He was the polite one from earlier and the tallest of the three, but only by a few inches. The other handsome demon, the blond one, stood with his hands behind his back. When their eyes met, he winked at her. She struggled to keep her face expressionless, though she felt the corner of her lips quirking upward.

For a few moments, she just watched them, deeply contemplating what she could do with them. She recalled what Kaiser and Hobson had both told her—that people would come for her, that she had inherited enemies when she had unknowingly fused with the pendant and absorbed its magic. Like it or not, she had powerful enemies now, probably far more than just Mara.

"Introduce yourselves," she said, her voice softly echoing inside the large room. "And tell me what you want."

Kaiser stepped forward. "You already know what I want, Sadie."

She nodded, remembering the conversation they had in her room. She still wasn't sure if he told her everything though.

"In addition to that, I'll offer you my loyalty and teach you more about your newfound power," Kaiser said.

"I appreciate your help, Kaiser." She nodded and smiled at him. She looked to the second one in line.

He seemed to take that as his cue and stepped closer. "Your Majesty." He bowed his head. "I am Prince Damien of Shardford. I have established numerous alliances with dignitaries and ambassadors of the underworld. And I want an alliance with you, too. In return, I also offer you my loyalty. However, I wish to discuss other matters of importance with you." He glanced at his brothers. "But it's integral I speak with you in private."

Sadie leaned back in her chair and drummed her fingers over the armrest. She scrutinized him, admiring the way he stood, the slight jut of his chin, the courtesy and brevity with which he spoke. She wondered what "other matters" he found necessary of her time.

Finally, she said, "I'll take your request under consideration."

"Of course, Your Majesty." Damien took his place next to Kaiser.

Next, Sadie regarded the man with the dirty blond hair. "What about you?"

He smiled and stepped forward as well. "Steele, at your service." He exaggerated his bow with a hand sweeping a nonexistent hat. He stood straight and stared at her, a mischievous glint in his eye. "As to what I want? Maybe, I also want an alliance." His gaze traveled down her body and looked her straight in the eyes. He smirked. "Maybe I want something *other* than an alliance."

Sadie rolled her eyes and suppressed a smile. His lightheartedness alleviated some of her stress. "What's in it for me?"

"Security. Training. Information." He grinned. "Lots and *lots* of fun."

She wasn't sure if she blushed, but her neck warmed from his gaze that insinuated a particular type of fun.

They all essentially wanted the same thing from her: their loyalty in exchange for her protection and teaching her more about what she was. An alliance, of sorts. She was sure there was more than what was simply said, and she would get to the bottom of it. For now, she thought it would be smart to align herself with at least Kaiser. He had proven himself a number of times. He still had more to prove to her, being in her newfound position. But she knew nothing of the other two and had no inclination to trust them at all. Especially with their little act at her gate.

However, in thinking about the people after her, about Mara, she knew she still needed to find Blair. Allies couldn't hurt. She needed all the help she could get. She may not have trusted Steele or Damien yet, but she could, with Kaiser's help, get to know them better, find out their secrets, and maybe discover their true desire behind an allegiance with her.

"Hobson?" she called out, knowing her fussy butler just lurked around the corner.

The gargoyle appeared from the shadows. "Yes, Your Majesty."

"Find rooms for these gentlemen, please," she said and returned her attention to the princes. "I need time to think this through. Meanwhile, make yourselves at home. But be warned, if you have ill intentions, I will find out and you will *not* like the consequences."

When Damien and Steele followed Hobson to their rooms, she pulled Kaiser aside. "Why do you look human when your brothers have wings and horns?" she asked.

In answer, he simply shifted into his demon self, his upper body curling as dark red wings sprouted from his back and darker red horns protruded from his brown hair and, beneath his wings, a red tail uncoiled, its metallic scales gleaming in the light of the room.

Demons could shift. They could change form to fit in. Fascinated, she stepped closer to him and raised her hand, stroking the underside of his left wing, feeling the soft membrane against her fingertips. She looked into his eyes. The hazel swirled and darkened, turning blood red.

"I didn't want to frighten you," he said, his voice soft.

Her heart skipped a beat. He did it to make her feel

comfortable. *How surprisingly accommodating for a fearsome warrior.*

She stepped back, forcing back the urge to move even closer. "I have to go," she said and walked out of the throne room.

Even in his demon form, she couldn't help being drawn to Kaiser. She couldn't risk trusting him completely just yet, but if anyone was going to help her find Blair, it would be him.

As she walked the fortress's hallways to her chambers, she touched the walls, feeling the connection she had with the place, letting the soft, electric sensations flow from the cold, stone walls to her fingertips and to the rest of her body.

Hobson had said the fortress held secrets she could discover and explore. And the butler had said she could summon him whenever, no matter where he was. Since she had powerful guests in her home, she needed to have fail-safes in place. Should it come down to it, she needed to learn how to fight with her magic. She had her MMA background to cover the physical sides of fights, but with this new world of hers, she knew that basic hand-to-hand wasn't going to get her very far.

Closing her eyes, she concentrated on the hum of the fortress beneath her palms, how it seemed to complement the rhythm of her heartbeats. *Hobson. Call Hobson.*

CHAPTER THIRTEEN

SADIE

*S*adie trained with Hobson in the castle's western courtyard under the crystal-lit, underworld sky. Its colors gradually dimmed to soft shades of orange, yellow, and pink—the colors of sunset.

Sweat dripped from her forehead as she shot fire at the stone discs Hobson threw in the air. He produced the small rock objects himself, lobbing them in the air from his forearms and sometimes from his belly or his knees. When Sadie hit the stone discs, they'd explode, and the fragments would fly back to him and meld into his skin.

The first five throws, Sadie missed, but from the sixth one onward, she finally got the timing right and hit every target. Even when Hobson feinted his tosses and pitched multiple discs at a time, Sadie's aims remained true. Once, she managed to take out six targets simultaneously.

"Very impressive, Your Majesty. I see you're a natural with fire." Hobson gathered the remnants of the marks. Rocky debris flew through the air, melted into his hard skin, and shifted to form more stony scales. "How about trying other elements? Smoke is a relative of fire. Let's go ahead and try that."

She thought about the suggestion for a moment, pausing to consider how powerful she felt, if there was a limit to the amount of magic she could do in a day without exhausting herself, and how late the day grew. But the feeling was better than anything she had experienced before. She smiled, wanting more of that.

"Okay," Sadie said, wiping the sweat on her forehead with the back of her hand.

Hobson extended his arms, deep lines appearing on his forehead. As he moved his hands, a small orb of smoke appeared between his palms and shifted until it took the shape of a thin dagger no bigger than Sadie's hand. Smoke billowed on the surface, and she gasped when she touched it, startled to feel the solid blade. She softly brushed a fingertip against its edge, marveling how it felt cold and hard like metal.

Hobson grunted, and the smoke dagger delicately exploded, dissolving into white mist.

"I can only hold it for so long," Hobson said. "The most common thing smoke casters do is create weapons out of smoke. Axes, swords, bows and arrows. With the demon queen's magic, you should be able to do more with smoke." He nodded toward her. "Try it. Make any weapon of your choosing. It's the same principle as casting fire."

Sadie nodded and inhaled, biting her lower lip. She put her arms in front of her, just as Hobson had, and focused on tapping into the now familiar energy concentrated within the ruby embedded in her chest. The air shimmered in front of her as particles collected, forming a tiny, swirling mass of smoke. She willed it to shift, to form the shape she wanted. The manipulation of the smoke really was similar to the way she could manipulate fire. The only difference was that casting fire had a sensation of heat while casting smoke had a cooler feeling.

A slender sword with a translucent blade began to form from the shapeless haze. She held the hilt with both hands. The edges glowed dark blue, and its crossguard spiraled. She altered the circular pommel to match the ruby in her chest. She smiled, proud of her creation.

"That's the easy part," Hobson said.

Sadie frowned. *That was easy?* "How so?"

"Observe." He approached a pomegranate tree beside a four-tiered, limestone fountain and picked up a fallen branch. He walked back to her side and extended the branch to her. "Cut this with your weapon."

"All right." Sadie raised the sword. She swiped downward, intending to cut the branch in two, but the sword had only passed through it. She pressed her lips together, focusing harder and trying again. The branch remained intact. Growing frustrated, she swung several more times, but it was no use.

"Concentrate, Your Highness."

"I'm trying. I just—" With a growl, she swung the blade once more, and again it only passed through.

The sword dissolved, shattering into white mist before fading into the atmosphere. Her mouth fell open. She looked at Hobson who shrugged.

"You'll get it eventually, my queen. Let's just go back to casting fire," he said. "We need to improve your concentration."

"I would rather do that while practicing my warmups."

Hobson nodded. "As you wish."

She moved through different poses while keeping her palms open and maintaining a small flame in both. Hobson held a wooden staff in his hands and tried to strike her with it. Her task was to parry and dodge his attacks while keeping the flames alive.

Hobson struck her calf, her knee hit the ground, and her casting faltered. Her shirt grew damp from sweat. Watery beads dripped from her hairline in near-constant streams. She stood back up, breathing heavily, and ignited two small flames in her palms again.

She dodged an overhead swipe of the staff and jumped back when Hobson jabbed at her. Hobson swung again, hitting her forearm. She winced. The flames flickered but remained alive. She sighed in relief.

Behind the shadows on the castle's façade, she caught silhouettes shifting. Sadie grimaced. The princes observed her training. Why couldn't they just leave her alone? She supposed she was going to have to set some ground rules before they get it in their heads she's to be disobeyed.

Earlier, when she and Hobson headed out to the courtyard, they had run into Steele closing his bedroom door as he stepped out of his chambers.

"Where are you going?" the prince asked.

"None of your business," Hobson said, looking down his nose at Steele. The butler walked past him in the hallway, Sadie following behind, both of them ignoring Steele's questions. Still, she had felt the demon prince trail them. She had rolled her eyes.

Upon reaching the hedge-decorated courtyard, they had stopped short to see Damien already there. Steele emerged from the hallway and stood next to Damien. Seconds later, Kaiser appeared beside her, seemingly out of nowhere.

She faced the princes, hands on her hips. "I'm going to train, and I don't want you watching me. You should all go back to your rooms."

But they didn't. And it distracted her. *Stubborn princes.*

Now, as she tried to focus and fight the distraction of the princes, she didn't see Hobson's strike that smacked her lower back, sending her crashing to the ground. She yelped.

Damn those men. She would have to find a more private place to practice.

She stood, rubbing her backside. She had enough training for the day. She brushed off her pants and walked out of the courtyard, ignoring the glances she knew the three princes gave her.

She made her way up the stairs from the throne room to the hallways that would lead to her chamber. Clam-shaped sconces along the walls lit her way, seemingly growing brighter as she neared them. As she turned a corner, an explosion of pitch-black shadows filled the room, swallowing her in darkness. Her pendant warmed in warning and she stiffened, hands buzzing with magic.

She kept her ears alert, listening for the faintest sounds.

Without warning, rough, strong hands grabbed her arms and spun her, smacking her back against the wall.

Though tired, Sadie had a better grip on her magic now. Her palms ignited in fire, and she aimed them toward her attacker and kneed him in the abdomen.

Just as fast as her assailant ambushed her, he jumped back, her hands and knees only hitting the air. The fire in her hands pitched the hallway in soft light, and she saw a broad-shouldered, handsome man staring at her. His lips twisted in a smirk behind his neatly trimmed beard. Sadie strengthened the flames in her palms and saw that he had silver horns with dark green wings and tail.

Great, another demon.

"How did you get inside my walls?" she asked.

He just stood there and smiled expectantly.

She needed to burn off more steam. Between the princes and now this intruder, her patience had run thin.

Sadie charged, gathering all the momentum she could muster to pin his massive body against the wall. Her proverbial hackles rose, and she stood ready to kill whoever dared enter her home uninvited.

He raised his arms in surrender and gave a smug smile. "I just wanted to see if you were as good as they claimed."

"Oh, for the love of—" Sadie backed off, stepping away from the stranger. "Who the hell are you?"

"Mordecai," he said.

"That means what to me?"

"You'll see. Soon enough." He leaned against the stone wall and crossed his arms over his well-toned chest.

Her chin jutted forward. "Why are you here?"

"Why, to be your ally, my queen." His canines glinted against the fire light.

"I don't have time or room for anymore demons knocking on my door wanting my allegiance. Especially you, who can't seem to answer a direct question of how the hell you got in my home."

Despite Hobson's crash course earlier, she was still new at this magic thing, and he was clearly experienced. She wasn't foolish enough to trust him. She didn't know if he really wanted to be her ally or if he had more sinister intentions that demons tended to have when dominating humans or whatever it was they did. Though, he did back off when she came at him. It seemed more like a game than to merely see if she was "as good as they claimed."

Who the hell are "they?"

She was going to speak to Hobson about this. Her impenetrable home had just been invaded by a demon. She knew there were going to be drawbacks to being queen, but three demons showing up at her home in one day was a bit much. She should be worried, but deep inside she couldn't help but admire how Mordecai managed to do it. She seemed to be more drawn to danger ever since she had fused with the pendant. And she wasn't entirely sure if that was going to be fun or bite her in the ass.

Just as she was about to call for Hobson, the sound of footsteps materialized from the other end of the hallway. Hobson, speak of the devil, and the three princes ran into view. The shadows dissipated around Sadie and Mordecai. Sadie eased the magic still burning in her palms.

Her butler and her guests reached her, panting.

"What the hell are you doing, Mordecai?" Damien asked, glaring at the intruder.

Mordecai shrugged, still leaning against the wall in all of his nonchalant attitude. "Whatever I want, Brother."

Brother. Sadie lifted her eyebrows. *There's another brother?*

"Exactly how many of you are there?" she asked Kaiser, voice full of accusation.

"Four," he said when Steele stood in the background saying, "Five."

"Well, which is it? Four or Five?" she asked.

Damien sighed and held up his hands in surrender. "There *was* five of us. But now, we are four."

"My spies told me you were dead," Kaiser said, stepping closer to Mordecai.

"Mine say you've retreated top-side, that you're a doctor or something. Rumor is you work as a stripper in your free time," Steele said, grinning like he was proud of his brother.

Sadie's eyes darted between them as she listened, one eyebrow lifted, and arms crossed in front of her chest. Hobson stood beside her, silently observing.

Damien repeated his question. "What the hell are you doing here?"

Mordecai stood silent, not giving away any answers.

"Oh man, you were running away from the bet you lost to me, weren't you?" Steele stepped in front of Mordecai, pointing a finger at his brother's chest. "You sore loser. You owe me a yacht."

Mordecai finally spoke up, grumbling, "I did *not* lose that bet…"

Eventually, Sadie's mind wandered, remembering what Kaiser told her that morning about their father threatening to kill his heirs. She wouldn't claim to know what each of them really wanted—justice, vengeance, a kingdom—but she was sure of one thing: she needed allies. If Mara had her sister stashed away, it was only a matter of time before she trotted her out as bait. And, if the demon king was willing to destroy his own sons, he undoubtedly would be a threat to her.

Hobson was great, but there was too much to this world that she didn't understand, so many answers her butler didn't have because he had been cooped up, waiting for her all this time. She needed someone who had been out in the demon realms, who knew this world, even her world above.

"But you cheated!" Steele cried. "Everyone knows turtles live in water and tortoises dwell on land. And—"

"I will pick an ally after all," she said, ending the bickering.

"Are you sure?" Kaiser asked as Steele asked "Who?" and Mordecai muttered, "I hope you make the right decision."

Sadie ignored that last one and held one hand up. "But just *one* of you. Over the next few days, I'll decide who I'm going to pick. I'm still not sure who to trust, so you had better impress me."

She wanted to leave it at that and go back to her room to get some rest but knowing how stubborn these princes could be from the small period they had been her guests, she had to state some rules. She placed her hands on her hips.

"No one comes to my room," she said, looking pointedly at Kaiser. "You will give me peace and quiet. Anyone who watches me train will be instantly disqualified, and—" she paused, deciding whether to add more or not. But the eyes of four handsome, strong demons staring at her made her mind empty.

She shook her head. "I just might add more later. Good night."

She was about to turn when Steele said, "But you're hot when you train."

Sadie rolled her eyes.

"Sadie," Damien said, "Isn't it only fair that we see you fight and know what your abilities are? You say you still don't know if you can trust us, but we can say the same about you. It's only fair if we are to have an alliance."

Sadie tapped a finger on the side of her chin. Damien had a good point. But nope. "I hold the cards here, don't I? Take it or leave it," she said. She looked at Damien. "Do you intend to join my little contest? If not, you can leave. I won't stop you. I'm sure you can find your own way out."

She met all of their eyes. They begrudgingly nodded, shooting dirty looks at each other. Sadie didn't consider Mordecai a real contender, but she needed him around long enough to learn how the hell he had gotten in.

She approached Mordecai and pointedly looked up at him, slightly craning her neck. His unwavering gaze shot an electric sensation through the base of her spine. She kept her breathing steady, ignoring his effect on her. "Because of the way you introduced yourself, you get to have a room in the dungeons."

The other princes laughed.

"I just may do that for the rest of you," she added, facing each of them in turn.

They stood more serious, finally taking the hint that she was in control here.

She turned to Hobson who had been silently standing beside her the whole time, patiently waiting until he was addressed. Pointing at Mordecai, she said, "See to it that he has the *appropriate* accommodations for the night."

Hobson bobbed his head up and down. His eyes lit up in excitement. Sadie wondered if she had inadvertently said the wrong thing, but then again, Mordecai did break into her fortress. A little punishment wouldn't hurt him.

"Come with me, young man." The butler grabbed Mordecai's wrist, dragging him to the other end of the hallway. Hobson's steps bounced lightly on the floor as he walked headfirst to the dungeons, as if he couldn't wait to get there. The prince had no option but to follow.

Sadie smiled. It seemed Hobson really enjoyed throwing people in the dungeons.

CHAPTER FOURTEEN

*S*adie gazed out over the underworld from her fortress's tallest tower, observing the now black sky and the scattered, shimmering crystals that acted as stars. In her opinion, they were better than stars. She barely got to see them in the business of the Seattle ghettos, working as a paramedic. She barely had time to see them from her apartment on her off nights and during the rare chance the sky wasn't covered in cloud and smog.

The tower was high enough that she could reach a stalactite jutting down just outside her window. She plucked one of the shimmering blue crystals and it pulsed brighter in her hand. She threw it out the window, watching it twinkle briefly in the darkness and wink out as it disappeared.

She sipped on her tea, savoring the taste of jasmine, milk, and honey.

Through her connection with the fortress, she called for Hobson. He appeared not long after, puffing out short breaths while he climbed up the tower stairs. It was so weird how she could summon him like that, no matter where he was in the fortress.

Insta-butler. She smiled. *So cool!*

"Your Majesty." The gargoyle bowed low.

"Oh, Hobson. Call me Sadie from now on, will you? I appreciate the formalities. I'm just not used to it."

"I—"

"Please?"

His eyes widened in shock, mouth forming a silent oh. "Of course, your—uh—Sadie."

The corner of her lips twitched. She placed the half-empty tea cup on the windowsill and faced him. "If my fortress is impenetrable, and no one can enter without my permission, how do you suppose Mordecai got in?"

He shook his head and sighed. "I have been working tirelessly to figure that out, S-sadie, but I still don't know how." He inhaled. "But I will, don't you worry."

"Thank you. That is all I ask."

Something about Mordecai seemed deadly and dangerous, and she wondered what he would do if she refused his offer to be his ally. He seemed like a dangerous enemy to have, but an equally dangerous ally. There was no telling what his motives were, especially with his entrance into her fortress in the first place. It wasn't a good first impression to make.

She continued to sip her tea. She noticed Hobson curiously watching her.

"Would you like some tea?" she asked.

The butler's scaly cheeks seemed to blush, though Sadie didn't understand how that was possible if he was made of stone. "Oh, no, thank you, Your Majesty. There's still a lot of work to be done."

"All right. Well, don't let me keep you."

As the butler left, Sadie returned to her observation through the opened window again and continued drinking her tea, placing one hand on the windowsill.

A few minutes later, footsteps echoed from the stairs behind her. Whoever it was walked steadily, his paces seemed confident. He came to a stop beside her, not talking.

Damien.

She didn't speak for a while, resisting the urge to berate him about interrupting her peace. But it wasn't her room, and she could use the chance to ask about him about his brother, but she also wanted to get to know him a little more. Questions shifted through her mind. She couldn't pick out one to start with.

"I'm surprised you're drinking tea and not blood," he said.

She almost spit out her drink. "What kind of society do you have down here?"

He laughed, and she smiled. After drinking the rest of her tea, she placed it back on the windowsill.

"Do you?" he asked.

She narrowed her eyes on him. "Do I what?"

"Drink blood." His question came out with a child-like curiosity, but there was a serious undertone to his words as well.

She snorted. "No."

Silence fell between them. She took a moment to narrow down a short list of questions she wanted to ask him while she had him alone. She leaned on the windowsill. "What do you really want, Damien?"

"I already told you, Your Majesty," he said.

Sadie nodded. "Yes, that you want an alliance, but not *why* you want it."

He stepped closer. "Isn't it obvious, Sadie? You're smart, you're clever. You think through a situation instead of reacting impulsively. I admire that."

She scoffed. "You've known me for less than a day!"

He didn't smile. The corners of his eyes didn't crinkle. His face remained stoic as he kept his eyes locked on hers. "I recognize power and strength when I see it. Call it a gift."

The weight of his stare made her uneasy, vulnerable. Like he could see everything about her. She cleared her throat and pulled her attention back toward the view out her window.

"I can see it when cogs turn in your brain, you know," he said.

"Really, now?" She chuckled, looking at him again. "How?"

Damien stepped closer to her. Too close. She wasn't sure if she wanted to back away or give in to the strange erratic behaviors her body seemed to fall victim to each time any of the demon princes were near.

"There's a small crease that forms here, for one." He touched the patch of skin between her eyebrows. The spot tingled. Everywhere else tingled, too.

"I see." Her voice came out breathless and light. Her mind and body played a game of tug-of-war. Her mind wanted to remain logical and clear, but her body seemed to want to move closer to him, close the gap between them. She pulled away from the windowsill, and at the last moment, her brain won the game as she stepped away and cleared her throat.

"Now, answer my question. Why are you here? I don't have time for guessing games. You seem the most level headed among your brothers, and I'd appreciate it if you told me the truth, Damien."

"I would love to. But I'm not sure you'll pick me, am I?" His smile didn't reach his eyes. "I'll tell you if, or when, we become allies. Otherwise, I could divulge secrets you may use against me."

Sadie nodded, admitting to herself his argument was reasonable. It seemed like he was a smooth talker, and she needed to be wary of him. He did break a rule, after all. She met his gaze. "How can I choose you when you already broke one of my rules? Spending time by myself is important, you know."

Damien grinned. "I couldn't resist." His smile faded. "I want you to know that I'm serious, Sadie. If you choose me to be your ally, you can always rely on me." He looked out the window. Her eyes followed. He added, "I want to show you something. As recompense for spying on you while you were training."

She raised an eyebrow, having no idea what he could possibly show her that would be remittance of his invasive intrusion during her training. "Go on…"

"There's Hobson," he said, pointing his finger at the butler's small form down below.

She returned to the window and followed the direction in which he pointed. The courtyard appeared so small from where she stood. If she put her palm out in front of her, it would cover the entire courtyard. Sadie narrowed her eyes to focus on the faraway target.

"After three to four steps, he's going to trip," Damien said.

True to his word, Hobson fell face first on the

ground. Objects that looked like gardening supplies clattered on the grass in front of him.

"You can't see it from here, but there's a pebble jutting out from the ground, and that's why he tripped. I also saw he wasn't looking at the ground while he was walking."

"You can see that from here?" Sadie asked, amazed. *That is some skill.*

Sadie realized, in that moment, Damien revealed a piece of himself. A skill, sure, but one that could be held against him in one way or another. She appreciated that.

"Yes. And the small butterflies and bees, even the tiny caterpillars on the blades of grass. Right now, I count four caterpillars."

She tried not to smile but failed. "Showoff."

"I can also smell emotions," he said.

"Of course, you can." It came out sarcastic.

"Right now, I can sense you're very impressed."

She gasped, feigning shock. "Impressive."

He drew nearer. "I also know that when I touch you like this," he said as his fingers grazed her arm, making her skin prickle with electricity. "You're ignited with desire. But you subdue it." His fingertips traveled upward to her shoulder, her neck, and then he cupped her cheek. "Smart woman."

Sadie resisted the urge to close her eyes. And God,

did she want to. His touch was quickly becoming addicting.

He began to lean forward, but Damien's hand fell when the flap of wings in the distance approached the window. Hobson hovered in front of them, his eyebrows drawing together. Sadie felt her cheeks warm.

"Your Highness," the gargoyle said, panting. When he saw Damien, his expression turned to one of annoyance, looking for all the world like a disapproving father. "Your people want to see you, Sadie."

Her eyebrows shot up. *I have people?*

Leaving Damien behind, she rushed to her bedroom to change into tight-fitting but comfortable black trousers, boots, and a soft, white linen tunic. When she reached the throne room with Hobson, she gasped as she saw three people waiting for her.

Three people made of *fire*.

They didn't shriek in pain as she would have expected them to. They moved naturally, the flames crackling on their skin as harmless as rain. They wore clothes that seemed made of malleable metal, and their eyes glowed orange.

Two of the three were women, and they closely resembled one another in appearance, although one was taller than the others.

"These are ifrits," Hobson whispered beside her. Behind the nearest column, Kaiser, Damien, and

Steele emerged, no doubt to be spectators for Sadie's latest unusual event.

Sadie nodded, as though it weren't the oddest thing she'd seen in her life—and given how the last couple of days had gone, that was saying something. Of all the things she had seen recently, the ifrits were the most amazing sight of all.

The shorter female stepped forward. Sadie looked in the ifrit's eyes, mesmerized, as the magical being curtsied. "Your Majesty. We have waited so long for you. The people in our village will rejoice tonight. All hail the demon queen!"

Sadie was at a loss for words.

The male ifrit accompanying them approached her and handed her an aluminum basket containing three large, red eggs. She took them from his arms with a nod and gracious smile, careful to avoid the flames that danced around his arms, but the heat didn't faze her. It was as natural as touching a warm sidewalk, nothing more.

"My name is Kiana, Your Majesty," the shorter female said. "This is our village's offer to you. We are grateful for your return. All hail the demon queen."

"All hail the demon queen!" the other two ifrits repeated.

Just as her visitors turned to leave, Sadie stopped them. "Wait!" She stood. "I want to go with you."

The ifrits looked at each other. Kiana tilted her head. "To our village, Your Highness?"

"Yes. I might not be able to celebrate with you, but I would like to see your village."

Kiana's mouth slowly opened. "O-of course, Your Majesty."

Sadie followed the ifrits outside. The three princes trailed behind her. "You don't have to come with me," she said as she faced them. But when she walked out, they still followed. She suppressed a groan. These princes were going to be the death of her. She had a feeling their disregard for her rules was just the beginning of the challenges she would have to overcome with them.

They walked around the fortress as the ifrits led her to a bridge with Damien, Kaiser, and Steele in tow. As they made their way closer, the noise of a large crowd grew louder. They emerged on top of a cliff, and in the valley below, an entire burning village sprawled across charred land. She knew she hadn't seen her entire fortress yet, and that she would come across surprising discoveries, but she hadn't expected *this*.

Stairs to the far right wound down the rocky cliff. They descended the steep steps and stopped on a hilltop. Little ifrit children played on the hill, but they paused and gaped at her when they saw her and her company. The children's gazes darted from the imposing princes to the pendant on her chest and they immediately ran to her, squealing with joy.

A small ifrit girl with flaming pigtails reached out a hand that held a burning dandelion. Sadie crouched and took it from the girl's hand. The flower remained in shape even when the child wasn't holding it anymore. Sadie twisted the stem in her hand and blew, giggling with the girl as the fire dandelion seeds flew in the air and flickered out.

The little girl looked at Sadie with glowing, twinkling eyes. The child extended her hand and aimed to touch the pendant on Sadie's chest, but the girl's hand faltered when Sadie looked at her. Smiling, she took the girl's hand, allowing her to touch the ruby. Sadie glanced up, finding Kiana and her two companions staring at her with wide eyes.

Sadie tenderly pinched the little girl's nose once and stood. She looked at the princes, only to find the children had turned the imposing demons into playground equipment. Sadie couldn't help herself—she laughed as three boys dangled off each of Steele's arms while he spun them around. A little ifrit girl giggled as Damien carried her on his shoulders. Kaiser chased three ifrit children on the far side of the hill, his hands held out, bending his fingers to form imaginary claws.

It seemed as though these ifrits weren't afraid of demons—for these children to approach her and her men so fearlessly, it must have meant they lived a charmed life here, secluded from the other demons of the underworld she still knew so little about.

Sadie was queen, true, but she knew so little about what that meant.

Her smile faltered, and she turned to the village below. Houses were on fire, streets were on fire. Everything was on fire. Countless ifrits danced in the middle of the town square. The whole village was alit with fire and celebratory noises. Kiana stood beside her.

Sadie took note that she saw more women than men, and it made her curious to know why. She wondered if she should ask Kiana such a question, not wanting to offend or bring up a sad tale of men dying in far off wars.

But these were her people. And to rule over them sufficiently, she needed to know all there was to them.

She tilted her head gently toward the ifrit. "Why are there so many women compared to men?"

"Because we are a village of soldiers, Your Majesty. Ifrit women are the fighters. Most of the men stay inside or in other villages. Though our men can also handle weapons, we find it more suited for them to remain at home and keep our village and children safe and cared for," Kiana said.

"What can ifrits do? What are your strengths?"

"We are made of fire. Of course, we can manipulate

the element and change ourselves to suit Your Majesty's needs," the ifrit said.

"You can change? Will you show me?" The excitement she felt bled through her voice.

Kiana grinned mischievously. "Of course, your Majesty."

In a heartbeat, Kiana grew wings made of fire and jumped down the hill, and waves of blazing heat engulfed her in a sudden, raging fireball. She soared like a comet and was so fast that Sadie could hardly keep track of her. Kiana landed exactly in the middle of the celebrations.

With that, the festivity stopped. Everything went silent except for the crackling of flames as the world around her burned. Every head turned in Sadie's direction, everyone watching her with wide eyes.

And, one by one, all of the ifrits knelt.

Sadie stood still, frozen in place, heart thudding as an entire people bowed before her. She didn't say anything, didn't do anything. After all, what could she say?

When the ifrits finally rose to their feet, a huge burst of light engulfed the entire village, brighter than it already was. The burst flashed even brighter before fading, the remnants of its heat forming a breeze that brushed Sadie's face. The inhabitants remained still, facing her, waiting for something Sadie had no clue about.

"All hail the demon queen!" they cried in unison.

Even as her body filled with a warming sense of joy that these people seemed to love her, Sadie couldn't move. In a day, she had gained all these followers. And they were *fighters*. Warriors. Soldiers.

Killers. Loyal to *her.*

She had inherited an army of ifrits. That gave her a sense of pride and protection, but also a sense of duty to make sure her people were well cared for and not made to feel like slaves. After all, it was becoming clear the previous demon queen had not been kind—who knew what she had done to these poor people.

Unsure of what else to do, she waved at the crowd and returned to her fortress. Behind her, the celebration started again, the noise increasing to the level it previously was before Kiana's demonstration.

Part of her wanted to join them, but more than anything, she wanted to let them have their fun. Sadie had a feeling that as time went on, and as the underworld became more aware of her existence, they wouldn't get much more of it.

On the way back, she walked in a daze, her hands floppy at her sides. *An army.* With that and the perfect ally, she just might be able to find her sister. The gears in her head began to turn. Damien walked beside her, and she caught him smirking. She guessed he really could tell when she began to piece things together.

To find the right ally among the princes, Sadie

decided she needed to get to know each one better. She needed to spend time alone with them individually and get a feel for them away from their brothers, since all they did around each other was bicker.

When they reached the fortress, Hobson opened the gate for them. Before they entered, she stopped and turned to face them. She gave each one a long glance, wondering if she was opening herself up to more resistance to what she would say next. But in the end, she was in charge. She said she would choose one ally. One it would be.

"In order for me to decide who to choose as an ally, I will be spending time with you individually, to see what you can do and whether or not you can be trusted."

The princes looked at each other.

"Since I'm the coolest, I should go first," Steele said.

"You met me before them," Kaiser said, addressing Sadie. "I think the first day belongs to me."

"Exactly," Damien said. "You got to spend time with her before the rest of us. I should go first."

Steele pointed a finger at Damien. "Don't think I don't know you were with her in the tower before the ifrits arrived. I'm the only one left who hasn't talked to her privately, so it should be me who goes first."

Sadie groaned. Grown men bickering like needy children. Not to mention acting like they had a voice in her decision. "You always speak as if I'm not here.

I'll pick the order *and* I'll change it on a whim if I want to."

The guys looked like they wanted to complain, but she glared at them, daring them to speak.

None of them objected.

Thought so.

Sadie thought about her handsome prisoner in the dungeons. She should probably spend time with him, too, if only for the sake of finding out how he got in. But she needed to be careful about it since she didn't entirely know what Mordecai was capable of.

She wanted to lay some ground rules for the remaining three, make a decision on who will go first, but she thought it best to make them wait. Stew on the indecision for a moment. She wanted to drill into their thick skulls that she was the one in charge here. Meanwhile, she could figure out a way to deal with Mordecai. He was the biggest threat of all of them so far. With that, Sadie entered and passed the butler. On her way past him, she whispered, "Keep an eye on Mordecai at all times."

The butler nodded once.

After taking a bath in her chambers, Sadie walked through the halls alone, letting the amulet guide her. She found herself in a beautiful garden surrounded by waist-high walls covered in moss and crystals. She felt the power of the amulet, of her new magic, running through her veins. She breathed all of it in as her old inhibitions faded away. Taking another deep breath, she allowed herself to absorb the amulet's power. She felt more in charge every single day.

Down here, she was the queen, after all.

~

MORDECAI

*M*ordecai sat in the dungeons, listening to the hubbub die down from outside, not bothering to watch it all through the little window in the cell. In front of him, his enchanted staff made of smoke floated in the air, its grey edges billowing and slightly sparkling against the faint light. When he got bored of playing with the weapon, he let it disappear. He shifted in his seat, leaning his back against the bars, lifting his feet up and stretching them on the makeshift bed. He bent his elbows and rested his head on his hands, making himself comfortable.

He knew Sadie was just testing him, letting him rot a little to get back at him for the way he introduced himself. He wasn't worried, though, because their tussle was the most fun he'd had in ages. She was human, sure, and brand new to the power she wielded, and yet, he could already tell she was immensely powerful.

More than that, the way her body pressed against

his when he pinned her to the wall, the way she kept calm even when he had ambushed her. Hell, the way she stopped him and his brothers from their worthless bickering… he wanted her. *Bad*.

And I always get what I want.

CHAPTER FIFTEEN

SADIE

*S*adie and Kaiser walked on a veranda in one of the fortress's many courtyards. Slender stone pillars embossed with curls and bars acted as window frames. Circular topiaries lined the outside. Sadie drew near one post and noticed the curls were serpents covered in scales. In the middle of the courtyard stood a statue of a demoness sitting on the fountain and reading a book.

The serenity of the place was freeing, and Sadie wanted to enjoy the peace a little longer, but she had a mission. Choose an ally. Spending time with the demon princes was worthless and time ill spent if she kept silent company with them.

She had a little more time to get to know Kaiser than the others. It made sense to her to pick him first. He was the most trustworthy. She just needed to figure out a way to get him to open up more. Find out his weaknesses, vulnerability, what really made him tick.

Glancing at his form from the corner of her eye, she couldn't help the smile that stretched across her lips. He had done so much for her, and she still had no reason why. Of course, she assumed it was to use her power for revenge. Maybe Kaiser and his brothers shared similar feelings? Perhaps they shared an equal desire for payback? What didn't make sense was how they acted toward one another.

"You mentioned that your father threatened to kill you and your brothers," Sadie said. "It's surprising to me that you all seem to hate each other." She stopped to face him. "Shouldn't you be closer because of it? I mean, don't you think you should stick together?"

Kaiser's lips tightened to a grim line. "He didn't just threaten to kill us, he *killed* one of us."

Sadie frowned as her heart broke for Kaiser. She was overcome with the urge to wrap him in a tight hug. Instead, she asked, "What happened?"

"We used to be close." A crease formed between his eyebrows.

She wanted to reach out to smooth it.

"When our brother died, we just... ran for our lives. I guess I felt like I couldn't trust them. So, I hid."

Sadie thought of Blair, wondering how she fared. Kaiser lost a brother. To his father, no less. She knew he understood how she felt. Maybe if she chose him, he could really help her. Of the four princes, she had known him the longest, and she felt inclined to trust him after all they had gone through. But she still had to be careful not to trust too much at this stage. She would be sending three of them away.

Sadie squeezed his hand and offered a sympathetic smile. He returned the gesture, and they continued walking.

As they turned the corner to a dark hallway, Kaiser gently pinned her against the wall. His hands propped against the wall on either side of her. Her heart quickened.

"You need an ally, Sadie," he said. "Someone you can trust."

"And that's you?" she asked, more breathless than accusatory.

"I know about Blair."

Sadie's eyes widened. "How could you possibly know?"

The back of his right hand brushed her neck. Sadie sighed. "That's what I was doing on the surface," he said, voice husky. "Tracking Blair Blackwood, one of the greatest demon hunters of all time."

"Demon hunter?"

His wings wrapped around the two of them, but she could still see his face. "Yes. My spies warned me she had finally gone in over her head. That she finally stole something she shouldn't have. I wanted—*needed* —to find it."

Kaiser knew more about Blair's secret life than Sadie. She tried to not let it affect her. But it didn't seem fair. Blair was her sister. She should have known more. Done more. The bite of jealousy hit her in the stomach and tears stung her eyes.

Blair had kept so much from her. Sadie worried she hadn't really known her sister at all. At least she could learn a little more from Kaiser and understand what Blair had gone through. Maybe he knew something that would help Sadie find her sister.

"What else do you know about her?"

"Demon hunters actively seek out the deadly creatures of the underworld. I don't know how she got hold of the pendant." He cupped her cheek and brushed her hair behind her ear. "Truth be told, I would have kidnapped you had I known your connection to Blair." His fingertips grazed the nape of her neck. Her nerve endings tingled. "I'm glad I didn't."

Sadie leveled her stare at him, standing as confident as possible. She kept her voice even when she said, "That didn't answer my question. And you don't scare me."

He could have killed her when he had the chance, and he had plenty of chances. But he didn't. And though that still puzzled her, she would forever be grateful to him.

A shadow of thought flickered through Kaiser's eyes. Sadie wondered what that thought was, but he pulled away, allowing her to stand away from the wall. The sudden cool air chilled her skin, and she wished for him to press closer to her again.

As they began to walk again, she said, "Tell me more about magic."

Kaiser nodded. "Some demons can get enhancements, advanced magic that sets them apart. Most who try, die, and most of the warlocks who perform the spells die in the process. So, it's rare that any two demons share the same powers."

"What's yours?" she asked.

In response, he held out his hand and ignited a small flame. She smiled, feeling more connected to him. They both had an affinity for fire. Destructive, cleansing fire. He could help her hone her ability, proving himself even more of an asset to her.

He hovered his other palm above the flame. It crackled like a campfire, even imitating the sounds. The sparks flew around the tiny flame, glowing like fireflies. Sadie stared in wonder.

He clapped his hands, extinguishing the fire, and dark smoke swallowed them. Her back slammed against the wall, and cold strips wrapped around her wrists, ankles, and waist.

As the smoke dissipated, Kaiser stared at her. Predatory. Fierce. Dark.

He stepped closer, closing the gap between them. He brought his face to hers. "Satisfied?"

His breath washed over her, warming her skin, setting her nerves on fire.

Energy brimmed from the wispy lines that shackled her to the wall.

Two could play this game... She focused her magic on them, trying to manipulate the smoke, but failed. He was definitely a strong caster. His magic rivaled hers most likely because she was still learning to control hers. She wouldn't let him know it, but she knew he would be an incredible ally if she chose him.

Smiling, she narrowed her eyes on his in what she hoped was a sexy and challenging look. "Is this the best you can do?"

CHAPTER SIXTEEN

SADIE

*T*hat evening, Sadie relaxed on a lounge on her balcony, drinking wine in her new favorite red robe. She reflected on her time with Kaiser, how he made her feel, the discussion they had, and that demonstration of his. Her nerves tingled with the memory.

She sensed someone entering her room, bursting her peaceful moment.

"My room is a private space," she said with a groan.

She removed herself from her lounge to further berate the intruder, but her eyebrows rose as she took in Steele, standing in the middle of her room, scratching the back of his head. She crossed an arm over her chest, watching him expectantly from over the rim of her wine glass.

She didn't know him very well. And so far, he wasn't off to a good start.

She set her wine glass on the balustrade and asked, "What are *you* doing here? Better yet, what part of my room is off limits is hard for you to understand?"

"I've wanted to get you alone since the moment I set eyes on you." He grinned. "I knew you were secretly waiting for me to visit you."

Hardly.

He held his arms out to the side. "Now, here I am. Sorry I took so long."

Steele was charming. Sadie had to give him that. But she set rules for a reason, and dammit, they were going to be followed. "Tell me why I shouldn't kick you out right now."

"Kick *me* out? How can you resist this?" He bobbed his eyebrows.

Sadie shook her head and smiled. And Steele smiled, too. He seemed hell-bent on disregarding the rule, but there was something carefree and weightless with his presence. Her shoulders felt less tense, and she seemed more relaxed.

"Fine," she said. "Since you're already breaking the rules, show me what you got."

"Finally," he said and removed his shirt. "I've wanted in your pants since I first saw you."

Her mouth fell open. "No that's not—"

He tossed the green shirt on her bed. His chiseled

abdomen and well-muscled arms were expertly displayed. Though she appreciated the sight, that wasn't what she meant at all.

"Okay, that's—" *Well, that's an amazing sight.*

Steele started with his pants, undoing the waist and pulling it past his hips enough to reveal the intricate, precise manscaping.

She burst out laughing.

Between breaths, she tried to form a full apology, but the words kept getting broken and coming out, "I... em... sar...," She panted for breath and tried starting over again. She excused herself to the balcony and forced herself to gain some composure before she returned, unable to keep the smile from her face.

She cleared her throat. "I'm sorry. I meant show me your magic."

He frowned. "Oh." He picked up his shirt from her bed and slipped an arm into the sleeve. He pulled the fabric down, covering up his delicious pecs and abs.

"Don't." She held up a hand. "Now, you have to do it with your shirt off."

He smirked and slipped back out of the shirt, throwing it to the side. She almost licked her lips.

"All right. Come closer, then," he said.

She didn't move. Instead, she crossed her arms over her chest and lifted an eyebrow. Oh, no. She wasn't going to follow his instructions. She was in control here. Not the other way around.

He chuckled. "Oh, *now* you're scared."

"Why do *I* have to come closer?" she asked.

"Because," he said, walking closer to her, eyes taking on a devilish glint. He closed the space between them and leaned in to whisper in her ear, "I want you to *feel*."

He leaned closer and kissed her neck. His hand drifted lower, parting the neckline of her robe and revealing her breast. She sighed, too consumed in pleasure to stop him. He had that effect on her. She wanted him.

Steele fondled her breast, and his thumb flicked her nipple. He kissed her ear, and she moaned. The apex of her thighs throbbed. *Don't stop. Don't stop. Don't stop.*

He growled as he removed her robe. The fabric collected at her feet.

His kisses drifted lower and she ran her fingers through his hair, urging him to continue. Needing him to. The pleasure was too much to halt. Too addicting.

He kissed her nipple and traced his tongue around the outside of it. She arched her back, pressing her breast farther into his mouth. Wetness spread between her thighs, and Steele groaned, digging his fingers into her back.

In an instant, he was gone. The immense pleasure that shook her to the core slowly ebbed. Sadie stood on her balcony, covered by her robe, and Steele sat on her bed, smirking. She gasped for air as her heart slowly returned to its normal pace.

"That was all in my head?" she asked.

He nodded and said, "I can make people see and feel things that aren't real. I wouldn't have done that if you had not wanted me to."

She didn't respond. Her cheeks flushed with heat as she thought about what it might have looked like to Steele to see her writhing with pleasure, gasping and moaning. She turned her back to him and looked over the railing to the courtyard below, steadying her breathing. His footsteps quietly approached. He brushed her forearms with his fingers and her heart skipped a beat. She wondered what he would do next.

"There is a much darker side to my gift as well. Do you want to see that?"

She wasn't so sure. To replace what he had done with something much darker, she didn't know if she could handle it. But it could prove useful to know the entire package of what he could do.

She faced him, leaning against the wall of the balcony. As she looked into his eyes, there was a light in them she hadn't noticed before. She wanted to give him a chance to see what his power could do, but that could leave her open and vulnerable. She didn't trust him yet.

He seemed to notice her hesitation and cupped her

upper arm, filling her body with warmth. "I'll teach you how to block it."

"How?"

"You can form a mental barrier, so I wouldn't be able to get into your head. Try to imagine a wall barricading your mind. Form that wall with unnecessary thoughts. Maybe you can use a song, or a poem, or just the same word over and over again. That way, when I try to breach your mind, all I'd hear is insignificant noise."

She slowly nodded. That could prove useful. Maybe she could allow him to show her that darker side of his skill. But first, she needed a song. Something she could repeat over and over to prevent him from getting in. She wanted something easy. Maybe a little ridiculous.

Finally, she settled on one. An old children's nursery rhyme.

"Let me try."

She bit her lower lip, focusing on following his advice. She imagined a wall and built it with the lyrics of *Ring Around the Rosie*. She nodded to signal that she was ready.

"I'll try to get through the wall, all right?" Steele said.

"Okay."

A claw scratched at her mental barrier.

"Good," Steele said. "You've got the hang of it. Let's see how strong it is now."

The claw scratched harder, and she concentrated more on the lyrics, strengthening the wall.

Now a fist seemed to bang on her barrier. Then two fists, and a huge blow.

All bounced off her mental block.

Steele stepped back a pace and cocked his head to the side, his lips pulled into a proud grin. "You're a fast learner, aren't you?" He raised a hand and his thumb brushed the edge of the amulet. "You have incredible access to magic, Sadie. New abilities may come to you faster than most people."

She nodded. "Yeah, but you realize I can teach this to whoever I pick, right?"

He shrugged, unfazed. "I'm sure you'll pick me anyway." He brushed her hair behind her shoulders and his fingers rested on her neck. "After the way I made you feel. You'll pick me."

Her eyes fluttered closed. If she ever chose Steele, that skill of his, for sure, would be the reason.

"Now, for that darker side. Care to give it a shot? If it becomes too much, you can always block it."

"Does it work that way?" she asked.

"Yes and no. It works better to practice having that barrier up at all times. It will get easier as you go."

She thought about it for a moment. Now that she knew how to block his mind invasion, she didn't mind seeing what he had to show her. She didn't trust him fully just yet, but boy did that thing he did help a lot. Not to mention, he showed her how to block it. She nodded.

Steele's expression turned serious, and his eyes darkened. He touched the back of her hand. At first, pleasure tingled through her skin. As the tingles moved, the pleasure shifted to sharp stings of tiny needles.

She looked at her hand as tiny black holes appeared on the surface, growing bigger as the pain increased. Sadie bit on the inside of her cheek to force back the urge to scream. Tiny, spike-covered worms squirmed out of those holes, biting and scratching as they moved. The pain became stronger, burning through her nerves.

Closing her eyes, she focused on the song again. Slowly the pain ebbed, coming back with greater force. A pinched formed in the center of her brow as she concentrated harder, shouting the song in the back of her mind as the image Steele put her through fought against her.

The barrier became solid as the mental attack faded away.

"That's enough for today," she said, shaking out the remaining effects of the imaginary pain and worms from her hands.

"Very well. We could always end on a more positive

note, like sending you into levels of pleasure you have yet to experience."

Sadie let out a nervous chuckle. "Maybe another time."

"I'll get you eventually," he said with a wink.

"You're always so sure of yourself, aren't you?"

He grinned and shrugged. "Then I bid you goodnight."

Leaving her on the balcony, he went back into her room and picked up his shirt. She hated watching him put it back on, but she also knew it was for the best.

As he opened the door to her room, he looked over his shoulder and said, "Oh. Interesting song choice, by the way."

CHAPTER SEVENTEEN

SADIE

*S*adie and Hobson stepped through the castle halls as he showed her more of the massive fortress. First, and to her appreciation, she was led to the private training area. Not far from there were some gardens, the dining room, sitting room, guestrooms, and courtyards.

She would probably need a lifetime just to see everything. But the general framework of the fortress seemed easy enough to remember. The north wing was hers. The east wing was for guests. And the west wing was the barracks for soldiers.

Sadie thought about her ifrit subjects. Her army. She wondered if that was something she really needed to build for herself. She rubbed the pendant, almost certain it would be a good idea, but she had enough on her plate for the time being. She needed to focus on the tasks at hand: align herself with one of the demon princes, rescue her sister if she wasn't already dead, and kill Mara.

In the south wing, the walls and archways were gloomy compared to the other parts of the fortress. The stone walls held an eerie shade of blue with dark runes painted in swirls throughout. The archways and pillars looked like gravestones, and on top of each sat a carved head of a snarling lion with glaring eyes that seemed to follow their every move.

An eternal mist permeated the air, guarding the metallic doorway that stood on the far end of the hallway. Sadie wrapped her arms around herself and shivered.

"This place had always been used for terror and torture," Hobson said beside her, his voice quiet. "I was never permitted to enter. It's reserved for the demon queen only."

Sadie wondered what the demon queen would need with such a place. For enemies, maybe? She wrinkled her nose. Though unnerved, she felt her pendant warm, calling her into the darkness.

"I'll take a look," she said. "You can go, Hobson. I can find my way to my chambers."

Hobson seemed to hesitate, but he eventually nodded and turned around. As soon as he was out of sight, Sadie spun in a slow circle, taking in every detail she could. It would help to have some sort of landmark for her to follow in case she ever did get lost in this gigantic place.

She opened the door and walked the cobweb-covered hallway, following the tug she felt on her pendant. Eventually, she arrived into a cobblestone courtyard surrounded by four majestic stone walls with ivy climbing up the posts and turrets. Shadows shrouded the place, and dim beams of light shined through cracks from the high ceiling. Hallways branched off in every direction. A fountain took up the center of the floor with a stature of a cloaked figure rising from its middle.

Anyone else would feel uncomfortable, if not scared, within this dark, lonely place, but she only felt curious. This was her domain. She knew it in her bones. The magic here obeyed her.

She sat on the edge of the fountain, breathing in the energy, letting it fill her body, taking in the ominous view. Movement pulled her attention to a white, wispy figure moving in one of the hallways adjacent to her. It floated toward her, taking the shape of a demoness, easily eight feet tall and towering over Sadie.

The ghost's white curls billowed around her face, and her eyes glowed white. Her sharp chin jutted out, her back ramrod straight. A circle of azure crystals sat atop her head. She lifted a hand toward Sadie, pointing a thin, ghastly finger at her. Whispers of a woman's voice echoed in the courtyard, all of it too soft and fast to hear clearly.

Sadie stood and watched the apparition. The ghost appeared paler, but she looked exactly like the woman in the portrait she saw on her first night in Bitterthorn. She knew this was the ghost of the last demon queen.

The apparition flew toward her. Sadie raised her arms and summoned a wall of smoke between them. The ghost scowled, disappearing into nothing, leaving Sadie alone in the room.

Looking around for the past demon queen to make another appearance, she considered why the ghost decided to appear to her in the first place or why she charged at her like that. She could probably talk to Kaiser about it. But until she could figure out more on her own, she decided to head back to her room and keep the event to herself. Sadie had to first figure out if the appearance of the previous queen was good or very, very bad.

CHAPTER EIGHTEEN

SADIE

*S*adie sat on her bed, examining the crystal ball in her hands, grateful for the warmth and light of her room after the cold darkness of the south wing. She wondered if the magic here really did obey her, or if it somehow still obeyed the will of her predecessor. Something about that ghost felt dangerous, and it wouldn't end well, but she didn't have enough information to go off of.

For now, she wouldn't tell the princes. Not even Kaiser or Hobson. If they knew the old queen was still here, in whatever form, they might be loyal to her instead. No. This wasn't something to share with anyone. At least, not yet.

Hobson entered the room holding a tray of croissants and a glass of orange juice. He placed them on the small coffee table in front of the plush couch. "Did you find anything of interest in the south wing, Sadie?"

She didn't answer, keeping quiet and somber for a moment, since she wasn't entirely sure what she had seen.

Focus.

"Do you know a demoness named Mara?"

The butler shook his head. "Why, Your Highness?"

She sighed, leaning back against the headrest. "She was looking for the pendant and almost killed me and my sister just to get it."

He went to a nearby chair and arranged the cushions. "All I know is that the pendant was locked away from the world and someone found it."

She lifted the crystal ball as she pondered over his responses. She knew who found it. Just not why. She also knew Mara had wanted it bad enough to kill. Just not why. The glass ball had shown her Steele and Damien when they arrived. But she only looked into it. Now, as she held the orb, it was just clear, plain, and still. No swirling smoke. No colors. No images.

She held it out toward Hobson. "How do you use this?"

"Simple," Hobson said. "Just place your palms on the surface and think of someone."

"Can I use it to find Mara or Blair?" she asked.

He shook his head. "No, but it can show their legacy."

"Then how did it show Steele and Damien at the gates?"

"Only you can tell me that, Sadie. I merely remembered the artifact in that room as I was cleaning. What were you thinking of when you approached it?"

She shook her head. "I don't recall."

"Well, perhaps we can try to use it now. Hold it just so and think of Mara or Blair."

Sadie sat the crystal ball on her lap and placed her palms on both sides. She focused her mind on Blair.

The green and red haze swirling inside puffed and shifted, forming a silhouette. Color spread on the image and a background formed. Sadie saw Blair, with two swords, fiercely fighting horned and winged creatures, leaving dead demons behind. Her sister fought humans, too. Sadie assumed they were fellow hunters, traitors who had aligned themselves with demons and betrayed humans for personal gain.

She watched her sister living off the bounties and sometimes the treasure she stole from her marks. She watched as Blair went to those in need, helping those who couldn't pay, merely wanting to make the world a little better. Sadie sighed, tears forming in her eyes.

I'll find you, Blair. I promise.

The images disappeared, retreating into the swirling, green and red cloud. She wiped her tears and placed her palms on the glass orb again. Sadie needed to know what she was up against and focused on the demoness, Mara. The cloud shifted, showing a rocky underworld desert littered with corpses.

"What is this place?" Sadie asked, her voice a whisper.

"That's called the Vale." Hobson gulped. "It's the home of the abyssians."

The crystal ball showed a war, an army of red-winged demons charging across a charred battlefield. This must've been the team Mara was a part of, the group that Kaiser mentioned. Sadie clutched the orb, watching as they burned their enemies. Mara fought at the frontlines, slaughtering hundreds of demons and monsters and anyone whose land they wanted.

Sadie observed Mara's cruelty, all the destruction she had left in her wake. Images of a razed village in the underworld shifted to view, all its inhabitants mutilated, damaged, and dead.

The cloud blurred again, and she saw her destroyed apartment in Seattle and Carlos's corpse lying on the floor. She held her breath. She remembered Blair's pained expression when Mara stabbed her in the side. The orb showed it, replaying the tragedy. She let go of the crystal ball, waving away the images.

Mara was a dangerous enemy to have. From what Sadie had seen, she was a seriously evil demoness, one that destroyed everything in her path. And right now, Sadie was next on her hit list.

Sadie thought about how Mara would approach things. A demoness like Mara would be smart—she would know she couldn't infiltrate the fortress, so she would bide her time, waiting for an opening.

Sadie clenched her fists. She wouldn't go down without one hell of a fight. And she would make sure Mara paid for the damage to her apartment and her sister. One way or another, Mara would suffer the consequences.

CHAPTER NINETEEN

*D*amien walked with Sadie through the woods on the east side of the castle. Acacias with silver branches and golden leaves filled the forest. Today was his time with Sadie, and she had suggested they go out because she didn't want to be cooped up in her massive fortress.

He obliged her, of course.

As they walked, they came across a tiny black rabbit, and it ran away from them. Sadie laughed.

"What's so funny?" he asked.

"Nothing. Things just seem to run away from you," she said. "I don't even know why I'm laughing."

Damien smiled, not at all offended. And it seemed to make her happy, which alleviated his mood.

They remained on the outskirts of the foggy forest,

walking alongside each other as they conversed. He could still see the eastern courtyard from here.

Sadie approached one silver tree and placed her palm on its trunk. "I can feel the grounds of the fortress extending out here. And for another half mile or so."

He stared at her fingers splayed out on the bark, controlling the urge to touch them. "That's a good thing. You can call on its magic if need be."

She stepped away and kept walking. Damien followed.

"Kaiser told me about your father," she said. "That he killed one of your brothers."

Damien's breath caught. He hadn't expected his brother to be brought up. It caught him off guard. After a moment, he regained his composure. "His name is Cedric."

Sadie gave his arm a reassuring squeeze. "I'm sorry for your loss. Not just for Cedric, but for your other brothers."

"I—" He stammered and sighed. "Yeah." He smiled at her. It wasn't a happy smile, but a sad one. "Why don't we talk about something else?"

"Okay," she said. "Well, you mentioned you had plenty of allies. Can you tell me about them?"

He held his bent arm out to her. She linked her arm through his as they trekked along a shallow dirt path, making their way through the forest mist and the sparkles of the trees' leaves.

"Through the years, I have forged alliances with various demon lords. They have pledged themselves to help me get the throne in exchange for favors and power. I have also established an alliance with the angels, but right now, it's very tense."

"Angels?"

He grunted. "Yes. Vain, self-entitled assholes."

She gasped. "Seriously? Where do they live?"

Damien gave her a sidelong glance. He gestured above them. "Why, in the heavens, of course."

They passed a bush of marigolds and he left her to pick one. Returning to her, he brushed her hair back, placing the stem behind her ear. *Perfect.*

"There, it suits you," he said. "Even if you are queen of the demons and all."

Her cheeks flushed, and she looked away. He, however, couldn't keep his eyes off her. She was absolutely the most beautiful creature he had ever seen. He didn't know what he would do if she didn't pick him as an ally.

She smiled at him, her eyes connecting with his. "What am I feeling?"

"Huh?"

"You said you can smell emotions," she said.

He almost growled. Oh, he knew. He sensed it from her and felt it himself.

Desire.

He leveled his gaze at her, pulling her closer to him. His pants grew tighter as he breathed in her scent and the intoxicating aroma of desire. "Are you sure you want to play this game, Sadie?"

"I only want to see you use your power again."

This woman... If he didn't get her under him soon—though he wouldn't mind above him, either—he just might go crazy. He took in a calming breath. On the exhale, he said, "All right."

"So, what am I feeling?" she asked again.

Her eyes were filled with so much curiosity. And he could get lost in them forever.

He stepped closer, marveling at the way she looked at him, gaze steady, chin lifted. His lips tugged upward. "Powerful."

She smiled at him, and he lowered his mouth toward hers. Just before their lips met, he pulled back.

What was he doing? He needed to focus. To be logical. She was only spending time with him because she needed to know if he was trustworthy. He shouldn't get too attached. With a sigh, he pulled away from her, ignoring the wounded light in her eyes.

Leading her down the path, the walk was silent. He mentally kicked himself for not kissing her. He should have. Judging by the way she looked at him when he pulled away, she wanted to kiss him too.

In the midst of his self-beratement, he sucked in a

long breath through his nose and stopped mid-step. Sulfur. Thick sulfur, too.

He drew Lightbane from his belt and the sword blazed to life. The flames cut through the fog, revealing a massive hellhound with fiery red eyes glaring at them as it lay on the ground. A deep sound rumbled from its chest, and when it opened its maw, fire billowed from its mouth. Its hackles were made of fire, and as it rose, the flames glowed brighter. The beast prowled toward them.

Damien had never seen a hellhound up close before, and he never wanted to as superstition stated hellhounds were harbingers of death. Now that he had one within a few yards in front of him, he noticed its body was like a gargoyle's—covered with rocky scales and spikes. Very much like a gargoyle, except for the veins of orange magma that meandered all over its skin. And at its chest, the magma was colored blue.

Sadie approached the creature, warily holding out her hands. Damien held up his sword, prepared for a fight, but when the hellhound looked at Sadie, it immediately stopped snarling, ears propping up instead. It bounded to her and bent its front legs, butt lifted in the air and tail wagging. The blurred red-orange light was a near constant arc of continuous light. With its tongue lolled out, the hellhound rolled over like a puppy, belly exposed.

She gasped and giggled.

Damien lowered the sword as Sadie knelt to rub the creature's belly. Its head reached for her cheek and licked her. She laughed.

It was the most beautiful sound he would ever hear. Damien had to smile, seeing her like that, though he wondered why the hellhound was alone in the forest. Hellhounds usually hunted in packs. The creature stood on its legs and snuggled close to Sadie. But when it looked at him, the damn thing growled.

"That's a good boy," Sadie said, chuckling as she petted the hellhound's head.

Damien sheathed his sword. "We should get going. I don't sense other creatures right now, but there could be more of them out there."

Sadie's lips pursed, but she nodded. She stood and gave the hellhound one final pet. "It's great to meet you. You can come back to the fortress with us if you want."

The hellhound nudged her hand with its nose and ran in the other direction. After a few meters, it stopped beside an acacia, pausing briefly to look back at her. But it turned around and disappeared, vanishing into thin air as mist covered the pathway once more.

"Strange," Damien said and offered Sadie his arm. "You seem to have a kinship with the most unique creatures."

"What makes you say that?"

Damien took the time to explain to Sadie the lore of hellhounds on the way back to the fortress. She seemed to absorb every word like a sponge. When they reached the gates, he and Sadie went their separate ways. While she went to do her own thing, Damien went back into the forest. He had to find out why there was a lone hellhound. An unsettling feeling filled his gut.

There was more to the random encounter than what met the eye. He was going to find out just what.

CHAPTER TWENTY

SADIE

*A*fter finishing a round of training, Sadie made her way toward her room, passing the door to the dungeon on the way. She paused, staring at the door. Mordecai might be willing to answer some questions now.

She figured she could at least attempt to get the answers she demanded. If he still refused, then so be it. He could rot down there for as long as it took. Though a part of her wondered if he could even be contained there. He managed a way into her home. He could have found a way out.

She would find out how he got in. One way or another.

With a sigh, she opened the door and descended the long stairwell, lighting a fire in her hand to chase away the thick shadow that covered the darkened corridor. Turning the corner after the final stair, she found him lounging in his cell, hands behind his head and one ankle resting on his knee. He seemed very much comfortable and at ease.

"Is it time to leave already?" he asked, feigning a yawn.

She leaned on the wall across from the bars and crossed her arms over her chest. "How did you get in? Do you work for Mara?"

He frowned, looking genuinely confused by the name. "I don't work for anyone but myself." He placed his feet on the ground, sitting up straight. "Who is she?"

"A demoness," she said.

He scoffed. "I don't work for some puny, little demoness's agenda."

"Then tell me how you got in," she said.

He stood up, grunting. "I'll do you one better."

Mordecai turned into shadow until only his eyes were visible and bled through the bars. He solidified then pushed Sadie against the wall. His tattooed forearm pressed on her chest. He looked down at her, smirking. But she didn't quiver. She stared at him head-on. Finally, she knew how he got in.

"How did you do that?" she asked. "Can you teach me how?"

He tilted his head. "No one else has my enhancement. It's passed on only at death."

"Oh."

Sadie thought that was good news provided she could trust him. Unfortunately, it wasn't some artifact she could take from him, but that meant no one else could, either. But if she rejected him, she wondered what he would do with this magic.

"Why are you here, Mordecai?" she asked. "What do you want?"

His arm pressing her chest moved, a thumb caressed her cheek. "Power. Vengeance."

His touch shot warmth through her body, she resisted the urge to close her eyes and lean into him. Instead, she kept her eyes on his and her voice steady. "And you'll get that with me?"

"There are many things you can give me, Sadie." He lowered his mouth to her ear and whispered, "More than you can imagine."

His breath sent chills through her body, gathering in the center of her apex. She fought against the urge to squirm and said, "What will you give me in return?"

His nose nudged her neck as his fingers drifted down her arm. Goosebumps formed all over.

"Protection," he said. "I have my own allies. Powerful warlocks that serve me. And I will teach you some of my magic. Not all of it, but some."

"Really?"

He stepped back. For a moment, she wanted to pull him back to her, to feel his touch again. The world seemed too cold without his nearness. "We can start now if you want," he said. "I saw you practicing with the shadow sword. Why don't I help you with it?"

Her body filled with the need to touch him. To feel him. She *needed* him. But he was willing to help her master the smoke sword. That meant he had other skills she could use. She clenched her jaw, willing her treacherous body to hold off on its pesky little desires for a while longer. She needed that smoke sword. Not to mention better control over her magic was a plus.

Finally, she said, "Okay."

He nodded, taking another few paces backward. "Show me."

She opened her palms and reached for her magic. A shadow sword appeared between her hands. Seeing that its pommel was spherical and ordinary, she transformed it to a shape she felt alluring, carving the pommel to the shape of the pendant.

Mordecai snorted. "Fancy blades won't make or break a fight, Sadie. Just focus on forming the sword. The power comes from you, not its appearance."

"All right," she said, allowing the sword to take its own shape. "What do I do now?"

"See the blue glow on the edges?" He pointed at the blade, tracing his finger along the length from a distance. "Focus on making it disappear. Try to make it all grey. If you do, it should be solid."

She did as she was asked. Biting her lip, she

concentrated on manipulating the color instead of the energy to harden the sword. Gradually, the grey smoke spread, and the blue glow faded, but it didn't disappear completely. Sweat formed on her brow.

"Try harder," he said.

She gritted her teeth. "I am."

The grey color kept spreading, but when it almost covered the entire sword, the weapon puffed into mist, disintegrating.

"Damn it," she said, panting heavy breaths.

"You'll get better with time." He smiled, though Sadie wasn't sure if it was a condescending smile or an encouraging one. "I'll teach you."

"Thanks," she said. "But I'm going to bed." That thought made her wonder when she should summon Hobson to give Mordecai a room of his own. Maybe he preferred the dungeons. Especially considering he had proven he could have left them long ago.

She turned to head for the stairway when she paused. Looking over her shoulder, she said, "Good-night, Mordecai. Thank you for showing me more about you."

He nodded. "My pleasure, Your Highness. But if it was all the same to you, I would prefer a proper room."

Sadie faced him as a devious smirk stretched across his face. She narrowed her eyes on him.

On second thought, I think I'll make him wait a little longer.

"No."

He shrugged. "Whatever you say, Captain."

She opened her mouth to ask why *captain*, but decided it had to be Mordecai trying to get under her skin. Assuming it was sarcastic, she would think of a way to handle that later. She snapped her mouth closed.

He shifted to smoke and seeped through the bars of his cell. Once solidified, he smiled once more as he reclaimed his spot on the lounge. "Once I do get a room, you should help me break it in." He winked.

Sadie shook her head and headed back to the stairs. She thought about each of the brothers and how they each seemed to have their own unique way of getting under her skin. She heaved a sigh.

Those men really are going to be the death of me.

CHAPTER TWENTY-ONE

SADIE

*I*n her scrying room, as Sadie had come to call it, she searched for Mara, taking in all the hints she could find from the images the crystal ball revealed. But she couldn't find much useful beyond the fact Mara was a force to be reckoned with. That helped Sadie to better understand Mara, but not *find* her.

She did the same for Blair, discovering more secrets and wondering how she could know her own sister so little.

Sadie yawned. It was almost midnight, and she knew she should get some sleep, but as she returned to her room from visiting Mordecai, and what the other princes had revealed to her, she wanted to see if she could glean anything to help her with the fight she knew was going to come knocking at her door.

She wasn't going to wait around for Mara to find a way in. To find *her*. And getting the jump on things seemed to be a good tactic. At least, until now.

If only there was a way to actively spy on her.

An idea came to her. If she asked the ifrits to send a small group of scouts to search for Mara and follow her from a distance, they may help Sadie anticipate Mara's attack and be better prepared for it.

She remembered how they had seemed very eager to please her. Although, she didn't really know them or whether she could trust them or not, their celebration earlier that evening was for her return. If they agreed to it, great. If not, at least she tried. She would consider a different approach if it came to that.

Sadie called for Hobson, and the butler came knocking at her door not long after. She beckoned him in.

"How may I be of service, Sadie?" Hobson asked.

"I would like you to bring the most faithful of the ifrits to me."

The butler nodded and left her room.

Not long after, another knock came on her door.

"Come in," Sadie said.

Hobson entered, followed by Kiana—the ifrit that had led their visit to the village—and four other ifrits she hadn't met yet. They all bowed before her.

"You summoned us, Your Highness?" Kiana said.

Sadie nodded. "I have a job for you, if you

would like."

"Anything at all, Your Majesty." She stood straighter, head held high. The three companions' expressions became ones of eagerness.

Sadie showed them the crystal ball with images of Mara's legacy shifting inside. "I need you to find anything you can on her. This is Mara. She attacked me and my sister just before I arrived here." She looked at each one of them. "Anything you can find. Even the tiniest details will help."

"Of course, Your Majesty," Kiana said. She bowed again and went off, the other ifrits following her.

"Thank you, Hobson. Please let me know as soon as word arrives."

"Absolutely," he said with a curt bow.

Yawning again, she excused herself to bed.

DAMIEN

*D*amien sat on the roof of the fortress, looking down at Sadie's bedroom, debating breaking her rules to go see her. He needed to win her favor. Not just to have an alliance with the demon queen, but because he refused to leave without her. Not now that he knew how it felt to touch her, to hear her soft sighs. Her laugh.

While lost in his thoughts, the hair on the back of his neck rose. His intuition flared, sensing something coming. He stared out into the darkness, beyond the rocky fields spread around the fortress, to see a convoy marching in his direction.

He stood and stared harder to gain a better look at the creatures heading for the fortress. Sharp-nosed demons wearing only loincloths stepped in rhythm behind a massive, red-orange dragon. The demons' long, pointed ears bobbed up and down as they followed along.

He inched closer to the edge, stretching his wings and balancing precariously. He sniffed the air, picking out the putrid scents that the lowest foot soldiers carried from weeks of not bathing.

His gaze shifted to the man riding atop of the dragon, heart skipping a beat.

King Zagan, Damien's father, marched toward the fortress. If he was showing up so soon after Sadie's arrival, that meant only one thing. Bad news. His father didn't like threats to his power, and with Sadie as the new demon queen, Damien knew his father came for one of two reasons. One: to kill Sadie and take her power. Or two: to gain alliance.

His father was about an hour's march out before he would cross into Sadie's boundaries. Damien had to get to Sadie before then. She needed a crash course in King Zagan 101. Her life could depend on it.

CHAPTER TWENTY-TWO

SADIE

*S*adie had just finished slipping into a new silk nightgown and was heading into bed when her bedroom door flew open. She whirled around, about to scream at whoever it was that *this was* her *fucking room* when she saw Damien panting, eyes wide.

"You have visitors," he said.

She rolled her eyes. *Seriously? All this excitement for visitors?* "It's late. I'm going to bed. They can come back tomorrow."

Damien rushed to her and grabbed her shoulders, forcing Sadie to look him in the eyes. "You don't understand—"

Hobson hurried, equally out of breath. "Your Majesty, the demon king has arrived."

"Demon king?" she asked, jaw hanging open. She stared at Damien. "Your father?"

He nodded, lips pressed into a grim line.

Though she didn't know much about the king, she knew enough to have a serious understanding of just how much his arrival meant bad news.

Shit. Her eyebrows knitted together. "What does he want with me?"

"Nothing good," Damien said, grumbling. "This is just the kind of move my father would pull—catching us off guard in the middle of the night, big pomp and show of force. Surely, he will ask you to submit to him, and he will consider it an act of war if you don't." He stood closer to her, keeping an eye on the window as if he could see something she couldn't. "Zagan probably heard you're human, and now he's going to try to intimidate you."

Sadie scoffed. "Fat chance."

Damien seemed stressed, but a slight smirk played around his lips in response. He gazed at her in a way that made her feel ready to show their father he made a mistake thinking he could bully her. She didn't know how, but she felt capable with him. Strong and unstoppable.

The gears turned in her head, quickly formulating a plan. She turned to Hobson. "Gather the ifrits and have them go to the wall. Space them out so it looks like there are more of them than there are."

The butler immediately left to carry out Sadie's orders.

"I should get dressed," she said, facing Damien.

"I'll wait outside." He turned on his heel and left the room.

Sadie opened her wardrobe, taking out the first attire she saw—a battle dress. She put it on, comfortable with its wide red and black sleeves, the long slit on the front parted to reveal the black leggings she wore underneath. She put on combat boots and clasped the outfit's black belt across her waist. On the topmost shelf, she noticed a blood-red tiara. She grinned as she placed it on her head.

I'll show him human.

When she opened the door to the hallway, Damien's eyes widened. Her heart fluttered, and her cheeks warmed. He didn't speak as she exited her room.

To be honest, she felt pretty damn hot in her dress.

"Let's go," she said and took a deep breath. *Time for my own show of force.*

They entered a tower along the castle's front. Sadie paused by a window overlooking the approaching army, the princes came to stand by her. Even Mordecai left his cell to show support and help deal with the matter at hand.

Sadie watched the king's convoy advance,

observing the demons' tiny silhouettes grow larger as they marched into her territory.

She felt it the moment they crossed onto her land, the shift in the air, the warning from the fortress. *Good.* That meant she could use her castle's magic against them if the need arose. And, even though she was still learning what it could do, she had seen enough to know it could contain intruders well enough.

Time to go. She turned and faced the men, giving them each a long, hard stare. "Stay here, all of you."

"You don't know our father," Kaiser said. "Let us come with you."

"He's right," Damien said.

Sadie didn't agree. "I'm going by myself. End of discussion."

The princes spoke all at once. "You're making a mistake." "This is madness." "He'll kill you."

She held up her hand. With as much of a command she could put into her voice she said, "If you come with me, I swear, this is the last time you step foot in my fortress."

They grumbled, but when she walked out of the tower to the ramparts, they didn't follow. Sadie smiled. *Now they're listening.*

When Zagan arrived, she took her time walking to the front gate, intentionally making him wait. She settled her eyes on the king as she approached the gate, stopping just a few feet away. He rode atop a dragon.

Pomp and show, my ass...

Sadie clenched her fists and took pity on the poor creature forced to walk on the ground instead of being free to do what it was made for. Fire burned in its throat, and its eyes seemed glossed over. Her heart broke for the poor creature.

Settling her eyes on Zagan once again, she called out, "Who goes there?"

"Demon queen, I would like an audience with you," Zagan said, puffing out his chest.

"Is that so? It seems more like you're looking for war." She pointed to the army that accompanied him.

"This?" He sneered, holding out his arms. "A mere precaution, given your predecessor's reputation."

She crossed her arms. "Then I hope you don't mind if I enact precautions of my own."

His sneer widened. "That's not very hospitable, is it? Won't you even let us in?"

"I will allow only you inside these walls, Your Majesty."

His mocking smile faltered. She had gotten under his skin which seemed too easy.

"No. You will bring my army inside as well."

"Then, goodbye." Sadie turned to leave. She didn't owe him any explanation. And she certainly wasn't going to be told what to do and who to let into her own damn fortress.

"Let me and my army in," he demanded, glaring at her, puffing his chest like a petulant child.

Sadie remained unperturbed. "You can enter alone or leave."

He huffed and stared at the ground for a moment, probably thinking of how to use Sadie's demand and refusal to his gain. Sadie was about to give up, take his silence and lack of moving as a sign that he still wouldn't budge when he shifted, turning his attention back to her.

She stared at him expectantly.

"Fine," he said.

Zagan rode in on his dragon. Sadie walked back to the tower she had observed the convoy from and came across the princes.

"All of you, remain hidden," she said.

Kaiser growled. "No. Not this time, Sadie. I don't care what you say. You don't know our father. I will go with you, and I don't care if you don't choose me as an ally."

"Same here," Damien said. "I'm going with you, too."

The other two agreed without a word. They nodded in unison, arms crossed over their chests.

Sadie sighed, certain she couldn't convince them to stay where they were. Mordecai and Steele followed her out to the courtyard. She approached Zagan, sitting straight on the dragon's back. A look of extreme displeasure deepened the lines formed on his forehead, and he frowned.

The king shifted his attention to the men behind and said, "Traitors!" He gave Sadie a threatening look. "I could ransack your fortress for hiding them."

The nerve. Sadie just laughed at him. "Go ahead."

Zagan raised his eyebrows but scowled again. "Did no one tell you that it's customary to meet important people in the throne room? You clearly don't know what you're doing."

Sadie rolled her eyes. This was all getting annoying. He was right, of course. She knew that she *should* bring him to her throne room, but Sadie ultimately wanted to ensure he didn't get to see much of her fortress. She figured he probably gave her a visit only to survey the place and needed him gone ASAP.

Mustering fake politeness, Sadie bowed. "Your Majesty, it's damp in my throne room. Very moist. And it smells. It doesn't do well for the lungs." She fluttered her lashes. She could've sworn she heard Steele snort behind her.

Zagan didn't reply immediately. Instead, he dismounted. Sadie looked at the dragon again, and she felt a tug. Like the creature was calling out to her.

"You need to ally with me," he said as he approached her.

Pushy asshole.

"You will die without my protection," Zagan continued, emphasizing die.

The men behind Sadie shifted. She held a hand up to keep them back.

"That is very noble and selfless of you," Sadie said. *Not.* "And what will you want from me in return?"

"Your powers, of course," he said. "If you even have any."

She gave him her sweetest, fakest smile. "Sure, I have powers. I do have to apologize that you're leaving here without an alliance. I'm still in the process of choosing an ally. And the decision will not be made tonight."

Zagan drew his eyebrows together. When he looked at the princes, Sadie knew he had pieced it all together. His face flushed. "If you ally with any of my sons, I will consider you an enemy and destroy you."

Okay, that's it! The veins in her neck throbbed. He wasn't going to just barge in here and threaten her. This was *her* home. "Well, I'd like to see you try."

Zagan curled his lip contemptuously and pointed at her. "Charge!"

The ifrits along the castle walls all raised their arms, ready to defend Sadie. The princes leapt into action, the four of them surrounding her. But when the dragon flew toward them, Sadie didn't feel violence from the creature, she felt defiance. And not toward her, but Zagan.

The dragon landed behind her and faced the demon king. She roared and blew a strong torrent of fire at the king. When it disappeared, the king stood with one hand held out, unaffected by the fire.

"I only wanted to test that gift of yours," Zagan said, sneering. "See if the rumors were true."

If he had been able to control the dragon, Sadie knew the princes and the ifrits wouldn't have hesitated to kill the poor thing. She clenched her fist, hating the king even more for bringing an innocent creature into this.

"I'm not here to kill you," Zagan said. "But I will give you an ultimatum to consider. Since you're new to this world, and I'm feeling generous, you are to join me or die. If you ally yourself with any of them," he shot his sons a look of pure hatred, "even one, I will consider it an act of war and respond accordingly."

Sadie's nails bit into her palm. "Why, pray tell, would *you* be so generous?"

"You'll come to your senses eventually," Zagan said. "Alliances aren't about trust, you know. They're about power. And no one can defeat me. Not even you. Not even all of you together."

Sadie scoffed. *How arrogant.* But the comment gave her an idea. What if they worked together? She briefly glanced at the princes. But no, they wouldn't share... would they?

Zagan turned his back and walked away. Hobson opened the gate for him. Sadie watched as her unwelcomed visitor retreated.

As soon as the gate closed, the princes huddled together.

"We need to strategize," Damien said. "Surely, he'll come back with a greater show of force."

"I agree," Kaiser said.

Steele nodded. Serious and not goofy for once. "If he doesn't get what he wants next time, there'll be hell to pay."

Mordecai grumbled. "I'll kill that son of a bitch."

Sadie should've been amused—proud even—that they did something besides bicker with each other for the first time. But she just stood there, silently waiting until she felt the last of his horde leave her land. Once the last foot of the intruders left her land, she silently headed to her room.

CHAPTER TWENTY-THREE

SADIE

*S*adie had finally removed the blue glow on the edges of the smoke sword she casted, but it only lasted for about five seconds. It had burst into mist like before. The stone statues of boar heads mounted on the dungeon walls seemed to watch her as she practiced.

"Again," Mordecai said, standing stern beside his cell.

Sadie wiped the bead of sweat that had formed on her brow. "I'm trying the best I can."

"If that's your best, it really sucks," he said. "Again."

Sadie grumbled, although thankful for his strict mentoring that helped her better cast. She may have had a hard time manipulating smoke, but she wasn't a quitter.

Holding up her hand and clenching her jaw, she

cast another sword out of smoke. It hardened and maintained its solidity but only for about thirty seconds until it dissolved once more.

Internally, she screamed.

"I think I know what you are doing wrong. The technique is to transfer magic to the sword and reinforce it from edge to center, not the other way around," Mordecai said from his perch within the cell. "Form a block along the border to contain the energy. Focus on the edges, not the body."

Sadie bit her lip. Taking a deep breath and keeping Mordecai's pointers in mind, she cast another smoke sword and concentrated on the sword's perimeter first. When the blue glow had faded, and the sword remained grey and solid for more than a minute, she lifted it and banged the blade against the wall. It didn't even hit the surface before disappearing from her hand.

She sighed and looked at Mordecai. "Maybe some other day?"

He shrugged. "If not a smoke sword, then a fire sword. It seems like fire's your specialty anyway."

"All right," she said. She closed her eyes and held out her hands. It was pretty much the same process, though crafting a weapon with fire was significantly easier.

When she opened her eyes and looked at the sword, she smiled. The hilt blazed, and the flames licked at her hand but didn't hurt her. And though completely made of fire, the blade had a metallic appearance. It glowed red-orange, like iron that just came out of the forge, while blue flames danced around the edges.

"Good," he said, leaving his post to approach her. "At least you learned one thing today. But now that you crafted a weapon, why don't you fight me with it?"

Sadie accepted the challenge. "All right."

Mordecai flicked his wrist, and a smoke staff appeared in his hand. She narrowed her eyes on the weapon, trying to gauge how he managed to produce it so quickly. A tinge of envy filled her gut. She wanted to be as masterful as he was. Hell, she was nearly there with her fire magic.

Sadie advanced first, confident of her speed and precision. Spinning around him, she swung her blade, but he whirled and parried the blow. She swung again and kicked his knee. He turned into shadow at the last moment, so her knee and her weapon only hit air.

"That's cheating!" she said, panting.

He solidified, no longer holding his staff, and grabbed her weapon that instantly disappeared in her hand. He swiftly tackled her to the ground but rolled so he was under her, softening her fall. He guided her head to him and gently bit her ear. She gasped, her entire body erupting in shivers, her heart picked up in pace.

"Fights aren't meant to be fair, Captain," he said, murmuring against her ear.

She inhaled, slowly puffing out her chest to loosen his hold on her, promptly exhaling a breath when she had sufficiently slacked his grip. Balling her hand into a fist, she went to jab him in the ribs. He turned to smoke again, forcing her to hit the ground. The blow knocked the air out of her lungs.

Sadie stood, blowing away the strand of hair that fell in her face, annoyed at how easily he escaped her blows. She created another fire sword and jabbed at him. He turned to shadow again, immediately solidifying back to his demon form as soon as he got out of her sword's range.

But this time, Sadie caught a tell. She noticed that his shadow form had swirled brighter before he changed back. She tried to get him to shift again by swiping the sword at him. Again, he transformed to shadow, the mist swirling in a brighter grey before he became solid again. Subtle, but there.

Sadie smiled. The shadow drifted to her left and she kept her eyes locked on it. When she caught the bright swirl of color, she reached into the amulet's magic and held up her arms. Ropes made of fire protruded from her fingers and wrapped around Mordecai like duct tape. He grunted as he fell to the floor. She dashed to him and pressed the edge of the sword against his throat.

He smirked. "Captain." A sparkling shimmer in his eyes revealed good humor.

Sadie lowered her weapon. "Why don't we take a rest?"

"Aye, aye." Mordecai crafted a smoke chair for her, even softening its smoke cushions to make them feel like real pillows. She chuckled.

"I'm surprised you don't just leave your cell," she said.

He sat on the floor in front of her and leaned back against the cell bars. "How do you know I haven't? Besides, I've grown fond of the place."

Neither of them spoke for a moment. Their breaths mingled together, echoing in the near-empty dungeon cell.

Sadie studied Mordecai's features, noting that each of the brothers had similar chins, high cheek bones, and noses. Just like Zagan. But they each had different eyes, colored skin, and hair. She wondered if Cedric had the same features, and if the softer features came from their mother.

"Where's your mother in all of this?" she asked as she realized she knew nothing of the woman that birthed them.

He shrugged as he scratched at his beard. "Died a long time ago. Why?"

"Just curious." Sadie fiddled with a sting that hung

lose from the seam of her shirt. "Were you close to her?"

"Not really. Were you close to any of your parents?"

Sadie thought for a moment. All her childhood, she had an equal closeness to both parents, never favoring one over the other. "I was close to both of them. Even my sister."

"Interesting…" He dragged out the last with a slight purr and narrowed his eyes on her.

She struggled not to squirm and fought against the blush that threatened to burn her cheeks. "Were you close with Cedric?"

Instead of answering her question, he stood and said, "Let's try to make a bow and arrow this time."

"Bow and arrow?" she asked, ignoring how he evaded her question. She realized it must have been prying. If he didn't want to answer, she would respect that.

"You were able to make a fire sword," he said. "Why not a bow and arrow too?"

She placed her hands on her hips though she felt a bit exhausted from the effort she had exerted. "I think I made good progress today. I should go rest. Maybe grab a tub of ice cream."

He approached her. "Nope."

Sadie sighed, but she appreciated the time and

effort he took to help improve her skills and make her a better fighter.

Mordecai pulled on her arms, so she could stand, the smoke chair billowing away as she did.

"You know what a bow and arrow look like, right?" he asked.

She snorted. "Of course."

"Then cast."

She glared at him and said, "Fine."

Sadie held up her hands again and bit her lip, but her focus wavered when Mordecai brushed her lower lip with his thumb.

"I love it when you do that," he said, his voice almost a whisper. She looked away, clearing her throat.

She took a step back and resumed her casting, producing a bow and arrow made of fire. She started with the bow's limb, curling it into an arch. She traced a line with her hand from one end to the other and crafted a bow string, imagining it to be a flexible cable. The weapon felt hot against her skin though, like the sword, the flames didn't hurt.

Recalling Mordecai's tips, she focused on the edges, containing the magic within as she strengthened the boundaries first. She held the bow and pulled the string. Flames danced along the surface, but it felt solid and effective.

First try, and a success.

She made an arrow next. It also felt solid in her hands.

Sadie grinned at him and he stared back at her, eyes alight with something she couldn't explain. It seemed like pride, and that filled her with joy.

"Shoot the arrow, then," he said. "Go ahead."

She lifted the bow with her left hand and notched the arrow with the other. She aimed at the far wall of the dungeon, but when she let go of the arrow, it shattered one of the stone heads that stared down upon them.

"Oops," she said and threw her head back, laughing.

Mordecai chuckled under his breath. "Now we have to improve on your aim."

Sadie let go of her magic's tether to the weapon, allowing them to disappear. She held her smile as she stared at him.

Mordecai isn't so bad. She actually enjoyed spending time with him. Too bad she had to be prudent and not trust him entirely.

At least, not yet.

CHAPTER TWENTY-FOUR

SADIE

*S*adie sat in her gardens the next day, peeling an orange that she had plucked from a tree. A tingling sensation, similar to the one she got when Zagan crossed onto her land, came over her. She stood and thought about Damien, wondering if she should ask him to observe who was coming. He knew about Zagan even before Hobson did, and his skills were beneficial, to say the least.

However, she didn't want to become dependent on any of the princes, so she called for her butler instead. He arrived swiftly, as always.

"You have visitors at the gate. Just six demons this time," Hobson said. "They said they would like to meet with you. Word had gotten around that you're looking for allies."

Sadie let out an exasperated sigh. Dealing with the

four princes' egos was work enough. But after the visit from Zagan, she could use all the help she could get. She nodded. "Go get the princes and some of the ifrits. I'll meet everyone in the throne room."

She hoped these visitors were like the ifrits and not the demon king. She had enough enemies inherited from the previous queen and a few of her own. The last thing she needed was more.

After changing into a blue battle dress, she arrived last, finding she liked to keep her visitors waiting. It felt like a good power move to remind them of who was in charge.

As she entered the throne room, she kept her head held high. She noted how deadly silent everyone was, and that made her weary of the visitors already. The princes stood beside a marble pillar as Hobson uneasily shifted near them. Five ifrits stood scattered across the room, lined up along the walls like guards.

When Sadie sat on her throne, the princes positioned themselves around her, glaring at the newcomers. She eyed the purple-clad demons—four men and two women, all of whom had pale, sharp features and wore spiked metal helmets around their platinum-colored horns. One skull hung on each of their necks. They glared back at her men, and that didn't sit well with her.

She paused at the thought of the princes as "her men" but dismissed it for the moment. There were more important matters to think about, and she was still set on only choosing one.

The male demon at the head of the small party stepped forward, his hand gripping the hilt of his sword. Sadie figured he must've been their leader.

"We would like to join your contest," he said. His voice sounded coarse and commanding. It repulsed her, made her skin crawl, and boiled her blood.

They were bad news and couldn't be trusted. That, Sadie knew. She listened to her intuition.

"I have enough on my plate for now," she said. "I regret to inform you that my answer is no."

The demons snarled.

"Self-important bitch," their leader said, lips curling. "You will never be queen."

That demon charged, soaring on his wings, claws out to get her. Sadie cast a fire sword and widened her stance, ready for a fight. Hobson hurried in front of her and grabbed the demon by the neck and threw him away with surprising strength. The demon hit the far wall on the back of the throne room and crumpled to the ground.

Sadie's gaze darted to the princes, hoping none of them were hurt as the visitors-turned-invaders attacked. One of the female demons charged at Damien and slashed his side, catching him by surprise. He sucked in a breath as he got knocked to the ground. Kaiser sprinted to his rescue.

As the demoness prepared to thrust her dagger into Damien's chest, Kaiser plunged his fist into the demoness's back and pulled out her heart. It beat once in his hand before going still. Kaiser flung it to the ground, dark ichor covering his hand.

Another demon advanced on Mordecai, but he dissolved into shadow and dashed pass his opponent. He solidified behind the demon who seemed suddenly petrified. Sadie stiffened as she watched the demon's body split in two, both halves thumping to the ground and dripping dark blood.

One robed demon ran toward Steele with sword held high. Steele smirked, not bothering to brandish a weapon. The demon didn't even get close to him before knees buckled and he screamed, clutching his head as he collapsed to the ground, blood flowing from his ears, eyes, and nose. The demon lay sprawled on the ground, eyes eternally staring into the distance.

Sadie swallowed hard as she realized the full weight of what Steele could do. He could have done that to her in a blink of an eye. But he didn't. That made her trust him all the more.

Her fire magic tingled and pooled in her hand as Kaiser fought the second demoness. Kaiser crashed to the floor as the demoness hooked her leg against his. She leapt toward him, her blade prepared to pierce his throat.

Sadie stood and prepared to launch a ball of fire as

Damien appeared, seemingly out of nowhere, flaming sword in hand. He swung his sword once, sending the demoness' head rolling along the floor. The now head-less body slumped forward with a thump.

Sadie sighed in relief, the pulse of her magic ebbing slightly.

The last demon stood in the corner, defending himself against five ifrits. One ifrit shot a ball of fire at him. The shot landed dead-center in his chest, slamming him against the pillar behind him. He screamed as the blow consumed him from the inside out.

The ifrits linked arms, joining together and forming a massive ball of fire. It swooped toward the demon and he burst into flames, screaming as his body combusted, slowly disintegrating to ash.

Hypnotized by the deadly grace with which the princes and the ifrits fought, Sadie didn't see the demons' leader attack her from her right. She was knocked to the ground. He jabbed at her with his sword stained with what she assumed to have been the blood of its prior victims.

Instinctively, she held her hands, palms out, in front of her. A bolt of fire struck her attacker.

The demon roared in pain as he jumped away from her, flailing his arms as the flames licked at the fabric of his cloak.

Sadie stood and flicked her wrist, fabricating another fire sword, already familiar with the process.

She swung, and the demon blocked the blow with an ill-formed parry. His weapon clanged to the ground when it met hers.

She didn't hesitate. She plunged her fire sword deep into the demon's shoulder. He scowled, but his eyes widened as his cloak caught fire.

She twisted the sword. "Why are you here?"

"To capture you, why else?" he said, his breathing ragged.

"Who sent you?" she asked, twisting the fire sword again.

"Mara's coming for you, and she won't show you mercy," he said through gritted teeth.

She yanked her sword from his shoulder and slowly plunged it into his chest. Instead of the screaming she anticipated, the demon laughed.

"I will not die in your hands," he said and spat at her.

He pulled out a strange trinket from his burning cloak.

Mordecai yelled, "Look out!"

A massive body slammed into Sadie. Arms surrounded her as she flew across the floor and rolled to a stop. A loud explosion burst from where she had been standing. The vibrations reverberated the throne room, shattering the surrounding three pillars. In the middle of a small crater in the floor, the demon's corpse bled and smoldered.

Sadie scrambled to her feet, coughing from breathing in the settling dust, smoke, and ash. She faced Mordecai who had saved her from the blast. "Thanks."

He winked at her.

Though rattled from her near-death, she rolled her eyes and smiled.

Kaiser ran to her. He gripped both her shoulders, his hold gentle. "Are you okay?" His eyes roved over her entire body.

"I'm all right," she said. But he didn't let go, proceeding with his own examinations. She held his arms and placed them back to his side. "Really, Kaiser. I'm all right. I promise."

His lips formed a grim line, but he nodded.

From the silence, Steele whooped. "That was the most fun I've had in *ages.*"

They all stared at him, not saying anything. Mordecai breathed a chuckle, and all of them laughed.

"Mordecai, I haven't seen you fight in *years*," Steele said. "I've forgotten how awesome your power is. Remind me not to kill you just to get it."

"Go ahead and try, brother," Mordecai said, the corner of his lips quirking upward.

Damien approached Kaiser. "Thanks for having my back out there."

Kaiser scratched his head. "Thanks to you, too."

Sadie glanced at each of them, watching them with

a raised eyebrow. *Huh. They're complimenting and thanking each other. What happened?*

Shaking her head, she walked to one of the ifrits who again stood with her back straight by the throne room wall. "Thank you for defending this fortress."

The ifrit bowed her head. "Of course, Your Highness."

"Can you do me a favor?" Sadie asked.

"What is it, Your Majesty?"

"I need more ifrits." Between Zagan and, now, these cretins, she needed to start building her own army. "Take two of your comrades to help you. Bring as many as you can from all the nearby villages."

The female ifrit bowed again and left, walking as calmly as if she hadn't just been in a fight. Sadie smiled to herself, thinking how lucky she was to have found reliable soldiers.

She turned her attention to the crumbling pillars blown up by the explosion, wondering what kind of artifact triggered it. Those demons must have come from Mara's own soldiers. She thought about Kiana and the other ifrits she had sent on the search for Mara but set the thought aside. These things took time. They would return with reports eventually.

CHAPTER TWENTY-FIVE

SADIE

*S*adie unlocked the bars of Mordecai's cell. Not that they did anything to keep him in the cell in the first place.

"What's this?" he asked. "You're here to interrogate me, or for more training?"

"Neither," she said. "Come with me."

Instead of going through the entrance of the cell, he shifted to shadow and bled through the bars. She snorted.

"What?" he asked. "I like doing it."

She shook her head and walked out of the dungeons.

"Where are we going?" he asked as he followed behind her.

She sighed. "To your bedroom. Unless you miss your cell. In that case, stop following me."

"Good to know I'm no longer a prisoner," he said. Even though she couldn't see him, she heard the smile in his voice.

"I'd love to keep you there," she said, halting in her steps to face him. "But you earned it after the fight today."

He didn't answer, so she turned her back on him again and they walked to the east wing in silence. When they reached his room, Sadie opened the double doors to his chamber, revealing a king-sized, ebony bed filled with soft cushions. The dark sheets and pillows were similar to hers. Dark grey and black silk fabrics hung from the ceiling, serving as the bed's canopy.

Sadie allowed Mordecai to step into the room and take a look around. When he faced her, she smiled and said, "Thanks for saving my life."

She turned to leave but stopped when he grabbed her elbow. She faced him again.

He smirked. "Thought you were supposed to help me break in the bed?"

"Or..." She glared at him, though she didn't think she did a convincing job because of the blush creeping up her face. "I can just send you back to the dungeons."

She tried to take her elbow back as Mordecai wrapped his arms around her. She twisted from his hold and tried to wrench his arms that locked her in place.

"What do you think you're doing?" she asked.

In answer, he opened his wings and flew them toward his bed. He pinned her to the mattress with him on top of her.

She yelped. "Mordecai!" She thrashed in his arms and tried to escape, but it didn't seem to do anything but burn energy.

Mordecai lifted his arm out to the side and flicked his wrist. Smoke shifted. It solidified, pushing the door closed. A spiral of smoke clicked the lock. She gaped and took in this handsome man's eyes, realizing he kept his eyes on her the entire time and not the door.

She should leave. But even though she kept moving and hitting his arm, trying to make him let go of her, a part of her didn't want him to.

This was madness. She shouldn't be pinned under him, completely at his mercy. Her body shivered with the way he looked at her. Even though she yearned for him to draw nearer every time he touched her, and even though being with him felt intoxicating, she teetered on the edge of darkness.

But he made her feel powerful.

He smirked. And she felt like he could see her internal struggle. That annoyed her even more.

She stopped thrashing and began to think of another way to get him off her, since she obviously couldn't move him through sheer strength. But when he brushed away stray locks of hair away from her face and kissed the corner of her left eye, she froze.

"Is this part of some weird training?" she asked, trying to make her voice authoritative, but the words came out breathless.

"Maybe," he said, voice husky. "Maybe I want you to give in."

He cupped her cheek with a warm hand. "I know you want this."

He leaned close and whispered, "Let go, Sadie."

His deep voice sent a shiver down her spine. She shut her eyes and took in a steadying breath. The darkness surrounding Mordecai felt familiar. It was a darkness that lingered within her, too. She had felt it since she arrived in Bitterthorn.

Maybe that was why she resisted him. Because being with him made her feel closer to that darkness within her. She knew the demon queen title had a history of cruelty and ruthlessness. But that wasn't her. She worried if she got close enough to touch the darkness that came with the amulet, she might change. And she might never come back.

As if he knew what she was thinking, Mordecai caressed her cheek with his thumb and looked at her so longingly. "Let go."

Her eyes softened with how he gazed at her. In that moment, she trusted him. So, she let go.

When his lips met hers, she felt herself fall toward

that darkness. She let it consume her. The magic. The power thrumming in her veins. She gave in.

And as this energy enveloped her, she didn't feel any different. She didn't feel cruel or ruthless. She only felt like herself. Maybe even better. She smiled against his lips, knowing in her heart and feeling it in her soul the magic didn't change her. It made her stronger. A darker aura seemed to surround her now, but she felt the same.

Mordecai's lips left hers to spread kisses on her cheek, her jaw, her throat. She wrapped her arms around his neck, wanting more. She moaned. His kisses drifted upward, and he nibbled on her ear, biting it softly, making her gasp.

Sadie hooked one leg on his hips and placed her arms on his chest. She guided him so that he lay under her. She kissed him the same way he did, spreading light kisses on his lips, his cheek, his jaw, because he should know how it felt, too.

Their lips met again and, this time, Mordecai's hands drifted to her breast, kneading, pressing his thumbs on her erect nipples. She whimpered needing more of him. His tongue explored her mouth. Sadie moaned again and clenched her thighs, trying to gain even the slightest release from the throbbing between her legs.

Mordecai's hands wandered down her side and slipped under the hem of her robe. He caressed her butt while playing with her underwear, stretching the fabric with his hands. She wanted to press against him, even closer than they already were. But before his hands could wander farther than they were now, Sadie took his hands and pinned them above his head. She looked at him with a teasing smile and pecked the tip of his nose.

Without a word, she sat up and left the bed. Mordecai growled, and she laughed under her breath. She smiled as she left his room, knowing he wanted more. She sauntered to her chambers with her head held high, very much so feeling like the queen she was.

CHAPTER TWENTY-SIX

STEELE

*S*teele strutted through the room, finalizing every minute detail to make sure his date with Sadie went off without a hitch.

The dining table was set with a lavish spread of roasted chicken and potatoes, wine, and a selection of cheeses that compliment his choice of pinot. Noir of course. The darker, the better.

Rose petals were scattered along the spread, with a sizable bouquet standing near center where Sadie would be sitting.

Standing back, he propped his hands on his hips and narrowed his eyes, scrutinizing every detail.

A throat cleared behind him.

Steele turned, finding Sadie looking ravishing in a midnight blue gown with a plunging neckline that showed off not only her pendant but her rather delicious cleavage. Her cheeks warmed, and Steele smiled.

So beautiful.

He wanted her. Bad. His gaze drifted back to the table as he considered taking her to the bedroom before dinner, but as things would go, Sadie pushed passed him and sat herself down in front of one of the plates.

"You've really outdone yourself, Steele. Everything looks wonderful."

"You look better than anything on that table." He approached her side and leaned over. "Care for an appetizer?"

Without waiting for an answer, he lowered his lips to hers, moving his mouth in the way that makes her moan every time.

And she did.

His hands slipped under the seam of her dress to cup a breast and massage it in the way that would make her come for him. It satisfied him when she crossed her legs and clenched them tighter.

Sadie pulled back, stopping Steele with a laugh. "I'm ready for the main course."

Steele groaned. "What are we waiting for then?" He held out his hand for her and she looked at it with a confused expression.

Her eyes widened as she blushed even more. "No. The food."

"It will happen, Sadie. And when it does, you will beg for more."

"We'll see," she said as she picked up a cube of cheddar and plopped it into her mouth.

"Care to place a wager on that?" he asked, taking his own seat adjacent to her.

"Is everything a game that you have to win? Are you not serious about anything?" She asked and took a sip of her wine. Her eyes rolled, and she let out a soft "mmm."

The look of pleasure on Sadie's face took control of Steele's already out-of-control sex drive. He had to get her soon. Else he would lose his mind. "I take plenty of things seriously. And I am serious when I said it will happen and you will beg for more."

"I'm sure." She smiled and set her eyes on the spread. "Nice touch with the rose petals."

"My pleasure."

She sat straighter. "So, what else do you take serious? Besides that."

He shrugged. "Things."

She shook her head. Her eyes focused on something on the table as she thought of something apparently dark. This wasn't what Steele was thinking when he had a romantic wine and dine type of date in mind.

She set her gorgeous black eyes on him, and his heart stilled for a moment.

"I'll make a bet with you then. Tell me the darkest

thing you can handle, and if I can show you something worse, I win whatever I want."

"And if you can't?" he asked, leaning forward, itching for the challenge.

"Let's cross that bridge when we get there."

Steele shook his head. "Nope. If you get whatever you want, so do I. And I think you know what I want, Sadie."

She narrowed her eyes on him, a thin smile toyed with the edges of her lips. "For me to choose you. I know. Not happening tonight however."

Steele shook his head. A chuckle rumbled in his throat. "Yes, there's that. But—"

"Oh, Damien and I found a hellhound in the forest. Did I tell you?"

Changing the subject didn't sway his goal for the evening. He played along. For the moment. She took a sip of the wine and licked her lips. Steele's pants grew even tighter. He groaned and fought to take her right then and there, show her the promise of what he could bring.

Damn, those lips. He wanted to lick them for himself, but he played the moment cool. Collected.

"Oh?" he asked, yanking his eyes from her lips to look her in the eyes.

"Yeah, such an adorable creature," Sadie said.

Not as adorable as you...

"Too bad he left not long after he showed himself."

He grabbed a cheddar cube from the cheese platter by the toothpick and ate it. He figured if he didn't attempt to eat something himself, she would probably think he poisoned her or something. It's not something he hadn't done before, but there was so much more to Sadie than he initially gave her credit for. If she didn't choose him—no, he wouldn't think of that. "Probably means Damien's going to die soon. That's good." He finished chewing the cheese and added, "One less competitor."

She smacked him on the arm. "And you wonder why I say you don't take things seriously."

He laughed, rubbing the spot, though it didn't hurt. Shrugging, he said, "Guess you'll just have to reconsider my end of the bargain."

"What about the stuff with your dad," she said. "What do you think I should do?"

Steele wiped his lips with a napkin. "Why don't we just run away and leave my three dork brothers to fend for themselves?" He smiled. "We could go to Ibiza. Party all night long."

Damn, he missed Ibiza. Maybe he could really take her there one day. But Steele disregarded the thought. He wanted to be chosen, more than returning to Ibiza. He just didn't want to get his hopes up on taking her with him.

Sadie shook her head, laughing under her breath. "Again. Not taking things seriously."

"Still waiting for you to agree to me getting what I want. Sure, I want to be chosen, but…" he settled his eyes on her and inched into her mind with the image of him satisfying his craving for her. The way he could make her feel.

She clutched the arms of her chair, eyes closed and leaned her head back.

He smiled, pulling away. Some things were better done than just shown.

She sat straighter again, panting for breath, setting her eyes alight with desire for him.

"Fine," she said through pants. She stood and walked to one of the massive halls.

He watched her walk through the door into the hall, eyes on her sumptuous hips as she walked and stood, stopping in the middle of the doorway to look at him.

"Chicken?" she asked.

He laughed, stood, and followed her, pulled by more than just the desire to win the bet, but by the need to be constantly near her. He was confident this fortress had many dark things to show him, but dark enough to unsettle him? Never.

They made their way to the south wing. Gloomier and darker compared to the rest of the fortress. Lion heads carved of stone silently roared from the top of each arch lining the walls. A massive metallic door stood at the end. It was colder, too. Steele tried to hide the shiver that quaked through him. He wouldn't admit that this place concerned him. Winning the bet wasn't his biggest concern for him anymore. Protecting Sadie was.

Sadie calmly led him inside the metallic door. She seemed unperturbed. But when they reached the entrance to what seemed like a dark, misty courtyard, her hands became uneasy. Her fingers fidgeted with her clothes. He took a hand just to help steady her, and it gave him the chance to touch her soft skin.

He thought she would lead them to the courtyard since he felt it deserved to be the darkest place in the fortress, but they passed it, and she hastened her steps. Steele drew his eyebrows together. He wondered what could possibly have been there that would cause such a reaction from her. Perhaps he would bring that up later. For now, he wanted to enjoy the dark things she wanted to show him. Besides, the courtyard concerned him as well.

Definitely bringing that up later.

Sadie stepped into another hallway instead, and they entered a vast, shadow-covered room with a ceiling ornamented with alcoves. Tall shelves filled with cobwebs lined the walls. The room lacked furniture, except for a lone couch covered in a white sheet stained with dust in the middle of the room. The one chandelier that hung from the ceiling was in complete disuse.

"What is this place?" Steele asked, his voice quiet though piercing the silence.

Sadie shrugged. Her face seemed inscrutable, but she pulled her hand from his and crossed her arms, betraying the discomfort she obviously felt. Steele went to put his arms around him, but she moved on, taking him out of the metal doorway, back into the hall that led to the south wing.

The air lightened and Steele sucked in a deep breath, warming up as they departed from the unsettling air from the south wing.

She kept walking along the south wing's hallways to another area he had never been before.

"Have you had enough?" Sadie asked. "You've kept your composure fairly well so far."

Steele looked at her. "Enough what?"

"Dark stuff."

He smirked. "Only if you've had."

She smiled at him. With that smile and her dark waves framing her face like that, he subdued the urge to run his hands along her cheek and pull her to him. He wanted to press her against the wall and take her right then and there. He wanted to grab a fistful of that beautiful hair and make her cum until she couldn't take anymore.

He wondered what she was thinking now. Quelling the guilt he felt for even thinking about breaching her privacy, he peeked into her thoughts. *Just a little bit of insight.*

The tiny piece of guilt he felt transformed to jealousy with Sadie in Mordecai's bed, his hands touching parts he shouldn't have touched. Steele left her mind immediately, unable to stomach seeing more of the images. He needed to step up his game. He was already losing. To Mordecai, no less.

Screw his imaginations of pressing her against the wall. He should turn it into reality. Steele approached Sadie, his hunger for this woman annihilated his practical sense. He wanted—no, needed— her. He needed her to himself. Sadie gently bit her lower lip as she stepped back until her back hit the wall, looking up at him through her long lashes. He couldn't take it anymore.

He pinned her to the wall and leaned down, pecking her on the side of her lips. "You're too irresistible for my own good."

"Not my fault you can't control your impulses," she said.

Her body arched against him.

"Good point," he said, voice low. "At least you understand my need to do this." His fingers traced her nipples through the fabric of her dress.

She leaned closer to him. He nudged her neck with his nose and planted another kiss on the side of her jaw. *This woman.*

"I hope you also understand my need to do this," she said, her lips close to his ear. She held his arms and planted them to the side.

Tease.

"You're very handsome, don't get me wrong," she said, smiling and looking at him with a mischievous glint in her eye. "But you haven't won the bet yet."

She stepped backward away from him, nearly tripping as she stepped on a loose stone on the floor. It lowered into the floor like a pressed button.

Instantly, his defenses rose on high alert. He knew what those were. He used the same triggers for his own castle's traps.

The floor under Sadie's feet opened to reveal a pit with yard-long spikes at the bottom. He spread out his wings, flying to her before she toppled to a deadly fall. He wrapped his arms around her and flew her to safety at the other end of the hallway. He carefully placed her on her feet and stepped back. His heart rammed hard against his rib cage at the thought that she nearly got hurt.

"What just happened?" she asked.

"Booby traps," he said, pointing to the place where Sadie had stood, now a gaping hole on the floor.

Sadie's jaw went slack, and she laughed. "Oh man, my fortress is so cool!"

He didn't speak for a while. That was definitely not the reaction he had expected. He smiled, wanting this woman even more. Because hell *yeah,* this fortress was cool.

In the back of his mind, he also knew he had lost the bet. The darkest thing he could think of was a world without Sadie. And that wasn't a world he wanted to be a part of.

CHAPTER TWENTY-SEVEN

SADIE

*S*adie took Steele to her room only to mess with him. She loved driving him crazy. That gave her a sense of power and control. Not to mention, she didn't mind the way he drove her crazy as well.

She figured the bet was a stalemate. They both got the bejeezus scared out of them. A win-win.

She sat on the leather lounge on her balcony. Steele sat beside her. She didn't look at him as he brushed her hair behind her ear and bent down to kiss her neck and shoulders. She sighed, eyes fluttering closed.

He gently turned her face toward him and they stared into each other's eyes. He kissed her again, letting his hand slide down her side to the hem of the plunging neckline. When he stopped, she guided his hand to her breast and he growled as he kneaded them, deepening his kisses with a hungry need.

She thoroughly enjoyed his warm touches and the tingling sensations that quaked through her body when he kissed her. She opened her eyes and looked at silver and gold trees extending from the edge of her courtyard to the horizon, and the river that flowed beside the forest, glowing orange and lavender and blue as it reflected the crystals that shone in her realm's ceiling.

Beside the river rolled a verdant meadow. A shadow shifted. Had she not been looking in that very spot, she would've missed the barely noticeable movement. She squinted as a silhouette seemed to approach her fortress.

There was something familiar about that figure. The limping gait, the strong shoulders and long hair.

She stiffened. *It can't be.*

Steele seemed to notice her change in demeanor and asked, "What's wrong?"

Sadie ignored the question as she sat up and leaned toward the edge of the balcony, narrowing her eyes on the figure. Steele removed his hand from under her shirt and adjusted himself on the seat.

Her breath caught. *Blair!* She wore the same tattered clothes she had on the night Sadie had found her wounded in her apartment.

Her pulse sped up, but she didn't run to her sister right away, even though her instinct screamed for her to move. First, she needed to make sure her eyes weren't tricking her.

"I'm not accustomed to this kind of role-playing, but I can get used it," Steele said.

She stood and ran to her scrying room where the crystal ball was placed on the table in the center. She touched the orb with her hands, demanding to see Blair. The green and red haze in the ball shifted to reveal her sister, holding her side, struggling to breathe as she stumbled toward the fortress.

That was all the confirmation she needed.

Sadie ran to the room's balcony, passing by Steele who clearly didn't know what was going on. The dragon Zagan had brought to her fortress flew by the balcony and halted mid-air in front of her, wings flapping, as if the dragon could sense her alarm. She jumped onto the dragon's back and they flew to her sister. She needed to protect Blair from the demons in the fortress and give her a heads up on the men.

She dismounted before the dragon landed and almost tripped on a fallen branch. Recovering, she bounded to Blair at full speed and wrapped her sister in her arms when she had reached her. Tears flowed from Sadie's eyes.

Blair clung to her.

Beside Sadie, the dragon roared and rose on her hind legs. Sadie jumped back and away from her sister. The dragon planted her feet on the ground and swiped her tail, slapping Blair's back and sending her flying over the boundary into the fortress land before Sadie could do anything to stop it.

Blair grunted as she stood up and doubled over in pain, clutching her midsection.

Sadie's intuition flared. This wasn't Blair at all, but an imposter. The dragon had sensed it before she did. Sadie was too consumed by the idea of seeing her sister that she didn't pause to think about whether or not it was really her. Sure, she checked the crystal ball, but that probably would only show what she wanted to see. And Sadie wanted to see Blair.

Her blood boiled. Partly because she had made a mistake and partly because the woman who pretended to be her sister had the audacity to show up at her front door.

"Who are you?" she asked, glaring at the woman. Sadie balled her hands into fists as she approached the imposter.

Sadie wished she could conjure the vines to keep the woman still. She would just have to make do without them.

"Drop your act and show me who you are," Sadie said, demanding.

The woman screamed as Blair's form shifted into Mara, adorned in skimpy armor and golden gauntlets. She glared at Sadie but didn't make a move.

"Where's my sister?" Sadie asked through gritted teeth, not even bothering to mask the hatred she openly felt for the demoness. Sadie flicked her wrist, and a smoke-sword appeared in her hand. Now was a good time for her training to pay off.

Mara sneered and lifted her arms. Sadie knew this move already. Mara prepared to cast fire, but Sadie didn't move. She also came prepared. And she would show Mara just how much she had learned over the past few days.

As a torrent of fire blew in Sadie's direction, she stood still and let the flames billow over her, knowing she wouldn't get hurt. She held her smoke sword in front of her, willing it to collect the fire. When the flames died down, she stood unharmed, her smoke-sword blazing and slowly dimming as the fire died.

Mara gaped.

Surprised? Good.

Sadie used Mara's surprise to her advantage, sending the same torrent of fire Mara had given her back to the demoness. Before the blaze ran out, she rushed to Mara and slashed at her torso with the smoke sword. Mara shook herself from her daze and had somehow avoided the fire but didn't move quick enough to avoid the wound that Sadie's sword made.

Sadie almost whooped that the smoke sword actually worked, but as her sword disappeared from her hand, so did her excitement. She sighed.

Great. Of course, it wouldn't work.

As she created a fire sword to replace her one of smoke, the dragon flew to Mara and used its claws to pin the demoness to the ground. Mara unsheathed her sword, swiping at both of the dragon's front legs. The dragon let out a painful cry and flew away before Mara could pierce the dragon's throat.

With her fire sword held in front of her, Sadie rushed at Mara. She leapt and thrust her weapon at the demoness's heart, but Mara parried it with a swing. Sadie jumped back, positioning herself in a fighting stance.

But Mara didn't come for Sadie. Instead, the demoness flew into the air, wings spread behind her. She screamed, "Charge!"

Yelling and the clanking of weapons came from the forest behind her. A knot of worry twisted in her chest. She should have felt their presence, but she had been so overcome with the idea that Blair had returned to her, she didn't pay attention to anything else. She pushed the worry aside. This was *her* territory. Whoever dared invade her home would pay for their transgressions against her.

An army advanced from the trees. A few dozen imps and horned skeletons appeared from the forest.

Sadie wrinkled her nose as their collective smell of sweat and decay pervaded her nostrils. She raised her sword, preparing herself for battle.

When the army reached the border of her territory, an invisible barrier prevented them from getting in. Sadie let out the breath she hadn't realized she was holding.

More imps and skeletons reached the border. They banged and slammed against the barrier with their bodies and weapons. As they assaulted the invisible wall, some of them managed to slip through.

The fortress produced metal vines, ensnaring the soldiers. Some of them were unlucky enough to get impaled by the sharp, metal vines.

As she watched the fortress defend itself from the intruders, a horned-skeleton approached her with a dagger in its bony hands. It must have been the undead remnants of what used to be a demon.

The skeleton attacked her with its dagger. She blocked it with a swipe and plunged her fire sword in its chest, but it only went through the bone harmlessly.

It must not be hot enough.

She concentrated and let the orange flames of her sword burn brighter until it turned light blue. She let the flames expand until it covered the skeleton's entire body, and eventually it burned to a crisp.

Another one advanced on her. She lifted her free

hand and summoned an orb of fire inside her attacker's chest cavity, making it as hot as possible. She let it grow, until it too turned to ash.

To her right, the dragon fought the brunt of the army, swinging her tail and snapping her maw at the enemies. She leapt and landed, crushing imps on the ground. She also kicked with her hind legs, dismembering a few boney soldiers.

The dragon kicked demons beyond the boundary that when they tried to come back, they couldn't cross the invisible barrier anymore. She defended herself, holding her own against the demons despite acquiring numerous slashes on her back, wings, and legs.

Sadie thought her dragon would be able to handle herself, but there were too many imps and skeletons. They climbed onto the dragon's back and she shook in an attempt to get them off her. She snapped at them with her teeth, but she was only slowly getting overwhelmed.

Above, Mara swooped in Sadie's direction. Sadie sidestepped and crouched. She struck her sword against Mara's and the demoness parried. Sadie swung again, this time slicing Mara's thigh. It didn't wound the skin, but the demoness hissed. Sadie slashed again, hitting Mara's left wing.

"I see you've gotten better," Mara said. The demoness smirked, but from the way her lip quivered, and her eyes widened, Sadie knew it was all bravado.

She *had* gotten better. And that thought filled her with hope that she could defeat this vile demoness and finally find her sister.

Advancing, Sadie jabbed at Mara's side. Mara blocked the blow with her gauntlet. Sadie turned in order to make a strike with her fire sword toward Mara's neck, but before she could lift her sword, the demoness's tail swung at her from the side. She knocked Sadie on the ground, and her ankle twisted in the fall. She winced and gritted her teeth as Mara's sword descended on her face. She rolled aside but didn't avoid getting her cheek cut. The wound stung like hell.

Mara lifted her sword. Sadie's pulse raced. She didn't think she could move fast enough to escape it. The dragon emitted a resounding roar, and the demon army shouted collectively. Sadie and Mara both looked in that direction.

Sadie relaxed as the four princes raced toward her at full speed. The princes tore into the army, slashing at the imps, killing them with single blows. They exploded to pieces with just a bash from a sword or a blow of fire. Kaiser fought at the forefront, killing most of the demons.

He fought with such a grim and determined expression, dead set on reaching Sadie and Mara. When Sadie met his eyes, he seemed to fight faster and more aggressively, killing double the numbers he already had. She felt a twinge of guilt for running off and getting him this worried. Gathering willpower, she used the upheaval the princes caused to stand up and step back within reasonable distance from Mara's sword.

Mara whirled and attacked Sadie. Shifting her weight on the uninjured foot, Sadie parried two of Mara's blows with her fire sword. The demoness's smirk had disappeared, now replaced by a wide-eyed countenance that seemed more like panic. Mara's moves became rushed and sloppy, as if she couldn't wait to kill Sadie and get out of here. Even with an injured ankle, Sadie dodged and slashed with her weapon, fighting with relative ease.

The demoness kept looking over her shoulder and at the princes. She had the same expression back in Sadie's apartment when Kaiser had appeared. Sadie snorted to herself. The demoness seemed to be really terrified of him, picking up her pace like that and with the expression of a small child afraid of the monster in her closet.

Sadie's blade struck Mara's hilt and hit the demoness's knuckles. Mara yelped, dropping her sword. Sadie caught the demoness's weapon with her free hand and attacked with both swords at once. Mara dodged the blow, tumbling to the ground.

Sadie knelt over Mara and dug Mara's sword into

her wing, pinning the demoness to the ground. Mara screamed.

A calm, ruthlessness, and consumed Sadie. The darkness she had embraced. "Where is my sister?" she asked. "Answer or pay with your life."

Mara didn't speak as she struggled to steady her breath.

"Suit yourself," Sadie said and lifted her fire sword, aiming to stab Mara's heart with it. Mara screeched in pain as she wrenched her wing free from the blade that rooted her to the ground. The pointed tip of the demoness's wing struck her across the face. Her vision blurred with tears from the unexpected blow. A jolt impacted her side as Mara kicked Sadie to the ground.

Sadie stood, raising her sword in defense even though her vision still blurred. Her eyesight cleared in time to see Mara disappear in a puff of shadow, leaving what remained of her army to die. Sadie stared at the spot where Mara had disappeared. She clenched her fists and the veins in her neck throbbed. She almost had Mara. But the wretched woman got away.

She bit the inside of her cheek enough to hurt. She stood there, livid, while the princes dispatched the remnants of Mara's army.

As Mordecai dealt with the last soldier standing, Steele rushed to her, yelling. "You shouldn't just run off into danger like that, Sadie!"

Her dragon flew to her and stood beside her,

keeping an eye on the horizon. She looked over her pet, relieved that, aside from shallow scratches and cuts, the dragon wasn't gravely hurt.

Kaiser ran to her. She opened her mouth to say something as he wrapped her in his arms as soon as he reached her.

"I'm okay," she said, her face buried in his chest. She pulled herself from his hold in time to see Damien and Mordecai approaching them, both glaring at her.

"Why would you put yourself in so much danger? You haven't even had a chance to learn more about your magic," Mordecai said.

She cleared her throat. She wanted to snap at them. Tell them it was none of their business. Why would they make it *their* business? They knew her abilities were limited, that she was still learning. But she had to think about everything they had gone through. After all, they could have just killed her, taken her power for themselves. But they didn't.

Little by little, they each showed her that they were good men. At least to her, they were.

She could've called on them. In the moment, she was too consumed by the idea of Blair being safe and showing up at her fortress gate that she didn't think about anything else. Emotion blinded her from considering it was a trap she had walked into.

Looking at each of them, she slowly nodded. "I know now. I should've counted on you. But I'm okay.

Thanks to you." She forced herself to smile though she felt guilty for making them all worry like that over her.

She shared a long look with Kaiser. "Did you see what happened?"

He nodded, lips in a grim line.

"I saw the whole thing, too," Damien said. "And that demoness pretended to be someone familiar."

Kaiser approached her. "I'm sorry, Sadie. But Blair's probably dead if Mara is taking her form." His eyes seemed so sad.

A lump formed in Sadie's throat.

"That's—" She choked on the words. She tried to swallow down the lump. "That can't be right."

Damien looked at both of them, his eyebrows knitting together. He turned toward her. "I don't know what's going on here, but he's right, Sadie. Demons can sometimes take the look of the people whose souls they steal or buy, though it's rare."

Sadie didn't speak. Dread wrapped around her heart, pulsing and swelling. Tears threatened to spill out from her eyes, stinging, and burning and itching. She clenched her teeth, trying her best not to break down in front of these men as she rubbed at her eyes to ease the tears and keep them at bay. She struggled to stay hopeful as she considered Mara taking Blair's form was just a trick. Maybe there was another explanation. There had to be another explanation. But deep in her heart, she suspected the worst.

"Do you know who Mara is?" she asked Damien and Steele.

"No," Damien said.

Steele shook his head.

So, Mara was probably unknown in the demon world, which likely contributed to her hunger for the pendant. Maybe she wanted it enough to steal Blair's soul to get it. If that's what happened. Sadie clenched her fists at her sides as she considered Mara using Blair as bait.

The dragon nudged her side and Sadie absently petted the scales on her new friend's side. "Thanks for keeping us safe."

The dragon gave what Sadie considered to be a dragon's version of a purr.

"You need a name, my fiery pet." she said, scratching the back of her dragon's ear. "Pyra. I'll call you Pyra."

The dragon lifted her head and roared, smoke coming out of its mouth. Sadie smiled at it, though her heart felt heavy.

She walked back toward her fortress. Although she should've felt relieved for successfully defending her fortress, her heart hurt. It broke for her sister. The hope she tried to hold on to ebbed away as Kaiser and Damien's words replayed in her mind.

Blair was probably dead. Her soul robbed from her body to feed Mara's desperate need for the amulet.

She felt her men and her dragon keep a watchful eye on her. Maybe she should check if they were completely unscathed. But her tears were falling now. And she couldn't let them see that.

CHAPTER TWENTY-EIGHT

KAISER

Kaiser stormed through the halls toward the guest sitting room, scratching his head in agitation, scrambling for any plan at all to avoid nearly losing Sadie like that again. He couldn't think of any way to keep her safe, but maybe his brothers had some ideas. He knew they cared for her just the same as he did. And it was high time they put their differences aside to protect the one person they all obviously wanted.

He opened the door without knocking, catching Steele, Mordecai, and Damien off guard. They each had looks of concern as they took in his storm-filled steps to the center of the room.

Steele sat on the couch with a book in his lap, his legs propped up on an ottoman. He chuckled. "Even when you open the door like that, we still don't see you coming."

Kaiser ignored his ever-jovial brother.

"Do you even smile, Kaiser?" Mordecai asked, smirking. He reclined on the sofa, casting two miniature smoke fighters atop horses that dueled with each other above his palm. Damien sat in front of him, a chess board set on the coffee table between them. Damien moved a piece Kaiser supposed was the bishop.

"Checkmate," Damien said, grinning.

Kaiser looked at his brothers. The room was relaxed, devoid of the animosity and irritation that crackled between them when they had been reunited because of the demon queen. Kaiser almost smiled as he sucked in a calming breath.

This feels nice. Very much like old times.

Mordecai swiftly sat straighter, the smoke figures on his hand puffing out. His eyes widened and squinted, scrutinizing the chess set. Kaiser approached and examined the pieces himself.

Kaiser pointed at Mordecai's remaining chess pieces. "See, if you would've just moved your rook here, you could've avoided losing, and you would've been able to checkmate him in three moves."

Mordecai's jaw fell open. He scratched his head. "How could I have missed that?"

Steele glared at him, but him being Steele, it only

looked comical. He scrunched his nose. "Maybe because you were too busy thinking about that make out session with Sadie."

Damien's eyebrows rose in high arches on his forehead. Kaiser noticed the twitch under his right eye.

"You made out with Sadie?" Damien asked.

Steele sniffed. "I know. Before *me.* And that's quite unfair." Steele looked at Kaiser. "Maybe she's not picking you after all."

A twinge shot through Kaiser's chest. He couldn't think about Sadie not choosing him. The mere mention of the possibility nearly crippled him each time. He would have loved to strangle Mordecai for making out with Sadie. Hell, he wanted to stab Steele for even mentioning the make out session, not to mention the threat of not being chosen, but he wasn't here to argue with anyone. He needed their help.

Kaiser shook his head. "I'm here because we need to make sure we're keeping an eye on Sadie. After what happened, we need to make sure she's safe." He looked at each of his brothers. "Correct me if I'm wrong, but that's what you want, too, right?"

Steele placed his feet on the floor and leaned forward, resting his elbows on his knees. "What's your plan?"

"I actually don't have one. At least none that wouldn't piss her off," Kaiser said. "I was hoping you would have suggestions."

Steele looked at Damien and Mordecai. Steele glared at them. "Forgive me if I say I'm not too inclined to help you."

Damien stood and began to pace. "I might agree with Kaiser. Dangerous demons are after Sadie. And she's too headstrong for her own sake. We need to put our differences aside and agree to this temporary truce, at least, just to make sure she's safe."

Steele breathed out an exaggerated sigh. The mischievous glint in his eye returned. "Fine. Do we spit swear?"

Mordecai grinned at Steele. "I will if you will."

Steele pocketed his hands. "Eww."

Damien looked at Mordecai. "I think it's time for you to go get it."

Mordecai seemed to understand because he nodded and disappeared into smoke and shadow.

"What are you up to?" Kaiser asked Damien.

"There's an artifact—a small, golden charm—that can track anyone, anywhere," Damien said. "It's deep in the vaults at one of my ally's castle, and I intend to borrow it. The catch is, it can only be placed on her and used by someone she trusts."

Kaiser mulled over this and didn't answer, not getting Damien and Steele's pointed looks right away. When he did, Kaiser stepped back.

"What? No." That would be a violation of her trust. He wasn't doing it.

"Sadie might have kissed Mordecai, but everyone knows she's clearly favoring *you* so far," Steele said.

"You're probably the only one who would be able to use it. Don't you want it? With the charm, you can use it to feel and sense where she is, anywhere on any world," Damien said.

Kaiser crossed his arms. "Why would you grant me this if you all want her?"

"I'll just have it removed magically when I win." He winked and smiled. "For now, all we need is to monitor her."

Kaiser opened his mouth to ask what he meant by removing it magically when Mordecai solidified beside him and grabbed his arm to place a small, golden symbol in Kaiser's hands. It was circular, like a pin, and embossed like a compass. Runes bordered the circle and intricate designs inlaid the compass symbol.

"Put it on her lower back, where she isn't likely to notice it," Mordecai said. "It won't hurt at all, she'll just feel warmth in the area for a fleeting moment and any time it's in use. Once embedded, it will look like a golden tattoo."

Kaiser pocketed the trinket. "I'm still thinking about it. I won't promise anything."

He got what he wanted—a way to keep her safe. Now, however, he wasn't sure if he should use it. Before he made his decision, he would consider his own option, which was to chain her inside her damn room.

SADIE

*S*adie lay in bed, staring at the coiling lines on her ceiling, mind buzzing with everything that had happened. She thought about Blair, and her chest ached. She wouldn't let herself cry anymore. All her life, Sadie had always been practical. Nothing would get accomplished if she stayed here, doing nothing but mourn her sister. It might've been a selfish way to grieve, but she couldn't let her sister's loss consume her while walking about the fortress halls or in the gardens, or with any of the princes.

Besides, without hard proof Blair was dead, she still held on to frail hope that her sister was alive somewhere, perhaps looking for her. If Mara really did kill Blair, wouldn't she have said so, in order to hurt her? So, until she had undeniable proof either way, she would prevent any more tears from falling and gain a strong sense of composure before showing herself to anyone.

Sadie's thoughts shifted to the princes. After the way her men had come to her rescue, she couldn't help but smile. She loved how they were there for her, and that made her choice even more difficult. She considered asking them all to stay again, but she still wasn't sure they would agree to that. Until she could decide on just one, or all, she would wait.

And Kaiser. Sadie grinned, feeling touched as she remembered how he had seemed so ready to rip the world apart just to get to her. To protect her. With the other three here, with everything happening so fast, she hadn't gotten to spend a lot of time with him. Sadie found that she missed him.

Sighing, Sadie got up from the bed and walked out of her room into the gardens nearby. She lay down on the soft moss, looking up at the countless crystals that glimmered in her realm's sky. She quickly became hypnotized, unable to look away, mesmerized by their colorful flickering. She found the purple crystals were the smallest in number. She traced constellations with them, smiling to herself when she formed a crown.

Beautiful. This place felt absolutely like home.

"Can I join you?" Kaiser asked.

Sadie gasped. *Damn him for always being so quiet.* Sadie didn't get up. Instead, she said, "Sure."

He lay next to her. Sadie felt a little calmer. She scooted closer to him, and she noticed him barely hiding a contented little grin.

Sadie twisted so she was lying on her side, facing him. They were almost nose-to-nose, so close that Sadie's heart skipped a beat. She looked into his eyes that shifted to a scarlet color as he stared back at her. She could compare his eyes to her stars, but she wouldn't do his gaze any justice. She would choose being mesmerized by his eyes over her sky full of stars any day. Sadie leaned over and kissed him. She sighed, grazing the shadow of a beard along his cheek.

This, too, felt very much like home.

Kaiser placed a hand on her hips, pulling her closer to him. Their lips moved against each other's. Kaiser held her like he might lose her at any second. He pulled her on top of him so that she was straddling him, not stopping their kissing. Sadie kissed him harder with more need and hunger. He responded, his own kisses becoming rougher, more passionate. His tongue entered her mouth and Sadie moaned. The sound she had made must have had an effect on him because he pulled her closer to him and his hand drifted lower, lifting her skirt and running his hand up her thigh, teasing her.

She pulled away enough to keep their lips separated. Everything was moving just a little too fast for her taste. Not that she minded being with him, just that she had yet to make a decision on who to choose and going further with him would make that choice much more difficult.

"What's wrong?" he asked, brushing his nose against hers.

"Nothing, it's just—"

"Do you want me to protect you, Sadie?" he asked, interrupting her.

She narrowed her eyes on him. "What do you mean?"

"Do you want what I have to offer? Do you want me to protect you no matter what?" He kissed her eyelids and Sadie's eyes drifted shut. His fingers grazed her neck.

"Yes," she said, sighing. She wanted that and so much more.

"Do you want me to watch over you by any means necessary?" He looked at her now, and it felt so intense that Sadie hesitated, sensing something deeper in the question. She set the thought aside. Because in her heart, she trusted him.

"Yes," she said, voice coming out soft.

He seemed to relax. Sadie didn't realize how tense he had been before he exhaled a breath.

"Is something bothering you?" she asked.

He caressed her cheek and kissed her ear. "I just wanted to know where I stand with you," he said in a whisper. "Just know that I'm going to protect you no matter what."

Sadie's heart skipped a beat. His words felt like a declaration of love and devotion. And she realized she couldn't see herself without him.

His hand pressed against the small of her back. Warmth radiated from his palm. She gasped as she felt her every nerve ending explode with the sensation. And all of it shot down her spine, to her core, and collected between her thighs. The spot became even wetter. But the entire feeling ended. It was over.

More.

She kissed him deeply, craving him.

"What did you do?" she asked in between kisses.

He smiled against her mouth. "It's a protection spell of sorts." He gently cupped her cheeks and stared her deep in the eyes. She fought the shiver as he asked, "Are you mad?"

"No."

She didn't care about that. She just *wanted.* Needed. She kissed him again. He shifted his legs, and she moved, adjusting, until the bulge in his trousers pushed against her entrance. She moaned.

Yes, that.

Her clit throbbed, and she ground against him, not caring that there were clothes between them, or they could be seen, or anything that resided outside of the two of them. She just needed to *feel.*

Kaiser growled. He sat up and wrapped his arms around her. Sadie yelped when he extended his wings and flew. He carried her up to her room through her balcony and gently laid her on the bed. Without a word, he crawled above her and stared into her eyes, the red in his eyes swirling.

"So beautiful," he said.

Yes, you are.

He spread kisses on her jaw and neck. He paused, sitting up again to look at her. "Tell me you want this."

Sadie reached for him, clenching fistfuls of his shirt as she pulled him back to her. She bit his lower lip. "If you stop one more time, I think I'm going to die."

"Good answer," he said against her mouth as he reached the neckline of her shirt. With a swift jerk, he tore the shirt from her.

Sadie gasped.

Kaiser reached behind her to unclasp her bra. He took his time sliding his hands over her shoulders, sending electrifying sensations all over her skin. He tossed the bra to the side and left a trail of kisses down her body as he shifted lower and slipped his hands up her thighs. His fingers pulled down her underwear.

He kissed the inside of her thighs, teasing her with need. He slowly made his way back up to her lips, busying his hands with a breast. His fingers traced a soft line along her belly as he occupied his mouth with her breast. His tongue flicked her nipples, and he gently grazed his teeth over the tips.

She arched her back, needing the release he promised her. His fingers played on the waistline of her skirt, further teasing her and enticing her nerves into overdrive. They drifted down again to the hem and inched up her thigh.

When their lips met, his fingers slipped inside her. Sadie moaned against his mouth. He explored her with his fingers, tracing a line from the entrance to her clit, rubbing back and forth. He was gentle, careful. And as her breathing grew ragged, she realized she didn't want careful or gentle.

She moaned a demanding, "Kaiser."

His fingers moved rougher, plunging one finger in, and two, and all along he played with her breasts and his thumb stroked her clit.

She moaned again, crying out his name and panting as she released the built-up pleasure. When the sensation ended, she needed more of him. All of him.

"Please." *Please, please, please.*

Kaiser took his time removing his shirt and pants, swirling red eyes deepening to nearly black as he held her gaze, rocking her body with shivers of pleasure and need. Her eyes drifted along his naked form and to his rock-hard erection. He climbed over her, hovering as he stared at her.

Sadie licked his lips. Kaiser moaned and crashed his mouth into hers, roughly kissing her as he toyed with her entrance with the tip of his shaft.

"I told you not to stop," Sadie said, pushing him off her and onto his back. With her palms on his chest, she held herself steady as she positioned herself onto him. She slipped him inside her, sighing as she became filled by his girth.

She moved up again, and down, all the while staring at his scarlet eyes that threatened to undo her. Her hips moved with a back and forth motion as she moved up and down.

Kaiser gripped her hips and angled his chin to the ceiling. A groan seeped through his lips and her climax grew even more. He guided her hips, moving her with steady rhythm as he pushed against her movements. She moved faster, and the pleasure threatened to release again, increasing every movement.

She cried out again, lowering herself to Kaiser's chest as he continued his heated thrusts, grunting as he moved.

He flipped her onto her back, managing to stay within her and moving without missing a beat. He moved in and out of her, thrusting harder and harder, sending Sadie through another wave of intense pleasure.

Sadie ground against him, in tune with his rhythm as he slipped his arms under her head, gripping handfuls of her hair and he buried his face into her neck. He grunted and shivered against her as warm liquid shot inside her.

A knot of trust and contentment became tied in her heart. She knew she could never let go of him now. And she wondered for a moment what that would mean for the other princes, but she left that thought as a blissful sleep came over her.

Kaiser kissed her lovingly and gently as he pulled out of her and laid next to her. Sadie rolled to her side and placed her head on his chest. He wrapped her in his arm, pulling her even closer, holding her tightly. She closed her eyes as Kaiser planted a kiss on the top of her head.

Too soon, Kaiser woke Sadie with a smile on his face. He kissed the top of her nose and helped her to sit.

"Are you okay?" he asked.

She looked at him with pursed eyebrows. "I'm more than okay. Why?"

He smiled. "I lost a lot of my self-control. I was trying to be gentler."

She wrapped her arms around him and leaned into him, taking in his scent mixed with that of their sex. "You were magnificent. But we didn't use protection. What if I get pregnant? I'm not sure I'm ready for a little demon-human spawn baby running around here, are you?"

He chuckled. "Don't worry. Demons have to take this special potion in order to get pregnant."

"Good to know," she said and climbed out of bed. She wrapped herself in a robe and went to look out over her balcony. Kaiser walked up from behind and rested his chin on her shoulder while she looked at her kingdom, the underworld. At her new life.

She thought of all her princes again. If she was being honest with herself, she was enamored of all of them and for very different reasons.

Her decision was supposed to be simple. A matter of allegiance. But damn it all if she didn't want each and every one of them. She still wasn't sure they would agree to all of them staying, but she knew she couldn't let any of them go. Especially Kaiser, now that she gave herself to him.

She touched her lips, remembering Kaiser's kisses.

She didn't regret this moment with Kaiser. Never in a million years.

The only regret she had was not killing Mara. She would pay for what she had done to her and Blair. She would kill the demoness once and for all. But she needed a plan. And that meant a decision regarding the princes needed to be made soon.

CHAPTER TWENTY-NINE

"Ten points to the awesome team, zero points to the not-awesome team," Steele said, laughing as he got the ball to his side of the court again.

He had smashed all ten crystals on Damien's side already. There were ten more multi-colored crystals to target, and he could finally destroy the orb, which was the main goal of the game. And as far as sports went, meracoan was definitely his favorite. Especially when he played against Damien, who *always* lost. Steele wiped tears of laughter from his eyes.

Damien bent forward, hands on his knees, panting. "I'm just letting you win, little brother. I hope you feel good about yourself."

Steele's smile faltered. "You're kidding."

Along the fortress wall beside the courtyard,

Mordecai chuckled and addressed Damien. "Try winning, then."

Damien shook his head. "This game is stupid."

Steele pointed a finger at his elder brother. "You think it's stupid and yet, you keep playing with me."

"It's because he's competitive to a fault," Kaiser said, leaning on the wall beside Mordecai.

Damien ignored Kaiser's comment. Steele supposed he just didn't want to admit it.

"I'm tired," Damien said.

One side of Mordecai's lips tilted upward. "Wuss."

"Not of the game," Damien said. "I'm tired of *losing.*"

Mordecai and Kaiser looked at each other and then at Damien. They spoke in unison, "Wuss."

"Hey, you should join us," Steele said, beckoning to Mordecai and Kaiser. "Maybe Damien can beat one of you."

"Fat chance," Mordecai said, but he walked to the court and began setting up Damien's knocked down crystals.

"I haven't played meracoan in a long time," Kaiser said, also departing his post to go to Steele's side of the court.

Steele was overjoyed, but he would never let that show on the outside. He missed this game, too. This was the first time he had played in years. But he didn't want his brothers to know that.

"Mordecai can be your teammate," he said to Damien. "Maybe then you'll have a chance."

Damien puckered his face but helped Mordecai fix the broken crystals by pressing the buttons on the brackets where they were supposed to be placed. Damien pressed a button and the bracket pulled back shattered pieces of crystal and recreated a solid one, forming an angular gem that sparkled with red, yellow, and green.

Steele and Kaiser watched as they fixed their side of the court, since nothing had gotten destroyed on Steele's side.

"I bet ten gold bars he's going to cheat again," Kaiser said, jutting his chin in Mordecai's direction.

Steele snickered. True, the last time they had played, and all the times they had played before that, Mordecai had cheated. Perhaps things had changed. Steele accepted the challenge, not really thinking he would win, but for the sake of opposition. "I bet you twenty."

They shook on it and Kaiser threw the meracoan ball at Damien. "You get the first shot."

Damien took the ball with a grim look in his eyes. "I accept your pity."

Steele shook his head, smiling. It was like nothing had changed. He couldn't even remember why they were supposed to hate each other. His thoughts drifted to Sadie, grateful to the demon queen for reuniting the four lost brothers.

The four of them got into position. Steele stood in front of the crystals to defend them and readied himself for Damien and Mordecai's offense. He caught Mordecai looking at the orb behind him, and Steele immediately felt like he was going to lose the bet with Kaiser.

Steele blocked the view of the first crystal because if it got destroyed, any of the nine crystals behind it were fair game. If that happened, they could easily lose. Damien kicked the ball, approaching Steele and Kaiser's court whilst continuing to transport the ball with his feet. Damien's eyebrows tilted down in concentration, keeping track of the ball as he kicked it toward Steele's court. Alongside Damien, Mordecai ran toward them, too, keeping an eye on the ball, the opponent, and the target at the same time.

Kaiser blocked Mordecai's path.

But it was no use.

Mordecai shifted into shadow and disappeared. The ball Damien kicked disappeared, too. Damien groaned. "Not again."

Steele felt a breeze pass by him as he saw mist dart behind Kaiser to the direction of the crystals. All at once, Steele and Kaiser's twenty meracoan crystals exploded. Mordecai reappeared for a second only to shift into smoke again. The shadow that was Mordecai rushed to the meracoan orb and it exploded, bursting into a million pieces so catastrophically, Steele raised his arms to protect his face from getting hit by the miniscule shards. He noticed Kaiser summon a wall of smoke, and Steele was grateful for it.

Kaiser let go of his casting of the smoke wall, and the shattered pieces that were embedded in it dropped to the ground.

"You owe me ten gold bars," Kaiser said beside him.

Steele turned around to find Damien gaping. In front of them, Mordecai appeared with the ball in his hands, smirking.

"Predictable," Steele said and laughed. He grabbed the ball from Mordecai's hands.

"You have to forgive me," Mordecai said. "I haven't done that in a long time."

He looked at the obliterated orb with an expression that seemed like longing. Steele found himself sighing.

Mordecai faced them but only stared at the ground. "I missed it."

None of them spoke for a minute.

Damien cleared his throat. "I have to go."

Steele scratched the back of his head. "Yeah, you probably have more meetings to go to or something."

Mordecai looked at Steele. "Farewell, brothers." He shifted back to shadow and disappeared.

"Good game," Kaiser said, patting Steele on the back and walked to the direction of the fortress.

"I should get changed," Damien said, not meeting his eyes. And he flew, leaving Steele alone in the courtyard.

"Good game," he said to himself, tossing the ball in the air with his knee. He tossed the ball a few more times and walked back to his room with the meracoan ball pinned between his arm and his side.

He sighed, wishing they would play a few more games at least. But he smiled, thinking he would never forget this momentary reunion. He remembered all those times they had played in the past, fondly recalling how Damien kept losing, Mordecai kept cheating, and Steele kept losing to bets with Kaiser.

CHAPTER THIRTY

SADIE

*H*obson appeared. He held a square, wooden box in his arms as he entered her bedroom. Its dimensions appeared about twelve inches long. "You have a package, Sadie. I found it at the front gate, and it's addressed to you. I already checked for wards and spells. It's clean."

Eyebrows pinched together, Sadie took the box from Hobson. Her butler kept his distance, silently standing in the doorway.

She sat on her bed, placing the box on her lap. She unwrapped the package warily, wondering what the hell it was. She opened the lid to find flaming hair strands surrounding a small pile of daggers with the outline of a flame carved in their pommels.

"No," she said, her entire body tensing.

She knew what this meant. The ifrits she had sent after Mara were dead.

She remembered Kiana, the first ifrit she had met, how she demonstrated her ability, how eager the ifrit had been to be dispatched on a mission. Sadie's ears burned.

Underneath the weapons, the corner of a piece of paper peeked out. She slowly removed it, finding a written note.

Her hands shook as she began to read it. She took a steadying breath to compose herself.

It wasn't even a fair fight.

I could have killed them as soon as they attacked, you know. But I didn't.

Sadie gripped the paper. She already knew who wrote this.

Mara.

She continued reading.

I kept them in a cell for days until they starved, extracting information from them. But they wouldn't talk, the wretches. Said they were loyal to the demon queen. To you. A human.

I told them they'd be fearsome and revered warriors if they surrendered to me, but they just spat at my face.

Can you believe it? They spat. At my face. The

audacity. I bound them in chains, hungry, weak, and alone. And still, they had the nerve.

My dear Sadie, you should know that they died the most horrible death there is. I made them suffer. I cut their fingers off, one by one. I flayed their skin, inch by inch. Oh, the screams they made were music to my ears.

And soon, it will be your turn, Sadie. Before I yank my amulet from your chest, I will make sure you scream even louder than they did. You will beg for your life. And even then, I will just laugh.

She stood, crumpling the piece of paper and throwing it in the package. She closed the lid. She couldn't stomach seeing the hair strands and weapons. Their deaths were her fault.

Her nails dug into the package. She clenched her teeth and fire erupted from her hands, consuming the box. The bright orange flames she casted grew hotter, turning into a white-blue color. The package combusted. The flames of the ifrit hair joined the fire in her palm, and the iron daggers melted from the sheer heat. Melted metal that had used to be daggers dripped to the floor.

She seethed, letting smoke seep in her room from the walls. The room shook, the paintings and adornments along the walls crashed to the floor. The glass from some of the framed decorations shattered. She had sent perfectly trustworthy ifrits to their deaths.

Sadie's breathing grew heavy. She couldn't stand having blood on her hands. She sat on the edge of her bed.

She took in deep breaths, calming herself. She dropped her hands to her sides, letting the flames die down.

She looked at Hobson and whispered. "I'm sorry."

Hobson nodded, and he held such sadness in his eyes. Sadie also felt guilty for her outburst.

"I'll fix the mess I made," Sadie said. "But can you please help me meet with the families? And please call the men and tell them to meet me at my study."

Hobson smiled, but it didn't reach his eyes. "Of course."

When Hobson left her chambers, she stood to rehang the fallen paintings and wall decorations. She swept the broken glass and collected them in a bag. This had calmed her further, finding cleaning therapeutic. As for the molten metal, she might need Hobson's help with that since it had hardened again and was now stuck on her floorboards.

She changed into black trousers and a simple pink, button-up shirt and walked to the study to find the four princes waiting for her. They sat on plush, yellow couches embroidered with petals and spiraling leaves. Their eyes followed her movements as she entered, looking at her with what seemed like worry.

She ignored it. "I need to know how to kill a

demoness."

The princes exchanged glances.

"Why?" Damien asked.

"I think you know why."

He knitted his brow. "Sadie, if you plan on running off to danger again, we need to know." Damien's voice grew deeper. "You're not putting yourself in harm's way like you did the last time."

She pouted. "Why do you care?"

Damien prowled toward her. He seemed to growl. And the way he stared at her made her want to shrink. "Trust me, I care very much."

Sadie didn't know what that meant, but she sighed, relenting. "I need to know how to kill Mara."

Steele stood and approached her. "Is this the demoness that attacked us two days ago?"

She nodded, her lips sealed in a grim line.

"Does she have any enhancements?" Mordecai asked.

She remembered shooting a round of bullets at Mara and how it didn't harm her. Sadie twisted her mouth. "She does. It's subtle, but her hide is almost impenetrable."

Damien clucked his tongue and shook his head. "That's a powerful enchantment. It would take an incredibly powerful artifact to kill her."

She hid her disappointment. "What kind of artifact?"

Before the guys could answer, Hobson flung the door open, eyes wide. "There's an angel at the front gate."

Sadie's eyebrows shot up. "Did you say angel?"

Hobson nodded.

Steele rolled his eyes and groaned. "Angels are douchebags."

"What's her name?" Damien asked Hobson.

"I think she said her name's Evangeline," Hobson said.

Damien pursed his lips. "If angels are douchebags, she's the epitome of douchebaggery."

Sadie didn't feel like meeting more of these creatures. She addressed her butler. "I've had enough visitors knocking on my door. Dismiss her."

Kaiser cleared his throat. "Not sure that's a good idea, Sadie. I think you should meet with the angel."

"Why?"

"Evangeline is a scout," Damien said. "She's a messenger, nothing more."

"Fine." Sadie faced Hobson again. "Bring her up here, please."

After a few minutes, Hobson opened the door to lead a sensual-looking woman inside. Clad in white armor that barely covered her body, she entered the room with her chin tilted high, looking at Sadie and the princes with disdain. Her sun-kissed hair billowed around her finely-chiseled face, and her golden, feathery wings were folded on her back. She eyed Sadie's form from top to bottom.

Though the princes convinced her that she should entertain this guest, she could feel how tense they were, shifting uncomfortably in the angel's presence. Mordecai didn't bother to mask his revulsion, glaring openly at Evangeline.

"Why don't you have horns?" the angel asked, crossing her arms and quirking an eyebrow. "Are you a human-demon hybrid?"

"So, what if she is?" Mordecai said, growling.

Kaiser placed a hand on Mordecai's chest, silently imploring his brother to back down.

Sadie stared at Evangeline, not at all rattled by the angel's haughty and discourteous demeanor. One, she had been warned. And two, Sadie was getting used to having guests with personality disorders.

"What brings such an esteemed guest to my fortress?" Sadie asked, smiling in the fake, polite way she had used to address Zagan.

"I'm just curious," Evangeline said as she lifted one hand and examined her nails, not even looking at Sadie anymore. Maybe the angel thought Sadie wasn't worth her attention.

Then why did she even bother coming here?

The angel blew on a nail. "You're not as intimidating as I expected, without the horns."

"Look," Steele said with a sigh. "If you don't have

anything important to say, why don't you go on your way? We're all tired of this."

Sadie looked at Steele, not expecting him to be the one to send Evangeline away like that. She also looked at the other princes, and they wore the same tight-lipped expression. They all seemed as impatient as Steele to see Evangeline on her way.

The angel could have been a demon with how her features twisted to an ugly snarl. "Fine." Evangeline exited the study without another word.

Sadie snorted. *Wow.* She turned to Hobson. "Make sure she leaves immediately and doesn't loiter around the palace."

When her butler left to carry out her order, Sadie sat down on the couch and leaned back on the seat.

"What did she mean by human-demon hybrid?" she asked the guys.

"It just means you are part-human, part-demon," Damien said.

Kaiser sat beside her. "You'll probably change eventually."

Steele sat at her other side. "And we're behind you, even if you don't. All right?"

She smiled, feeling touched that they stood up for her. She knew they were four of the most powerful demons in the underworld. And for them to stand by her like that, she knew it was both a statement and a sacrifice.

CHAPTER THIRTY-ONE

SADIE

*S*adie sat on her throne, watching as the family members of the fallen ifrits walked the length of her throne room. There were a few men and a few women, some holding the hands of children walking alongside them. Mothers, fathers, siblings, daughters, and sons.

Sadie swallowed the hard lump that had formed in her throat and wished away the guilt-filled tears that stung her eyes.

She only knew Kiana from the ifrits she had sent, but she had asked Hobson who the rest were. Irithel, Zoe, Adela, and Edmund. Their names deserved to be remembered.

When the group reached the foot of the dais, they bowed in unison. Sadie stepped down from her throne and approached them. The woman in front seemed to be on the verge of tears. She had white strands of flaming hair and a slight stoop on her upper back. Sadie assumed she was elderly. But what caught her attention was how much she resembled Kiana. Sadie stepped closer and embraced the woman. The woman stiffened in her arms. The ifrits behind her stared at Sadie with wide eyes and shifted uneasily from their posts.

Sadie stepped back and held the ifrit's hand. She looked at each of the ifrits and to the one that appeared to be Kiana's mother. "I'm sorry for your loss."

The woman looked at her, seeming a bit shocked, and broke down crying, letting her tears fall. Sadie hugged her again, rubbing the woman's back. The other ifrits looked at her with sad eyes. Some cried with the elder ifrit.

For once, Sadie was grateful the princes weren't here. She had ordered the guys to not be present. She told them she wanted it to be a private matter regarding her people. The princes had stared at her with a kind of skepticism. Steele said he couldn't believe she was being so compassionate. But, in the end, they agreed and respected her decision.

She went to the others and hugged each one of them, even the children. Each time she embraced one, they seemed to cry harder. Her own eyes burned, but she kept her tears from falling because she wanted to stay strong for them.

She returned to Kiana's mother. She held her shoulders within arm's length and looked into her eyes. "You are always welcome in the fortress." She glanced at each ifrit. "Your son and daughters are honorable heroes."

The woman tried to speak but choked on her tears. She took a deep breath, swallowed hard, and tried again. "Th-thank you, Your Majesty."

They whispered their thanks under their breaths, but Sadie heard it. She smiled softly, sympathizing with the pain they felt.

The ifrits bowed one last time before leaving.

Sadie walked up the dais to her throne and sat, watching the ifrits' figures disappear from the throne room. She wanted to do more. Just saying sorry and offering them a hug and open invitation into her fortress whenever they wanted didn't seem enough. She just didn't know what else to do.

Mordecai appeared from the shadows beside her. "You know, demons will think what you did is weak. Kindness is not respected down here."

Sadie turned her head to look at him. "And what do *you* think it is?"

"Curious." One side of his mouth tilted up. "Curious, indeed."

There was a glint in his gaze that mesmerized her.

She wanted to get closer to him. But this was not the time. Instead, she stood.

"Goodbye, Mordecai," she said, turning around and walking out of the throne room.

She had planned the night before that, after apologizing to the ifrits' loved ones, she would return to the south wing to ask the ghost about being demon queen. Maybe if she asked questions, she would get real answers other than eerie whispers. She moved through the halls, dragging her feet, a bit nervous of going to that courtyard again. She wasn't entirely sure it was a good idea to go back there again. But she had enough of trying to figure things out on her own. The previous demon queen was her only shot at getting some real answers to the problems she faced. Killing a demon being one of them.

Sadie reached the south wing and opened the metallic door, shivering from the cold that saturated the dark place. But she also felt its magic. She had her questions whether it obeyed her or not, but she felt it, and it seemed like it listened to her. It called to her.

She walked to the courtyard, taking a deep breath as she approached the statue in the middle. The ghost was nowhere to be found.

She surveyed the entrances of the dark hallways that led out from where she stood.

"What does it mean to be the demon queen?" she

asked the silence. "What are her powers? Who are her enemies?"

She waited, hoping being straight-to-the-point merited an appearance from the ghost. A cold breeze blew against her and she hugged herself, rubbing her arms. She sucked in a breath.

When she thought no one would answer, the sound of vague whispers emanated from the hallway in front of her.

She's here.

From the shadows, the silhouette of a tall, wispy woman appeared and floated toward Sadie.

The ghost appeared to be a little more solid as she hovered to the center of the courtyard. She was getting stronger. Sadie thought that pretty alarming, if that was the case. She hoped her observations were wrong, knowing if the demon queen was amassing strength and physical form, that could spell disaster for Sadie and her new position as demon queen.

The ghost spoke, her voice deep and echoing. "I am Hecate. I am no longer the demon queen."

The ghost admitting the title had passed on eased Sadie's feelings a little. Still, it was possible the ghost who called herself Hecate might've been playing with her.

Hecate continued. "You have power over every world, and you have the power of the gods."

Sadie cocked her head to the side. "What does that mean?"

"Your magic is transcendent. You are envied. You are lost. You are alone. And because you have that amulet, you are a thief."

"What?"

The ghost smiled, revealing a set of sharp, pointed teeth. She soared toward Sadie.

Sadie held her arms up instinctively to shield herself, but the ghost disappeared.

That ghost is so creepy.

Sadie wondered whether Hecate was her ally or her enemy. It made her weary to know there was more of a chance to her being enemy than friend.

Sadie left the garden, deciding to set aside Hecate's useless guidance for now until she had more to go on.

As she walked the hallways, she resolved to continue keeping the ghost a secret from the princes. After all, she was still undecided on only picking one and didn't need to tell them all her secrets just yet. She exited the tower and walked the ramparts to her room, needing a bit of fresh air for a change after the secluded and dismal environment of the south wing.

Hobson had said it was reserved for the demon queen only. And even though Sadie felt a certain connection to the magic of the place, there was also a feeling of malice that didn't quite sit well with her. She had a feeling Hecate had something to do with that.

Perhaps the fortress was torn between obeying Sadie or continuing to obey Hecate.

From a window in the rampart, she looked down at the castle's front courtyard and saw Pyra curled up in the middle. The dragon crushed shrubs of daisies under her weight. Sadie smiled to herself, thinking how Hobson would throw a fit when he finds out about the wrecked foliage in the gardens. He tried too hard sometimes, but she still enjoyed the unusual personality Hobson had.

Upon reaching her room, she neared a bookshelf on the corner, realizing for the first time that because of the activity and events of the previous days, she hadn't been able to examine the books yet. It was filled with books covered and written in glyphs and runes, languages she couldn't understand. But amid these tomes was a selection of classics from her world. She ran her hands along the spines, grabbing a book she hadn't read yet, and laid on her bed.

She was halfway through *The Metamorphosis* when one of the princes interrupted her.

"Enjoying the book?" Damien asked as he emerged from her balcony.

Sadie closed the book, chuckling. She wondered if she should bother having set days for any of them since they kept breaking that rule, especially the one about staying out of her room. Surprisingly, though, she didn't actually mind. For once.

"This man woke up to find he's a beetle," she said.

He smiled. "I know. I also know how it ends."

She glared at him. "You wouldn't dare."

He sat on the edge of the bed. "I wouldn't. I know I'd be in trouble." He ran his fingers on her knee and up her thigh. She smacked his hand away, but she laughed and placed the book on her bedside table. Perhaps this was just the distraction she needed. Time with Damien.

"Let's go to the gardens." She stood and put on her slippers.

CHAPTER THIRTY-TWO

KAISER

Kaiser stood on his room's balcony, watching Damien and Sadie strolling through the gardens below. Damien looked up and caught Kaiser's eye. His brother glared at him, probably thinking Kaiser unwelcome even as a spectator during his time with Sadie.

Kaiser remembered what it was like growing up with his brothers. His heart broke, as it did every time he thought about Cedric. He missed him. He missed his other brothers, too, if he was being honest. He missed the sense of family they had shared when they were still together and complete. Cedric was the glue that kept them together. The dutiful, older brother. The oldest of them.

Then, Cedric died, and everything around Kaiser had fallen apart.

Damien returned his attention to Sadie and whispered something in her ear. Sadie laughed, and Kaiser's heart skipped a beat. After having placed the protection spell on her, he followed her everywhere. He might have felt guilty for doing something she wasn't completely aware of, but he *had* asked for her permission, albeit vaguely. He convinced himself he did the right thing by affixing the charm to her. Because of it, he could feel her every movement, and it calmed him to know she was safe.

He could also feel her emotions, so he knew she had been in the south wing. Something about that place unnerved her, and there was a hidden danger she refused to tell him about. She was uneasy and confused while she was there. He thought about going to her there, but the feelings ebbed, and she left the wing for her room.

He wondered what she did in that part of the fortress and what about that area concerned her. He decided he should take a look. If he saw anything that would prove a danger to Sadie, he would then convince his brothers to help him take care of it, before Sadie put herself into harm's way again.

Steele appeared on the adjacent balcony, stretching his arms and yawning. When Steele saw him, he flew to Kaiser's balcony. Steele stood beside him and looked at Sadie on the grounds below.

"Jealous?" Steele asked.

"That's your move," Kaiser said.

Steele snorted.

Kaiser smiled to himself. *Yeah, he's jealous.*

Both didn't speak for a while. They just watched Damien and Sadie pick apples from the trees. For the first time in a very long time, Kaiser felt comfortable just having Steele beside him, relaxing in silence.

"You know, this is kind of nice," Kaiser said. "We're more like a family now than we have been since Cedric died."

"Yeah," Steele said with a sigh.

Kaiser faced his brother, sympathizing with how longingly Steele looked at Sadie. They all loved her. He would be an idiot to think otherwise. And far as Kaiser knew, Sadie had yet to make a decision on who she was going to make her ally.

"I guess we need glue to keep us together, one way or another," Steele said, nodding at Sadie.

Kaiser returned his gaze to Sadie. Now that Cedric was gone, *she* was their glue. Kaiser couldn't be happier. He would do anything to keep Sadie within arm's reach and protected. That reminded him of the south wing.

"I have to be somewhere," he said. When his brothers had agreed that Kaiser should place the protection spell on Sadie, they also placed their trust in him. As much as he didn't want to let Sadie down, he didn't want to let his brothers down, either. "I should go."

Steele nodded. "Take care, brother."

Kaiser spread his wings and flew. Whatever it was that got Sadie riled up, he needed find out what and why.

CHAPTER THIRTY-THREE

SADIE

*S*adie strolled along the garden pathway with Damien. She contemplated the colorful leaves of the canopy above her. White and golden vines hung from the branches. She breathed in the sweet fragrance of the flowers lining the cobblestone path. What a beautiful day.

While she approached an elm tree, a roar rung out in the distance. She stiffened, the sound chilling her bones. It seemed to come from the back of the castle, from the ifrit village.

Sadie looked at Damien. Both stood still, waiting for another roar, perhaps as a sign that they didn't just imagine it. Sadie shook herself from her daze and, without another word, sprinted toward the direction of the sound.

She sped around her fortress and crossed the

bridge that led to the ifrit village. Once she reached the cliff that overlooked their burning city, she halted, panting, eyes widening at the massive blue dragon that spurted frost from its mouth to the ifrits' houses. The ice covered the buildings, some of them crumbling from the weight and momentum of the ice.

The dragon leapt toward the square in the middle of the settlement, spreading its wings that were formed like an array of sharp icicles. Ifrits raced toward the dragon, shooting fire at the creature, but the balls of fire bounced off the dragon's hide.

Braver ifrits drew weapons and ran to the creature only to become victims of its claws, teeth, and frostfire. It wasn't long before the inhabitants seemed to have given up, running away from the dragon and hiding in any crevice they could find. Some reached the outskirts of their town to evacuate.

Damien joined Sadie at her side. His eyes widened, and he panted for breath. They descended the cliff, hurrying down the steep, stone stairs carved along its height.

As they ran, Sadie considered how she had been able to tame Pyra and that hellhound they saw in the forest. She hoped she could do the same for this creature too, before any more lives were lost.

Her heart thudded, and her throat stung from the force of the air she took in. Her legs burned from exertion. She ignored the pain as she ran as fast as she could, hoping to stop the dragon from causing even more destruction.

She neared the dragon as it blew out another gust of frost at a building filled with screaming ifrits. She raised her arms, palms burning with the energy of fire magic. She let it build and shot streams of red flames into the dragon's frost. Steam sizzled and cracked in the air.

Though she had saved the hut from utter destruction, she had only managed to bring attention to herself as the dragon snapped its head in her direction. Its eyes were white-blue, wild with unhinged fury.

Aiming her hands toward the dragon, she built up fire magic in her palms, increasing the heat and intensity until they glowed blue. She held onto the magic, not wanting to release it unless she absolutely had to. She screamed, "Stop!"

The creature tilted its head, mouth parted enough that she saw a bright blue ball of light glowing at the back of its throat. Sadie gulped and approached with her hands held up, walking as slowly as possible, hoping to placate the creature. To further show her willingness to help and not hurt the creature, she slowly let the energy within her hands fade.

Please don't attack me... I'm a friend. I won't hurt you. She tried to plead with the creature, hoping to mentally reach it and ease the turmoil within him.

There was a bit of chaos that overwhelmed the poor thing. It was in complete defense mode.

What happened to you?

No response. Only the increasing turmoil. She had to defuse the situation before more lives were lost. Including hers.

Just as she thought she was succeeding, the dragon snarled and glared at her. It opened its maw. The bright ball of blue increased in size. Sadie froze in place.

Damien shouted, "Sadie!"

Sadie bent her knees to jump to the side and avoid the dragon's icy blast, but a body slammed into her. She shut her eyes as her feet left the ground, bracing for the impact of the fall. Wings flapped, and strong arms surrounded her body. Damien's heartbeat pounded on her back.

"You're safe," he said and set her down out of the path of the dragon's wrath.

"It wouldn't listen to me," Sadie said. "I don't understand why."

Damien stared at the creature. "Let's worry about that later." He unsheathed his sword and it blazed to life. "For now, we should stop it from destroying the city."

"Right," Sadie said, and cast a smoke sword for a weapon. She curled her fingers around its hilt as it solidified in her hand. She charged, weapon held high.

Once again, she reached with her mind to communicate with the dragon, but she still didn't sense any kind of friendliness. Only the need to destroy.

She reached the dragon and ducked the claw that descended on her. Tumbling to the front of the creature, she aimed to slash at its throat. It reared back, avoiding the blow. She quickly jabbed at its scaly belly, but her sword hardly scratched at the ice that covered the scales like armor.

The dragon rose on its hind legs and leapt back, front legs descending to crush Sadie. She rolled away, tucking her arms closer to her to lessen the shock of her collision with the hard ground.

Climbing to her knees, she noticed the dragon had turned its attention to Damien who fought in the air, black wings spread wide behind him.

He dashed from side to side, striking the creature's body with his weapon wherever he could. Flying directly above the dragon, he raised his sword and descended, pushing his blade through the dragon's back. His weapon sank halfway through the creature's scales, but it only seemed to irritate the dragon instead of hurt it.

Sadie stood as Damien yanked his sword out of the dragon's back and flew up again, away from the creature's gnashing teeth, narrowly missing the heels of his boots.

The dragon stooped and inhaled a deep breath. A

blizzard erupted in a short radius around the dragon. It let out a terrifying cry.

Sadie's teeth chattered, and her breath formed a slight foggy cloud in front of her. Icicles formed around her smoke sword as the weapon crystallized and cracked, bursting into fragments of ice, disappearing in her hand.

Shivering, she reached for her amulet's magic, tapping into the warmth she had always felt every time she cast fire. Two flames materialized in her hands. In need of a weapon, she molded the flames to create swords. The weapons blazed to life within her hands. She let the warmth surround her and protect her from the cold that the creature relentlessly emitted.

She sprinted to the dragon's side, ducking the creature's tail as it swung at her. With a swipe of her sword, she hacked off a piece of the creature's frozen wing and it fell like an icicle to the ground. Golden ichor spilled from the wound.

The dragon's other wing crashed into her abdomen, knocking her aside. Her back hit the ground and the shock reverberated through her. The breath was knocked from her lungs. Her casting faltered, and she gasped for air as pain rocked through her core.

Damien screamed, "Sadie!"

He flew in her direction. The dragon whipped its tail. Damien ducked and lashed out with his sword, scratching the dragon's shoulder. It growled in response.

Damien landed as Sadie stood. She coughed and summoned a fire sword in her right hand and a blazing shield in her left. Her torso was tender and was more than likely bruised, but she wasn't giving up. She needed to save the village and try to get the dragon to snap out of whatever came over it.

"Are you all right?" Damien asked.

She thought he shouldn't have flown to her.

"Focus, Damien," she said, and she ran toward the dragon with her shield in front of her. She used the flames on her shield to shoot a bolt of fire, hitting it in the face.

The creature shook its head and shrieked. Scales melted and cracked. Sadie shot another bolt of fire, landing in the dragon's chest.

Damien bolted past her, his cloak swinging with the breeze. He jumped and shot a stream of fire of his own. It hit the dragon's throat. The creature staggered to the side but didn't collapse. It growled and snapped at Damien, again missing him by mere inches.

Sadie cast a ball of fire that the dragon's leg. The creature snapped its head at her and opened its mouth. Another ball of frost appeared in the creature's throat. She ducked and raised her shield, intensifying its heat.

The stream hit her shield and it jarred her arm, but she gritted her teeth and summoned more energy for her shield's flames. Her shield burned white and steam surrounded her as the ice cracked and fizzled. She poked her head around the shield as the dragon paused to take in another breath. Through the fading mist and flames, she caught an exposed spot on the creature's chest. The scales surrounding the area had separated while the dragon inhaled, revealing a patch of soft skin.

That gave her an idea. An unfortunate idea, but an idea none the less. If she could get the dragon distracted, she could use the moment to stop the dragon permanently. Albeit, she would've preferred to save the creature's life. But it refused to respond to her mental pleas.

Searching for Damien, she found him on the other side of the dragon. He slashed at the creature with his sword.

"Make him shoot ice at you, Damien! I have an idea!" Her voice came out muted, though she exerted herself to get her voice to carry as much as it could through the chaos of screams and magic, and roars from the dragon.

Damien had heard her though. He lowered his weapon and darted into the air from one point to another, pausing for a split-second before flying to another space. He reminded Sadie of a hummingbird, never staying in one place long enough to get snipped by the dragon's sharp teeth.

Taking her opportunity, she sneaked up on the dragon, hoping she was stealthy enough that the creature wouldn't notice her creeping. So far, it worked, since the dragon was too distracted by Damien's movements. As Sadie neared, she had to constantly step out of the way of the dragon's legs, wing, and tail.

When the creature's chest was within her reach, she struggled to keep her position.

Please work...

"Now," Sadie said in a whisper, silently praying Damien heard it.

Damien swooped down, sword angled at the creature again. His weapon found its target within the dragon's shoulder. He twisted the blade. The dragon roared and blew a long stream of frost at Damien. Sadie kept her eyes glued to the dragon's chest, waiting for the scales to part and reveal a patch of skin.

There.

Sadie angled the tip of her sword toward the unguarded area that had just opened up. She plunged her fire sword through the soft skin until it was hilt-deep in the creature's chest. Smoke and golden ichor seeped from the wound. The dragon reared back and let out an ear-splitting scream.

Sadie's chest tightened.

That was the first sign of a true connection she felt with the dragon. Sadie almost regretted what she had done.

I'm so sorry...

But this wasn't time for grieving. Sadie broke her hold on the fire sword and jumped out of the way before the dragon collapsed and crushed her on the ground. The dragon crumpled to the ground. Its head lay still, eyes wide and focused on Sadie.

The poor thing stared at her in a way that made Sadie's heart break. She attempted to reach out again, to communicate with it. She sensed the creature's life ebbing away. She also felt something unexpected.

Freedom.

The creature blinked once before its eyes closed for the last time.

Sadie's eyes drifted to Lightbane still within the dragon's shoulder.

Damien! No!

Her pulse quickened as her eyes scanned her surroundings for him. She wondered if he was hurt. He was nowhere in sight. That made her panic rise a bit more.

Just as she started to assume the worst, a voice spoke from behind her. "Sadie."

She whirled to find Damien staring at her. She ran to him. He grunted as she slammed against him and threw her arms around him, holding him as close as she could.

He stiffened in her arms before surrounding her in an embrace of his own.

"We're all right," he said, murmuring against her hair.

Around them, ifrits appeared from their houses and buildings. At first, it was only a small group, but more kept coming until it seemed like the entire village's population surrounded them.

Everyone just stood around, staring at her, at the dragon, and back to her. Some checked on each other while others held their injured before turning their attention to the defeated dragon and demon queen. Sadie stood still, worried a single move could tip the moment in the wrong direction quickly.

A collective cheer broke out. Sadie smiled at them, but she didn't feel like rejoicing. She wanted to save the creature from its demise, not aid in it.

She turned her attention to the body of the beautiful blue dragon, now at peace and lying on the ground. Golden liquid pooled from underneath it.

Such a majestic creature. She wished she didn't have to kill it.

Above the corpse, the fortress's silhouette loomed above a cliff. Beside the castle's shadow, three flying figures appeared. Damien placed a hand on her shoulder as he watched his brothers fly toward them.

Kaiser reached them first. He panted for breath as he said, "What happened? Are you okay?"

Sadie smiled at him. He seemed to always be the most worried out of all the princes.

"I'm fine," she said. "We're fine."

Mordecai and Steele landed in front of her. Mordecai looked over her shoulder to the corpse of the dragon. He raised his eyebrows. "You killed that?"

Damien answered. "Sadie did."

Sadie opened her mouth to say that they both did, but Mordecai walked around her and approached the body. He knelt and opened its jaw to examine the creature's mouth while she looked away. She didn't want to watch whatever it was Mordecai was going to do to him.

But curiosity had gotten the better of her. That, and she didn't want to show how squeamish she was in front of the ifrits. She and Damien had just killed the creature to save them, after all. She turned her attention back to the dragon.

Mordecai pressed his palm over the dragon's chest. When he found whatever it was he wanted to find, he nodded to himself and stood.

Mordecai walked back, a dire frown on his lips as he looked at his brothers. "Edreatrum."

Sadie's eyebrows pursed.

Mordecai caught the look of confusion and said,

"It's a fungus that makes creatures wild and blood-thirsty."

"How did you know?" Sadie asked.

"There are black spots in its tongue. It's usually the most prominent sign of poisoning."

Now I know why he was looking in its mouth.

"But who would do such a thing?" she asked. She instantly thought of that demoness and her incessant need to destroy everything Sadie was trying to build. "It's Mara, isn't it?

Kaiser shifted beside her. "It's possible. Especially since this fungus is only found in the Vale."

The Vale. Where Mara lives.

She clenched her jaws and formed fists so tight that her nails bit into her palms.

The demoness was coming after her people now. She had to end Mara, once and for all.

CHAPTER THIRTY-FOUR

SADIE

*S*adie stood by the largest window in her room, lost in thoughts of how to take care of Mara as she looked over her land. She had to find this artifact the princes had talked about, so she could kill the demoness.

The dagger Blair had given her back in her apartment had hurt Mara, but she didn't remember seeing it when she went back there with Carlos.

She sighed, frustrated. She wondered what else she could do.

Lost in thought, she almost didn't notice the sound of footsteps outside her room. She turned around and watched the doorknob twist. The door opened a crack and Steele peeked inside.

Oh great.

When he saw her, he entered her room, closing the door behind him.

She rolled her eyes and groaned. "What now? I thought I made my rules clear."

"You called?" he asked.

She scoffed. "Actually, no. I didn't. But since you are here, you might as well stay."

"You can drop the act, you know," he said.

She propped her hands on her hips. "What act?"

"I know you secretly pine for me." He scratched the nape of his neck. "Even though you clearly look annoyed that I broke your rules again."

"You got me," she said. "Maybe I'll let you sleep in the dungeons for a night."

Sometimes this man got on her nerves, but sometimes she also liked him. Very much. Everything felt light around him. Especially now, as the air lightened and the tension in her shoulders eased a bit. She knew what he was doing… and she let him when the gentle scratch at her mental barrier came. He affected her in that way, and she trusted him enough to know he wouldn't hurt her. Not with his power. And she could use the break from planning for the moment.

Sadie returned her gaze toward her window to look at the dark crags beyond rolling, green hills covered in pink flowers. She felt Steele come up behind her. He placed his hands on her shoulders. His fingers began to move, massaging her. She didn't stop him, because it felt nice. She just enjoyed his touches and the break from the plotting and danger.

"You're stressed out," he said. "Just relax, will you?"

Sadie sighed. "It's kind of hard to relax when everyone seems to want me dead."

"You can't keep worrying about the demons banging at your door," he said. "You have this incredible, newfound power."

Steele stopped kneading her shoulders only to set aside the thin strap of her chemise and bend his head to kiss her shoulder.

"You have a castle, a reliable butler."

He pressed his lips on her neck. She could feel him smile against her skin. "

You have a handsome man in your room with you right now."

She chuckled.

He nudged her ear and whispered. "I'll help you relax. Let me distract you."

Sadie closed her eyes. He scratched against her mental barrier again, soft and gentle. Asking permission.

She didn't hesitate. Her barricade fell. Steele's fingers traced lines on her shoulder and drifted down her arm. His tender touches created goosebumps along her skin.

In the back of her mind, a collection of memories played like a movie flashing in front of her eyes. She saw her and Blair as children, chasing each other on a playground their parents used to take them to.

She remembered her first heartbreak, the boyfriend that cheated on her and how Blair stormed to his house with a golf club in hand. Sadie had followed Blair then, pleading with her sister to just leave it alone. Blair hadn't hurt him, but she screamed a plethora of verbal threats, promising to beat him to a pulp if she ever saw his disgusting face again.

Sadie relived the several nights, back in college, when Blair had appeared on her dormitory steps, asking if she could crash for the night because she missed her sister.

Now, Sadie knew better. Blair had probably been on the run and hiding.

The memories played in her mind, and she recalled them with fondness and a few of them with regret. But even with the bad memories, she still felt lighter, holding on to these moments with her sister. They were the only thing that she had of her sister now.

As the movie of memories ended, she wiped away the solitary tear that trickled down her cheek. She blinked away the dampness welling in her eyes. She faced Steele and lifted onto her toes to kiss his cheek.

"Thank you."

When she stepped back, Steele placed his hands on the small of her back and pulled her closer.

"Thank you isn't enough," he said. Two fingers held

her chin and tilted it upward. He drew nearer and kissed her lips.

And this *is more than enough,* Sadie thought as she smiled against his mouth.

She rested her hands on his shoulders. He pulled her closer and kissed her more deeply. She moaned. His touches always made her feel lighter and so very much more. Every worry that dragged her down dissipated. He had that effect on her, and she loved it. Even amidst all the craziness that was happening around her he made smiling easy.

His lips traced kisses on her neck. She arched her back.

As if his kisses weren't enough, Steele knocked on her mental barrier again. She let him in. She gasped as an explosion of scenarios burst in her mind.

Images of him and her. Sexy ones. Tempting ones.

Of her underneath him. Above him. Beside him. On the bed. On the floor. Against the wall. Outdoors. *Everywhere.*

Steele's imaginary kisses and touches felt as if they were real. She moaned as a surge of desire shot down to the space between her legs. She curled her toes.

Damn.

When the images ended, she opened her eyes, his arms around her, chin resting on her shoulder. He kissed her neck and looked at her with a knowing smile on his face.

He stepped back but still held her hips. Her hands still rested on his shoulders. They seemed like they were about to dance for a slow song. The music was the only thing missing.

Steele's eyes crinkled as he smiled at her, and a tune began to play in her head. A slow, romantic song. Piano notes danced with the graceful humming of a violin. Her eyebrows shot up.

Bastard is in my head.

He began to sway from side to side. She giggled but followed his steps, letting him lead. She just relaxed and enjoyed the moment with him.

She thought of all those times she had spent with Steele. It was obvious. She liked his company very much. He always ignited her sexual desires every time he got her alone, and even with such a sexual beast like him, he never ceased to surprise her with how soft and gentle his touches could be, instead of rough and harsh and rushed.

Sadie rested her head on his chest and listened his heart beating. He planted a kiss on the top of her head before resting his chin on that very spot. She smiled and sighed. She wouldn't mind if this went on for hours.

The music stopped. She looked at Steele, wondering why he ended things there.

"This is just the start, you know," he said. "Sex, itself, is even better."

Sadie laughed. "Maybe I'll let you enjoy it with me someday."

"Playing hard to get, I see."

"Of course," she said. "I'm a queen. I *should* be hard to get."

Steele cupped her cheek. "I'm kind of liking the taking things slow game."

He took her hand and led her to the bed. He sat down and propped his feet up on the sheets as his back rested on the headrest. Sadie sat on the edge of the bed next to him. He placed a small red pillow on his lap and gestured for her to lay down.

She lay her head on the pillow and he played a soft piano piece in her mind. His thumb softly traced small circles against her skin. Combined with the music, his touches made her drowsy. What astonished her most was how much she trusted him, though grateful for him all the same. Lying in his arms, she fell asleep, knowing her prince would watch over her.

CHAPTER THIRTY-FIVE

Sadie woke surrounded in silk sheets, feeling well-rested and happy. She reached an arm out to rub Steele's chest, but the space beside her was empty. She sat up on the bed and rubbed her eyes.

"Good morning, beautiful."

Sadie followed the sound of Steele's voice to the balcony. He grinned at her, his chiseled torso was bare. The waistband of his trousers hung low on his hips. Her gaze lingered on the lines of hard muscle that led down his pants.

She stood, wearing only her black chemise. She thought to question him about that, but then he probably only wanted to make sure she was comfortable. Instead, she strode to where her robe hung on the back of a chair. As soon as she had the robe on and was tying its ribbons around her waist, Steele sauntered to her and held her hands to stop her.

"Don't put it on," he said.

She pecked his lips and finished tying the robe's ribbons. "It's cold, you know. Besides, we have work to do. Can you go find the others? I'll just shower. I'll be along in a bit."

He pouted. "Why can't I shower with you?"

"Steele." She gave him in what she hoped was a reproachful expression.

He laughed. "Of course, my queen."

He grabbed his shirt, put it on, and locked his lips with hers for a few seconds before leaving.

After showering, Sadie opened her wardrobe and put on a long, black gown with red brocade spiraling over its bodice. Two slits ran along the length of the tight skirt from ankle to thigh, baring an ample amount of skin as she walked the halls to meet with her men. She opened the double doors to the dining room, finding the princes sitting around the dining table, laughing at something Steele had said.

Hearing their laughter made Sadie happy. Across from her, Steele caught her gaze. His eyes wandered down her legs and returned to her eyes. He smirked. When she walked toward him, he pulled out the chair beside him. He stood as he guided her to her seat before sitting down beside her. To her other side, Mordecai took a sip of what she hoped was wine, but knew it was probably blood. That was a thing here, apparently.

"What were you talking about?" she asked as Hobson poured red wine in her glass. She whispered her thanks before he left to stand along the wall.

"We're planning our next game of meracoan," Steele said. He looked pointedly at Mordecai. "And this time, shadow-shifting is banned."

He took a bite off a loaf of bread and spoke around his food. "We're planning to give Damien permission to use his powers."

Mordecai chuckled, and Damien grimaced.

"What's meracoan?" Sadie asked.

"It's a game we used to play when we were younger. Kind of like soccer, but different. It's pretty known in the underworld. We should teach you," Kaiser said. He looked around the table at his brothers. "Don't you think so?"

This cordial exchange was so far from their usual bickering. Sadie's eyebrows shot up. It was the first time she observed them so at ease with each other.

"I would love to play with you guys," she said. She turned toward her butler. "Maybe Hobson can join, too."

"If I'm to join, I should be on your team to keep an eye on you," the gargoyle said.

Sadie crinkled her nose. "I can keep an eye on myself, thank you very much."

"Uh-huh," Hobson said and smiled. "And you should wear armor when you play."

Sadie's jaw went slack. "Armor?"

The guys laughed, no doubt imagining her playing an outdoor sport covered head-to-toe with metal. She visualized herself wearing armor, too, and she found herself laughing with them.

It felt good, being around the guys when they were friendly with each other and not fighting over the silliest things. They could be controlling idiots some-times, but damn she adored them.

Her smile faltered, and she realized that thought was true—she deeply adored them *all*. She had vowed to take only one ally, but what would the others do if she refused them? She would lose them, and she couldn't imagine what her life, what the castle would be like without them all here.

She bit her lip, deciding to stall her decision. She still needed more information on each of them. At least, that was the lie she told herself.

CHAPTER THIRTY-SIX

DAMIEN

*D*amien stood outside the fortress walls, hidden in shadow as he waited for the small silhouette sneaking its way toward him from the forest nearby. The figure sprinted from tree to tree, careful not to be seen by the ifrit sentries walking along the castle walls. A few feet to the side of the figure, Damien saw something else shift within the trees. He peered through the darkness, waiting for the shadows to move again, but the imp came into view, dashing at full speed toward him. The creature stopped in front of him, catching its breath that billowed into mist from the coldness of the night.

Damien looked down his nose at the creature. The top of its head hardly reached Damien's waist.

"What took you so long?" Damien asked.

"Sorry, Your Highness." The imp fidgeted with the

hem of its dirty brown tunic. "I thought someone was following me."

Damien furrowed his brow and stared into the shadows of the forest again, waiting for that movement he saw. Nothing shifted for a good, long moment. He mentally shook his head. The imp was probably just making an excuse. Though that didn't explain him seeing something else move too.

"Do you have it?" Damien asked the creature.

"Yes." The imp didn't elaborate.

Damien grew impatient and growled out, "Well?"

The small creature uneasily shifted. "C-carleset Hollows."

Damien's eyebrows rose. He had to admit that Carleset Hollows was a clever hiding place. It was well-hidden, and it had been abandoned for centuries. He wasn't sure it even still existed.

"You're certain?" he asked his spy.

"I should be asking *you* that question. You're too invested in this queen," the imp said. "Do you want to fuck her that much?"

He leered at Damien. "Can I have a go?"

Damien's blood boiled. No one should talk about Sadie in that way. "Do you like having a tongue?"

The spy continued, as if Damien hadn't made a threat, in a more serious tone. "You have allies enough. You can make a move against your father now and secure the—"

He shut the imp up with a stern glare. "You're dismissed."

"I'm only trying to say—"

"You're dismissed," he said again. He kept his monotonous tone and the imp's eyes widened, no doubt feeling the roiling anger underneath Damien's words.

Finally.

"Leave, before I change my mind and kill you after all."

The creature left without another word.

He leaned against the fortress wall, lingering in his post for a few minutes. He arrived here with the intention of a mere alliance, but his mission had been interrupted by the unexpectedness of Sadie and the arrival of his brothers. He smiled, as he always did every time he thought about the most incredible woman he had ever met.

The woman he was falling in love with.

Damien furrowed his brow. *Was* he falling in love?

He thought about all the times he had spent with her. How he felt every time she was near, every time he touched her, and every time she touched him back. When he found out she had run out into battle to fight Mara, he had felt fear unlike anything he had ever felt. He remembered hoping, wishing, and his version of praying that she remained safe, unhurt. He realized at that moment he wouldn't know what to do if something terrible happened to her.

He really was falling for Sadie. He had never felt this kind of emotion before, but he knew.

Now he was stuck. What would he do with this realization? It was a dangerous thing—a demon falling in love. He would raze cities and destroy empires in his passion. He had heard stories of similar feats during his childhood. His father drilled it into his head that love was a waste, it made you weak.

But he was in love. And he felt stronger than ever.

And his brothers. He took in a steadying breath, knowing full well they were drawn to her as well. Mordecai had made out with her, Steele had said so. Steele, on the other hand, was obviously smitten with her. He sucked at hiding it every time she walked into a room. And Kaiser had a bond with Sadie.

Though he knew things for him couldn't possibly end well, he still couldn't help himself. He needed her. And he refused to lose this contest. Not just for his father's crown but to win *her*, too.

CHAPTER THIRTY-SEVEN

SADIE

*S*adie cast a spherical shield of smoke around her. Since she didn't have anything else to do, aside from brood over her lack of ideas to kill Mara, she decided to head to the west courtyard and do some warmups with smoke casting. Hobson helped her train, launching more of his stone discs in her direction. The discs struck her shield.

The impenetrability of her shield's surface wasn't consistent, so every now and then, Hobson's stone discs passed through and hit her limbs. She bet she would be bruised after this. But she pushed through, knowing she should exert herself to improve.

She kept in mind some of the pointers Mordecai had taught her, and those helped. The more she practiced, the better she got.

Footsteps ruffled the grass on her right. Sadie

raised her hand. The flying discs halted. She let her shield dissolve and faced Damien as he approached from the fortress. He held a determined expression on his face. He stopped a few steps in front of Sadie. "I know where we can find the weapons to kill Mara."

Her heart thudded with excitement. "Where?"

"It's a place called the Carleset Hollows," he said. "A cave. And apparently it contains the mageblades—it's a collection of four daggers. They're strong enough to kill the demoness."

Sadie narrowed her eyes. "How do you know this?"

Damien winked and smiled. "I called in a few favors."

Sadie took in a deep breath. Since the dragon attacked the ifrit village, she had spent most of her time stewing on the most random ideas, grasping at any plan at all, no matter how futile, just so she could do *something*. This news changed everything. Now, defeating Mara was possible.

"I always have someone who owes me." His gaze turned serious as he stepped closer. "I'll spend all these favors on you if I have to. Without thinking twice."

Sadie smiled. "I got you wrapped around my finger, don't I?"

"You have no idea."

She shook her head, unable to understand that he would do such things for her, but she appreciated the gesture.

She faced Hobson, who stood by silently as they talked. "Please, gather the others in the sitting room."

The butler nodded and left to carry out his orders.

"What's your plan?" Damien asked.

She tilted her head to the side. "What do you think?"

He snorted. "I shouldn't have asked."

Sadie and Damien walked to the sitting room together. She opened the door to find the other three princes waiting, sitting comfortably on the posh couches. The princes stood when they entered.

"What's up?" Steele asked.

Sadie said, "We know where the mageblades are."

Mordecai's eyes widened. "What?"

Steele's mouth hung open.

"We need to leave immediately," Sadie said. "We have to get our hands on those weapons."

The three princes looked at each other, not answering.

She placed her hands on her hips. "I'm going without you if I have to."

Kaiser, Mordecai, and Steele seemed to snap out of their surprise.

"Of course, we're going," Mordecai said.

Kaiser frowned at her. "You're not going alone."

Sadie smiled. *I knew they would see it my way.*

Hobson chimed in. "Then you all need weapons."

Everyone looked at the butler.

"Thanks a lot, Sherlock," Steele said.

Hobson rolled his eyes. "Just follow me, will you?"

The butler turned on his heels and headed out the door. Sadie and the princes exchanged glances before following him.

Hobson led them to a hallway she had never been in before. They stopped in front of a vault that extended from wall to ceiling. He faced Sadie. "Only you can open it."

He pointed to a shallow, circular depression on the door. "Place your palm here."

Sadie stepped closer and did as she was instructed. Her hand fit the space perfectly, almost like the depression was made to her hand. The sound of a latch opening clicked inside, and the vault slid open, revealing a massive, square room filled with an array of various weapons.

Behind her, one of the princes sucked in a breath. Steele whistled.

"Holy shit," Damien said, rushing to the farthest shelf. He touched every weapon he could get his hands on whilst muttering under his breath, "Bone reavers, justifiers, modulators. *Moonbeams.*"

He faced Sadie with a glint in his eyes that reminded her of a boy on Christmas morning. He practically bounced in the place he stood. "You didn't know you had this room?"

Hobson said, "I didn't have the chance to show it to her yet."

"Well," she said. "Take the weapons you think you would need."

Damien's eyes lit up. "Don't mind if I do."

He scanned the shelves and took a belt that could hold numerous daggers. As Sadie watched, he attached no less than a dozen knives to the belt and a few small grenades. He pocketed a few more weapons she didn't recognize.

Steele approached the shelves on the left wall. He grabbed two short-handled axes and holstered them. He grabbed another weapon: a hammer encrusted with diamonds. He grinned as he spun it with his fingers. He took a few daggers and tucked them in his boots and sleeves.

On the right wall, Mordecai finished lining his belt and tunic with different colored gemstones. After tucking daggers and circular throwing blades inside his boots and pockets, he perused a tall, mahogany shelf filled with books.

"You have the Verity Scrolls," he said. "They have been lost for millennia."

His hand twitched on his side as if he wanted to touch the tomes but restrained himself.

Sadie smiled and shook her head. *Boys and their toys.* "Take a look then."

His eyebrows shot up. "You sure?"

"Yeah," she said, chuckling.

She didn't think these princes could be nerds, but she had been wrong before. Kaiser stood beside her and had already grabbed two daggers, tucking one in each boot. Other than that, he didn't seem interested in anymore weapons, to which Sadie found interesting. He turned and watched his brothers, too. The corner of his mouth lifted.

Hobson approached Sadie. "There's a small room down here."

Sadie nodded and followed him to a special back room. As soon as he opened the door, she was captivated by the battle dress adorning a mannequin in the middle of the room. It was made of flexible, blood red fabric, and metal spikes lined its sleeves. Like all her other battle dresses, a slit opened up on the front of the skirt, revealing dark tights with a webbed pattern.

A black belt cinched across its waist and it had numerous attachments where she could holster weapons. The sleeves were wide and billowy, also with a slit up the side as not to hinder her in battle. The dress was the most badass thing she had ever seen.

Daggers, swords, and arrows lined the walls of the small space. Any of these weapons would look good on the outfit. Their hilts glimmered with jewels or shining stones. She approached a pure white dagger and touched it. She assumed it had been carved with a very pale looking wood, or some kind of metal, but it was made of bone.

A creeping, itching sensation traveled up Sadie's arm, and the eyes of the carved skull on the dagger's hilt glowed red. She spun it in her fingers, feeling comfortable and weirded out at the same time. She put it back on the shelf and took the dagger beside it.

This one's hilt was covered in moss and vines. It felt different in her grip. She felt warmth and her blood rushed.

The next dagger was made of water. She held its hilt which shimmered against the room's white light. She didn't expect it to feel solid, but aside from its cold and damp hilt, the blade didn't feel different than ordinary knives. When she was about to put it back on the shelf, it shifted and turned into a shield made of ice. She gasped.

She shifted the shield, letting it catch the light of the room in various prisms of color before it shifted back into dagger form. She set it back on the shelf and hovered her hands over the other daggers.

Each was different from the others in appearance and ability. One's hilt had multi-colored gems that resembled a rainbow, another dagger had a handle that looked like a key, and there was a sword that seemed to hum violin tunes. Each weapon also reacted to her differently, but all were equally powerful.

As she walked around the mannequin, she saw a

sword strapped to the back of the dress. She unsheathed the dark blade outlined in silver. A blue pearl glowed in the pommel, casting a dull light over its cross guards that were shaped like arrowheads.

It was light as a feather and felt so natural in her grip. Unlike the other weapons, this one seemed to have a direct connection with her amulet. Her chest warmed, and a chill crept down her spine. When she held the hilt with both hands, the blue pearl glowed brighter, and the blade erupted in light blue flames.

She stepped back, lowering her arms, nearly dropping the sword. The tip of the blade touched the brick floor and immediately formed a small crater on the surface. The affected area turned to ash. Having casted fire hot enough to turn skeleton to ash, Sadie realized the fire that came from this weapon transcended even that. She smiled, certain she had found her weapon.

She sheathed the sword and set it aside in order to put on the battledress.

This queen was ready for war.

CHAPTER THIRTY-EIGHT

SADIE

*S*adie sat on the head of the table of the war room with the four princes surrounding her. All of them were dressed and geared for the mission. Before leaving the castle, they agreed to go through a dry run of what they would do once they arrived at Carleset Hallows.

"Here's the plan," she said. "Once we get there, Mordecai will scout the entrance to see if we have company. He will then return to our hiding place and notify us of what he sees."

"Noted," Mordecai said.

Sadie continued. "Whatever his report will be, determines what we do next. If we have the all clear, then we will proceed to the caves. If not, then we will have to fight."

She faced the shadow shifter. "Mordecai, your task

after that is to scout the remaining parts of the cave for the artifacts. The rest of us," she said, motioning to the other princes, "will enter together and meet up with him inside. Let's hope the odds are in our favor."

They promptly left for Carleset Hollows. Sadie flew with Kaiser and the other three men flew alongside them. They landed a few miles away from the location and walked through a dense forest of elms and aspens toward the hollows. When they reached the clearing where the cave was located, Sadie and the princes hid behind the brush lining the fringe of the glade.

"Ready?" Sadie asked Mordecai.

He nodded.

She placed a hand on his shoulder. "Please, be careful."

His eyes softened before he shifted into smoke and disappeared.

Sadie and the rest of the princes waited in silence for about ten minutes before Mordecai reappeared. He grumbled under his breath and said, "Empusa."

Steele sighed. "This won't be easy, then."

"What are empusa?" Sadie asked.

Damien said, "They're creatures that are part human, part snake. But this can be a good sign. They're commonly relocated to areas where demons want to protect things."

Steele snorted. "It's funny, really. When you see a

hoard of them, it's usually a sign of something worth stealing."

"Still, they're mindless and bloodthirsty," Kaiser said. "Perhaps, you should stay here, Sadie."

She glared at him. "Stay here? Are you freaking kidding me?"

"We just don't want you hurt," Kaiser said. "The four of us can take them. You don't have to lift a finger."

Sadie inched closer to him and jabbed a finger into his chest. "Listen here, mister. I didn't wear this dress just to sit around and look pretty while you boys have all the fun."

Behind Kaiser's shoulder, Mordecai grinned.

"Now, now, brother," he said. "Don't baby the queen. Even if you tie her in chains, she'll still probably find a way to get to the artifacts before us."

Damn straight.

Kaiser ignored his brother and kept his eyes on Sadie. "If something happened to you, Sadie, I don't know what I'd do."

She took in a deep, steadying breath. Though she was irritated with him, his genuine care and need to keep her safe was touching. On the exhale of that breath, she cupped Kaiser's cheek with her hand. "Believe in me for once, will you?"

"I do. I just—I don't want a single scratch on you, do you hear?" His eyes became stern and serious.

She smiled but kept the giggle bubbling in her throat from coming out. "I promise I won't die. Happy?"

He groaned, looking at her like he would chain her after all. But he turned around and grabbed the dagger he slipped under his boot. "Let's go kill some demons."

Steele already had his axe in one hand, and he unholstered the hammer he had grabbed with the other. Mordecai twirled his staff. Damien unsheathed his broadsword but kept it from igniting in flames. Sadie supposed he didn't want to draw any unwanted attention toward their group.

"What now, Captain?" Mordecai asked.

"Let's try to sneak into the cave and hide from them," Sadie said. "If we get caught, I'll attempt to speak with them and hope they listen to me. But if not, then I guess we fight."

"Sounds simple enough," Steele said.

Sadie looked at Mordecai. "You can go." She placed a hand on his elbow. "And please take care."

He winked before shifting to shadow and disappearing again.

"I'll lead the way," Damien said.

Sadie agreed, knowing his enhanced senses would help them navigate.

Sadie, Kaiser, Steele, and Damien sneaked into the cave, keeping their footsteps as light as they could. They walked through the dark entrance. A tense silence enveloped their small group. Sadie held her black sword on her side, gripping the hilt harder than she should. It unnerved her how dark and silent the cave was.

Around her, the men held their weapons at the ready, all of them prepared for an ambush. She wasn't sure if that made her feel better or worse.

Damien took the lead. He seemed lost in his own thoughts, turning his head or turning up his nose every once in a while, perhaps listening for movement or catching a scent only he could detect. All of them trusted his sense of direction more than their own.

In the middle of their group, Kaiser held out his palm and summoned an orb of yellow light, small enough to illuminate a short distance around them and, Sadie hoped, faint enough that creatures lurking in the dark wouldn't notice before Damien caught sight of them. But the place felt empty, like they had no other company besides the damp tunnel walls that surrounded them.

Sadie wondered if Mordecai had somehow been mistaken or if the empusa had managed to travel deeper into the cave or left when everyone wasn't looking.

Damien stopped in his tracks. He held out a hand, signaling them to halt. Then, she heard it. Sounds of soft hissing began to echo from the numerous tunnels in front of them.

Around Sadie, the guys raised their weapons. She raised hers too, and she focused her hearing on the hissing whispers. At first, they sounded muffled, but the voices grew louder, becoming more distinct. Sadie knew they were getting closer to them.

She strained to hear what they said through their thick accents and odd dialect.

"Demon queen."

That was it. Spoken in a chant or mantra.

Sadie stiffened.

The dark tunnels in front of them became lit with bright, yellow light as slightly more than a dozen women with burning hair similar to the ifrits' appeared. True to Damien's description of the empusa, these women's lower bodies were scaly serpent tails.

Really, *really* big serpents.

They slithered toward Sadie and the princes. Sharp blades of scales that glinted and reflected the light coming from the flames of their hair covered their forearms and hands. Kaiser dropped his hand to his side, letting the small orb of light he casted die out. With all the light the empusa emanated, his tiny orb wasn't useful anymore.

Here goes nothing. She took in a deep breath and stepped in front of Damien. She stood taller, mustering confidence she hoped was convincing. "Halt!"

The empusa stopped and swayed from side to side.

Their whispers continued to assault her ears. "Demon queen... Demon queen... Demon queen."

The largest empusa of the group slithered closer to them. She looked at Sadie and bowed. Sadie exhaled the breath she had been holding.

"What bringsss her Majesssty here?" the empusa asked, voice high and screeching.

"I'm looking for something," Sadie said. But as soon as she spoke, something shifted in the air, and the empusa's demeanor became more tense and aggravated.

The empusa looked at each other and back to Sadie, tilting their heads and furrowing their brows. They all snarled, their flaming hair glowing brighter. Something had set them on high-alert.

The empusa that had addressed Sadie bared her sharp, jagged teeth and pointed a finger at her. "You are *not* the demon queen."

The others hissed behind her. "Fake. Impossstor. Fake."

What do you mean fake? Who else would I be?

The empusa raised their arms and rapidly slithered toward Sadie and the princes. The men wasted no time in sprinting past her, no doubt to take the first blows from the monsters and keep them away from her. Even with the erupting chaos, she rolled her eyes.

Of course, there would be an issue.

As Sadie dashed toward the melee to fight the

demons, she mulled over the empusa's reaction. Maybe they greeted her nicely at first because the amulet had confused them. Maybe they were still loyal to Hecate. She couldn't think of any other demon queen that still existed. Or, rather, still had some form of life.

An empusa slithered to Sadie and swiped with its arm. Sadie raised her sword to block the blow. She whirled and slashed with her sword, decapitating the monster's head. Nearby, an empusa slithered behind Steele. She lifted a blade into the air, readying to thrust it into his back.

Sadie rushed over and plunged her sword between its shoulder blades. The monster collapsed to the ground. Steele glanced behind him, eyes wide. His gaze drifted to Sadie, and he nodded to her in thanks. She pulled her sword from the creature's corpse. From her left, another empusa charged at her. She swung at the creature's neck, slitting its throat.

Sadie looked around. The princes slaughtered empusa. Damien dispatched five of them, Steele killed four, and Kaiser took out three. Even Mordecai fought his own share of the creatures. He must have heard the commotion and came to help.

One last monster remained, fighting Mordecai with its bladed arms. Mordecai sliced the empusa's shoulder and stabbed the creature in the heart, killing it instantly.

The flames of the last empusa's hair died as the creature gave out its last breath, leaving Sadie and her princes in darkness. And without the empusa's hissing, their group became wrapped in silence again. Dead empusa lay scattered in the darkness surrounding them. Sadie's heart grew heavy. They had caused another massacre.

She summoned a flame in her hand, casting soft orange light on the five of them and the littered corpses around them.

"Is anyone hurt?" she asked.

She made the flame grow brighter as she looked at each of the princes, scanning their bodies for any major injury. But the princes shook their heads and she felt relieved that none of them were seriously hurt.

"We should leave," Damien said. "There might be more."

Sadie pursed her lips. "We're not leaving without the weapons."

"Worry not, Captain. I found it," Mordecai said. His enchanted staff dissipated to mist as he turned to face them. "Follow me."

He led them to a small cavern with a single chest on the far end.

"I haven't opened it yet," Mordecai said. "But it's free from any kind of trap or enchantment. I checked."

Sadie approached the chest, knelt in front of it, and opened the lid. She stared into the cavity a bit dumbfounded. It was empty, except for a small piece of paper on the bottom. She picked it up and read the message scrawled onto its surface.

Good job for finding the treasure!
   - B.B.
   XOXO

The guys looked over her shoulder.

"Blackwood," Damien said, growling. "That woman ruins everything."

Sadie wasn't sure what "B.B." had meant until Damien said Blackwood. That was her last name. And the first B had to mean Blair. She crumpled the piece of paper. "Shit."

That was a whole lot of effort for nothing. She felt like laughing and crying at the same time. Blair had probably intended to trick one of her enemies, but she ended up tricking Sadie instead.

Sadie thought of places Blair might have hidden the mageblades, but her sister had kept so much from her that she had no idea where the things could be. Sadie recalled the fight at her apartment. If Blair already had her hands on the mageblades, that meant the knife Blair had given her in the apartment was definitely one of the artifacts. And there were three more daggers out there somewhere.

Sadie looked at Kaiser and frowned and rubbed her forehead.

"I already had it. One of the mageblades. I had it, but I didn't know what it was." She paced as she muttered to herself. "Shit, shit, shit."

Steele, Mordecai, and Damien stared at her. They seemed confused.

"What do you mean?" Mordecai asked.

Steele's eyebrows met. "Do you know Blair Blackwood?"

She dropped her hands to her sides and faced the three men. "My full name is Sadie Blackwood. Blair is my sister."

Damien gaped. "You—" He ran a hand through his hair, staring at her as though he had been betrayed.

Steele completed his sentence. "Blair Blackwood is your sister?"

"Why didn't you tell us?" Mordecai asked, snarling.

Sadie's eyebrows rose. She didn't understand why they were upset. There were more things to worry about than Blair being her sister. She stopped pacing to glare at them. "Why is *that* the issue?"

Damien looked at Kaiser and pointed a finger at him. "You knew all along and you didn't even mention it once?"

Kaiser just shrugged. "It wasn't my business."

The three of them seemed hurt. Perhaps, because Kaiser knew, and they didn't.

Sadie groaned. "Are you kidding me? This isn't important right now. Will you please focus?"

She must have appeared really annoyed because they didn't pursue the topic further. Still, she suspected she hadn't heard the end of it.

Mordecai grumbled. "Fine." He crossed his arms. "What now, *Captain*?"

Sadie ignored the way Mordecai had said captain and shifted her attention to Steele and Damien. "Can we agree to leave this behind for now and focus on how we can find the daggers?"

"All right," Damien said. His jaws clenched, and his lips were pressed tightly together.

They were really pissed at this discovery.

Steele wrinkled his nose, but he nodded.

"The only thing we can do now is retrace your sister's steps," Kaiser said beside her.

Damien agreed, but he still seemed quite pissed. "Worth a shot."

"Okay then," Sadie said, choosing to ignore their accusatory stares. "How about we start with my apartment?"

CHAPTER THIRTY-NINE

SADIE

*S*adie held Kaiser's arm as her world shifted into rapid blurs of shapes. She felt weightless the moment before her feet touched the ground. Her knees buckled, but Steele's strong arms kept her steady. As far as going through portals went, this was her third time. She wondered if she would ever get used to the vertigo that came with it.

In front of her stood the building she had inhabited not even a month ago. Looking at the place now, nostalgia overwhelmed her, and a slight tinge of nausea as she remembered the fight with Mara. In the night sky above, a quarter of the moon shone, peeking through silver clouds. She wondered how her apartment had fared since she last fought with the demoness.

"Lead the way, Captain," Mordecai said in human form.

All of the princes had changed form to their human shape in order to remain inconspicuous. Sadie thought that was a good idea. Halloween would've been a much easier night to walk around in their normal forms. Maybe even win a few contests for best costume. But it wasn't Halloween.

The five of them approached the side of the building and climbed up the fire escape, keeping as quiet as they could, hoping not to gather any kind of attention from the few people on the streets or inside. Mordecai shifted to smoke and passed through the wall. He opened a window leading to the hallway for them. Once each of them had climbed through, Sadie led them to her flat.

The last time she had seen her door, the edges and doorknob were stained with blood, and yellow police tape covered the door. Now, the tape was gone, and her door had been painted brown.

"Can you check for new inhabitants?" Sadie asked Mordecai.

He nodded, shifted to shadow again, and the rest of them waited in the hall shifting weight from foot to foot, or shooting casual glances down the hall on either side.

Mordecai returned a few moments later, opening the door and gesturing everyone inside. "We're alone."

When Sadie entered, it didn't at all feel like the place she had lived in for years. The wall paper, the lighting, and the flooring had been renovated already.

That didn't take long.

And she was thankful it wasn't still the charred, blackened remains of an apartment it had been, because she remembered Carlos and the stains his blood must have left on the old flooring. She remembered Mara and Blair, and the fire. It would likely have been too much for her to step into so soon after the events themselves, but she would do anything to get her hands on those daggers, facing the burnt apartment or not.

The guys walked around, looking at shelves and tabletops. Sadie roamed the place, forcing back all the memories she had here, both good and bad. She already knew they only wasted their time coming here. If someone had cleaned and reconstructed everything, to the point that even the walls and overhead lights were different, and the dagger was definitely not here. If it was, whoever had cleaned should have gotten it, or Mara must have kept it.

Sadie sighed. "We aren't finding anything in here."

"Then, where to next?" Steele asked.

Kaiser said, "The safehouse."

Kaiser knew the place, so he made the portal to get there. All five of them held hands as Kaiser transported them to the safehouse where Sadie had fought the demon hunter.

When her world began to spin and distort, she bent her knees and readied herself for the tough landing. Once she set foot on level ground, her legs didn't buckle, and she didn't topple over from losing her balance. She suspected it was because Steele and Kaiser held each of her hands, but she was still proud of herself for having made that improvement.

They landed inside the abandoned house. Sadie looked around the place. Nothing had changed. Even the pile of ash that had used to be a demon hunter remained on the floor, though it was a significantly shorter pile this time, perhaps because of the breeze that, from time to time, blew in from the broken windows.

She didn't want to stay longer than necessary, so she searched everywhere, looking at anything that might seem suspicious. Her eyes traveled over the broken debris on the floor, to the pile of discarded clothes and items, the shelves on the walls and the cabinets. But she didn't see anything that would help.

Sadie noticed Mordecai scanning the symbols on the wall, at the graffiti of an ouroboros that filled the entire surface.

She approached him. "What is it? What does it mean?"

"The owners of the house converted," he said, not looking at her. "They belong to a demon now. The symbol is a warning to other demon hunters who stop by here that it's not safe anymore."

"How do you know that?" Sadie asked.

Mordecai looked at her then. He smirked. "I've converted a few demon hunters in my time."

Sadie snorted but wondered why she wasn't bothered by the revelation. Though she suspected Mordecai had done terrible things, she didn't feel scared or disgusted. She shook her head. This wasn't the time to analyze her views about the princes. It was time to focus on where Blair might have hidden the daggers.

From what Mordecai had said, she guessed multiple hunters had used this place. So, Blair would have hidden her stash well. But, if Blair had used this place as a safe house for a while, then she must have hidden things here. At this point, there was no telling, and things started to look pretty grim for them.

Sadie needed to find the daggers. She needed to kill Mara and be done with her once and for all. The only thing standing in their way was her sister.

Sadie and the princes tore the place apart, looking inside cabinets and drawers, checking the floor and the walls for any loose boards, holes, or hidden latches.

She was looking for said holes in the wall beside the back window when she looked out and saw a concrete slab in the grass outside. She remembered how Blair liked secrets, contingency plans, insurance, and extra precautions. On a whim, she stopped her search and just stared at it, scrutinizing the edges. In her gut, she felt that there was more to it. There was something off about it. More than just a slab of concrete.

Beside her, Steele had just toppled a rickety shelf and was perusing each book. "Steele, come here."

"What's up?" he asked, standing up and approaching her.

Sadie pointed to the slab. "Help me break it, will you? It's just a feeling."

They went out through the back window and stood beside the concrete slab. Damien noticed and followed. "What did you find?"

"Not sure yet," she said.

Steele raised his axe and slammed it on the concrete slab. It broke after one blow. Sadie had expected it to crack, not to wither and crumble down a hole in the ground. Steele kicked on the fragments that remained, widening the hole.

Sadie opened her palm to cast a small flame. It glowed, brightening the darkness inside the hole. She peeked and saw a small hollow, a room, all its walls covered in shelves containing all sorts of trinkets. It reminded her of a treasure trove.

Steele jumped in first. She followed. Steele held his hand up to help her, but she just rolled her eyes and waved it away. Damien called Mordecai and Kaiser before jumping into the hollow himself.

When Kaiser and Mordecai jumped inside, the four of them had to minimize their movements because of the narrow space. Sadie began to look around when Damien held his hands up.

"We have company," he said.

Just as they were about to leave the confined space to be safe from an attack, if there was one, a small, metallic object dropped down from the small entrance they had created and clanked on the floor.

A grenade.

Kaiser quickly grabbed the object and threw it into the air. It reached such an extraordinary height that when it exploded, it looked like a lone firework bursting in the night sky. Sadie knew fireworks were illegal in Seattle, and she wondered if anyone would be reporting the sound or if authorities would even bother to reprimand people in a place such as this. She didn't think so, and she let the thought go.

She was about to tell the guys to get out of the small room when Kaiser wrapped his arms around her and jumped out of the hole. The two of them landed on the grass a few meters away from the broken, concrete slab. The other princes followed soon after. They immediately shifted back into their demon forms.

Sadie looked around her. The abandoned house

stood behind her and the princes and surrounding them was a group of men and women clad in dark clothes, armed to the teeth with knives and pistols. They formed an arc around them and reminded her of the man she had fought in this place not long ago. They were demon hunters, and there were at least thirty of them.

Sadie wondered how they knew she would be here, and tonight of all nights. Maybe a scout was always stationed near this place, lying in wait so that if someone appeared, the scout would raise the alarm. Either way, Sadie didn't know for sure. All she knew was that this was going to be a big fight.

A man, middle aged and wearing an eyepatch, stood in the center of the line of demon hunters. He seemed to be their leader. He approached but kept his distance from Sadie and her princes.

"Thanks," he said. "We have been looking for Blair's stash for a while now. She stole a lot of shit from the wrong people, you know."

If Sadie should think of one good thing that had happened today, it was the confirmation that they had finally found Blair's stash. This man didn't seem friendly at all, though, and he didn't seem like the type of guy to let her group take a look at Blair's hideaway, even if they only took what they needed…never mind the grenade, hello.

"Who are you working for?" Damien asked. "I have

friends in high places that would be pissed if their servants dared to attack me."

The man only shrugged. "No worries. You're fair game." He looked at Sadie, smirking. "You all are, especially Sadie."

The way he said her name and stared at her made her skin crawl. She was about to snap back, but the man pulled a gun from his back and fired at her. She held out her arm in a reflexive move. She almost laughed at her reaction, thinking her arm could block a bullet. Thankfully, with his inhuman speed, Kaiser sprinted in front of her and parried the bullet with the blade of his dagger.

The man snarled and fired the remaining bullets of his pistol at her. Kaiser became a blur, parrying all the bullets with his blade. Most fell to the ground, but some of them hit a few men in the arms, shoulders, and legs. One bullet that ricocheted from Kaiser's blade hit a man in the forehead. He dropped down dead, his mouth hung open in a silent scream.

The man's gun clicked empty. Kaiser paused in front of Sadie, holding up his dagger that was now crooked and dinted. He let it drop to the ground. The man threw aside his gun and pulled out two knives from his boots. He charged at Kaiser who now held his fists in front of him. The rest of the demon hunters followed their leader and charged.

Sadie unsheathed her black sword as the leader

sidestepped Kaiser's blow and made his way toward her. She slashed her sword at him and jabbed at his chest, but he blocked it with a swing. She turned to reduce the impact that resonated through her arm. The man threw one of his daggers at her. She sidestepped, narrowly missing the knife as it whizzed past her shoulder.

She ducked and crouched, and she shot a ball of fire at the demon hunter. It hit him in the abdomen. His shirt caught fire, which distracted him. Sadie stood with a hand held out in front of her and concentrated on the man's flaming clothes. She willed the fire to spread from his abdomen to his chest and to his sleeves.

A shadow loomed over her, forcing her to halt her casting so she could face her new attacker. At the very last second, a blade descended on her. She raised her sword and blocked the blow only to kick the attacker's kneecap and swing the sword at his wrist. He screamed as his hand fell to the ground.

The woman nearest her saw what had happened. Shrieking, she ran toward Sadie and swung her sword. Her movements were furious, but that made her weaker in strategy. Perhaps she was a lover to the man she had injured, based on the way she behaved. Sadie blocked each one of her blows. The woman pulled her gun from its holster. Sadie expertly kicked the gun out of the woman's hand, forcing it to land in the grass a good five to ten feet off.

Guns. Why didn't we bring guns?

She groaned. She was too caught up in the moment of finally finding a weapon that could take care of Mara to think about grabbing a *gun*. She almost laughed. But she had to compose herself and collected all her deranged thoughts, subduing them until a more appropriate moment to let them out. She could cast fire and smoke. Who needed guns when there was that?

The woman scrambled for her dagger, but in her panic, she couldn't seem to find it. Sadie jabbed her sword under the woman's sternum and felt the tip of her blade pierce the woman's heart. She kicked the woman's body away from her weapon as her blade slid off the body with a sickening sound.

The one-handed man, who Sadie supposed was the woman's lover, attacked. His face twisted in a mixture of grief, fear, and anger. In a normal day, Sadie would have been sorry. But right now, she just didn't have the time when all these people were trying to kill her.

She leapt in the direction of the woman's gun. She picked it up, crouched, and shot the man straight in the throat. He collapsed with a gurgling sound as she climbed back to her feet. Her heart raced as two more demon hunters sprinted toward her, weapons at the ready. She held her sword at her side. The blade dripped red on the grass.

Just as she stepped forward and prepared for another fight, a piercing sensation struck her shoulder. Someone had stabbed her from behind. She lost hold of her sword, and it fell on the grass. She yelped as a blow hit the back of her knees and caused her to collapse to the ground. She raised her arms up to soften the fall, but that had only sent searing pain through her shoulder. She rolled on her back, clenching her teeth, and she tried to reach for her weapon on the grass beside her. But a half-naked figure kneeled over her.

The eye-patch guy, the leader of the group that had attacked her. His entire torso was now covered in blisters and burns.

The man leered at her. "Bitch. Look at what you've done."

His visible eye blazed. Spittle flew from his mouth as he spat his words.

The man pressed on her wounded shoulder. Sadie gritted her teeth. He thrust his blade in her other shoulder, and Sadie groaned. Her body begged for the pain to stop. Her breathing grew shallower. And she got pissed.

She refused to die. Not at the hands of a random demon hunter.

She screamed, gathering all her magic. She had

once turned a man to ash and she couldn't even control her fire abilities then. Now that she could, it should be easy. She reached for the energy brimming in the amulet in her chest. She tapped into its magic and let it consume her. The power sizzled and flowed from her chest to her hands. She held her palms up and, with all her strength, she let everything out.

Bright light enveloped her, but the flash ended soon after it started.

The outburst left her drained. The weight above her thankfully disappeared, but both her shoulders stung from the wounds. Ash rained down on her. She coughed and spat, tasting the vile remains in her mouth. Groaning, she rolled to her knees and stood and walked away from the remnants of that man.

CHAPTER FORTY

SADIE

*H*er shoulders hurt, but she raised an arm to shoot bolts of fire at her enemies. She struggled to maintain focus as she worked through the pain, suffering more throbbing sensations each time she lifted an arm. Burning sensations erupted from her chest and she felt her wounds slowly start to heal.

"Sadie," Steele said. "Are you all right?"

She nodded, but it didn't feel convincing. Kaiser stood beside him within seconds. Mordecai appeared from mist beside her. Damien flew toward them and landed beside Steele.

I'm fine, she wanted to say, but she staggered. Steele caught her before she fell.

"Don't even speak," he said.

Sadie gathered her focus, and speaking slowly, said, "I can still fight."

Steele kissed the top of her head. "I know you can. But we fight together, all right?"

She felt him caress her mental barrier and she let him in without a second thought. It was Steele, after all. A blissful warmth built on the back of her head, and the pain in both her shoulders disappeared. She looked at him and opened her mouth to speak but didn't know what she would say.

He kissed her cheek. "Can you cast?"

"Yes," she said, sounding stronger.

Mordecai, Kaiser, and Damien surrounded them, backs facing each other. The dozen or so demon hunters that were left surrounded them. She scanned each of the princes' bodies, checking for any wounds. She noticed Kaiser shifted his weight on his right leg, and Damien had a shallow gash on his thigh, but aside from that, they didn't seem hurt too much. She didn't care how hurt she was. She was just relieved that none of them had been lethally injured.

The rest of the demon hunters charged at once. Kaiser blocked the bullets that sailed toward them. Some would have hit Mordecai or Damien, or even her and Steele, but Kaiser blocked them all. The three of them fought a duel of their own but at the same time protected each other whenever a demon hunter got too close. Now that she was observing them fight together, she understood why they fought so efficiently and how they avoided injuries like what had befallen her. Unlike her, who had fought pretty much alone and just looked out for her own hide, they fought as a team.

Now as she fought with them, she was a part of that team, and she felt stronger with their aid.

Steele, aside from using his mind to ease her pain, also mentally attacked some of their assailants. A few of the demon hunters doubled over in pain and collapsed to the ground, holding their heads. Some screamed for no apparent reason, swinging their weapons at non-existent attackers.

Sadie recalled her own little torment from Steele's demonstrations and forced back a shudder. She didn't envy the hunters one little bit. In fact, she was glad she wasn't experiencing the images they were succumbing to.

Sadie shook herself from her reverie. She should be fighting with them.

Raising a palm, she shot bolts of fire at some of the demon hunters that got to close to her and her men. She hit one on the chest and let the flames grow, consuming the woman's entire body. Now, she had the princes surrounding her back, so her concentration didn't falter. The risk of being hurt from behind was removed. Steele easing the pain in her shoulders had also helped a lot.

She hit another one in the forearm. Her shot got extinguished immediately, so she tried again and shot the him in his head. His hair combusted. Still, she let the flames grow until it covered his entire body. The man screamed, flailing his arms and running away from her until he fell, writhing on the grass before eventually lying still. The smell of charred remains didn't affect Sadie in the least. If anything, it encouraged her.

Fighting was definitely easier with the princes. She marveled at their efficiency while working together. Even after so many years estranged from each other, they still had that undying, brotherly bond. She had noticed that very bond growing stronger, uniting them again, since coming to her fortress. They all made an incredible team, and she was grateful for it.

When only three of the demon hunters were left, they had their weapons drawn but looked around at their fallen comrades. The three of them looked to each other, hesitating on making the next move.

Damien stepped forward. The hunters seemed to have nearly shat themselves, dropped their weapons, and ran away.

Mordecai shifted to shadow and rushed toward them. Their running figures stopped and tumbled to the ground.

Sadie guessed he had to kill them before they could bring more reinforcements. She wasn't sure if it was completely necessary, but being new to her position of demon queen, the move was probably for the best.

Mordecai reappeared in front of them, his fists bloody. He wiped them against his pants and approached Sadie, looking her up and down.

"I'm fine," she said.

She seemed to always say "I'm fine" every time she was with these guys. She had to think hard as to why they cared, but she didn't want to stray on the thought. She didn't want to assume anything. And she certainly didn't want to get carried away with the idea they truly cared for her in case it would make her decision harder.

"Let's check the place and get out of here," she said.

"Wait," Steele said. He still held her arms and he kept her in place. "Let's tend to your wounds first. I can alleviate the pain, but we also need to stop the bleeding."

Fair point.

"Right," Sadie said, forgetting her injuries because Steele had removed the pain. "But you can leave my mind alone now. I can take it." She smiled, hoping to convince him. She didn't want his attention lingering on her. Although she felt he could be trusted, she didn't want him to see how she felt any more than he already had.

Toward them, toward her sister, toward her whole situation.

He seemed to understand as he nodded and backed off in her mind.

"Thank you," she said.

Damien ripped a piece of his shirt and parted it into two. He wrapped one of her shoulders with the fabric and Kaiser wrapped the other shoulder with the second half.

Steele let go of her and said, "You'll feel the sting again. Are you sure?"

She nodded, and he counted to three, and the pain returned at once. She clenched her jaw. She almost wanted to ask him to go back in there again, but she restrained herself. She didn't want the princes distracted in case of another attack. She would bite against the pain until they were back at the fortress. Then she would do something about it.

They walked back to the small concrete room buried underground and jumped inside. Kaiser helped her get down and she didn't object because she needed it this time. Kaiser summoned a small sphere of light to illuminate the room.

She walked to the nearest shelf and began to slowly scan the trinkets and random items. Daggers were strewn all over the place, but she doubted they were mageblades. Still, she took and examined each one, wincing every time she moved her arms too much. She felt so exhausted. Fatigue crept up her body, and all she wanted to do was sleep.

Aside from weapons and trinkets, numerous boxes lined the walls. The five of them assigned corners and areas for themselves and looked around the items and boxes, hoping to find the artifacts.

Sadie had just opened the fifth box and saw only grenades. She felt like giving up. The last four boxes only contained scraps of metal and plastic. But when Sadie had removed enough grenades to see the hilts of two daggers peeking through the explosives, her breath caught in her throat.

Encouraged, she removed the rest of the grenades. The hilts already looked iridescent from the scant light that entered the room. She took out the daggers. The same ouroboros that was carved into the one her sister had given her was carved on the base of each blade.

They were the exact same blade.

"Guys," she said, her voice quiet. They looked at her and approached her from their respective areas. "I found them."

She handed the weapons to Damien. He looked at the weapons with clear fascination. "I never thought I'd ever see one of these."

Sadie returned to the box and reached in. A single journal was at the bottom. She opened it and scanned through the entries, already knowing full well it was Blair's.

Tears welled up in her eyes, not just for finding

something Blair had left, but for finding a clue that could help her find her sister. At least discover more of the secrets that she held. Sadie closed the book and held it to her chest. Now that she had found the daggers, the only thing she had to do now was find Mara.

SADIE

Sadie sat on her ebony bed, reading through the diary she had found with the mage-blades in Blair's stash. Both her shoulders had been patched up as soon as they returned to the fortress. The shooting pain from the wounds had gone and been replaced with a dull itch under the bandages. By morning, they would be completely healed.

She had Mordecai to thank for that. Because after they got back, he asked for permission to peruse her vault of tomes and search for a particularly strong healing spell that would regenerate her injured tissues and speed the healing process. He had performed the spell himself, although she had noticed he stood a bit wobbly after. He had insisted he was fine, but Sadie knew he only pretended to be fine for her sake. But she was grateful for what he had done, and she definitely owed him.

She wiggled her toes under the sheets as the fireplace on her right crackled and surrounded her with a comforting warmth. She flipped through the pages and read each of Blair's entries—about the fights she had with various demons, about her fellow demon hunters that had betrayed her, and about all sorts of missions to steal relics and artifacts she supposed were rare and lethal.

Her sister had lived such an eventful and dangerous life. Sadie read her sister's stories like they were written by a renowned author. Her eyes flew through the words, and she gripped the journal's edges harder than she should've. It felt like a fiction novel, but it was her sister's life. And knowing the words were Blair's truth made them even more impactful.

After reading about Blair's journey to the former demon queen's tomb to steal the amulet, Sadie flipped through one more page of the journal to find the last of Blair's entries. It was written the same day she found Blair in her apartment that night Mara tried to kill them. Sadie hesitated to read the entry at first, not wanting to finish the journal and lose that connection with her sister.

For the first time, she truly understood what her sister had gone through, the lengths she had taken to protect Sadie and even strangers from the monsters that lived underground. Sadie wanted more of Blair's words. She wanted to feel more connected to her sister. She hoped the last entry might have clues on where Blair could be, so she bit her lip and read it.

> *The amulet rejected me. I know it doesn't fuse with just anyone, but I never thought that I, myself, would be unworthy. Stealing it was a stupid idea. Because of it, I've made a bunch of new enemies. More than I already have.*
>
> *I can sense this won't end well for me.*

Sadie turned the page, already knowing she wouldn't find a continuation, but her heart felt heavier nonetheless. She absently turned the blank pages. She imagined her sister breaching that tomb alone then hiding somewhere in the underworld to wear the amulet, only to be rejected by it. Sadie wondered why her sister even wanted to wear the amulet in the first place. Did Blair want to become demon queen? Was that her intention? And if not, what was?

As she turned the pages, her thoughts and endless questions were interrupted by a piece of paper falling on her lap. She set Blair's journal aside and picked up the note that was folded in two. She opened it to see messily scribbled letters and dark brown smudges on the right side of the note. It looked like dried blood.

She read it.

Dear Sadie,

She stiffened when she read her name. She sat up straighter and continued reading.

If you're reading this, I'm probably dead. Don't come for me. Assume I'm gone and that I'm never coming back.

Her hands began to shake.

And I know you. You won't listen. So, please stay as far away from this as possible. Some of my contacts are working for demons now, and I'm not sure which of them betrayed me.

I don't know who to trust anymore.

Don't trust anyone either, little sister. Please stay safe.

The note's edges crumpled from her grip. Blair couldn't be dead. She read through the words over and over again, lingering on the last three words of the first sentence.

I'm probably dead... I'm probably dead... I'm probably dead...

Sadie's vision blurred over the letters. She didn't know what she was looking for as she kept re-reading the letter. For some reason, she just couldn't move. And things couldn't have ended like that.

A knock sounded on her door. Her trance ended. She looked up and blinked her tears away. "Come in."

The door opened, and Damien entered her chambers. His lips were set in a grim line. He looked a bit grumpy. Sadie supposed it had something to do with her and Kaiser not mentioning Blair was her sister. Or maybe it was her injuries. Either way, she didn't address his expression.

She wasn't in the mood for any of his complaints. Not now.

"If you're here to lecture me or anything, can we reschedule it?" Her voice sounded monotonous and devoid of energy even to her own ears.

Damien must have noticed she wasn't feeling quite well. He frowned, and his eyebrows drew down. "What's wrong? Are you all right?"

"I'm fine," she said. Because she was always *fine*.

Damien didn't buy it. He approached her and looked at what she was still holding—Blair's note to her. He read it and sat on the edge of her bed. Damien rubbed her back.

"I'm sorry," he said in a whisper.

She looked into his eyes and smiled. She placed her hand over his and was grateful that he set aside his own emotions to cater to her bad mood. She wasn't sure what she might have done if he didn't arrive after she had read Blair's letter. She might have burned her room to a crisp or something much, much worse.

"I don't know what to think," she said.

Damien brushed aside a lock of dark hair that

strayed in front of her face and tucked it behind her ear.

"When we lost Cedric," he said. "It was like a hole grew inside my heart. It hurt too much. And the pain." He shook his head. "It never really disappeared."

Sadie didn't answer.

"I'm sorry for getting mad at you," he said.

She squeezed his hand. She scooted closer, so she could lean her head against his shoulder.

He wrapped his arms around her and continued, "The demoness that attacked you, she's an abyssian, isn't she?"

"Yes."

"And she was after your sister, Blair Blackwood, not you." Damien sighed. "I just wished you'd told me," he said roughly, but his voice softened when he added, "I don't want to lose you, Sadie."

She tilted her head back to look at him. He looked back at her and dropped one arm to intertwine his fingers with hers.

His gaze grew stern. "Don't keep information like that from me again."

She couldn't help but smirk. "What are you going to do about it?"

He growled. "Never ask such questions, Sadie. You might not like the answer."

She felt the need to challenge him. "And what answer will that be?"

His look almost made Sadie melt. He didn't answer, only stood and walked to the foot of the bed. He grabbed both her ankles and pulled down. She yelped. Damien removed his shoes and got on the bed, crawling until he was on top of her. He grabbed her wrists and pinned them above her head. She kept still.

"This is your answer?" she asked, keeping eye contact with him. The blue of his eyes swirled into a bright red color. He bent down and kissed her neck. He traced a line of kisses from her collarbone to her shoulder where he gently bit. She gasped as tingles erupted from the bite. It still felt a bit tender from her past injury. Oh, but the pleasure was simply delicious.

His gaze threatened to consume her. "Promise never to keep anything from me ever again."

Sadie opened her mouth to retort that it wasn't his business, that it was her decision to make, but his eyes looked so serious. Pleading, almost. So, she didn't say what she had intended. Instead, she felt the urge to agree.

She wrenched a hand free and held his cheek, caressing his lower lip with her thumb. She smiled and whispered. "I promise."

In answer, he leaned down to kiss her. And boy, did he *kiss* her.

His lips were sultry, powerful, *addictive*. She moaned against his mouth.

He held her neck and let his fingers move down so he could caress her breast. She pressed her body against him, arching her back, wanting more. But when his hand drifted down to lift the hem of her skirt, she reached down and stopped him. She smirked.

"As payment for that promise, I will stop you right now."

At first, he just stared at her with his crimson eyes, seeming confused, but then he began to laugh. "Such a cruel woman."

He kissed her again and she let him. She let him until she couldn't feel her lips anymore. When that happened, she gently pushed him away and pecked the tip of his nose.

"Let me breathe, will you?" she said, teasing.

He smiled. "I wish I didn't have to, but anything you want, my queen."

Damien lay on the pillows beside her, and she snuggled closer to him. She placed her head on his chest as his arms surrounded her. He kissed her forehead and his fingers began to absently trace circles on her arms. The little movements almost drove her crazy, and she debated whether she should let him continue with what he had started earlier.

Sadie chased the thought away. No matter how much she wanted him, now wasn't the time. Besides, her eyes were closing. After the empusa cave, going back to her apartment, and that fight with so many demon hunters, who wouldn't feel exhausted?

She placed her hand on his abdomen. Through his shirt, she traced tiny circles of her own. She heard him hum through her hair.

"You're powerful, you know," he said.

She smiled. "I know."

"I mean it."

She looked up at him and whispered, "I know."

"Everyone wants you. The whole underworld is after you," he said. His arms tightened around her.

What he said flattered her. She felt empowered. But at the same time, because of the way he said it, it felt like everyone wanting her unnerved him. And from the way he held her now, it felt like he was holding on to her for dear life, afraid he would lose her. She took his hand and kissed each of his fingers.

"I'll kill Mara myself," he said. He nudged her hair with his nose. "I'll prove myself worthy of you."

She didn't say anything. It wasn't because his declarations didn't touch her. They definitely did. But she had no intention of relying on others to solve her problems. And she definitely wouldn't let the men she was quickly falling for die in her place.

Falling for.

What was she thinking?

But as she thought about it, she knew it was the

truth. She was falling for Damien. She was falling for Kaiser, too, and Mordecai, and Steele.

Maybe she *had* already fallen for them. Because in her heart, she loved them all. And instead of feeling rattled from that realization, it only filled her with newfound strength. She loved all four of them. And if she ever returned from killing Mara, she would ask all four to stay.

CHAPTER FORTY-ONE

SADIE

*S*adie opened her wardrobe to dress for the day. All she had ever worn since arriving here were satin robes, chemises, and battle dresses. All that royalty stuff. She wondered if there were any casual, outdoor clothes hidden in here somewhere. The wardrobe was so huge, she only ever visited the main chamber and grabbed the first thing she saw.

Her wardrobe had, in total, seven mahogany closet doors lining the walls in equal distances from each other, and their lengths extended from floor to ceiling. She hadn't really opened any of them—it had completely escaped her mind—because of how busy things had been. She looked around the dark-walled and mirror-filled chamber, examining the lack of variety of the displayed clothes. Sleepwear, armor, and five skirts and shirts.

That's it.

Perhaps the former demon queen always had a reason to prepare for battle and little time for recreational activities.

She walked to the leftmost door and twisted the latch. She expected it to be a bit big, but she didn't expect it to be a whole different room. Her breath caught in her throat. It was even larger than the main chamber.

And this room's cream walls were lined with rows of shelves containing shoes of all sorts. Stilettos, wedges, boots, sandals. She gaped as she took in the view. She approached one shelf and grabbed a pair of strapped sandals made of brown leather. She played with the small, brown tassels lining the ankle strap. She liked it so much that she took it with her when she exited the room and opened the second door. Each room was a collection of something. Sweaters, jackets, jeans, skirts, dresses, ballgowns, more armor and battle dresses, and jewelry.

She had just inherited a wardrobe filled with thousands of clothes she probably wouldn't be able to wear in her lifetime.

But that wouldn't stop her from trying.

Sadie returned to the second closet to grab a smooth and flowy, off-shoulder top from the second closet and made her way to the third for a pair of tattered, denim, skinny jeans. She returned to the wardrobe's main chamber to put them on.

Back in Seattle, she rarely got the chance to dress up because of work. She mostly just wore her uniform, and during her days off, she would just wear the usual shirt, leggings, and sneakers because they were comfortable and practical. Especially during emergency calls.

Now, she couldn't contain her happiness. It was her dream come true.

After putting on the blouse and jeans, she sat down on a soft, white futon. As she strapped on the brown sandals, she reached out for her connection with the fortress to call Hobson. And when she walked out of her wardrobe to her room, the butler was already there, standing beside her door.

Hobson looked over her outfit and smiled. "You look dashing, Sadie."

She curtsied, even though she was wearing pants. "Why, thank you."

But she summoned Hobson to her room for a reason. Now that she had the mageblades, she had to know more about Mara, so she could plan on how to use the daggers.

"Have you gained more intel on Mara the past few days?" she asked.

Hobson shook his head. "Sorry, Sadie. It has been very difficult to track her."

Sadie frowned. "I see."

Hobson stood straighter and clasped his hands behind his back. "I sent more ifrits to gather information on her, but they haven't found any, either."

"You what?" Sadie asked, her eyebrows shooting upwards. She wouldn't have been surprised if any of the princes pulled something like this, acting behind her back after what had happened to the last ifrits she had sent after Mara. But this was Hobson. She never actually thought he would do something like this.

The butler kept his eyes on her and said, "I know you didn't want to send more ifrits out after what happened—"

"You're damn right," she said, her words carrying a bite that caused Hobson to flinch.

"But they are your subjects, and they were ready to serve you. They also wanted to do something to avenge their fallen comrades, and they were more than happy to have received the mission."

Sadie didn't answer right away. If she had known that was how the ifrits felt, she would have agreed to let them go. She bit her lip. "Are they safe, at least?"

"Don't worry," Hobson said. "All of them have returned safe and sound. They volunteered, Sadie. They are as furious with Mara as you."

Sadie sighed and glared at him. "I will let this pass, Hobson, but only as a warning. You are not doing anything behind my back ever again."

Hobson walked to her and placed a stony hand on her elbow. "I'm sorry, please forgive me. You were so sad from brutally losing those ifrits to Mara that I thought you wouldn't have allowed more to go. This won't happen again."

Hobson was right. He should've told her what he had planned on doing. But she knew his intentions were good. He only wanted to help and give the ifrits a chance to avenge their fallen friends.

Sadie sucked in a deep breath and smiled on the exhale. "I forgive you." She looked at him pointedly. "But consider yourself warned, Hobson."

The butler relaxed. "Of course."

"You're dismissed, then," Sadie said. "I need to think."

When Hobson left Sadie to her thoughts, she went and sat in front of her vanity table and began to brush her hair. If neither Hobson nor her ifrit spies could gather more info on Mara, then she needed a new plan. She thought about all the resources she had. She had the mageblades, but they were useless if she couldn't find Mara.

She thought about the castle's inhabitants. Her ifrit spies hadn't found anything, and she doubted they would have more progress if she sent more, so just sending ifrits was probably not her best option.

She could send the princes out to gain intel on Mara, but she doubted any of them would want to leave. She suspected none of them would volunteer to go out because that would mean leaving the fortress and, possibly, their chance to become her ally. Besides, she liked to think they had already sent out spies of their own to find Mara to earn her favor.

Then, she thought of the south wing and the ghost of Hecate. It was probably a crazy idea, but what if Hecate knew about Mara or at least some spells that would help Sadie find the demoness?

Technically, this was *Sadie's* fortress now, so that ghost could be her resource. Her feet dragged her out of her room and through the hallways to the south wing. Before she knew it, she felt the familiar chill of the place. The lion heads along the walls always felt like they were watching her, and they definitely made her feel unwelcomed. She grimaced.

When she reached the massive metallic door at the end of the hallway, she paused, hesitating to go in. She thought about the last time she visited Hecate, and she didn't get much useful information or guidance. But maybe her approach was off back then. Maybe if she talked to Hecate in a forceful and more demanding way, she could command the ghost's respect.

She took a deep breath. If she approached this correctly, the results might go in her favor.

Sadie pushed the metallic door open and strode straight to the middle of the courtyard where Hecate's ghost seemed to linger. She approached the marble statue and stood beside it.

Here goes nothing. "Hecate," Sadie said, calling out the ghost's name. Her voice filled the place for a second before reducing the place to silence once more. And it was so silent, her ears rang.

She waited for a while until she heard eerie whispers coming out of one hallway to her right. She wondered where those hallways led. And "hallway" probably wasn't the right term since *tunnel* fit them better.

The wraith floated toward Sadie. Even with its pale, translucent color, and its wide, blank eyes that seemed to look into her soul, the ghost still moved gracefully. Sadie should have felt honored, standing in front of the ghost of the previous demon queen, a great figure of the underworld's history.

But as the ghost approached her, she noticed that, though still translucent, Hecate's ghost had gathered a bit more opacity and color. Sadie's eyebrows shot up. Hecate's eyes weren't completely white like before. They were now red and staring right at her. Sadie kept still.

She had to focus. Remembering her earlier plan of being more forceful and commanding, she took a steadying breath and stood straighter. Hecate had made a lot of enemies and, therefore, might know a lot about how to track them.

When the ghost of the demon queen had reached her, Sadie stood a little straighter. "How do I find Mara?"

Hecate floated in circles around her. She had to turn around to keep up. The ghost whispered her answer, and her voice brought chills down Sadie's spine.

"Nothing is free, youngling."

"What do you want?" Sadie asked.

"Just a little life."

Without asking, Hecate raised her arms and began to cast. Sadie saw bright, red light come out of her body and stream toward the ancient demon queen. And as soon as she noticed, she felt light-headed. It literally felt like the life was being sucked out of her.

Sadie lifted her hands to summon fire. A flame burned in her palm, but it flickered out as soon as it had ignited. The attack had been too fast. It seemed like Hecate had gathered quite a bit of energy while Sadie had been in the castle. She could feel her body growing heavier. All she wanted to do was sleep.

Sadie tried again. She raised her hands to cast. Fire, smoke, anything. But she couldn't concentrate. And for some reason, she couldn't reach her stores of magic. She couldn't feel the amulet's power. Right now, she just felt cold, and sleepy.

She hadn't realized that her feet had been dragging

her to Hecate's direction. She tried to stop herself, but the drowsiness made her want to be closer.

So, this is what it feels like to die. It's not that bad.

Just as she had accepted her fate, the attraction to the ghost stopped. The need to be closer ended.

What just happened? Did she really think she would let this ghost kill her?

Not a chance.

She attempted to stand up, to get up and defend herself, but she couldn't feel her body. When she saw Mordecai race to her side, everything became surreal. She felt so sleepy that she thought all of this was a bizarre dream. She was barely aware of Mordecai casting smoke bars around the ghost to keep her contained.

The prince bent down to carry her. Through closing eyelids, she saw his mouth moving.

Such a sexy mouth.

She might have muttered it. Because he really had *such* a sexy mouth. And she might have passed out in his arms after that, because that was the last thing she remembered.

CHAPTER FORTY-TWO

MORDECAI

*M*ordecai sat beside Sadie's bed, holding her hand as he waited for her to wake up. After just one bad encounter with a ghost, her skin had grown pale, her face grew thinner, and there were dark lines under her eyes. He intertwined his fingers with hers and brought her hand to his mouth to kiss her fingers. Her veins were visible through her skin. His heart broke looking at her like this.

The feisty, sexy woman he had met just got her life force drained by a ghost. And not just a regular ghost. *Hecate*. The most ruthless of demon queens.

Ever since their father arrived and the incident with the abyssians, Mordecai had begun patrolling the walls of the castle during his free time. He had examined traps, checked all sorts of stuff out, and made a mental map of the fortress. He needed to set up contingency plans to protect Sadie if visitors ever dared ambush them again.

This morning, before he had seen Sadie almost die in front of his eyes, he had decided to roam the hallways of the south wing. It was his third time going to the place. He avoided it as much as possible because every time he went there, it seemed like he wasn't alone. Like some kind of sentient power lurked in its halls.

He shifted to smoke, feeling weightless and spacious as he floated through the cold, dark blue walls and looked at the stone gargoyles that hung on them. Most of the hallways here were empty. They didn't even have torches, and if there were, few of them were ever lit. He passed through numerous chambers filled with withering skeletons and torturing mechanisms, but with the place's foreboding atmosphere, it didn't really surprise him.

When he reached a hallway that he hadn't seen before, he changed back to his demon form and walked the hallway. Its tiles were made of marble and not from the same damp bricks that seemed to be the place's style. He examined every part of the area. To anyone else, it might look like a boring and dark hallway, but he remembered every detail and updated the mental map that he had created of the south wing.

After walking for a few minutes, he noticed a faint

light glowing at the end of the hallway. He took his time getting there, a bit wary of the light and what it was. When he reached the end of the hallway, he hadn't expected to see Sadie's life force getting drained by a ghost.

She stood in front of the spectral figure, frozen in place with hands clenched beside her as she attempted to cast but couldn't. The ghost became more and more solid as she sucked bright red light from Sadie's amulet and skin. The ghost's spell heavily affected Sadie. The effects were instantaneous. Her cheeks had already grown hollow and he watched her hair fade from black to grey to white.

Mordecai summoned his enchanted staff out of thin air and cast a cage made of smoke to confine the ghost. He ran to Sadie's side to catch her before she fell.

"Hecate," she said in a whisper. Mordecai stiffened.

He whipped around to see if the ghost really was Hecate. He looked at the ghost with wide eyes. The ghost smirked, not exactly looking like her translucent self anymore.

The first demon queen stood semi-solid before his eyes. The wraith floated, her white hair billowing around her pale, translucent skin. Even in this form, she looked exactly like the portraits he had seen of her in the fortress and his warlock allies' houses.

He gasped. *Impossible.*

As he held Sadie steady in one arm, he held up his enchanted staff and cast smoke bars to contain the ghost. He prepared to defend Sadie if Hecate tried something. But the demoness only snarled at him and disappeared. He stood stock-still for a moment, unsure if he should believe what he had just seen. He got snapped out of his reverie when Sadie grew limp in his arms. He carried her, and she seemed to mutter something before passing out.

He had wasted no time after that. He took her back to her chambers and lay her down on the bed. He darted through every place in the fortress to look for anything that might help.

Now, he rested his head on the bed beside her, feeling completely worthless. He didn't know any spells to cure what Hecate had done to her. Still, he did everything he could. He scanned every page of the grimoires he owned and all those in the fortress's vault and library. He cast every spell that he thought would help, but she still hadn't woken up.

Besides, why was Sadie in the south wing anyway? How had she encountered Hecate? Had she known the demon queen stayed there all along?

As he sulked over what happened to Sadie, he felt a hand brush his hair. He jerked in his seat, snapping his head back to look at Sadie smiling faintly at him.

He had never felt so relieved in his entire life. He

hugged her. When he heard her suck in a breath, he let her go. "Sorry."

"It's okay," she said, voice cracking.

He looked her over. "How are you feeling?"

She took in a deep breath. "I feel like shit."

She held her forearms right in front of her to examine the veins that were visible through her skin.

"I guess I didn't dream it then." She placed her arms to her sides. "How long have I been stuck in bed?"

"Not long. Just this morning," he said. "It's almost midnight now."

"Oh." Her voice was flat and emotionless.

He knew he should probably let her breathe, but he had to know what had happened.

"Sadie," he said. "Did you know all this time that Hecate was in the south wing?"

Sadie sat up, wincing. He reached out to help her, but she waved his help away. She leaned back on her pillows and pulled the blankets to her waist. She fumbled with the fabric of her blanket, picking at a loose thread, and didn't look him in the eyes, only at the numerous paintings on her bedroom walls, as she confirmed his suspicion.

"Yes. I've known for a while."

He shook his head. This woman was unbelievable. His hands balled into fists, and he wanted to shout at her. But he swallowed down his emotions. He knew he should give her a break after what she had gone through.

I'll get angry later.

As much as he tried, though, he had never been particularly good at suppressing his emotions. And they boiled over.

"Why would you keep this from us?" he asked through clenched teeth.

She glared at him and crossed her arms. "One: because it wasn't your business. Two: because I'm only choosing *one* of you as an ally, and I might not be able to trust the other three with the information."

Mordecai scoffed. He knew her reasoning made sense, but what resounded most in his ears was the fact that she still didn't trust him *enough*. "And now look what happened! You almost *died* because you have fucking trust issues."

She frowned. "Even you can't deny my logic."

Mordecai almost laughed. The woman had just come from a near-death experience and still she found the energy to hold her ground. She never lost, did she? Well, neither did he.

"It doesn't matter!" he said, and his voice continued to rise in volume.

Sadie's voice rose to match his. "What do you mean it doesn't matter?"

He threw his arms up and groaned. "Because!"

She huffed out a breath. "Damn it, Mordecai! I don't know why you're shouting!"

He stood, looking down at her. "Because I'm furious that the woman I love would expose herself to so much danger!"

Mordecai shut his mouth, catching himself, and sat back down and leaned back on his chair. Dumbstruck, he stared at her. He was never one to use that word. Did he really just say that?

Sadie gaped at him.

"I—" she said but closed her mouth and didn't speak. He supposed she didn't expect that he, of all people, would admit to loving her.

He kept staring at her. Even with pale skin and even paler hair, she still looked absolutely beautiful. Her dark, wide eyes looked at him in disbelief, and he could've drowned in them. He always drowned in them.

Sadie pouted and bit her lip in the way that drove him crazy.

What the hell.

He rushed to her and kissed her. He cupped both her cheeks with his hands. At first, she didn't respond, but it didn't take long for her to wrap her arms around his neck and lean in to him. She moaned against his mouth. He growled and deepened his kisses.

This woman.

He couldn't believe he had nearly lost her. He

wouldn't let it happen again. Because he knew within himself that if something happened to her, his whole world would be destroyed. His lips left hers only so he could move back, sit on the edge of the bed, and wrap her in his arms. He rested his chin on the top of her head and brushed her hair.

"We'll tackle Mara together."

"I won't let you," she said, but her voice was muffled since her head was pressed against his chest. Still, he didn't let go. He needed her in his arms right now. Right now, and possibly for a long time. She was his strength, and if he let go, he wouldn't make it.

"I won't take no for an answer," he said. "I care about you too much."

She laughed and looked up at him. "*And* my power."

He moved back and looked into her eyes. "Sadie, I care about you, not your power. *You.*" He kissed her one more time. "I love you."

Her eyes seemed to soften. She smiled and placed a hand on his cheek. "I believe you." His body leaned in to her touch. "And I love you, too."

He positioned himself to lay on the bed next to her. He reached for her hand and guided her, so she could lie down again and snuggle against him. She had said she loved him, and he couldn't ask for anything better than that. But he also knew in his heart that if she loved him, she loved his brothers, too. He snorted.

This alliance thing had gotten so out of hand now. He wondered what she would do.

Sadie placed a hand on his chest and lay her head in the crook of his neck. "I won't let you die for me. You didn't ask for this madness."

He laughed under his breath. "Well, this is who we are." He kissed her forehead. "We're all mad and surrounded by madness. We breathe it."

She chuckled. "Is that so?"

His lips smiled against her hair. Everything felt so right when he was with her. "You're the demon queen," he said. "You and anyone who loves you needs to expect a little crazy."

"Still," she said. "I don't want Mara to hurt you."

He shook his head. "At this point, you can't escape me. I won't let you out of my sight." He held her tighter. "You're not going through this alone."

CHAPTER FORTY-THREE

SADIE

"What are you all doing here? Get out!" Sadie screamed as she lay in bed, surrounded by all her men. She kept trying to get them to leave, but they just wouldn't listen.

After finding out that she had finally woken up, the other three guys—Steele, Kaiser, and Damien—had barged into her room to find her and Mordecai sitting on the bed together and eating popcorn while watching a horror film.

Earlier, she had convinced Mordecai to do a movie marathon with her even when he had urged her to rest. Her room didn't have a television set, but all Mordecai had to do was go to the human world and get one. It didn't even take him twenty minutes. As soon as he arrived and began setting up the TV, he still tried to get her to go back to bed.

"All I did the entire day was sleep," she said. "Unless you want me to spend the night alone, you should probably let me call Hobson, so I could ask him to get us some popcorn and soda."

He just muttered something under his breath and disappeared into shadow. About ten minutes after, a knock came on her door and she opened it to find him carrying a huge tray with a bowl of popcorn and two grape soda cans on it.

Sadie and Mordecai had just reached the part of the movie where the first of the main characters die in the woods when the other three princes flung the door open without knocking. Sadie raised her arms, prepared to attack the intruders. She let down her guard when she saw the guys enter, looking wide-eyed and out-of-breath. She blindly reached an arm through the pillows to find the remote control, and when she had, she turned the television off.

She held the bowl of popcorn toward the guys. "Popcorn?"

Damien growled. "Are you serious?"

Steele arched an eyebrow and walked toward her to get the bowl from her hands. "Why, thank you very much."

"You almost died, Sadie," Kaiser said, glaring at her. "We heard what happened."

"Here we go," she said, rolling her eyes. "I don't have time for this."

"Well," Steele said, putting a handful of popcorn in his mouth. "You should've thought about that before getting yourself nearly killed." He got a bit of powdered cheese on his white tunic, so he handed her back the bowl of popcorn to brush off the powdery mess.

Damien faced Mordecai. "Did you at least catch Hecate?"

She should have guessed Mordecai had told them the news. She sighed, hoping he would have done it tomorrow instead. Or a week after. Or never.

Mordecai reached over the bowl on her lap to grab some more popcorn. "No."

Kaiser scoffed. "And?"

Mordecai looked at him blankly.

"How can you just sit here and do nothing?" Damien asked, nose flaring.

"I already sent out my warlock spies to search for her," Mordecai said. "And I'm not doing nothing, I'm watching a movie."

Damien's voice rose. "In that case, we're all okay then!"

Sadie placed the bowl of popcorn on her bedside table and stood. "That's it. That's enough." She took Damien and Kaiser's hands to lead them out the door, but it only felt like she was pulling two trucks with her arms. "Leave."

Mordecai leaned back against the headboard. "She's right, guys. Leave."

She pointed a finger at him. "You, too." She motioned to them all. "Everyone, leave, right now. Or I'm not choosing any of you at *all.*"

Kaiser crossed his arms. "I'm not leaving until you tell us what the hell you were doing in the south wing, Sadie."

The other three stood their ground, waiting for an answer.

"Fine." She sat down on her bed and motioned to the numerous chairs in her chamber. "Sit down, then."

When the princes had made themselves comfortable, Sadie crossed her legs and began talking. "I've known about Hecate for a while now, and I didn't tell you because I was only going to choose one ally."

All their lips seemed to be uniformly set in a grim line.

She continued. "I have the mageblades now, and all I got to do is find Mara. I figured Hecate could help with that."

Kaiser snorted. "Well, we found out how that went, didn't we?"

"Yes, we did," she said, rolling her eyes. "Now, you know what I was doing there. Happy?"

"And what are you planning to do if your plan worked and you found out where Mara is?" Damien asked.

"Then I guess I'll set out and find her."

"All by yourself?"

"Of course, it's my fight," she said, jutting her chin out a little bit.

Kaiser sighed. "We know and admit that you're powerful, Sadie. But Mara is dangerous. She could legitimately kill you."

"That's a possibility. But I'm ready to do whatever it takes to kill Mara." She looked each of them in the eye to show them that she meant it. "For my sister."

The four of them sat or stood straighter, and they collectively growled at her, loudly declaring their protests over each other's voices.

"You can't just say that," Damien said.

"You're not going anywhere by yourself," Kaiser said.

"I'll just shift to shadow, find her, and kill her myself," Mordecai said.

It became so obvious that they were all related. She groaned and stood up. "Stop it!"

To make sure they listened, she raised her arms to the side and let fire flare in her arms for a second before extinguishing it. They shut their mouths.

"Don't you realize you're all so... so..." She scrunched her nose. "Annoying!"

They didn't answer, only simultaneously looked at each other and grumbled to themselves.

At last, Damien sighed. He was the first one to

realize their berating wasn't doing any good. "I guess she's right," he said, dropping his arms to his side. Maybe were just stressing her out a little bit."

"A little bit?" she asked, placing her hands on her hips.

"Fine. A lot," he said. He faced his brothers. "And I assume none of you want to leave this room, so why don't we just come up with a plan. We can scold her all we want, but we all know we won't win."

Steele muttered under his breath, "Which is unfair."

"I heard that," she said.

Steele winked at her.

She just shook her head and faced Damien. "Thank you."

Mordecai got up from her bed. He walked to a chair, flipped it around and sat, resting his arms on the backrest. "What's the plan then, Captain?"

She shrugged. "I'm not really sure. I'm out of ideas."

"Mara lives in the Vale," Kaiser said. "How about we make a portal to get there?"

Steele placed an ankle over his knee and leaned back on the couch. "Well, has anyone ever been to the Vale?" He looked at his brothers, but they only gave him blank stares. "I see. So, no one's really been there. But there are maps somewhere. I guess, we just have to learn the geography."

"Right," Damien said. "We'd definitely have the

element of surprise on our side, assuming Mara isn't expecting us. But how do we find her, exactly?"

Steele scratched the back of his head. "That's—a big hole in the plan."

"I can scout the area and find her," Mordecai said in suggestion.

"That could work," Kaiser said. "And if she finds us first, we could handle her. Especially with two mageblades."

"Right. There's that," Mordecai said. "Now that you brought it up, we have two mageblades. Sadie gets the first one, of course, but who gets the second one?"

"I think Kaiser should hold it," Damien said. "He's the fastest among the four of us and would reach Sadie first if something did happen."

Steele and Mordecai agreed.

Sadie listened to them with a fixed gaze, marveling at the way they strategized together. They all talked so amiably toward each other. She hoped it was always like this between them.

"That's assuming Mara would be anywhere in the Vale," Mordecai said. "What if she was near here? Or in the human world? We'll only be wasting our time if we teleport to the Vale blindly."

Kaiser shrugged. "Well, so far, it's better than nothing."

Damien rubbed his chin with his fingers. "That's actually very possible. The night I met with a spy to procure for me the location of the mageblades, I saw shadows shifting in the forest. I thought it was just me, but the imp mentioned he had seen it too. It could be Mara or a scout she sent."

Sadie piped up. "If that's the case, I think I should be bait."

"No," Kaiser said. "Out of the question."

She rolled her eyes. "What? It's easy enough. And it makes sense."

"You're not doing it."

"Well, you're not the boss of me. Besides, Mara's cunning. She definitely has a scout out there somewhere just observing the fortress if she's not doing it herself. She would have eyes on me."

"You're probably right, Sadie." Damien grimaced. "But let's brainstorm some more. We'll think of a better idea."

Sadie shook her head. "Think about it. *If*, and I think it very likely, Mara has eyes on the fortress, or if she's around here somewhere, she's not going to come out unless she thinks she has the upper hand."

Damien and Kaiser ran their fingers through their hair.

Steele crinkled his nose. "This is crazy. You could really get hurt, Sadie."

She looked at Mordecai. His eyebrows were drawn downward, but he didn't protest. He just sat there silently. She knew he was on the same page. When

Mordecai caught her gaze, he nodded, albeit begrudgingly. "She's right… as much as I hate the idea."

Kaiser sighed. "Fine."

"It's a good plan," Sadie said.

Steele winced. "Keep telling yourself that. Though, I'll be there, don't worry."

Damien acquiesced, too. "It's the best plan we have." He looked at her. "But if we're going to do this, you have to bring Pyra with you. And we'll just be along the castle perimeter. I'll be scouting from there, and the four of us will be ready to fight if it comes to it."

She smiled at them, thankful for their help and support.

That wasn't so bad.

She took a deep breath. Now, it was just a matter of her walking into the eye of the storm.

CHAPTER FORTY-FOUR

SADIE

*S*adie walked through the fog outside her fortress, beyond the boundary of her lands. Underneath her white, long-sleeved satin robe, she wore a leather corset to serve as lightweight armor. It was the more practical choice since it wouldn't be as conspicuous as real armor. She also wore leather leggings, hoping the material would help make it harder for sharp weapons to get to her skin.

She had to walk carefully because the forest floor in this part of the woods was strewn with sharp rock fragments and the spiny surface roots of evergreen trees. Treading the forest was especially hard with sneakers on because the rock fragments grew bigger and sharper the deeper she went into the woods.

This part of the forest was connected to the place

she and Damien had walked one time—the one with the golden and silver trees. It was hard to believe, because the forest she was walking through now felt like a different place.

Aside from the evergreens, there were also cherry trees and narrow hornbeams, and they were spread so far apart that the forest canopy was close to nonexistent. If she had visited this place under normal circumstances—perhaps in a time where she wasn't purposefully serving as bait for a deadly demoness—she would have enjoyed how the pink cherry blossoms melded with the red-orange glow of the crystals that covered the ceiling of the underworld, and how the fog accentuated the glow.

Pyra trudged through the forest floor alongside her. Fallen twigs broke and rocks cracked under the massive dragon's feet. Pyra snorted, causing a puff of smoke to billow out of her nostrils. She sensed her dragon was tense from the way her tail stood at attention, twitching at the slightest noises. One time, Pyra snapped her head back and almost roared out a stream of fire toward a green rabbit scurrying away to hide in the bushes. She did it again when a squirrel, that looked more like a bat, ran up a tree. Pyra was so tense that Sadie had to keep close and pet her every once in a while, just to calm her.

"Easy girl. I know what we're doing."

As Pyra remained attentive with her surroundings, Sadie looked through the fog as well, wary of any kind of movement. She focused to stay alert for any surprise attack.

The guys were nearby, hiding in the part of the forest that was still inside her fortress's compound. She had specifically told them to stay where they were and that it was as far as they could get. They were *not* to cross the boundary until she had instructed them to. They would only go to her aid when she had said so. She and the princes had agreed beforehand that she would whisper her instructions to Damien.

A cold breeze flew past her, and Sadie hugged herself and rubbed her arms. She looked around, walking as ordinarily as possible, pretending to take a normal stroll through the forest with her dragon. But underneath the billowy sleeve of her robe, she clutched the mageblade's handle tighter. She knew that even if the princes were nearby and, literally, one call away, ready with their powerful demon magic, they still might not get to her in time. So, she prepared herself for an ambush. Out here, she was pretty much alone.

Of course, there was a chance that Mara wouldn't show up. After all, their mission for today just relied on the assumption that Mara was lying in wait. It was even possible that the demoness didn't even set up spies or scouts along the fortress's perimeter, but she doubted that was the case.

As she walked and waded through the fog, she felt Steele claw against her mental barrier. She knew it was Steele because of the way he scratched softly to get into her mental block, and it had become familiar to her. She heard Steele's deep voice whisper in her mind at the same time Pyra stiffened and halted in her tracks beside her.

"Damien says someone's there."

Sadie stopped walking and peered through the fog. She clutched the mageblade so tightly her nails dug into her palm. Then, through the mist, she saw it—a silhouette.

Steele spoke inside her mind again. This time, instead of a mere warning, she heard a touch of pleading mixed in his voice. "Now's probably a good time for us to step up, Sadie."

But she didn't think so.

"No," she said in reply, muttering under her breath, knowing Damien was listening. Hell, he probably could smell her right now. "You'll blow our cover. Wait for my signal."

Sadie reconstructed her mental barrier, so she could keep Steele out of her thoughts. And based on the lack of handsome demons flying to her rescue, she concluded they listened to her instructions.

In front of her, the silhouette grew bigger, and as it got closer, she began to distinguish a pony-tailed figure limping toward her and Pyra. The woman seemed to notice them since the figure stopped and seemed to scrutinize Sadie and her dragon through the fog.

The woman called out. "Sadie?"

Sadie's breath caught in her throat. She tried to speak but couldn't find her voice. She took a steadying breath. "Blair?"

Beside her, Pyra let out a soft growl. Damien had suggested she bring the dragon because Pyra had sensed Mara's pretense the last time the demoness had taken Blair's form. The dragon's reaction now meant that this woman was yet another impostor. Still, Sadie couldn't be sure. The woman could still be Blair, and Pyra would still be a bit aggressive toward her because she was unfamiliar.

Sadie placed a hand on the dragon's spiky neck and rubbed the rough hide. She reached out with her mind to plead with the dragon to keep calm and let things happen as they should. That Pyra should let Sadie handle the situation. She didn't want their plan to fall to pieces. She breathed out a sigh of relief when the dragon seemed to understand and calmed down.

Blair walked closer, keeping her weight on one leg as she limped toward them. Her sister's clothes looked different from the last time she saw her back at her apartment in Seattle. Now, Blair just wore a regular purple sweatshirt and jeans, although her clothes were filthy, and some parts of the fabric were tattered. Sadie's heart twisted.

When Blair seemed to realize her guess was correct, that it was indeed Sadie that she saw, Blair's lips opened in a wide-toothed grin.

"Sadie!" she said and bounded toward her. Blair hugged her tightly. "You're alive. You're all right."

Sadie kept her arms to her sides and tried to gently extricate herself from Blair's embrace. She wasn't falling for this charade again. This woman looked exactly like her sister, and she sounded exactly like her. She even smelled like the Victoria's Secret perfume her sister was obsessed with.

But Sadie couldn't trust what she was seeing or hearing or smelling. She couldn't even trust was she was feeling. It was hard, but she had to be objective. This was too much a coincidence for this person to be really her sister.

Blair stepped back from her and frowned. "What's wrong with you?"

Even though she believed this wasn't Blair, she still had to act friendly, that she believed she wasn't Mara and was Blair after all. She had to trick her that she was being fooled.

She smiled. "Nothing. I—I just can't believe you're actually here."

Blair didn't look convinced. "Did you know what I had to endure to get here? It was lucky I still had an arsodite stone with me, so I could teleport myself to where you were supposed to be. But somehow, it didn't work, and I got transported to Beijing. The residents took me to—" She shut her mouth, interrupted by what she must have seen in Sadie's expression, whatever it was.

"Oh," Blair said, wrapping her arms around herself. Her body seemed to droop. "You think I'm Mara."

Sadie stepped closer. "No, Blair."

Blair shook her head. "It's okay, I understand. Demonesses are tricky, vile creatures." She smiled, but her eyes looked sad. "Sadie, I'm so proud of you. You're such a fast learner. You were always the smart one."

Deep down, she knew it wasn't Blair. But it was difficult giving up seeing her face, hearing her voice, even if it was a lie.

She pretended to let her guard down. "Is it really you, Blair?"

The impostor arched an eyebrow. "What do you think?"

Her tone and body language reminded her too much of Blair that Sadie's act threatened to waver. She hugged Blair's look-a-like instead.

"I can't believe it," she said, letting out fake laughter.

Blair tightened her arms around her that Sadie had difficulty swallowing.

"Look at you now, little sister," Blair said as they embraced. "You're *royalty*. I knew you could handle this power and assume the throne as the demon queen. That's why I gave you the pendant."

Sadie looked over Blair's shoulder and admired how the shades of sunset cast the entire forest with bright orange light. It made the forest look like it was on fire. The fog added to the effect, giving the illusion of smoke. She took a deep breath, enjoying this moment even though she knew it wasn't real.

"I miss you, Blair," she said while gripping the mageblade's handle tighter. She stealthily drew the artifact out of her sleeve.

"I hope you're happy, wherever you are," she whispered. A tear streaked down her cheek as she thrust the dagger into the impostor's abdomen.

Blair screamed.

Sadie stepped back, for a second wondering if she had just killed her sister. But Blair clutched Sadie's shoulders, gritting her teeth through the pain. Blair's face dissolved, her features morphing into a paler complexion and sharper bone structure, revealing Mara's face that twisted in an ugly snarl.

Blair's figure grew taller, slowly shifting to the demoness's original height.

The mageblade was already hilt-deep in the demoness's abdomen, and dark blood seeped through the sweatshirt. The wound underneath hissed as if the dagger burned Mara's skin. Sadie gripped the artifact tighter and buried it deeper into Mara's body, resolving to end this bitch once and for all.

CHAPTER FORTY-FIVE

SADIE

*M*ara's face crumpled as her red, bat wings unfolded, and her thorny tail uncoiled from her back. She grunted and opened her mouth. Sadie saw a small, yellow orb form inside the demoness's throat. Knowing she was about to get burned to a crisp, she removed the dagger from Mara's abdomen and immediately climbed onto Pyra's back.

The dragon leapt to the side, avoiding the stream of fire that erupted from Mara's mouth. Pyra rose on her hind legs and attempted to crush the demoness under her feet and claws. But Mara unsheathed her sword and, with one hand on her abdomen, slashed Pyra's thigh.

The dragon roared as her legs buckled. Sadie held on to one spike on Pyra's neck, but the demoness sliced with her sword again, and the dragon leapt away. Sadie wasn't able to keep her hold this time, and she fell to the ground. She tucked her arms and rolled to decrease the impact. She saw Pyra swipe her tail at Mara, but the demoness spread her wings and flew away from the thorn-covered attack.

The demoness held her sword high and soared toward her.

Sadie hastily stood and ducked as a ball of fire shot past her shoulder. The sleeve of her robe caught fire. She patted it repeatedly in an attempt to quench the flames, but it didn't work. So, she just tore it off and threw it aside. Now, merely clad in her leather corset and stretch pants, she shivered as a cold breeze brushed her shoulders.

Above her, Mara cast multiple balls of fire in her direction. The demoness still held a hand against the stab wound on her abdomen. Sadie smirked, even as she leapt from side to side, ducking and turning to avoid the fireballs. Some flew too closely by her that the hot temperature singed her skin.

She had dodged what seemed like the twelfth fireball when she turned around and wasn't able to dodge the next one. It hit her abdomen. The sheer force of the impact knocked her off her feet. She groaned, folding in on herself, but immediately got up, not wanting Mara to have any kind of advantage.

As she stood, the demoness used the distraction to

rip the red fabric of her own top, exposing her gashed midriff that spurted black ichor. Mara cast a small flame in her hand and used it to burn her skin. The demoness winced as she closed the wound by cauterizing it.

Sadie held her dagger high as Mara tended to her wound. She ran as fast as she could, preparing to strike under the demoness's sternum. But Mara looked up with enough time to fly up and avoid her attack.

in the air, high enough for Mara to fly above the trees, she heard the demoness yell out something. Then, she heard rumbling all around her, followed by the arrival of imps and horned skeletons. There were hundreds of them running from behind trees and shrubbery. They sprinted toward her.

She braced herself. If Mara brought company, she had backup of her own. She couldn't see the princes yet, but she knew they were on their way.

She sheathed the mageblade, so she could cast fire. The flames licked at her forearms. She held her arms in front of her and shot long streams of fire at the imps. Those that got hit stopped in their tracks, flailing their arms as they let out high-pitched shrieks. Eventually, they dropped to the ground, unmoving. She kept casting, trying to stop more of them. But there were too many. She looked to her left and to her right and saw more of them coming out from the trees and running toward the fortress.

Her eyes widened, knowing the barrier wouldn't be able to hold off this many soldiers. When she caught sight of her four men flying through the trees from the fortress's direction, she breathed out a sigh of relief. She knew she wouldn't be able to handle all of this by herself, and she was grateful that the princes were there to help her defend her home.

Mordecai shifted to shadow and appeared behind a skeleton that immediately burst into pieces of bone.

Sadie returned her attention to six of Mara's soldiers that surrounded her. The skeletons held spears and scimitars, attacking her in unison.

One of them swung its sword at her head. She sidestepped and whirled around the skeleton. She swung her sword over and over again, decapitating the skeleton and amputating its limbs. She aimed at its torso, swinging her sword, hacking at the bones until the skeleton stopped moving. She concentrated on disarming the skeleton soldiers first and moved on to dismembering them one by one.

To her right, Pyra and the princes fought their way toward her.

The men fought side by side, their backs to each other. They kept an eye on each other as they fought, protecting one another each time a dangerous blow got in too close.

Kaiser moved at inhuman speed, dismantling skeletons with his bare hands. Damien held his flaming broadsword high, fighting the imps with it and killing most of them with just one blow. Steele fought with his hammer, bashing skeletons and breaking them apart. Mordecai held his enchanted staff, casting cages made of smoke, ensnaring enemies to dampen the flow of soldiers running toward them. They defeated wave after wave of soldiers, and Mordecai would release those that he caged so they could fight all over again.

Beside them, Pyra crushed imps and skeletons under her weight. She swung her tail back and forth, demolishing skeletons and sending imps flying through the air. The dragon also opened her maw every now and again to breathe fire at the enemies. As they fought, they moved closer and closer to her. There were just too many soldiers.

She would have dropped her weapon then and there to just watch them fight because she thought they were brilliant. But imps rushed to her with their axes and hammers, and she had to dispatch them. It didn't take long.

She slashed an imp's throat and stabbed another from behind, between its shoulder blades. Taking a deep breath, she wiped a bead of sweat that dripped down her hairline. As she prepared to fight more soldiers, a weight slammed against her from behind and arms locked around her.

It was Mara.

The demoness's claws dug around her arms as she flew her away from the melee. Sadie gritted her teeth and thrashed, desperately trying to get away from Mara's hold.

The demoness hissed in her ear. "You want to escape, do you?"

Mara's nails dug deeper into Sadie's arms. Warm liquid trickled down her skin.

"Why didn't you say so?" Mara careened to the nearest tree. The demoness slammed Sadie against its trunk.

Her chest and forehead hit the tree. Her ears rang from the impact. She fell and hit the forest floor face-first and rolled. She spasmed in pain. Still, her survival instincts kicked in.

As she tried to stand up, a jagged rock sliced her right palm. She sucked in a breath. She stood, even though she had a hard time keeping her balance and focus. She limped around the tree, finding shelter behind it just as the demoness cast a beam of fire on the spot Sadie had fallen.

Sadie crouched behind the trunk. She held her palms up and gritted her teeth as she parted the beam of fire Mara shot at the tree. Her head throbbed and the slice on her palm stung. She coughed. Her breathing turned more and more labored by the second. She must have broken a few ribs in the collision with the tree.

Breathing be damned, she got up and ran through the woods as the tree behind her creaked and crackled as it caught fire and threatened to fall on her. She ran in the direction she hoped the princes were. She hid behind the largest tree she could see.

Behind her, more trees had caught fire, but she had spread quite a bit of distance between her and the demoness. The sound of fire crackling and trees falling on the ground came from behind her. To her right were the sounds of screaming and weapons clashing against one another.

Crouching behind the trunk, she fought to catch her breath. When the sound of a fallen branch snapped, she inched a bit to her right and leaned her head to the left to see what had made the noise. Mara's wings folded as the demoness landed on the ground. She looked from left to right and began to walk slowly.

"Your cowardice just proves you're unfit for the throne."

Sadie breathed through her nose, trying to quiet her panting as she unsheathed the mageblade. She pressed her left palm on the ground and grabbed a fistful of dirt and gravel.

"Come out, come out, demon queen," Mara said, voice set in a mocking tone.

Sadie slightly shifted from her hiding place, so the demoness wouldn't see her.

Mara approached the tree she currently hid in.

Sadie took slower and softer breaths, growing more conscious if she breathed too loudly.

Once the demoness got close enough, Sadie took in a deep breath and dashed in front of Mara from behind the tree. She threw a handful of dirt into Mara's eyes.

The demoness let out a screeching noise, holding her hands out reflexively to block the dirt that was already in her eyes. "You fucking bitch! I'm going to enjoy ripping you apart, piece by piece."

Sadie turned to the side and slashed Mara's arm. She turned again to slash Mara's side. The demoness snarled, holding out a hand to claw at her, but she was no longer there. She crouched and dealt another gash on the demoness's calf. When she came face-to-face with Mara again, the demoness's eyes were opened, but they were teary and red.

Mara bared her teeth and glared at her. "You pest. Why are you so hard to kill?" She extended her claws and slashed at her.

Sadie sidestepped. "I could ask you the same thing."

Mara snarled and shot a ball of fire at her.

She ducked and swung her dagger at Mara. But the

demoness spread her wings and flew back, dodging her blow. Sadie sprinted closer to Mara and jabbed with her dagger. As they fought, she noticed that the demoness's eyes sometimes darted to where the princes were, and they widened, and Mara would hasten her attacks as if she was in a rush.

Sadie scoffed. Even if she wouldn't be able to kill Mara, maybe all she had to do was stall long enough for the princes to get to her and frighten Mara to death.

As Sadie reached out to slash the demoness's throat with the dagger, Mara grabbed ahold of her wrist. Mara wrapped her arms around Sadie, pinning her arms to her sides. Sadie flicked her wrist, using the dagger that she held to wound Mara's thigh. The demoness winced but otherwise maintained her hold on her.

"I will get that amulet, one way or another," Mara said against her ear.

She bent her knee to step on Mara's foot. Her world began to swirl and morph into blurry shapes. Somewhere in the distance, she heard one of the princes scream her name.

She looked up in time to see her four princes staring at her with wide eyes. Kaiser's figure ran toward her, but his form began to blur as well. The out of focus shapes vanished, and she was cast in darkness.

She felt the familiar weightlessness of going through a portal as she disappeared, sucked into the void between worlds to wherever Mara was taking her.

CHAPTER FORTY-SIX

KAISER

Kaiser held the skeleton's ribs with his bare hands. He pulled, dismantling the torso. He could kill one with little effort, but Mara had brought so many soldiers that his blue tunic was now drenched in sweat. When the head of the skeleton he had just dispatched dropped on the ground by his foot, he kicked it away and watched it land near Mara and Sadie fighting in the distance.

An overwhelming need to get to her overcame him as Mara flew Sadie into the forest, farther away from them. His mind became swarmed with the very real danger that the demoness was killing the woman he loved and cared for. But another group of skeletons and imps had approached him.

No matter, he would hack his way through the

rising horde to get to her, and he knew his brothers would do the same.

He had made his way through the onslaught of creatures in time to watch Mara conjure a portal with Sadie wrapped in the clutches of her hold.

Adrenaline coursed through his veins. Helpless, he screamed her name. More imps came his way, and he slashed through them as desperation took over. He needed to get to her before the portal closed. Knowing his time ran short, and Sadie would soon be left to a dire fate, he left the fight to rush after her.

Sadie disappeared into the portal and was gone.

His knees hit the ground, and he pounded his fists into the dirt, gravel, and roots of trees. "No!"

He stood, breathing heavily, and tore through the imps and skeletons that emerged from within the shadows of the woods. There was no thought to how he would kill them. He just moved and fought on instinct. And he couldn't seem to stop screaming. All he saw was red.

Hundreds of demons were still alive and fighting. Some of them surrounded the fortress, blocked by an invisible barrier. They clawed at it, forcing themselves in. Some were able to get through because of their sheer number. Thankfully, metal vines protruded from the fortress ground and caught them, immediately strangling the imps and taking down the skeletons. But some got away and ran toward the fortress gate.

Kaiser growled and sprinted toward them. Within in a split second, he stood in front of them.

He dodged their knives, swords, and axes, catching imps by the ankles and throwing them away from the castle compound and above the forest canopy. Grabbing a rib from a skeleton's torso, he flung it against the fortress gate, decapitating its head. He slammed the body on his leg, breaking the torso in two. Using the sharp shards of bone, he stabbed the remaining imps charging him straight through their hearts.

Blood covered everything.

Pyra roared, drawing Kaiser's attention to her. A circle of dead imps and broken bones surrounded her on the ground, but she was losing ground with the group that still surrounded her. Light glistened off the gashes from the attacks the creature had endured, and it seemed she was growing weaker.

An imp dug its small axe in one of her hind legs. The dragon roared and snapped her head, catching the imp between her teeth and shaking her head from side to side. The imp's body flew from Pyra's mouth and landed on the ground beside Kaiser's feet. More climbed onto the dragon's body, hacking and slicing as they moved.

Kaiser ran to Pyra's aid, reaching her side as her legs gave out from under her.

"Hang on, Pyra."

He grabbed the imps by their necks, hair, arms or legs, and threw them in the forest's direction.

"Can you fly?" he asked.

She let out a small growling purr and lowered her head to the ground. Taking that as a yes, he climbed onto her back as more imps ran toward them.

"*F*ly, Pyra!" Kaiser said.

The dragon roared and opened her wings, flapping a few times before taking to air.

Kaiser hadn't ridden a dragon in a long time, but it was a skill difficult to forget. He held one of the spikes on Pyra's neck and leaned to the left to urge her to fly left. Up here, he could see there were still hundreds of imps and skeletons left.

The outlook wasn't good. A decision had to be made. Stay here and protect the fortress, whatever the cost, or grab his brothers and search for Sadie before it was too late.

If Sadie managed to survive, she would likely be furious he and his brothers didn't stay behind to take care of the fortress.

Then again, if anything were to happen to Sadie, Kaiser knew not a single one of his brothers would be able to live with themselves if she fell at the hands of Mara.

Somehow, almost as in answer, Hobson and a fleet of ifrits emerged onto the fortress grounds just inside of the gate, easily dispatching dozens of imps and skeletons within moments.

Kaiser let out a sigh of relief and led Pyra beyond the fortress to help his brothers. Most of the soldiers were gathered around his brothers who stood back-to-back with each other.

He yelled, "Look out!"

They looked up at him, spread their wings, and flew up beside him and Pyra. He reached out to pat the side of Pyra's neck, a gesture dragon-owners often did to urge their pets to blow out fire. At first, Pyra didn't seem to understand his intention, but then the dragon reared her head back.

A rumble came from underneath him, along with a strong torrent of hot, blue fire that erupted from Pyra's mouth.

Warmth enveloped him. As the fire consumed most of the soldiers and plants below them, the other demons ran deeper into the forest or toward the direction of the castle. At first, there were sounds of screaming and clashing metal, but eventually, the screaming ended. Meanwhile, the stream of fire coming out of Pyra's mouth showed no signs of ending.

She must be as pissed and worried as we are.

Remind me not to piss you off...

He patted the dragon's neck again. "It's all right, now. Good girl."

Kaiser led Pyra back to the ground. They landed on ashes and charred land. He climbed off Pyra's back as Mordecai, Steele, and Damien landed on the ground around him.

Steele coughed as his feet touched the ground and swatted his hand in front of his face. "Even their ashes smell bad."

Kaiser approached him. "Make a portal. Now."

Steele nodded and held up his hands, muttering a spell.

"Where to?" Steele asked. "I got the entrance ready but not the exit gate," he said through gritted teeth. Keeping one palm up, he used the other to wipe a bead of sweat from his forehead.

"I can still feel her," Kaiser said, pacing. He closed his eyes and concentrated. He reached out for the connection he had with Sadie and used it to track where she was. He saw it in his mind's eye. A rocky desert filled with lines of magma. There's no other place like it.

"The Vale," he said, opening his eyes to look at his brothers.

Steele sucked in a breath. "It has been ages since I've done this. And I've only ever flown above the Vale or through it. I've never really set foot there."

Kaiser knew that portal magic was rare. He and his

brothers could do it, but mostly just between here and the human world. Sometimes, they didn't even know where they would land when they got there. They could also use it to go to places they were familiar with, but only if they tried hard enough.

The Vale was a mostly barren land. He never found use in going there before, and he guessed his brothers felt the same. Now, they were paying for it. They could all fly to the Vale, but it would take half a day to get there. Unless they didn't want to get there and save Sadie quickly—which was impossible—they needed to make a portal.

Around them, dozens of warriors peeked out and came out from the trees, perhaps because the fire attack had finally ended. They began to run toward him and his brothers again. Pyra swiped her tail to send them flying back to the forest.

"Keep doing that," Damien said to Steele. "We'll handle the rest."

"Right." Steele said, not even looking at them. "Don't die."

Without a word, Mordecai shifted to smoke. He flew toward the soldiers, killing them with little effort. Damien's blazing broadsword hacked at imps and dismantled more skeletons. Behind them, inside the fortress boundaries, Hobson and the ifrits picked at the soldiers who succeeded in getting through the barrier.

"Kaiser," Steele said.

He looked at his brother who had his face scrunched up in concentration as he created the portal. "I need a map of the Vale. Do you think you can point out where she is in the Vale if you're looking at a map?"

Kaiser thought for a second and nodded.

"Good. There might be some in the library," Steele said through clenched teeth. "Run like you've never run before."

Kaiser kicked the sternum of the skeleton running toward him and turned to give it a kick to its head. He punched through the skeleton's ribs and it exploded into pieces of bone.

Once he had the room, he flew toward the fortress. Landing on the ramparts, he ran the length to a tower and jumped inside. He ran through the halls so fast that the walls blurred. Once he reached the double doors leading to the library, he flung them open and quickly scanned the massive book cases.

Where the hell is that map?

CHAPTER FORTY-SEVEN

SADIE

*S*adie's knees hit the ground. She held her arms out to protect herself from the harsh landing, but it didn't do any good, especially with her already-cut palm and exhausted body. The mageblade clattered on the cold stone, not far from where she had landed. She scrambled to her feet, wincing as she stood, and prepared for Mara's next attack.

But the demoness didn't seem to be in any kind of hurry. Instead, she leaned against the back wall, calmly staring at her. The demoness seemed unfazed by the cuts on her arm, calf, and sides, and the blood soaking though the fabric of her robe.

Mara smirked. "No one to save you now."

Whatever makes you sleep at night...

She lifted her palms in front of her and summoned a torrent of fire, aiming it toward Mara. But the demoness flicked her wrist and the fire Sadie had casted sputtered out like it was nothing.

Sadie stared wide-eyed at her hands and tried again. She summoned another beam of fire and urged the flames to grow brighter, for the temperature to rise. The color changed from red to blue.

Mara held her palm up again. Sadie's casting faltered. The flames died in her hand.

Sadie gasped. "What—"

Mara snarled. "You're in *my* domain now."

I'm in the Vale?

Sadie's gaze quickly raked over the area. The cavern had dark gaping tunnel entrances lining its walls. Its ceiling was covered with light blue and green crystals, much like the crystal-filled ceiling above her fortress but fewer and with a less variety of colors.

For some reason, the light that emanated from them wasn't blue or green, but red, and it cast them in blood-colored light. She supposed it was because the entire cavern was hewn of red stone.

She could feel the crystals pulsing with magic. But it wasn't the kind of magic she felt with her pendant. This magic felt weak, diminishing, and reluctant. It felt like it wanted to break free from the constraints of the crystals.

In the spaces between the tunnels, numerous swords and daggers adorned the walls. At least she would have a weapon if she lost her dagger. But that meant Mara did too.

She took in a steadying breath as Mara smiled at her.

"Do you like my collection?" she gestured around her.

"It's okay. I've seen better though."

Mara walked away from the cavern wall and Sadie took note of a circular space behind the demoness. It was framed with smaller blue and green crystals.

Sadie peered at the odd frame. It looked like it was meant to house something. Inside the circle of wall, there was a small shape embossed in it. Her eyebrows shot up when she realized it was exactly the same size as the ruby on her chest.

Mara followed her gaze to the strange area and traced her fingers along the empty, teardrop-shaped hole.

"It should have already been complete." Mara glared at her. "But you Blackwoods are the worst."

Sadie subtly walked to her left, in the direction the dagger had fallen. She taunted Mara to distract her. "You don't deserve to be queen."

Mara laughed. "Tell me, who exactly *deserves* to be the demon queen? It's such a rotten world down here. Violence, torture, darkness. It's all there is in the underworld." She crossed her arms and arched an eyebrow. "And you're cocky for a weak human. You deserve the title even less than me."

Sadie balled her hands into fists but didn't speak.

Mara didn't seem to notice. The demoness kept tracing the outline of the ruby with her fingers. "You know, I can end this, Sadie."

"Yeah? How?" Sadie asked, her tone sounding more curious than she felt. She only had to keep Mara talking anyway. She crept closer to the mageblade.

Mara gazed at the space she had meant to put the amulet in, caressing the edges as she would a lover.

"I can make you wake up at home with no memory of this." Mara paused and smiled. "I can even give Blair back."

"Right," Sadie said, curling her lips.

"Oh, you don't believe me?" Mara asked and stood straighter.

Mara rolled her head and, as she did so, her face morphed, her features gradually shifting into Blair's. The demoness's height shrank, and her wings and tail subsided, until they completely disappeared. She transformed, and it resembled Blair's exact physique. Even her tattered and bloody robe changed into the sweatshirt from earlier.

"Don't you miss me, Sadie?" her sister asked. "Don't you want to have your old life back? Don't you want *me* back?"

But the woman wasn't her sister. Still, her throat

tightened. This person's eyes looked at her, pleaded with her, as if she wanted to be free—to be with her.

Oh, Blair.

The woman standing before her looked exactly like her sister. She sounded *exactly* like her sister.

But this was all wrong. This wasn't Blair. And although Sadie's heart broke, she wasn't tempted by Mara's offer at all. Her sister had never felt so unreachable as she did now. Sadie also knew that the underworld, even the human world, would suffer if Mara got ahold of the power in the amulet.

"No," she said, holding her head up high. "You will never be queen. Not on my watch."

She threw herself to the side, closing the remaining distance between her and the dagger. She picked it up and stood in time to see Blair's face twisted in an ugly snarl, baring her teeth at her.

"Then you should know that your sister suffered. Even more than your ifrit bitches."

Blair yanked one longsword from the wall and advanced on Sadie. When Blair reached her, she swung the sword at her neck.

Sadie held up her dagger. Her arm shook with the impact as she parried the blow. She relaxed her arm, giving into the sword's weight, and twisted aside. She jabbed her dagger at Blair, aiming for her already-wounded side, but Blair blocked it. She swung again, aiming for her abdomen this time.

But, again, Blair blocked the blow.

Sadie couldn't believe she fought her own sister. Although she knew that this wasn't really Blair, it still shattered her inside, seeing her sister's face, knowing that Blair died in her apartment, alone and in tremendous pain. That she died at the hands of this vile woman.

She bit the inside of her cheek, trying to keep the tears from falling. She would let them fall later. Right now, she needed to focus on defeating this impostor, so she could avenge her sister and herself.

She held out her hand and cast fire toward Blair's face, but Blair ducked and dodged the fire. She tried again, shooting out bolts of fire here and there, but the magic in the room seemed to help her opponent.

Mara in Blair's form swung the sword at Sadie's head, and she crouched to avoid getting decapitated. She cast fire again and hit her stomach, but it didn't seem to hurt. The sweater caught fire and eventually died, exposing fake-Blair's midriff, but the skin remained smooth and unharmed.

She swung again, and Sadie held up her dagger, her arm getting closer to Blair's weapon every time she parried a blow. This time, Blair's weapon cut her hand. She winced. It was difficult fighting with a dagger when one's opponent fought with a sword. And a pretty long one at that.

Blair swung again, aiming for her neck. Sadie

turned around in time to avoid getting her throat slit but not in time to prevent her cheek from getting gashed by Blair's blade. A lock of her dark hair fell to the ground. She definitely needed a longer weapon.

While dodging and blocking all of her fake sister's advances, she retreated toward the weapons. She reached to grab a weapon from the wall when Mara in Blair's form stopped moving and held out her arms to the side. Numerous daggers from the wall shook, dislodged from where they hung, and shot toward Sadie. Their glinting tips were aimed straight at her.

Her eyes widened. She reflexively dropped face-first to the ground and rolled aside to where the least daggers flew. A blade whizzed past her and cut her shoulder. She flinched.

She stood and looked at Blair's form who held out her hands again. Sadie prepared herself this time. As Blair caught a flying dagger with her hand, Sadie raised her own dagger. Blair dashed toward her.

She blocked the first swing from Blair's sword but not the second one from the dagger which sliced her left thigh. She stepped back and jabbed at her fake sister's chest, but her attack was parried.

It was difficult enough blocking blows from a longsword. Blocking attacks from both a longsword and a dagger wasn't much easier. She barely held her own. And in contrast, Mara seemed to grow stronger.

Whatever magic this cavern contained, it was obviously helping the demoness.

Mara tirelessly wielded her sword, swinging it at her constantly. Sadie was pushed back as she labored to fend off the blows.

When the demoness swung her sword in an overhead swipe, Sadie ducked and raised her sword to block it. At the same time, Blair thrust her dagger hilt-deep into Sadie's thigh. She cried out as her legs failed her and she fell on her back.

Blair struck again, so Sadie held up the mageblade. She blocked the blow, but the tip of Blair's sword sliced her wrist. Her grip on her dagger failed, and it clattered on the floor beside her. She reached out for it, but Blair stepped on her wounded wrist. Sadie screamed as the pain rocked through her entire body. Her thigh throbbed from the dagger stuck in her flesh.

Blair bent down to pick up the mageblade and examined it with a snarl.

"This weapon really stings, huh?" Blair looked down on her and smirked. "I haven't felt pain like this in years. I'm not used to it anymore."

She twirled the mageblade with her fingers. She stopped playing with the only hope Sadie had of killing her and summoned energy from the cavern's reserves of weird magic. Blue light streamed from the crystals to Blair's hands and collected on the iridescent metal of the dagger. It filled the dagger completely until the mageblade shattered into pieces.

"Poof," Blair said. "No more."

Sadie's breathing grew ragged as she looked up at her sister's likeness.

"Enough talk," Blair said, smiling like a deranged serial killer, and raised her sword to strike the final blow.

CHAPTER FORTY-EIGHT

SADIE

*S*adie wrapped her free hand around Blair's ankle and yanked as hard as she could. She threw Blair off balance, knocking her to the ground.

She promptly rolled aside, away from Blair's sword. With the dagger still embedded in her leg, she stood and limped toward the cavern wall. She removed two swords and held them in front of her.

Blair recovered, glaring at her, and ran to her with sword held high. She screamed. "Why won't you just die?"

Sadie parried her blow with the sword on her right hand. Her sister swung again, and she blocked it. Through clenched teeth, she said, "Maybe you're supposed to die first."

She swung her sword and hit Blair's shoulder. She swung again and struck Blair's neck. She jabbed her sword at Blair's chest, but it felt like she was hitting hard stone. Her sister winced but wasn't really wounded.

Meanwhile, she blocked Blair's blows with increasing effort. She kept her mind away from the stinging wound on her thigh, trying her best to focus on not dying. She gritted her teeth as she parried more of Blair's blows.

This isn't working.

She had to think of another plan. She couldn't defend herself like this forever. She was rapidly losing what strength she had. Besides, her injured leg affected her concentration and limited her movements. And the demoness's strength showed no signs of wavering. She had to get out of there, catch her breath, and think of a new, effective plan.

Now that her mageblade was gone, she was in deep shit.

She quickly glanced at the numerous tunnels that shot off from the room she was in. Though she didn't know where they led, since there were so many, maybe she could use them to play to her advantage. She could probably hide in one of them, assuming those tunnels wouldn't just lead to dead ends. If they *did* lead to dead ends, well, then... she would just think about that when it happened. But for now, those tunnels were her best shot.

Staring at her sister's form, she took a deep breath

and hoped her MMA training wouldn't fail her. As she blocked another blow, she retreated to collect momentum and sprinted toward Blair.

Roundhouse kick, here we go.

She jumped with her wounded leg, and the pain almost made her collapse to the ground. She screamed and pushed through the pain. She twisted in the air and kicked Blair's head with her uninjured leg. Blair's head snapped back, and she staggered.

Sadie landed on her good leg and ran to whatever tunnel she would end up reaching first. Well, it was more like half-limped, half-ran. As soon as she entered one, she cast a stream of fire behind her. She cast smoke, too, in hopes of blocking Blair's vision.

Her pulse raced, and she fought to keep up with her breathing. Her leg throbbed as she ran, and warm liquid trickled down her leg. But even with the pain, she felt so relieved that the tunnel kept going on and on. There weren't any signs of it being a dead end—yet.

With the ever-increasing pain in her leg, she reconsidered removing the blade and creating a makeshift tourniquet. But stopping now would give Mara the advantage and time to catch up. Plus, Sadie really didn't have anything to use that would apply enough pressure on the wound to stop the bleeding. She bit her cheek against the pain and forced herself to move faster.

Ahead of her, the tunnel split into two. She moved faster, reaching into the amulet's magic reserve to shoot fire and smoke behind her. As she got closer to the entrance of the two tunnels, a dagger flew past her, dangerously close to her head. She ran faster.

When she reached the divergence, she entered the left tunnel with little thought. The tunnel bent to the left, and she came across another divergence. This time, there were three tunnels. She took the one in the middle and kept running.

The temperature rose the deeper she went. Warm smoke began to seep out of the dull-red ground and walls. Along the way, the number of cracks within the smooth surfaces gradually grew in number until they webbed the walls in semi-intricate designs. As she kept going, she noticed the end of the tunnel she ran through glowed a distinct orange.

That was when she allowed herself to slow down.

Panting, she crept toward the orange glow. It seemed like Mara wasn't able to follow her here. Either that, or it was just a matter of time before she would creep out from the shadows, sauntering like a beast having finally trapped its prey.

But the tunnel behind her was only dark and quiet. There were no sounds or signs of pursuit. Her heart rammed against her chest. Warily, she approached the end of the tunnel turning out to be, yet again, another turn.

Turning the corner, the tunnel walls made of the same cracked stone, but the cracks were wider and filled with flowing magma. The ceiling had the exact same appearance. She wondered why the magma didn't drip to the ground even though she was grateful it didn't.

The floor of the tunnel was the odd one out, since it was made from the same dull-red granite of the tunnels she had run through to get here.

Her skin tingled as a sensation of déjà vu wiggled through her senses. The walls and heat felt familiar, though she didn't know why.

The sound of footsteps behind her pulled her from her thoughts. Following that came the sound of metal scratching stone, and Blair's voice.

"Sadie," she said in a singsong tone. "Come out, come out, wherever you are."

So much for not being followed.

The screeching sound of metal against stone grew louder.

"You keep hiding from me," she said, high-pitched and mocking.

Sadie walked faster, limping and following the magma-lined walls toward whatever lay waiting beyond the tunnel. She had only walked a few feet, but beads of sweat already dripped down her face, chest, and back. The heat made her light-headed. She had to find somewhere to hide fast. She needed to regroup, make a new plan, and hopefully surprise the demoness with an attack.

Meanwhile, Blair's voice kept taunting her. "You can't run forever, Sadie."

There was another bend in the tunnel. When she turned it, she came across charred footprints on the ground.

At first, she stopped dead in her tracks, tightly clutching both swords in her hands. Her eyes darted from left to right, looking around for the beast that caused the prints. She remembered the day she had walked with Damien in the forest and met a hellhound.

That's why they seemed familiar. The lines of magma were similar to the hellhound's hide. Maybe there was one nearby.

Desperate for a plan, she reached out with her magic. She walked and searched using her connection to the amulet until she felt a tug on her magic. She hoped it was a hellhound responding. She strode deeper into the cave, keeping her weight on her good leg, following whatever force tugged on her pendant.

When she reached a small cavern with walls and ceilings filled with lines of flowing magma, a massive beast prowled toward her from the far wall. A grumble emanated from the hellhound's chest. It looked far bigger than the creature she saw in the woods, and it stared at her with such piercing, orange eyes that she debated whether her plan was a good one.

Blair's voice rang out from the tunnel behind her, and all she could do was pray she made the right decision. She already had one enemy that was nearly impossible to kill. If worse came to worst, she wouldn't know how to kill a hellhound. She hoped her magic worked on the creature, because right now, she couldn't think of any more plans.

"Sadie," Blair said with her annoying, mocking tone. "Stop running, will you? I still have to skin you alive, like I did your sister."

That horrific little—

Sadie curled her fingers until her nails bit her palms. She reached toward her connection with the hellhound. With all her might, she communicated her need for help. For vengeance. She pleaded with the creature.

Help me. Kill Mara. She repeated that thought over and over again.

The hellhound tilted its head, and Sadie mentally crossed her fingers that this one was an ally and not like the afflicted ice dragon that had attacked the ifrit village.

Please, please, please.

The creature remained unresponsive, but she kept pleading with him in her thoughts.

She gripped her weapons in front of her until her

knuckles turned white. She faced the tunnel where Blair would soon enter. When the demoness finally walked into the small, magma-covered cavern, she smiled at her. "There you are. You made quite a chase."

She ignored her and kept communicating with the hellhound. *Please, help me. You're my only hope.*

Just as she thought her plan had failed, and that she was probably going to die, the hellhound snarled at Blair and leapt at her, digging its sharp teeth into Blair's calf, though it didn't draw any blood.

Blair yelped as she fell to the ground. The hellhound shook its head with Blair's leg still between its teeth. Blair struck her sword against the hellhound's back, but it only clanged on hard stone. The act seemed to have gone completely unnoticed to the beast.

While her opponent was distracted, she dropped her weapons to the ground and took a deep breath. She remembered that time Mara had first ambushed her fortress with the imps and the skeletons. She had been able to weave a smoke sword and use it. Before her casting wavered, she had wounded Mara with it. Maybe she could do it again now.

She closed her eyes and tapped into the magic the amulet contained. She created her weapon from smoke. When she finished crafting it, she looked at the weapon she created, all grey and smoke and heavy in her hand like a real sword.

Her eyes drifted to her sister's figure and her sister's face as Mara tried her best to fend off the hellhound. Blair slammed her sword against the creature, but it harmlessly ricocheted off the hellhound's leg.

Sadie didn't waste another second. She sprinted toward her opponent and funneled all her magic, rage, and power into the smoke sword.

She drove it into Blair's heart.

Her sister's eyes widened. Blair clutched the smoke sword embedded in her chest and looked at it and then Sadie. She reeled back and quickly turned back into her own form as the hellhound let loose of her leg. The demoness opened her mouth, and it seemed like she wanted to say something, but only blood poured out between her lips.

Sadie extracted the sword from the demoness's chest only to plunge it into her body again. And even then, she kneeled over the body and stabbed again and again, for everything Mara took from her, knowing Blair would finally be freed when Mara was dead. For being the constant pain in the ass that she had proven herself to be.

Sadie's vision blurred, and she let out a painful, rage-filled cry. She continued to shove the sword into Mara's body, because it was the kind of death Mara deserved. And it felt good to give Blair the vengeance she deserved.

Mara's body grew still.

Sadie released the weapon, and it dissipated. Her shoulders heaved as she looked at the demoness's corpse. Her eyes burned.

I'm sorry, Blair. I'm so, so sorry. Now you can be free.

She stared up at the ceiling, not even caring that there was no sky. And she laughed even as tears ran down her cheeks.

It was over. But it wasn't enough.

She no longer had her sister. But now that she had avenged her death, at least Blair wasn't stuck in a demon's body anymore. That was all she could have done, and she had finally succeeded.

The hellhound approached her and licked her hand with its sloppy, warm tongue. She smiled as she petted the creature. "Thank you. You saved my life."

Footsteps echoed from the tunnel she had come from. She stiffened. Climbing to her feet, she prepared herself for another fight.

As the princes came into view, she released the breath she had been holding, and the energy that burned through her veins eased. She relaxed, dropping her arms to her sides. She smiled at them, grateful for them showing up, albeit a moment too late. Still, grateful nonetheless.

"It's about time you got off your asses," she said, smiling at each of them.

Kaiser, who stood at the head of the group, looked from the demoness's body to her. His shoulders drooped, and he hurried toward her. He held her against his chest. "You're safe."

She stepped away from him. "Do you think I would just let Mara kill me?"

She peeked around Kaiser to see Mordecai smirking. "That's my girl."

"I've been waiting for a moment to say this my entire life," Steele said. He opened his arms. "Group hug!"

He bounded toward her and Kaiser and wrapped them in a bear hug.

Damien and Mordecai laughed but joined in. More tears streamed down Sadie's face, but they were happy tears. She smiled.

It's over now.

CHAPTER FORTY-NINE

SADIE

*S*adie stepped out of the bathroom and into her massive wardrobe. She let her plush red robe fall to the floor, and she put on the black, silk evening gown she had chosen to wear for the night. She looked at her reflection in the mirror, brushing her fingers through the soft skirt that flowed to the floor. She traced the spirals of red and gold brocade covering the bodice and grabbed the black tiara from the top of her vanity table.

After putting it on, she turned her head from side to side. Its tiny diamonds glowed and sparkled along its sable spirals as they caught the light with her movement.

She took in a steadying breath. Even though she had just faced a demoness, she felt more nervous about what was ahead.

Tonight, the princes waited in her study. It was time for her announcement on who she had chosen as an ally among the four princes. She had a difficult time choosing, because all of them had fought by her side. All of them had risked everything for her. Now, she wasn't sure if they would like her decision.

When she walked out to her chambers, she found Steele sitting comfortably on her bed. He whistled as soon as he saw her.

She laughed as she approached him. "You could never stay out of my room."

He stood, his eyes wandering all over her body. She stood a little taller.

"I was hoping there was something I could do," he said. "You know, so I could be sure to sway you in my direction." He winked at her.

She chuckled. He was such a rule-breaker, but she was glad he was here with her right now. His mere presence eased her nerves.

"My mind is made up, Steele," she said. "There's no longer anything you can do."

He sighed and took her hand from his cheek and kissed it. With a smile, he offered his arm. She placed her hand in the crook of his elbow, and he led her out to the sitting room where the other guys were.

When Steele opened the double doors to her study, she entered to find Mordecai wearing a white shirt and black jacket, sitting on an ornately carved alder chair. His feet rested on the long, rectangular, wooden table in front of him, and his head rested on the back of the chair. An open book lay on top of his face.

Steele walked toward him and patted his shoulder. Mordecai jerked up and the book covering his face fell on the floor. He looked at the door to where Sadie stood. He yawned and stretched out his arms. "Done deciding?"

To her left, Damien stood in front of a bookshelf and glared at Steele. "You better not be cheating."

Kaiser sat on the largest orange sofa, his elbow resting on the armrest, his temple against his knuckles. He also glared at Steele. "Did you go to her room?"

Steele just shrugged and didn't answer.

Sadie smiled at their antics. They had no idea what she was going to say. She wondered how they would react after she made her announcement. She really hoped they would agree with her decision.

She walked in the middle of the room and took in a deep breath.

Now or never...

"Listen," she said.

Damien and Kaiser instantly left their Steele-glaring to give her their full attention. She looked at each of them. Steele and Damien stood beside each other on her right, Kaiser sat on the orange couch in front of her, and she twisted around to watch

Mordecai pick up the fallen book, place it on the table, and walk to sit beside Kaiser.

She cleared her throat. "You all know why you're here tonight. It's time for me to announce who I choose as an ally. But before that, I would like to say a few words."

Her palms began to sweat, and she wiped them on her skirt. She clasped them in front of her. They felt cold, but she continued.

"At first, I didn't trust any of you, but you proved to me, time and time again, that I could. You've done so much for me. You stood by me against your father, against Mara, Evangeline, and even when you found out about Hecate, you still chose me. You saved my life so many times, and you defended this fortress when I couldn't. I'll always be grateful for that."

She looked at Kaiser who sat ramrod straight on the sofa, looking at her as if he didn't want to miss a word she said.

"Kaiser, I've known you the longest. And out of all your brothers, you're the most protective. Annoyingly so." She smiled. "But you also saved me from Mara when my friend betrayed me. And many more times after that. You were the one who led me here, to my fortress."

The fondness she saw reflected in his eyes reassured her that she had made the right decision.

"You brought me home. I don't know how I could ever repay you for that."

Kaiser nodded. "It was my pleasure and duty, Sadie. I would do it one thousand times more if necessary."

Sadie smiled and turned to Damien.

"Damien," she said.

His posture was straight and imposing with his hands behind his back.

"You have very impressive allies. Practically speaking, choosing you would be very advantageous, since an alliance with you would mean an alliance with them, too. You're diplomatic, and you're a leader."

His chest puffed out a little bit.

"But you're also very protective, and I don't want you looming over my head all the time, because I can protect myself. You have to trust me on that."

Damien's lips tightened, but he nodded.

"I also worry that you're too focused on your diplomatic ties that you forget to have fun," she said.

His eyebrows knitted together.

Mordecai scoffed. "Oh, he can have fun all right. Just not very good at it."

Damien crinkled his nose, and Kaiser and Steele laughed. Sadie shook her head and chuckled.

"You have also saved me and protected me. I owe you my gratitude."

Damien nodded. "Of course, Sadie. Anything for you."

"Next." She looked at Steele.

He leaned on the bookcase with his arms crossed in front of him.

"Steele," she said.

When he heard his name, he stood tall and placed his arms at his sides.

She smiled and winked. "Good news or bad news first?"

He narrowed his eyes. "Bad news."

Sadie played with her bottom lip. "Well, it seems like you're the polar opposite of Damien. You have *way* too much fun." She placed her hands on her hips. "It's like you don't take anything seriously."

He pouted, and she tried not to smile.

"But you bring so much light and humor to this dark place," she said, features softening toward him. "You make me laugh, and I think you're a wonderful stress-reliever."

Steele smirked.

"At first, your power was my concern," she said. "Because it's so dangerous, I couldn't be sure you wouldn't use it against me. But you surprised me by teaching me how to block it. And it proved to me that I could trust you. And I owe you my thanks for all that you have done for me."

"I will always be there for you, Sadie. Regardless of who you choose."

That made her smile and it encouraged her even more. She held her head higher. Lastly, she turned her attention to Mordecai who leaned back on the sofa. He seemed rather disinterested in what she had to say about the others. He sat with his arms crossed over his chest and a bored expression on his face. His eyes connected with hers, and her knees damn near gave out from under her.

"Mordecai," she said. "You have a certain darkness around you. A certain danger. I wonder if that's something to look for in an ally."

He frowned.

"You're strict when you train me, but I'm thankful for that because you push me beyond my limits. Because of your training, I finally learned how to sustain a smoke sword. And that helped me defeat Mara. I'll always be grateful to you for that."

She smiled at him, and he nodded in acknowledgement.

"So, having said that," she said, looking at each of them in turn. "The person I choose is…"

Steele and Damien stood straighter, if that was even possible, and Kaiser and Mordecai leaned forward in their seats.

She cleared her throat. "I choose you all." She braced herself for their reaction.

They gaped at her, speechless.

She opened her mouth and talked, afraid their silence meant they disagreed.

"I never thought it would be this hard." She nibbled on her lower lip. "But I can't imagine how empty this fortress would be if three of you were gone."

Kaiser stood and growled. "Demons don't share, Sadie."

Damien walked to her and held her elbow. "He's right. This is a bad idea."

"Why?" she asked. "How is sending the three of you home a better choice?"

"I—" Damien said, stuttering. "Just—I refuse to share you." He tugged on her arm. "Come with me, right now."

Kaiser blocked his path. "You're not taking her anywhere."

Mordecai yawned. "Even if you do, you realize I can just go to her and break her out anytime I want, right? Then I could take her somewhere you would never find her."

Kaiser snarled at him. "I'd like to see you try."

Oh, for the love of...

"Enough!" Sadie snapped her arm back from Damien's grip. "No one is taking me anywhere. Why are you all so against this?"

"Not me," Steele said. "I'm fine with the idea."

The other three men gawked at him.

"What?" he said. "Think about it. We've never been this close since Cedric died. We're just learning to be a team again, to be brothers again. Am I the only one who wants that?"

No one spoke for a while.

Damien sighed. "I suppose you have a point."

"I've nothing against it," Mordecai said, still leaning back on the chair, looking very much relaxed. "I never really planned on following her decision anyway. My original plan was to kidnap her whether she chose to ally with me or not."

She glared at him. "You had better be kidding."

He shrugged. "I wasn't, but, if you choose all of us, that's pretty convenient too. No more kidnapping plots. And that's fine with me." He stretched out his legs.

She rolled her eyes and looked at Kaiser pleadingly. "Will you stay? Please?"

He grumbled but held her hand. "If it's what you want."

She smiled at him.

Mordecai stood. He approached her and lifted her over his shoulder without warning.

She yelped. "What do you think you're doing, Mordecai?"

"Why, to consummate the deal," he said. "What else would I be doing?"

"What?" Her voice came out an octave higher as her eyes widened.

She looked at the other princes over Mordecai's shoulder. Kaiser and Damien looked at each other, but they were smiling and shaking their heads.

Steele wrinkled his nose. "Why didn't I think of that?"

Kaiser and Damien burst out laughing. Mordecai didn't put her down, and he showed no signs of stopping, but she found herself laughing, too.

CHAPTER FIFTY

SADIE

*S*adie spread a thick wool blanket over the cool blue grass beside the makeshift tent she and Kaiser had made out of more wool blankets. Well, it looked more a fortress than a tent, if she was being honest. They had been hanging out in her bedroom when she suggested they go camping in her backyard.

"Finally," she said, brushing her hands together. "I didn't think we would take this long setting up."

She plopped down on the green blanket and patted the space beside her. Kaiser obliged and sat down on the blanket. She lay down, and Kaiser did the same. Above her, glinting bronze strips spiraled and intersected each other. They formed multiple circular patterns and steepled at the center. The structure looked like the skeleton of a huge circus tent.

Surrounding the metallic frames were honeysuckle and sweet pea vines, winding and twisting around the bars, racing their way to the spire at the top. Through the spaces between the vine-covered metal strips, and through the thin canopies of the red cedars and cypress trees, she gazed at the underworld night sky riddled with colorful crystals.

She and Kaiser lay in silence. With these crystals, she traced constellations of her own, and as she did so, she felt Kaiser's fingers intertwine with hers. She smiled and shifted to look at him.

"Do you have constellations here in the under-world?" she asked.

He propped himself up with his elbow and raised her hand to kiss her knuckles. The corner of his eyes crinkled as he smiled at her. "Actually, yes."

"Really?" she asked, eyebrows lifting up. "Will you show them to me?"

Kaiser lay back down again. He beckoned her closer. She obliged him.

"See that bright blue glow, right there?" he asked as he pointed at the crystal stars. "And the two small orange ones on the left?"

She traced a line between his index finger and the underworld sky. "Mm-hmm. I see it."

"Imagine that as a bow," he said. "Now, there are four yellow gems that form a horizontal line, intersecting the bow." He briefly looked at her and back to the sky. "Imagine it as an arrow."

She nodded to herself. "I'm following."

"Beside it, there are tiny, white gems that form a person holding the bow," he said. "Four for the head, three on each arm, five for the body, two on the right leg, and three on the left."

She counted with him, and she saw how the collection of stars resembled a body that held a bow and arrow. "I love this constellation already."

He laughed under his breath. "The constellation's called The Archer. Legend says it points to the one thing you want most in life, if you follow it."

Her eyes lit up. "Oh?"

"Many travelers in the underworld had attempted to," he said, continuing his story. "And they've all gotten lost. They never came back. It's one of this world's greatest mysteries."

"Interesting," she said. "What else is there?"

"Hmm... let's see." He pointed somewhere farther down from the Archer. "There."

Again, she followed with her eyes.

"See that group of purple stars that form the outline of a bulb?" he asked.

She searched for a few seconds before she found it. "Yes."

"There are tiny white stars surrounding the bulb. Imagine them as tentacles."

"All right," she said.

"That one's called the Kraken."

"Yeah?" she asked. "And what's the story behind that?"

"No story. It just looks like a giant squid."

She giggled. "I see."

She sighed and sat up. Her eyes wandered to the statue in the middle of the garden, a few meters past the large skeleton of a tent.

The day after she had defeated Mara, she had asked Hobson to have a statue of Blair erected in her private gardens. The marble statue of her sister wore a pony tail, her sister's usual black shirt, leather jacket, and jeans. It held a mageblade in one hand, and a small, circular orb in the other—the orb Blair had given her the last time she saw her, the one that had teleported her to the abandoned house.

Blair's statue was fierce, like the warrior and hero she truly was. That was how she wanted to remember her sister.

Kaiser sat up, too, and brushed her hair with his fingers. "I know you must really miss her."

"I'm just happy that she's finally free of Mara," she said before giving him a sad smile. "And wherever she is right now, I bet she's kicking ass."

Kaiser laughed softly. He caressed her neck with the back of his hand. "And I know she's proud of you, too."

"Thank you," she said.

He began to play with her hair, twisting her locks with his fingers.

She started to talk about a different topic, because if they kept talking about her sister, she would probably lose it.

"I can't believe the four of you agreed to share me," she said.

He groaned. "No need to remind me."

"Why? You work so well together," she said, laughing at his reaction. "Besides, don't you think it's nice that you've become brothers again since you arrived at the fortress?"

"I suppose," he said begrudgingly. He wrapped his arms around her and nudged her neck with his nose. "But I'm not saying it would be easy." He placed his hands on her waist to pull her closer. "It'll be very hard for me to share such an amazing woman like yourself."

"I'm blushing," she said, giggling. "But you're going to have to. From now on, we're on the same team. All of us." She moved away to look into his eyes. "Promise me you'll try."

He sighed. "I promise. For my queen, anything."

She smiled and moved away from Kaiser a little bit, so she could remove her maroon cape. She was beginning to sweat from the warm night. She kicked off her white slippers and wiggled her toes in bliss. The night breeze kissed her bare shoulders, and she folded the thin skirt of her red gown, so she could sit more comfortably. Beside her, Kaiser also discarded his black vest and folded the sleeves of his brown tunic, revealing well-toned, muscular arms. She folded her cape and placed it behind them to be used as a makeshift pillow.

Kaiser lay his head down on the folded cape. He held his arms out to her and guided her, so she could rest her head on his arms.

She sighed happily. "This feels nice."

"I could stay like this forever, Sadie," he said, murmuring against her hair. "At least I'd have you all to myself."

She playfully hit his chest. "You promised."

"What? They could sit on those stone benches right there."

She laughed, and they didn't speak for a while.

After a few minutes, she broke the silence. "What do you think will happen next, Kaiser?"

"What do you mean?" he asked. "What will happen with what?"

"With me as queen, with us, with the fortress," she said. "With the entire underworld."

He sighed. "So many answers to your question."

He brushed her hair absently. "Well, there were those ifrits you sent out to find more ifrits. By the way, have they come back yet?"

"No, I don't think so. Hobson would have told me if they came back. So far, no news from him."

She felt him nod against her head.

"Do you think they met the same fate as the spies I sent after Mara?" she asked.

"It's possible. But if she had, she would've sent you proof of their deaths, right? Just to taunt you? It's possible but unlikely. Maybe they're just taking a long time. Maybe they're looking at a lot of places. There are other explanations."

"You're right. The best thing to do now is to wait and be patient."

"What we *should* be thinking about is how my father will come for you when he learns that you didn't take his deal."

She snorted. "Let him try."

Kaiser wasn't amused. "He's childish and it seems ridiculous, but please, don't underestimate him. He's a dangerous enemy to have, Sadie."

She tilted her head back to look at him. "I know that, and I won't underestimate him. He's just so awful." She cupped his cheek. "I don't believe for a second that he raised the four of you. He doesn't seem like your father *at all*."

His eyes softened. "There's something else."

"What?" she asked.

"You also have to know that after the alliance you made with all four of us, we'll be losing allies of our own."

"Really?"

"Yes," he said. "Some of our allies are mortal enemies with each other, and now that the four of us are together again, they wouldn't accept we're all on the same team now."

"Bummer."

"I know. It's a complex web of grudges and pettiness down here."

"Well, we can try to convince them to set aside their differences, so we don't lose any allies," she said and shrugged. "But if we end up losing them, then it's their loss, I guess."

"And then there's the issue with Hecate—"

She had asked him the question, but his answers began to exhaust her. It turned out she had so many things to worry about. Right now, she just wanted to enjoy the rest of her night with him.

She laughed softly and placed a hand on his shoulder and pecked his cheek. "All right then, let's just stop worrying for five minutes."

"I don't know, Sadie," he said. "There's a lot of things to worry about." He kissed the top of her head. "But at least you don't have to worry about us anymore. Me and my brothers, that is. Whatever happens from now on, I'll always be here for you. And I know you can count on my brothers as well."

She smiled. "Thank you, that means a lot." She

rubbed his chest. "But you should relax. Sure, there are plenty of things we should be thinking about. But let's just enjoy the victory right now."

He smirked. "You're right, as always."

"Besides, we have a great view up there, and you're still not done telling me about the rest of the constellations."

"Of course," he said, and pointed to another star.

She smiled as she snuggled closer to him, feeling safe in his arms.

A war was coming. Possibly several. But between her magic and her men, Sadie was more than ready.

YOU'RE MISSING OUT...

Olivia Ash occasionally takes over the Wispvine Publishing social media channels on Facebook, Instagram, and Twitter. She also has her own Facebook page.

Olivia also likes to hang out with Lila Jean in their Facebook group specifically for readers like you to come together and share their lives and interests, especially regarding the hot guys from their reverse harem novels. Please check it out and join in whenever you get the chance! Everyone in there is amazing, and you'll fit right in.

https://www.facebook.com/groups/LilaJeanOliviaAsh/

Sign up for email alerts of new releases AND exclusive access to bonus content, book recommendations, and more!

https://wispvine.com/newsletter/demon-queen-saga-email-signup/

Enjoying the series? Awesome! Help others discover the Nighthelm Academy by leaving a review at Amazon.

ABOUT THE AUTHOR

OLIVIA ASH

Olivia Ash spends her time dreaming up the perfect men to challenge, love, and protect her strong heroines (who actually don't need protecting at all). Her stories are meant to take you on a journey into the world of the characters and make you want to stay there.

Reviews are the best way to show Olivia that you care about her stories and want other people discover them. If you enjoyed this novel, please consider leaving a review at Amazon. Every review helps the author and she appreciates the time you take to write them.